Royal Games

USA TODAY BESTSELLING AUTHOR

T.K. LEIGH

ROYAL GAMES

Published by Carpe Per Diem, Inc. / Tracy Kellam, 25852 McBean Parkway # 806, Santa Clarita, CA 91355

Edited by: Kim Young, Kim's Editing Services

Cover assets:

olly © 2020

Romolo Tavani © 2020

trekandphoto © 2020

Used under license from Adobe

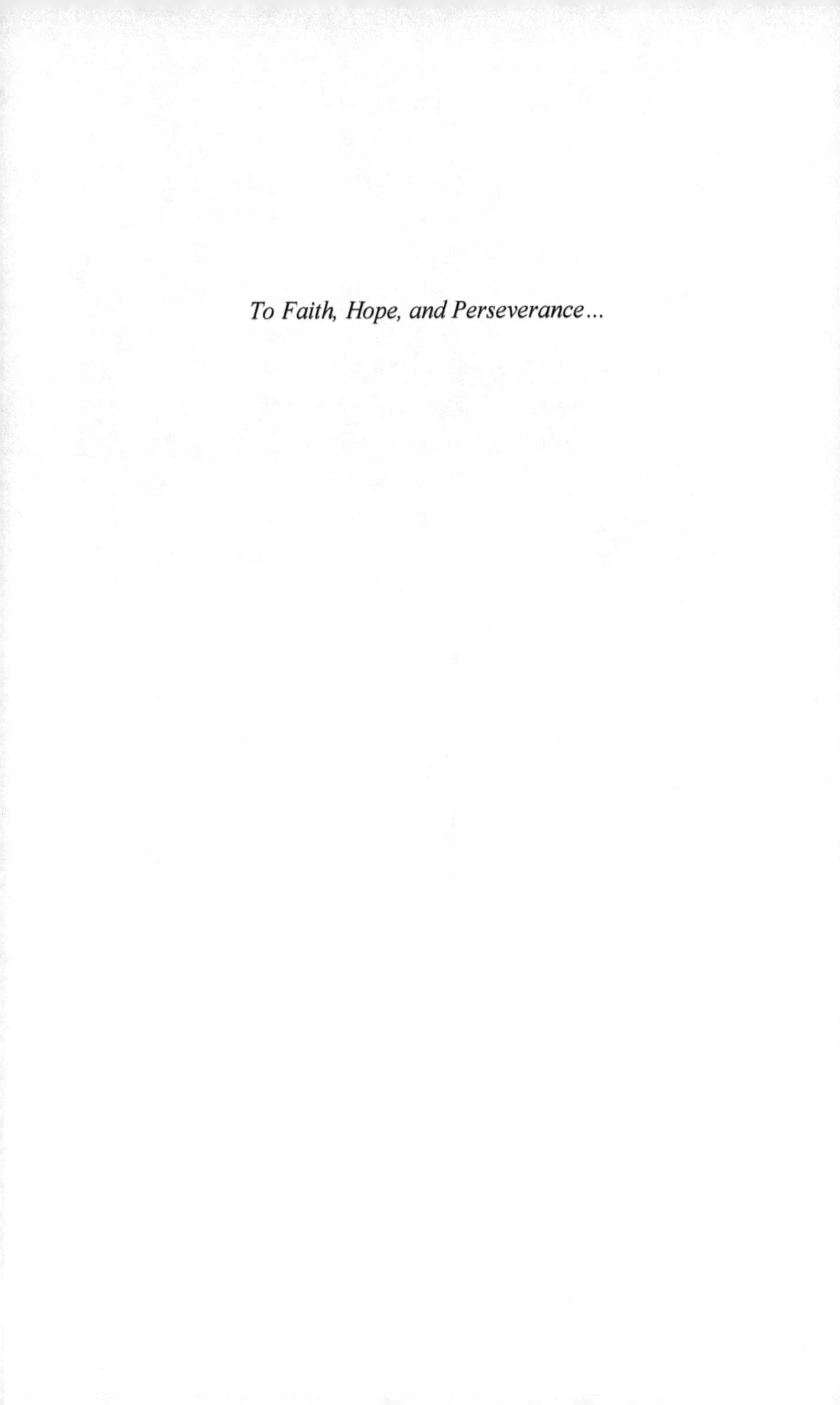

To Faith, Hope, and Perseverance...

Chapter One

NORA

YOU CAN'T LIVE *in the present if you're still held captive by the past.*

Sounds fairly straightforward, right?

Unfortunately, I've found that living in the present is easier said than done.

All our lives, we're trained *not* to live in the present. To either long for the past or look toward the future. It's rare we're allowed to enjoy the moment. To stop and smell the roses, so to speak.

We count down the days until we move into our college dorm and bid farewell to our parents' rules.

Then we count down the last few months of college until we're free and can start our career.

Once we have that career, we count down the hours at work until we can go home or on that date.

And we count those dates, wondering when he's finally going to pop that all-important question so we can start the next chapter of our lives.

When you think about it, that's all life is. A series of chapters. When one ends, another begins. The story continues. Your life goes on.

Except for me.

Ever since that night six years ago, I've been stuck in the past, struggling to turn the page.

I'm not sure I *want* to turn the page.

I'm not sure I'm ready to say goodbye to the only time in my life I've ever felt happy.

* * *

"Congratulations!" A boisterous cheer assaults me, nearly knocking me over.

I'd expected to walk into Chloe's apartment in Chelsea to a subdued atmosphere, my three friends hanging out in the kitchen, each sipping a glass of wine.

That is not the scene that greets me at all.

P!nk's voice blares from the surround sound, belting out that she's had enough and to blow her one last kiss. Black balloons fill the industrial-looking space, a banner boasting "Ding-dong, the dick is gone" displayed prominently along the wall over the couch. Centerpieces of a hand sticking up its middle finger decorate the coffee table and a few side tables. However, the *pièce de résistance* is a three-tiered cake, like one would expect at a wedding. That's where the similarities end.

Instead of figurines of a madly in love bride and groom, the bride has pushed the groom off the cake, red frosting made to look like blood following the path of the groom's untimely demise all the way to the scene of the crime at the foot of the bottom tier.

My gaze shifts to the three women standing proudly beside the kitchen island, "Divorce Support Group" scrawled on the front of their matching black t-shirts.

"Welcome to your divorce party!" Evie dances up to me, her expression bright, red lips curled up in an animated smile. She grabs my hand, dragging me farther into the apartment.

"Divorce party?" I arch a brow, glancing at a few of my coworkers, who salute me with their drinks. I lean toward my friends, lowering my voice. "I told you not to make a big deal out of today. It's just another day."

"No, it's not," Chloe insists, her gray eyes trained on me as she slings an arm around my waist, moving her hips in time with the music. "Today is the first day of the rest of your life, and it must be celebrated!"

"So put on your shirt and let's get this party started." When Izzy throws a black t-shirt at me, I scramble to catch it. "Because if you don't, Evie will pout all night long. Seriously. Since she heard about the divorce, she hasn't shut up about this party and these damn t-shirts."

"That's not entirely true," Evie interjects, scowling playfully. "I commiserated at first. Then I started planning your freedom party. I am a planner after all." She winks.

Shaking my head, I shrug off my blazer, leaving me in just a tank and skinny jeans. I hold up the t-shirt in front of me and burst out laughing.

"Divorced A.F.?"

"I wanted to spell it out," Chloe tells me, "but Evie thought someone might find it offensive."

"We will eventually be leaving your apartment tonight. There could be children around."

"At a bar?" Chloe shoots back dryly.

"Still, I didn't want to offend."

"Says the girl who used to write articles for the magazine about techniques to give a blow job that will have him begging for more."

I smile at my friends' bickering, grateful for this small slice of normalcy.

Since I no longer have Jeremy to return home to, I've struggled to find a new normal. Sure, we were only together a few years, such a brief time compared to some couples, but his absence has drawn into focus all the trivial things he did. Like make me coffee in the morning. Or empty the dishwasher before leaving for work. Or even change the lightbulbs. To most, these acts are insignificant, but now that I do them, I'm reminded that Jeremy's gone.

I pull the t-shirt over my head, smoothing back the few tendrils of strawberry blonde hair that escape my low ponytail, then spin a slow circle, arms stretched wide. "Happy?"

Evie beams. "Definitely."

As cheesy and cliché as these shirts seem, I appreciate the symbolic gesture. The knowledge that my girl gang, my tribe, my sisters from other misters will stand by my side as I navigate the uncertainty facing me as a thirty-year-old divorcée is exactly what I need.

"Okay. Let's celebrate." Chloe grabs a wine glass off the kitchen island and hands it to me.

I bring it to my lips, stopping when I notice the words "Just Divorced" etched on the glass. "You guys went all out, didn't you? Although, I have to admit, I like the decorations." I nod at the cake, surprised how realistic the "blood" dripping down the side actually looks. I turn to Chloe. "Was this your handiwork?"

"Can you imagine me baking?" She bursts out laughing, the sound echoing off the walls, everyone joining in at the ridiculousness of the suggestion. "I do *not* bake."

"I'm more than aware of that. But why do I get the feeling the design was your idea?"

She shrugs, flipping a few blonde locks behind her shoulder. "Because you know I have an active imagination."

"That, and when I told you about the divorce, you offered to pull a few favors with some of your contacts who know how to make people 'disappear'," I counter, using air quotes.

"What? Jeremy's a prick for what he did."

I narrow my gaze. "I told you. He was just confused. And scared of his family disowning him."

While I was initially hurt to learn my husband had been seeing another man behind my back, my heart couldn't help but break for him when he explained everything. How he'd always felt like he was different. How he'd pretended to be someone he wasn't for years. How he was tired of wearing that mask. I somehow found strength in his ability to finally be himself.

It gives me hope that maybe I'll soon stop pretending, too.

"That's no reason for him to be unfaithful to you, Nora." She grips my biceps, forcing me to face her. "I love you, and I am absolutely sympathetic to how difficult it must have been for Jeremy, considering how close-minded his family is. Hell, at your wedding, they kept mistaking Izzy for a member of the waitstaff because, according to them, all Hispanics look the same."

I float my gaze to Izzy's dark eyes, gritting an apologetic smile. When I look at her, I only see an amazing woman, one who's made a career out of helping some of the most vulnerable people as a pediatric oncology nurse. I can't wrap my head around anyone only seeing the darker tone of her skin or the fact she's not blue-eyed and blonde-haired.

"Don't forget that Jeremy made a promise to *honor* you," Chloe continues, forcing my attention back to her. "*Honor*, Nora. He broke that promise. And now it's time to rid yourself of the negativity surrounding those broken promises." Looping her arm through mine, she drags me to the center of the room.

"What is this?" I eye what appears to be a miniature casket sitting amongst a model graveyard straight out of the attic in *Beetlejuice*.

"Isn't it fantastic?" Evie asks excitedly. "It's a ring coffin. Companies actually make them. Who knew?"

"Who knew indeed."

"But Evie couldn't leave well enough alone," Izzy explains. "Thought if we were going to make you bury the ring, we needed a graveyard, too, so…" She gestures to it, "there ya go."

"My brother used to make model railroads growing up." She shrugs, her red curls bouncing with the movement. "I made a model graveyard."

I step closer, noticing the engagement ring Jeremy had bought me while we were both in a St. Patrick's Day alcohol-induced fog sitting beside the wedding band I'd worn for less than a year. The diamonds still glitter and sparkle, not having had enough time to grow dull from years of wear.

The music cuts out, and I glance around the room to see everyone step closer, expressions of forced solemnity crawling across their faces.

"We've gathered here at my apartment, surrounding this really creepy, tiny graveyard, to pay our respects to the dearly departed… Nora's marriage to Jeremy the Fuckface," Chloe begins in as serious a voice as she can muster.

I open my mouth to argue, yet again, that I don't blame Jeremy, but her hand shoots up, cutting me off.

"But this isn't a sad occasion, friends. It's a momentous one. One in which we celebrate not the separation of two people who never should have been together in the first place, but Nora's freedom to live the life she was meant to live. To be the person she was meant to be. Even if she doesn't quite know who that person is just yet." She offers me an endearing smile, then picks up a yellow rose petal from a nearby bowl.

Closing the lid on the casket, she places the petal on

it. "Today, Nora Jean," she continues, love in her gaze, "may you be happier than a bird with a french fry."

Everyone erupts in laughter, including myself, even as I wipe the few tears tricking down my cheek. Not from losing Jeremy, but at the length my friends went in order to make sure tonight isn't marked with regret and sadness but hope and laughter.

"May you be happier than a fat cat in a small box," one of my co-workers, Claire, says, tossing another yellow rose petal on the casket.

"May you be happier than Daryl Dixon with a crossbow," Gretchen, another woman from work, offers. We chuckle, all too familiar with her obsession with *The Walking Dead*.

"May you be happier than a dog chasing a squirrel," Marcy, one of the women who works with Evie and Chloe, states as she tosses her own petal.

I smile in thanks, watching as each one of the dozen or so women steps up to offer their own wish for my happiness, all of them amusing. Finally, we reach the last few people in the circle. Evie steps forward, grabbing a rose petal.

"May you fly high and never let anyone clip your wings again." The tone shifts from fun and humorous to sincere and earnest as she places her rose petal on the overflowing pile.

"May you find the strength you need in the people who love you," Izzy encourages, then glances at the two women at her side — Evie and Chloe. "In your friends. In us."

I nod, swiping at the tears escaping.

"May you dream big," Chloe begins. "Sparkle more. And shine bright." Then her grin turns conniving. "And have some mind-blowing sex, even if just for a night." She waggles her brows as the room erupts in cheers and whistles.

Once they settle down, Chloe picks up the bowl and extends it toward me. I grab the sole remaining petal and place it on top of all the others.

"May I find the happiness I deserve." I close my eyes, as if making a birthday wish, allowing my hope for the future to fill me with peace.

When I open my eyes, Chloe's standing in front of me, holding out a shot glass, as Evie makes her way around the room with a tray, offering everyone a shot, as well.

Once everyone has one, Izzy holds up hers. "To Nora," she toasts. "Never forget that walking away from something unhealthy is incredibly brave, even if you stumble a few times as you make your way out that door. Trust me." She laughs under her breath. "I've stumbled more than a few times. But I've also learned that it's never too late to find your happily ever after."

"It's truly not," Evie joins in. "Sometimes you have to kiss a lot of frogs to find the prince you deserve."

"Now, say it with me…" Chloe lifts her shot glass. "Fuck Jeremy."

"Fuck Jeremy," I laugh, my voice barely audible.

"Louder," Chloe instructs. "With meaning."

I roll my eyes, then quickly say, "Fuck Jeremy."

"Is that the best you can do? For once in your life, stop bottling it up and let it all out. It's okay to be mad."

Licking my lips, I square my shoulders, about to inhale a deep, calming breath.

"And none of that 'positive energy in, negative energy out' bullshit, either. Breathing exercises only mask the problem."

With determination, I level my eyes on Chloe. "Fuck Jeremy," I say firmly, my tone icy.

She grins in satisfaction. "Louder."

"Fuck Jeremy," I repeat with more tenacity and strength.

"Again."

"Fuck Jeremy!"

"Again!"

"Fuck Jeremy!" With each repetition, my voice grows louder, more fevered, more excited, more animated. This is the most emotion I've shown in ages. This is the most I've allowed myself to feel in ages, too. Even when I walked in on Jeremy with another man, I kept myself in check, refusing to show even a hint of weakness.

"Again!" Gretchen calls out.

"Fuck Jeremy!"

"One more time," Chloe encourages, eyes brimming with pride.

"*Fuck Jeremy*!" I screech at the top of my lungs, all the frustration and annoyance that's built up over the years of hiding my true feelings spilling out of me like lava, burning yet satisfying at the same time.

When applause breaks out around me, I return to the present, smiling at all these people who care enough to support me during this trying time. That should be all that matters, shouldn't it? Don't they say you find out who truly cares about you when you're at your lowest?

These women have always been there for me, even when I tried to keep them out. They didn't have to go through the trouble of throwing this party to commemorate my failed marriage. Yet they did because, somehow, they realized I needed it. Isn't that the mark of true friendship? Realizing what you need when you're too stubborn to admit it?

I wrap my arms around Chloe, Evie and Izzy joining in on our group hug. "I love you girls."

"Hoes before bros," Evie says.

"Chicks before dicks," Izzy adds.

"Pussy before… I got nothing." Chloe laughs, and we all follow.

I glance at my circle of friends, my family. Until this moment, I'd been apprehensive about the divorce being finalized and being thrust into the next chapter of my life. Now I look forward to it. Because no matter what's written on the pages, these three amazing women will be a part of it. They'll be with me until the last word.

That's a love worth celebrating.

Chapter Two

NORA

"IS THAT THE sun?" I slur, taking a swig out of a bottle of champagne as I rest my head on Izzy's shoulder. We must be a sight, all of us collapsed on a spacious patio sofa on the rooftop terrace of the Gramercy Park townhouse Izzy shares with her boyfriend, Asher.

After leaving Chloe's, my friends dragged me out to Staten Island, where they'd rented out a paintball arena for the night. Mannequins with photos of Jeremy's face were set up throughout, allowing me to take out my frustrations on inanimate objects. As if that weren't enough to help me release this pent-up aggression, Chloe had snuck into my apartment and stole my wedding dress, which waited for me toward the end of the course.

When I first saw it, I hesitated, not wanting to damage the dress I'd dreamed of wearing since I was a little girl. But this would always be another memory of Jeremy. If I wanted to turn the page on this chapter, I had to let go of those memories.

Now, as I stare at the wedding dress covered with splats of paint, the rising sun illuminating it from behind, I feel less bound to Jeremy and more like the woman I was before I swiped right on his picture.

"Impossible," Chloe responds in a lazy voice. "It's

probably just the bright lights of Manhattan or some shit."

"No. I definitely think that's the sun," Izzy remarks.

"What time is it?" Evie asks.

"That would require me to move." Chloe takes another long pull from her bottle.

"But you can find the energy to take a sip of champagne?" Izzy snips playfully.

Chloe shoots her a pointed stare. "I have priorities."

It's silent for a moment as we bask in our denial over the fact we managed to drink the night away, something I doubt we've done since our college days. I glance around the rooftop terrace that's now littered with bottles, as well as the remnants of the Jeremy piñata I'd obliterated after just a few smacks with a stick. It will take me at least a week to recover from tonight's festivities.

"So, what's next?" Evie asks in a scratchy voice, floating her gaze toward mine.

I take another large swallow from my champagne, the liquid having grown warm and flat over the course of the past few hours, but I can't be bothered to get up to find a fresh bottle.

"Maybe I'll take a page from Jeremy's book and turn gay," I joke, then scowl. "But I like the dick too much."

"So did Jeremy," Izzy snort-laughs, and we all join in, the sound echoing against the relative stillness of early morning.

"But seriously," Evie continues after a beat. "What *is* next for you, Nora?"

I sigh. "I wish I knew. It probably sounds stupid, since Jeremy and I were only together for less than three years, less than the time it takes people to earn a college degree, but he was such a big part of my life during that time. Sure, we haven't lived together for several months now, but…" I expel a breath. "It's hard to explain. There's something so final about the divorce being, well…final."

"You should go on a divor-cation," Evie suggests.

"Divor-cation?" I ask in a drawn-out voice.

"Well, couples go on a honeymoon to celebrate the start of their marriage. You should take a trip to celebrate your independence and the fact you're no longer beholden to anyone, except yourself. It's what the main character did in *Eat, Pray, Love.*"

"We're not resorting my life to some cheesy romantic comedy or self-help book."

"I'm not suggesting you should. But some time away might be good for your soul."

I stare ahead, watching as New York City comes to life with the dawning of the day. The sound of cars increases, a few dogs barking as their owners take them for a walk.

"If you found out Julian were gay, where would you go to clear your head? On your own personal *Eat, Pray, Love* trip?"

"Do I have to pick three different places like in the book?"

"Whatever you want. No rules."

Evie nods, pulling her bottom lip between her teeth as she considers the question. "This is really difficult," she admits with a laugh. "You don't want to choose a place that will have overwhelming memories of your ex."

"And you probably want to avoid places where all you'll do is sit by the ocean or pool without anything to keep your mind occupied," Izzy adds.

"And there should be nothing romantic about it," Chloe states. "It should be the antithesis of romance."

We nod in unison, a pensive expression falling over

all our faces as we consider the perfect divor-cation location.

"I'd go to California." When Evie's voice cuts through, we all look toward her. "I'd eat my way through the Mexican food in San Diego. Find clarity of mind hiking around Yosemite or camping in Big Sur."

"And love?" Chloe waggles her brows. "Where would you find love?"

A playful grin tugs on Evie's lips. "I'd fall in love with wine in Napa Valley." She lifts her bottle to her mouth. "Oops. Too late." Then she takes another long sip of her champagne, which causes us to erupt in laughter.

"How about you?" Evie asks Chloe.

"Vegas," she replies without hesitation.

Izzy whips her head toward her. "What? Have you forgotten you met Lincoln *in Vegas?* Hell, you guys also eloped and got married there. Pretty sure all you'll have are memories of Lincoln."

"I'd want my divor-cation destination to hold memories of my ex. To remind me why I'm better off without him. To show him he can't ruin a place for me."

Her response doesn't surprise me. Chloe's not the type of woman who wallows in heartbreak for too long. Her divor-cation would be one big "fuck you" to whomever hurt her. But based on the way Lincoln adores her, I don't see that happening anytime soon… Or ever.

"Well, I wouldn't choose Vegas," Izzy remarks. "Even though Asher and I kind of…reconnected the same weekend you hooked up with Lincoln."

"Where *would* you go?" I inquire.

She furrows her brow, shaking her head. "I'm not sure. I think I'd just go to the airport and pick somewhere."

"Without any planning?" Evie asks, aghast.

Out of our circle of friends, Evie's the one who finds joy out of making itineraries and lists. Chloe's more spontaneous, preferring to live life to its fullest. Izzy's the compassionate one, as evidenced by her career. And me? Well, I'm not sure who I am. On the outside, I'm a calm, collected woman who seems to have her life together. But the more I think about it, that's who I want people to see. On the inside, I'm still the naïve teenager who clung onto every man who looked familiar after a psychic told me my soulmate would be a stranger I recognized. It's part of the reason I agreed to marry Jeremy after only knowing him three months.

"Yes, Evie." Izzy rolls her eyes. "Without any planning."

"But what if it reminded you of Asher?"

"Truthfully, I doubt there's a single place on this planet I could escape to that wouldn't hold any memories of Asher, considering he's a musician who tours around the world. Not to mention, I can't turn on the radio or bring up a random Spotify playlist without at least one of his songs coming on. But some higher power brought us together back in Vegas after over eight years apart. If something ever happened between us, which I doubt, I'd want some higher power to steer me in the direction I should take." She shrugs, then levels her gaze on me.

"Your turn, Nora. Where should you go on this divorcation? Where should you begin the next chapter of your life?"

A gentle breeze brushes against my skin as I consider where to go to reboot my life. "Maybe Paris." I scrape at the label on the champagne bottle.

Chloe scrunches up her nose. "Paris?"

"Why not? I've always wanted to go."

Her eyes narrowed, she assesses my response, then

shakes her head. "That doesn't work for me."

"Well, what *does* work for you?" I retort lightly.

"Route 66."

Her answer nearly takes the breath from me, my chest constricting, a lump building in my throat. "Route 66?" I respond in a small voice.

"Yes, Nora." Her tone drips with sympathy. I float my eyes to Izzy and Evie, both of them wearing the same reassuring smile. I get the feeling they've discussed this amongst themselves. "It's what you need to move on."

I briefly close my eyes. It doesn't escape my notice that she doesn't say it's what I need to forget about Jeremy. She's talking about finally moving on from my first love. Finally mourning everything I lost when I watched all our dreams go up in flames mere hours before we were supposed to move to California. We'd planned to drive Route 66 then. But we never got the opportunity.

"I don't think I—"

"I can't even begin to imagine what that must have been like for you." Chloe places her hand over mine. "But you've pretended you're okay long enough. You never allowed yourself to grieve him. Instead, you tried to fill the void Hunter's absence left by finding someone to take his place, hoping meeting someone you could pretend to love would be enough."

I want to argue, but I can't. She's not wrong. Once I made the decision to move to Manhattan mere months after losing everything, I'd downloaded a few dating apps. Not a single man I dated carried the same spark I experienced with Hunter, but at least I felt *something*. And something was better than the utter despair and misery that seemed to consume me.

Then I saw Jeremy's profile. Everything about him

reminded me of Hunter, from his deep-set eyes, to the square shape of his jaw, even his love of Mel Brooks movies. Maybe that's why I clung onto Jeremy like I had. Maybe I so desperately wanted him to be Hunter that I'd been blind to everything else.

It's been six years, but I still find myself imagining Hunter lying beside me. Still move my hand to my stomach where our baby once grew. Still haven't made good on the promise I made to his mother to dispose of his remains. They still sit on the dresser in my apartment. Even during my marriage to Jeremy, Hunter was there. Hunter's always been there.

"It won't be an easy trip," she continues when I don't say anything. "But it's something you need to do. Isn't that what Hunter would have wanted? What would he say if he were here and saw how miserable you are?"

"I'm not *that* miserable," I protest.

Chloe tilts her head. "You don't look miserable. But inwardly, I know you're falling apart. Even six years later." She offers me a compassionate smile. "We repeat what we don't repair, Nora. It's time to repair yourself. You can't start the next chapter if you're still stuck in the last one. And you've been stuck in Hunter's chapter for years now. It's time you turn that page. For Hunter."

I nod, peering into the distance. "For Hunter."

Chapter Three

NORA

"**M**OTHER FUDGE OF all that is crap!" I exclaim, clenching my jaw tightly when I see the name flash across the screen of my phone. The anger in my voice is jarring against the tranquil music playing in the background at the yoga studio where I work.

"If it's a telemarketer, just ignore it," Lindsay, the receptionist, says.

"It's not." I close my eyes and exhale deeply. "It's my mother."

She grimaces. She's only worked here a few months, but in that time has learned all she needs to know about my rather tenuous relationship with my mother.

"I'm sorry."

"No more than me," I mutter under my breath.

This is the last thing I need today. Which is exactly why she called. She tends to reach out at the worst moments, if only to have a front-row seat to my misery. It's like she gets off on watching people suffer. Which is an interesting notion, considering her line of work.

As much as I'd love to ignore her, I'm smart enough to know it's not an option. She'll view my reluctance to speak with her as using avoidance as a coping mechanism…or whatever other term she'll come up with in her analysis of my supposed distraught state.

The drawback of being a psychiatrist's daughter.

Finding my AirPods, I place them into my ears, wave to Lindsay, then push open the glass door, leaving the tranquility of the studio behind, exchanging it for the frantic atmosphere of Greenwich Village. Tourists and commuters scurry along the sidewalks like ants, everyone walking with purpose. No one acknowledges one another. Here, I'm nobody.

I like being a nobody.

Summoning the strength to get through a conversation that will undoubtedly take ten years off my life, I plaster a fabricated smile on my face, smoothing back a few wisps of my mid-length hair that had escaped the ponytail set low on my nape. At least I took a shower after teaching my last class. Otherwise, I'm sure she would have had something to say about my flushed skin or the sweat on my brow. She acts like she doesn't ever sweat or have blotchy skin. Then again, she'd have to be human. I'm not quite sure my mother qualifies.

"Nora, sweetie," she soothes in a voice of forced compassion when her heavily Botoxed face pops up on the screen. Her pink lips are thin, eyes tight, barely able to blink. Her cheeks are abnormally high and full, like they belong on one of those creepy dolls from scary movies.

"Hello," I reply, joining the crowd of people and beginning my five-minute walk toward my apartment near Union Square.

"How are you holding up?" She tries to look concerned. It might work for her patients, but I know better.

"Today's just another day," I lie.

Today's never been just another day. Instead, today is the day I'll always remember as not only the day Hunter died, but also a part of me.

It still drives me crazy that my mother feels the need

to call me every year on this day when she couldn't manage to pull herself away from whatever midlife crisis she was screwing at the time to be with me when he actually died. When I was in the hospital with my own injuries as a result of the car wreck that took Hunter's life.

When the doctor delivered the awful news that our baby no longer had a heartbeat.

"So, unless there's something important…"

"This *is* important," my mom insists. "It's the anniversary of Hunter's death. And the first one since your divorce from Jeremy. I need to know you're okay."

I do my best not to roll my eyes. All my life, this woman has analyzed every tiny thing I've done.

Like when I was six and decided to give my Barbie a haircut. She said I was intimidated by her beauty and that's why I butchered her appearance. I just wanted to give my Barbie a haircut.

Like when I was twelve and broke my leg during the ballet class I hated but she insisted I attend so I could maintain a slim figure. She claimed it was a cry for attention. I had simply landed on it wrong.

Like when I was twenty-four and survived the car wreck that killed my fiancé, only to learn the baby I'd been growing inside me for six months didn't make it, either. According to her, I didn't try hard enough to save the baby. In reality, I would have given anything to have both Hunter and our baby with me.

To *still* have them with me.

It was then that I swore to never give this woman any more ammunition to use against me. To make me feel like I'm less of a woman, of a person, of a human.

"I told you. I'm fine." No thanks to her. The only reason I'm not a complete wreck is because of the amazing network of support I built myself.

She wasn't always like this. The memories are fuzzy, but I remember a few moments of happiness we shared as a family. But when my father died just after my fifth birthday, she changed. She grew distant. Not just toward her friends, but her kids, too. My brothers probably didn't notice. They were all teenagers at that point, considering there's a seven-year gap between me and my next youngest brother. Regardless of the fact I was so young and it was years ago, I remember wondering what happened to my mother. It was like that woman died along with my father, leaving an imposter in her place.

At first, I tried to bring that woman back. I thought if I did everything she asked of me, it would make her happy, would make her love me again.

It took me years to realize she's not capable of loving anyone.

Not anymore.

"And I told *you*..." She brings a martini glass to her lips, and I recognize the pool area of the enormous house where she now lives with husband number five, whom she married last year. The same day I married Jeremy.

If that's not an indicator of the type of woman she's turned into, I don't know what is.

"It's not healthy to keep these things inside," she continues. "It's important to talk about your feelings. Don't let it fester."

"I'm not. It's been six years since Hunter died." I force a smile so she can't read between the lines.

Sure, I've had more than enough time to mourn losing him and our baby, but have I done so? I wish I could say I have. Wish I could say I've accepted what happened to them. Some days, I feel like I have. But others, I still find myself wishing I would wake up and learn it's all a dream.

"Then what about Jeremy?"

"What about him? We parted ways amicably."

"Yet you didn't attempt to reconcile your marriage first."

I try to stop the look of astonishment and annoyance from crossing my brow, but it's impossible. I've become a master at pretending to be someone I'm not. At wearing a mask, if only to avoid this woman's criticism. But not even the most accomplished actor can fumble their way through this conversation with a straight face.

"What was there for us to reconcile? I walked in on Jeremy mid-coitus. With a man."

"All the more reason you should have worked harder on your marriage."

"Says the woman who's on husband number five," I mutter as I approach my building. I grab the keys from my purse and unlock the front door, heading inside.

She glares at me, then brushes off my statement. After all, it's okay for Elaine Marie Harcourt-Tremblay-Duval-Corbet-Thibault-Vaughn to marry as many times as she wants. But if anyone else does, they're a failure. She's a classic narcissist, but her head is shoved so far up her ass that she refuses to see it.

"At least none of my husbands left me for someone else, let alone a man."

"That's low, Elaine. Even for you," I snip out, climbing the stairs up to the third floor. She hates it when I call her by her first name. In my mind, the title Mom should be earned. This woman hasn't earned it in years.

"What is that supposed to mean?"

"You're the therapist. Feel free to psychoanalyze my statement and prepare a full report on everything that's wrong with me. In the meantime, I'm going to enjoy my night. Send my love to Dan."

"Your step-father's name is *Dean*."

I snort. "Step-father?"

Upon entering my apartment, I make a beeline for my tiny kitchen and pour myself a glass of wine. I'm tempted to forego the glass to cut out the middleman, but I can only imagine what my mother would have to say about that.

"In case you've forgotten, Dean's only a few years older than I am. We went to the same high school. Hell, he asked me to go to his senior prom."

"Is that what this is all about?" she asks as I take a long sip of my wine, tilting my phone away from me. "Did you only marry Jeremy because you were jealous of my relationship with Dean? I can understand how that might be difficult, especially when you realized you let go of someone who became a right-fielder for the Yankees."

"I was engaged to Jeremy before Dean was in the picture. Plus, I turned down Dean's invitation to prom because I thought he was a creep, considering he had a reputation for sleeping with anything with a pulse." I pause, then go in for the kill, the alcohol coating my stomach momentarily decreasing my "give a fuck" meter. "I guess some things never change." I grit out a smile, giving myself a mental high five when I see the offended look on her face. "Have a nice night," I sing.

"Nora, wait!" she calls just as I'm about to end the FaceTime session.

I clench my jaw, but stay on the line, nonetheless. "What?" I grind out.

"I was wondering what your plans are this weekend."

"This weekend?" I blink, caught off guard by her question.

"Yes. It's the playoffs, so I'll be heading up to New

York to watch Dean."

I snort, finding it laughable that this woman who's always adamantly refused to leave Miami for New York can now find the time to do so. It's why I chose to move to Manhattan. Not just because my college roommate and friend, Chloe, lives here. But because it's the one place my mother would never willingly visit.

"Would you like a medal?"

"Sarcasm isn't an attractive quality, Nora. Perhaps that's why you can't seem to hold on to a man."

I pull the phone away, taking a moment to draw in a deep breath, pushing out all the negative energy that always seems to accompany my mother. Instead, I focus on the good things in my life.

My apartment… It may be small and have its quirks, but it's all mine.

My job… It's not what I pictured doing years ago, but it's brought me peace when I needed it most.

My friends… They've been an incredible foundation of support. Not once did they ask what I did to cause Jeremy to seek out companionship from a man. They offered me a shoulder to cry on, then a bottle of wine to drown in. As any friend would.

"Dean and I would like you to join us for dinner Sunday night." My mother's voice rips me from my moment of serenity.

"Why?"

"Because you're my daughter and I miss you."

It takes all my willpower not to bark out a laugh.

"Don't worry. You won't be a third wheel. One of Dean's teammates will be joining us. Play your cards right and you might just hit a grand slam." She waggles her brows.

Maybe if I had a better relationship with my mother, this wouldn't make my skin crawl. Wouldn't make me feel like she was whoring me out.

"I'm busy Sunday," I lie.

"Monday then."

"That won't work, either."

"When *will* work? I'll be in New York all week. Possibly longer if they proceed to the next round."

I look past the screen, floundering to come up with some reason why I'm not available to see her at all. Even if I tell her I'm too busy with work, that won't stop her from showing up at the yoga studio or, God forbid, my apartment. I've fought for several long years to make a life for myself in New York. To make it my own. I fear it will only take my mother mere minutes to dismantle everything I've built.

It's a special talent of hers.

"I'll be out of town," I lie.

"Out of town?" She scowls, obviously taken aback that I won't drop all of my plans to cater to her, as she's used to from me.

I hold my head high. "Yes."

"Where are you going?"

I part my lips. I hadn't thought this far ahead into my fabrication. My mother normally doesn't ask questions unless they revolve around her.

I blurt out the first thing that comes to mind. "Route 66."

"Route...66?" Her voice is laden with disgust. Of course she'd turn up her nose at the idea. Roadside diners. Cheap motels. Driving for hours. Certainly not my mother's idea of a vacation.

"Yes," I answer with more confidence than I've ever shown her. "Years ago, I made a promise to Hunter's mother that I'd take the trip and spread his remains along the route. Unfortunately, life got in the way, so I never got around to it. Now I am."

"You're driving Route 66 to spread your dead fiancé's ashes?" She scrunches up her nose.

"I sure am."

"The psychiatrist in me wonders if the only reason you're doing this now is because you've realized you're a failure at forging strong relationships with another person and are leaving town to further avoid having to try."

I pull my lips between my teeth, biting back the words I'd love nothing more than to unleash on her. I've learned she's not worth the time or effort.

"And the compassionate person I've grown into, no thanks to you, would tell you I'm doing this because I made a promise to someone I care for. Something you wouldn't understand the first thing about. So, as enlightening as this conversation has been, I need to pack. Enjoy New York."

Before she can utter another syllable, I end the FaceTime call, shaking off the invisible bugs crawling on my skin. I always get itchy talking to her.

I fall onto the couch, taking a minute to calm myself. Deep breath in. Satisfying breath out.

But with each breath, I ruminate on the lie I told my mother. How I wanted her to see that, despite her influence, I am nothing like her. That I'd drive thousands of miles across the country to fulfill a promise I made, whereas she couldn't even be bothered to get on a plane to visit her daughter mere hours away. Until now.

Earlier today, driving Route 66 was the furthest thing from my mind, even after Chloe mentioned it a few weeks ago. Now, I can't stop thinking about the trip Hunter and I never got to take.

Gingerly rising from the couch, I set my wine glass on the coffee table and make my way toward the bedroom.

Focused on the dresser, I step toward it, lifting the envelope from beneath the simple canister containing Hunter's ashes. Dust has settled on the paper from years of being left untouched, the corners yellowing with age.

For several minutes, all I can do is stare, not wanting to open it, knowing what I'll confront once I do. But I can't keep running from my past. I can't pretend it doesn't exist. Like Chloe said weeks ago, we repeat what we don't repair. It's time I finally repair the hole Hunter's death left in my heart.

My hands tremble as I turn the envelope over and lift the flap, pulling out the worn pages within. A tear escapes when my eyes fall on Hunter's handwriting for the first time in years.

It's amazing how something you once thought to be common and insignificant can spark such intense emotions, bring forward such powerful memories. I can almost feel the summer sun beating down on my skin as Hunter and I sat on the beach, writing this very list, planning the first adventure of the rest of our lives.

One he never got the chance to take.

But I do.

It's time I take it. For Hunter.

And myself.

Chapter Four

NORA

THIS IS A *mistake*, I think as I sit in a Chicago diner, staring at the list that started me on this path less than a week ago.

The past few days have been a whirlwind. One second, I was happy to continue on in my normal existence. Wake up. Workout. Head to the yoga studio. Go home. That all ended yesterday morning when I landed in Chicago.

Now I'm about to set out on the adventure I never got to take with Hunter.

In the comfort of my tiny apartment, it seemed like a good idea, if only to get me out of the city while my mother was there. But now that I'm here, the reality hits me. At every turn, I'll have no choice but to be reminded of Hunter, the first man to possess my heart, my soul, my everything.

"More coffee?"

I pull my attention away from Hunter's list, looking up at the waitress holding up a pot.

Forks scratch against plates as boisterous conversations fill the large diner located mere blocks from the start of Route 66. This spot was first on the list of places to visit — Lou Mitchell's. Apparently, it's a ritual for all travelers on the Mother Road to fill up with a greasy breakfast here before setting out on their journey.

"Thanks." I smile as I tuck my list into the leather-bound journal the girls had surprised me with. They'd also given me a vibrator, which shouldn't have shocked me. They have a tendency to be irreverent, yet poignant at the same time. Case in point, my Ding-Dong Divorced Party.

"You got it." She tops off my mug, the nutty aroma fighting for attention over the scent of bacon and pancakes. Then she places the check in front of me. "Take your time, sweetie. No rush."

"Thanks," I say again as she heads off to check on other customers.

I bring my coffee to my lips, closing my eyes, taking this opportunity to find peace using the techniques I teach in my meditation classes.

Rather than dwelling on the memories of Hunter this trip will inevitably evoke, I force my brain to only focus on the present. I don't think about the past. Don't worry about the future. As I've learned, no one can be prepared for what life has in store for us. I couldn't have prepared myself for losing Hunter like I did. Or learning Jeremy was gay, although in retrospect, there were quite a few signs. Regardless, it's useless to dwell on any of that.

I clear my mind and make a list of things in my life without judgment. Rather than wishing this coffee was stronger and more like the local coffee shop in the Village I've grown addicted to, I appreciate the fact I'm alive to drink coffee. Instead of questioning my decision to overindulge in a greasy omelette and breakfast potatoes, I give thanks that I can afford food in the first place and still have a healthy metabolism.

"Driving Route 66?" A deep voice cuts through my moment of reflection.

I open my eyes, looking down the counter to my left, a pair of vibrant blue orbs peering back at me from a few seats over. Thick locks of hair frame his distinguished face, the hue a mixture of various shades of brown, turning to copper and blond toward the ends that fall just over his collar. Days-old scruff dots his jawline and upper lip, but not in a way that makes it seem as if he doesn't care about his appearance. It's more like…organized chaos.

"I noticed your list," he adds in an accent I can't quite place. It sounds British, but there's a hint of American inflection, too. "Judging by how faded it is, seems it's been several years in the making." He brings his mug up to his lips, sipping on what I assume to be coffee. "Am I right?"

Goosebumps prickle my skin as his gaze locks with mine. There's something that draws me to him when I'd normally politely answer his question, then disengage. As I peer deeper into his eyes, I see it, as unmistakable as the rising of the sun. Heartache. Despair. Grief. I can physically feel the sorrow rolling off his body.

"I am," I breathe, curious about his story. Why doesn't his smile light up his face like it should? What caused the dark shadow that seems to cloud everything about him?

"Well…" He lifts his mug in a toast. "May the road rise to meet you. May the wind be always at your back. May the sun shine warm upon your face, and the rains fall soft upon your field." He offers me a slight smile. "Until we meet again."

I mirror his movements, sipping on my own coffee. Then I tilt my head, brow furrowed. "Why does that sound familiar?"

"It's an old Irish blessing my mum used to say to my father before he left on a business trip."

"A more eloquent way of saying have a good time, I suppose."

"She was a very eloquent woman." His expression falters briefly before he recovers, plastering a smile on his face I can tell is forced, despite being a stranger. But grief has become an odd bedfellow of mine over the years. I can see when it's befriended someone else.

Fighting the urge to delve deeper into this mysterious man's background, I offer him a smile of my own, then slide off my stool, placing enough cash to cover my breakfast and a tip on the counter.

"Until we meet again," I say. It's the only part of the blessing I can recall.

He tilts his mug at me. "Until we meet again."

I hold his gaze for a beat, something keeping me rooted in this spot. When the bell over the door chimes, I manage to pull myself away from the mysterious stranger, making my way past booths filled with diners and out onto the busy Chicago sidewalk.

It's the first week of October, but summer is hanging on, the air warming as the day goes on. But it's still comfortable, the sun shining through textured clouds. The perfect day for a drive.

My phone in hand, I check the map to make sure I'm heading in the correct direction. Sirens blare in the distance, and I inhale the smell of car exhaust, but it's not as overwhelming as the pollution I'm used to in Manhattan.

After walking a few more blocks, my destination comes into view. I slow my steps as heaviness settles in my chest. This is why I sat in that diner for nearly two hours, struggling to summon the courage to start my journey instead of heading back to the airport to book a flight home. I've already put this off for six years. I can't put it off any longer, especially now that I'm finally here.

Drawing in a deep breath through the thickness in my throat, I stare up at the brown road sign with the Route 66 insignia on it, the word BEGIN in bold lettering below it. A breeze picks up, wrapping around me as the wind changes direction. I close my eyes, an unexpected warmth filling me. Something about this moment makes me feel like my life's about to change. Like this adventure will alter everything.

Isn't that what I'd hoped for when I decided to do this?

Withdrawing the canister from my bag, I lift the top and look at all that's left of Hunter. He was once this vibrant, sympathetic, selfless man I was lucky enough to receive a wrong number text from my freshman year of college. Now he's reduced to a can of ashes. His memories will live on, but it's time I stop clinging to those memories and make new ones. And I deserve to move on, don't I?

I tilt the can, pouring a handful of his ashes into my hand, allowing them to sift through my fingers as they fall to the ground around the road sign.

"Here's to the start of our adventure."

Chapter Five

NORA

TURNS OUT, THAT Irish blessing from the mysterious stranger was exactly what I needed. All day, as I made my way along the approximately two-hundred-mile route I'd planned, the wind has been at my back, the sun shining upon my face. At least as much as it could through the windshield of the compact car I'd rented.

To say I've been nervous about this trip is an understatement. The idea of thinking about what Hunter would say or do at certain stops, of watching the amount of ashes slowly dwindle, knowing that he wouldn't be with me at my apartment when I returned home, made me edgy. But once I was on the road, all that trepidation vanished. I can almost feel him beside me, hear his laughter, smell his cologne. He may not physically be with me, but his spirit is here, guiding me along this adventure six years in the making.

Tom Petty's voice comes over the speakers, and I'm drawn to the words as he sings "Square One". The lyrics fill me with determination and encouragement. In a way, I'm on square one. This journey marks the start of the rest of my life. It took a while for me to take that first step, but now that I'm here, I feel peace wrapping around me.

I glance out my window as wind feathers through the

tall grass, the sky a beautiful shade of blue interspersed with picturesque, fluffy clouds. The sun sparkles brightly in the west as I enter Springfield. While it's technically a city, I'd be hard-pressed to categorize it as one. It's remarkably quiet. I suppose any place would seem that way after living in Manhattan.

I follow my phone's directions, turning off the main strip and driving through a residential neighborhood, American flags hanging from every house. Thick trees line the road, the lampposts on the median of the divided street announcing to all that this is the home of Lincoln.

As I approach the gates of Oak Ridge Cemetery, a solemn air greets me. I turn off the music and slow my speed as I meander along the roadway through the cemetery, marveling at how green the grass is. Nearby signs direct me toward a parking lot reserved for those here to pay their respects to President Lincoln, and I pull into a spot.

Killing the ignition, I step out of the car, stretching my arms skyward, tilting my head from side to side to work out the kinks in my muscles after hours of driving. I grab my bag and follow the marked path toward Abraham Lincoln's resting place. And my final destination for today.

The building reminds me of the Washington Monument. A white obelisk rising into the sky, the setting sun casting a beautiful pink glow over it.

I start toward the mausoleum as a man in a park ranger uniform approaches. "I'm sorry, ma'am. The tomb closed to visitors at five."

I check my watch to see I'm fifteen minutes too late.

"We open again at eight tomorrow morning, but feel free to look around the grounds and rub Lincoln's nose."

I furrow my brow. "Rub Lincoln's…nose?"

"Yes, ma'am." He nods over my shoulder. "For good luck."

I follow his gaze. Several yards in front of the mausoleum stands a bronze bust of Abraham Lincoln's face. Most of it is a dull copper, apart from his nose, which seems to shine from being constantly rubbed. It's more than apparent this is a rite of passage, something everyone who comes here must do.

"Thank you."

The man tips his hat, then heads off as I stroll along the paths, admiring the landscape. The lush grass. The overgrown trees providing shade and a serene resting place for the inhabitants. The stunning flowers in red, white, and blue that wrap around the building where Abraham Lincoln has lain for over 150 years.

I grab the canister out of my bag, checking my surroundings to see if anyone's paying attention, unsure about any rules regarding spreading human remains in a cemetery. Certain I'm alone, I sprinkle a handful of Hunter's ashes along the grass by the mausoleum, pausing to consider what he'd do or say if he were here. He would have found some way to charm the park ranger into allowing us into the mausoleum. That was Hunter. Always charming everyone he met.

Except my mother. She didn't like him from the moment she met him. Probably because he made me happy, and she can't stand the idea of anyone being happy.

Releasing a long sigh, I suppress all thoughts of my mother. They have no place on this trip. Hell, they have no place in my life. Period.

I take my time as I make my way from the building, walking around the bust of Lincoln with its luminous nose. Stopping in front of it, I lift my hand, joining the ranks of millions who came before me as I rub it.

"It's said to be good luck."

I whirl around, the sudden interruption catching me off guard. "Wha…" I stop short when I'm met with the same stunning blue eyes from the diner this morning.

"Rubbing his nose," he continues, as if it's not a strange coincidence that we ran into each other again. "It's said to bring good luck."

A sly smile builds on his full lips as he steps toward me, his frame towering over me by nearly a foot, making me estimate him to be around six-four. His broad shoulders fill out his button-down shirt, the sleeves rolled up his forearms. A few tendrils of chest hair are visible from where the top button is undone. A pair of khaki shorts hangs from his hips, revealing sculpted legs, making me wonder whether the rest of his body is as toned. Judging by the way his biceps stretch the fabric of his shirt as he crosses his arms over his chest, I imagine it is.

When I hear him clear his throat, I inhale sharply, whipping my eyes toward his to see him smirking, a cockiness about him from having caught me checking him out.

"So I've heard," I reply nonchalantly, holding my head high.

"Have you also heard the story about the plot to steal his body?"

"Steal his…body?"

"In the late 1800s, a counterfeiter named 'Big Jim' Kennally hoped to ransom it for two hundred grand and a pardon for his engraver, who was locked up at the time. That was a lot of money back then."

"Some would say that's a lot of money today."

"Well, in the late 1800s, it was a… What's that saying you Americans use? Shit ton?"

"Sounds about right." My cheeks warm, a blush blooming on them. "Did he succeed? In stealing Lincoln's body?"

"Unfortunately for 'Big Jim' and his associates, they were really bad criminals."

I tilt my head. "Bad?"

"Not bad as in dangerous. More like they were…daft."

"Daft?"

"Yes. You know… Dumb."

"How so?" I angle toward him.

As I peer at him in the glow of the late afternoon, I notice there's something different about him. He seems more…vibrant than he did this morning. It could be because the caffeine finally kicked in, but that doesn't seem to be it. Hours ago, sadness consumed his tone. It lacked life, energy. Like he was just going through the motions. But now, the eyes that had been clouded with grief exude a renewed vitality.

"The men didn't have body-snatching experience. Sadly, this was before the days of being able to find a reliable body snatcher on Yelp."

A laugh escapes my throat at his serious tone, and he flashes a debonair smile. It steals my breath. Full lips framing perfect teeth that shine brightly against his tan skin.

"So they formed an alliance with a man who purported to be a grave robber, Swegles. Unfortunately, they didn't run the necessary background checks, because Mr. Swegles was actually a paid informant of the Secret Service."

"Good help really is hard to find, isn't it?" I quip sarcastically.

"That it is." He shoves his hands into his pockets, rocking on his heels. "When Swegles told his contact at the Secret Service what was going on, they put a plan into motion to have agents waiting for them. What unfolded then was like a comedy of errors." A chuckle rumbles from his chest, as if he's recalling a humorous personal memory, not a historical anecdote. "The men had hoped to steal a body, yet they struggled to even pick the lock of the tomb. When they finally did manage to get inside, they couldn't lift the coffin. Not to mention, a group of lawmen were lying in wait."

"So they didn't steal Lincoln's body?"

"No, they didn't. Even so, the custodian of the tomb was worried. What if more…experienced people decided to make a go of it? He couldn't stomach the thought, so to protect Lincoln's remains, he created the Lincoln Guard of Honor."

"Guard of Honor?"

"Precisely." He briefly catches my eye before shifting his attention to the mausoleum. "Five ordinary men got together to relocate Lincoln's body to a shallow, unmarked grave in the tomb's basement. They all pledged to keep the location secret, and in the years that followed, they did just that. It wasn't until twenty-five years later that they were relieved of honoring their duty."

"What happened then?"

"Robert Lincoln had his father's body placed into a steel cage, which was lowered ten feet below the ground and covered with cement." He nods at the obelisk. "And that's where he still rests to this very day."

I turn my eyes toward the building, neither one of us saying anything for several moments as we pay our respects to the man buried and protected within its walls. A slight breeze blows, the aroma of fresh-cut grass and wildflowers surrounding me. It's a stark change to the stench of garbage and stale cigarette smoke that seems to permeate the streets of New York.

"They never taught that in history classes. At least not in *my* school."

"What can I say?" He shrugs, dimples popping. "I'm a sieve of useless information."

"Well... Thank you for the lesson. It was rather educational."

"Glad to be of service..." His voice rises in pitch, making it apparent that he's asking my name.

"Nora."

"Anderson." Pulling his hands from his pockets, he offers me one, a single brow arched in anticipation.

My eyes trained on his, I extend my own hand, allowing him to wrap his fingers around it. His grip is firm, but not overly so. There's a tenderness in the way he touches me.

"Nice to meet you, Nora."

"Likewise, Anderson."

We stop shaking, but don't release our grasp. It's not because I don't want to. All reason says I should. But something keeps my hand fused to his, some bigger force at play. Something familiar about him that speaks to my subconscious, pulling me toward him instead of pushing me away as it normally would. My heart rate picks up, those same goosebumps from earlier returning, but this time they're stronger, the chill trickling down my spine more pronounced.

I try to look away, to break this spell his mere presence seems to cast over me. By the awe and curiosity in his stare, he appears just as bewitched by me. His eyes are a myriad of shades, compelling me to get lost in them. Light hues of blue more clear than the most stunning ocean. But the more they flame, the darker and stormier they become, until they're nearly as dark as midnight. I can't help but feel like I've seen these eyes before. But where? Wouldn't I remember them?

He parts his lips, his Adam's apple bobbing up and down as he leans closer. But before he can utter a single syllable, I yank my hand from his, severing the connection.

"I have to go." I turn, practically running away from the mausoleum and toward my car, ducking inside like I'd just robbed a bank. Why did I run from a simple handshake?

Because, deep down, I know it wasn't a simple handshake.

A handshake doesn't make your knees weak.

A handshake doesn't make your heart ricochet into your throat.

A handshake doesn't make your core clench.

A handshake doesn't allow you to peer into another person's soul.

Yet I felt all that with him.

Which is why I have to leave, not looking back until the cemetery, and Anderson, are safe in my rearview mirror.

This is not how I expected to end my first day of saying goodbye to Hunter.

Chapter Six

ANDERSON

I STARE AT the pill bottles on top of my toiletry bag, my daily reminder of the new trajectory my life has taken.

Corticosteroid. Receptor modulator. Muscle relaxant. Anti-depressant. Sleeping pills. Drugs to help control my bladder. Oh, and my favorite, drugs to help with any sexual dysfunction I may experience as a side effect of my recent diagnosis, one I still struggle to come to terms with. What I thought was simply a terrible migraine that caused me to pass out and hit my head, resulting in a mild concussion, was a symptom of something much worse.

But there's nothing I can do. This is now my life.

I'm not sure I want it to be. To lose control of my muscles, my bladder…hell, my entire body. It probably won't happen for years, my progression slow, which is why it took so long to diagnose me in the first place. According to the neurologist I saw back in New York, I've had MS for several years, but my flareups were too spread out to raise any suspicion. I'd written off the random pins-and-needles sensations, blinding migraines, and occasional dizzy spells as being caused by stress or lack of sleep. I should have known better.

After all, my mother had MS. She was my age when the disease took her life twenty-five years ago. All I can think about is how, one day, she was this vibrant woman who made everyone she encountered smile. Then, practically overnight, she was gone, having fallen to the disease that now plagues me.

A phone chiming cuts through my growing denial, and I glance at the screen to see my younger sister calling. It's not unusual. I talk to her quite a bit. But not in the middle of the night. It's only eight at night here in Illinois, but back home, it's nearly five in the morning.

"Esme," I answer quickly. "Is everything okay?"

"Of course," she responds. "Why wouldn't it be?"

"It's early. You know what Dad says."

"I know. I know. The only people who call you between the hours of midnight and seven in the morning are those with bad news," she recites. "But it's evening where you are. And I couldn't sleep, so I figured I'd call to check in on you." She pauses, lowering her voice. "How are you?"

"I'm…good."

"Like, good good? Or 'I hate this question so I'm just going to say I'm good' good?"

"A little of both."

She blows out a long sigh. "I wish you'd come home."

"I know," I respond, running a hand through my disheveled hair that's had a chance to grow out these past few months I've avoided public engagements. Couple that with my overgrown facial hair, and I barely resemble the persona of the man I was molded into years ago.

"I'm worried about you, especially about you driving."

"I told you… The neurologist said I can still drive for now. He even thought it might help with some of the psychological effects, with the stipulation that if I encounter any muscle spasms, difficulty with gait, or extreme dizziness to call him immediately."

"Maybe I just want to give my brother a hug to let him know he's not alone. You don't have to go through this alone," she reminds me. "Hell, you haven't even told Creed, and he's in charge of your safety."

"Because there's no way he'd let me drive on my own, Esme. You know that damn well. I just…" I expel a long breath, falling onto the bed of the tiny motel room a few blocks away from Lincoln's final resting place. It's a far cry from the luxurious surroundings I stayed in last night in Chicago. But this is what I need right now. To be normal.

If I were born into a normal family, I wouldn't feel forced to keep my diagnosis to myself for the time being. But I wasn't.

When you're not only part of the Royal Family of the Western European Nation of Belmont, but also Crown Prince and next in line to the throne, things are never normal. Every choice must be carefully weighed before a decision is made. For now, I don't want anyone other than my sister to know. That includes my oldest friend and chief protection officer, Creed.

We may have grown up together, our mothers having been close friends, but as a member of the Royal Guard, Creed takes his oath seriously. If he knew the truth, he wouldn't hesitate to follow protocol in order to ensure my safety. And that would include informing my father. I'm just fortunate this incident happened while traveling under an alias here in the States and Creed believed me when I told him the doctors didn't find anything serious. That it was just a migraine brought on by the stress of it being around the anniversary of my girlfriend's death. Otherwise, I doubt I would have been able to keep this from hitting the headlines. And there's no way he would have been okay following behind me in a separate car as I drove across the country.

"I need a little more time to process everything," I tell my sister. "Need some time to myself. Before everything changes."

"Speaking of changes, Creed mentioned you had a change of plans."

"You've spoken with Creed?"

"I, well… Yes, I have."

"I bet you have," I tease, breaking through the growing tension. I don't have to worry about her telling him about my MS. We made a pact years ago to always keep each other's secrets, and it's one we still honor, even though we're both in our thirties. "I never knew you to be the type to go for phone sex, Esme, but whatever works."

"Anders!" she gasps, using her nickname for me. "That's sick. I'm your sister."

"Yet you're not denying it."

"There's nothing to deny. As I've told you time and again, there's nothing going on between us." Her voice falters. "It's not allowed. Anyway, this isn't about me, or Creed, or whatever." Her tone brightens. "He mentioned you're driving Route 66."

"I have to take the opportunity while I still can."

"Are you sure you're not doing this to avoid facing the truth?"

"I'm not avoiding anything," I protest, although my voice lacks the conviction I wish it held. "I have to face the truth every damn time I get out of bed and wonder if the soreness in my arm is from sleeping on it wrong or if it's another symptom. There's no avoiding this. Not when it's forcing me to question everything in my life, Esme."

"Then come home," she pleads. "Be with your family. Don't push us away. While I can understand why you'd want to take this time to process everything, to do things you've always wanted to do, your family needs you. Your country needs you."

"Until they learn their future king is a goddamn cripple."

"Just because you may eventually have trouble walking—"

"And shitting and fucking," I interject, but she ignores my outburst, remaining as levelheaded as always.

"I did my research. Your progression is slow. And you have relapsing-remitting MS, which is easily managed with drugs and diet. This isn't the death sentence you make it out to be. Even if your symptoms do deteriorate, it doesn't mean you'll be any less qualified to rule this country."

"We both know it might. At least in some people's eyes. It might be best for all involved if I abdicate now before it becomes a bigger deal than it needs to be."

The line goes eerily silent for what feels like an eternity. "Why would you do that?" Esme squeaks out.

I slowly raise myself from the bed, padding along the dingy carpet toward the water-spotted window and peering out at the traffic on the main road abutting the hotel. I'd like to believe what Esme says is true. Hell, in my humble opinion, Roosevelt was one of the best presidents the United States ever had, and he managed to do it all from the confines of a wheelchair. But that was before there was a television in every home. Most people had no idea he was even in a wheelchair.

These days, it's all about appearances, especially for the Royal Family. Especially for my father. After all, he abandoned my mother during her own battle with MS. He never came right out and told me why, but he's always been a man who prided himself on never showing vulnerability, no matter what. He viewed her condition as a show of weakness.

"I thought you'd be happy." I push out a laugh. "After all, you'd become next in line. Crown Princess. Finally a woman in charge. First ruling Queen of Belmont. You've always been rather vocal about the need for gender equality. This would be your opportunity to show all those men how effective a woman leader can be."

"But not at that price, Anderson. I won't allow it."

"You may not have a choice," I manage to get out past the lump building in my throat. "You know, I'm beginning to think this is what I deserve. That the universe is making me pay for all the mistakes I've made."

"How could you say that? You've never done anything in your life that would make you deserve *this*."

"Really? What about Kendall?"

"That wasn't your fault. No one could have seen the signs."

"I lived with her. I *should have* seen the signs."

I squeeze my eyes shut, rubbing my temples, feeling the same guilt now as I did when I watched my girlfriend, the woman I planned to marry, fall to the ground during a beach volleyball match. She'd hoped to make the Olympic team. Instead, she was carried out on a stretcher, never to open her eyes again.

"But, Anders—"

"You remember what Mum always said whenever we acted out as kids, don't you?" I interrupt.

"Karma is like a rubber band," she recalls, a lightness in her tone.

"You can only stretch it so far before it comes back and smacks you in the face. Maybe this is my smack in the face."

"Maybe it is," she agrees contemplatively. "But not as

payback for whatever perceived wrongs you committed in the past."

I open my mouth to argue, but she cuts me off.

"Maybe this is the smack in the face you need to finally get over Kendall. To finally allow yourself to live again. Despite anything you *think* you may deserve, you deserve to live most of all. And you will live a long, happy, *healthy* life. Don't you ever forget that."

I lean my head on the glass of the window, wondering if she can somehow read my thoughts. If she knows that every day since my diagnosis I've been consumed with what it means for my future. If I *have* a future.

Until today.

When a stunning, strawberry blonde caught my eye in a Chicago diner and changed my trajectory. I've always liked the idea of driving Route 66 but never allowed myself to slow down long enough to do it. It was a crazy notion, but the temptation was too strong. Before I knew it, I'd downloaded a Route 66 app onto my phone and set out on my cross-country journey. I'm not sure why, or what I hope to get out of it. Clarity? Peace? Acceptance?

"I'll never forget it," I tell Esme, mostly to placate her.

Seemingly satisfied with my affirmation, she exhales a relieved breath. "Be good, Anders."

"Being good is boring," I answer, as we've always said between each other. Our inside joke.

"Then be extraordinary," she responds. "Because, my darling brother, you are extraordinary. And no ridiculous diagnosis will ever change that. Please believe me."

I clutch my phone tighter, basking in her words. "Good night, Esme."

"Good morning, Anders."

I stay on the line for another beat, then end the call,

about to turn away from the window when I catch a movement out of the corner of my eye. Normally, I wouldn't think anything of it, wouldn't pause to watch a figure walk the perimeter of the outdoor pool, then lay a towel on one of the lounge chairs. It's not the fact it's nighttime that makes me stare in curiosity. It's because I can *feel* this woman. And when I notice her sit "Indian-style" and rest her hands on her knees, as if meditating, I know this isn't just a manifestation of my deepest desires.

Nora…

Running into her once was luck. Twice was a coincidence. But a third time?

I spin from the window and dash toward my suitcase. Ignoring all the pills, just as I've done every other night, I grab a bottle of wine I'd purchased earlier and leave my room, determined to find out what running into someone a third time could mean.

Chapter Seven

NORA

DEEP BREATH IN. *Close eyes. Liberating exhale out.*

I usually don't have any trouble finding a cocoon of peace whenever I meditate. It's the one place I can forget everything. The one place I'm able to focus only on the present instead of allowing myself to be consumed by the past. Perhaps that's the problem. Because, presently, all I can think about is Anderson's brilliant blue gaze.

I came out to the pool at my hotel hoping to clear my mind, something I had trouble doing in my room. It didn't help that a framed print of the obelisk from Lincoln's tomb hung across from my bed, reminding me yet again of the mysterious stranger. I'd hoped some fresh air would help. Instead, as I sit cross-legged on a lounge chair, a strange energy surrounds me. The same energy I felt at the mausoleum. The same energy I felt at the diner.

I need to replace that energy with something else. *Anything* else. So, instead of focusing on those sparkling blue eyes that seem to peer into my soul, I meditate on the events of the day. Events that don't include the handsome stranger with a spine-tingling smile and full lips that have me wondering how they'd feel against mine.

I reflect on the woman at the restored gas station who

shared stories of her late husband and how they used to drive Route 66 at least once a year. I admire the incredible artistic ability of those who painted the murals along the brick buildings in Pontiac. I give thanks to the sixteenth President of the United States who governed our country through one of the most trying eras, only for his life to be cut short.

And of course, as I think of Abraham Lincoln, my mind finds its way back to Anderson. His penetrating gaze. His sexy, disheveled hair. His deep, accented voice that makes my toes curl.

I fling my eyes open, aggravated that this man I'd never seen before this morning has somehow infiltrated my thoughts, no matter how much I try to clear my mind. Perhaps meditating isn't what I need. Perhaps I need to find some sort of…other release. Then my mind and body will be at peace. Or, at the very least, my libido will be.

Frustrated, I jump up and sling my bag over my shoulder, keeping my head lowered as I curse under my breath.

"Stupid blue eyes and full lips and gorgeous body and—"

I'm cut short as I slam into what I can only describe as a human wall, throwing me off balance. Hands shoot out to my hips, steadying me, preventing me from toppling over backward.

When I snap my head up to see who belongs to the body against mine, my gaze meets those same stupid blue eyes and full lips. Thankfully, I'd run into that gorgeous body before I got my next words out, considering I was about to curse what I assumed was a giant dick.

"We need to stop running into each other like this…" He arches a single brow, everything about his demeanor calm and confident. "Wouldn't you agree, Nora?"

Words. I need to make words. A sound. Anything. But nothing comes out, the warmth of his hands on my body sending liquid heat coursing through me. I try to summon my vocal cords to vibrate and make sound, turn those sounds into words, then string those words together into a complete thought. But they refuse to listen, Anderson's proximity leaving me devoid of thought, of mind, of body.

A horn honks in the distance, breaking his spell, and I scramble away. "How are you... Did you... What are you doing here?"

He chuckles. "Surprised to see me? Safe to say the feeling's mutual."

He brushes past me, settling on the lounge chair beside the one where I'd just attempted to find clarity. No wonder I couldn't. Because he's here.

"Would you like some?" He raises a bottle of wine.

"Thanks, but it's unwise to accept a drink from a stranger." I cross my arms over my chest, pulling my sweatshirt closer to my body. "How do I know you didn't drug it with roofies or something?"

He frowns. "Roofies? People seriously do that?"

I shrug. "Apparently so."

"Trust me, gorgeous..." The combination of his debonair smile and the sound of him calling me gorgeous in his accent has my knees weakening. "I don't need to drug women to get them to sleep with me." A flash of something washes over his expression, but it's gone in a heartbeat.

"Spoken with the cockiness of someone who'd drug me."

"You know what, Nora?" Reaching into his pocket, he retrieves a corkscrew and starts opening the bottle. "I like you. You're opinionated." The sound of the cork being yanked with a *pop* echoes around us. Then he fills a plastic cup halfway with a deep, red liquid. "I consider that an attractive quality. Lately, I seem to find myself surrounded by women who don't have a mind of their own. If I said jump, they'd ask how high without a single question as to *why* I want them to jump."

"How awful for you," I joke, rolling my eyes. "You must hate being with a woman who will do whatever you want."

When he looks at me, I expect to see a hint of amusement. Instead, his expression is serious, gaze even, lips formed into a tight line. "Actually, I loathe it. A relationship should be a partnership. Not a…dictatorship. In my opinion, there's nothing sexier than a woman who knows what she wants." He brings the plastic cup to his mouth and takes a long sip. My eyes are drawn to his Adam's apple as he swallows, releasing a satisfied "ah" on the finish.

Then he stretches his arms wide. "Now, what do you say to a glass of wine?"

I scrunch my brows. "Weren't you paying attention? You could be trying to drug me."

"And weren't *you* paying attention?" His voice is as smooth as velvet and as deep as the ocean, causing my insides to vibrate with want. "You just watched me not only open this bottle, but also pour from it, then take a drink. Yet I'm still functioning."

"You could have an immunity to whatever you put in it. Could all be part of your game." I bite my lower lip, my demeanor shifting to more playful. It's hard not to fall under Anderson's spell. He's charismatic. His smile alone has me wanting to agree to anything he asks. And the idea of some wine sounds incredibly appetizing.

"True, but the Dread Pirate Roberts I am not."

I give him a sideways glance, but before I can say

anything, he holds up a hand.

"If you're about to ask who that is, I rescind my offer for a glass of wine, as it's obvious we'll have nothing in common."

With a sly grin, I saunter toward him, swaying my hips more than necessary. More than I have in quite a while. I didn't come on this trip to flirt with a man, but it's empowering to feel desired again, especially after everything I've been through this year. By the way Anderson's gaze rakes over me as I sit down and gradually lean toward him, his jaw clenching with want, he absolutely desires me.

"*The Princess Bride* is one of my favorite movies," I murmur in a breathy voice. "But the book's better." I pull back, grinning.

He winks. "It always is."

"And it's a plastic cup," I add.

"Excuse me?"

"You're holding a plastic cup. Not a glass. And if the offer still stands, I'd like to take you up on it now."

"The offer most certainly still stands." Barely looking away, he pours wine into a fresh cup, then hands it to me. He raises his "glass", and I do the same. "To the road."

"To the road."

I maintain steady eye contact as I sip the wine. I'd expected some cheap "church" wine, as I always called the stuff tucked away on the bottom shelf of the liquor store. Instead, this is good. I steal a glance at the bottle and recognize the label — Grgich Hills.

"That's one of my favorites."

"Life is far too short to drink subpar wine." A thoughtful look pulls on his expression, then he refocuses on me. "Plus, I don't drink to get drunk. I drink wine because I enjoy the flavor."

"Same." I tip back my cup, taking a larger gulp than I normally would. But I need the alcohol to loosen me up, to make me ignore the heat of Anderson's gaze scalding my skin.

"So what's your story, Nora?"

"Story?"

"Yes. Why are you driving Route 66 all by yourself?"

"I just got divorced and decided to go on a divorcation." I don't look him directly in the eyes.

"You're divorced? You barely look old enough to be married."

I snort. "Thanks, but I'm thirty." On a long sigh, I sip my wine. "Divorced at thirty."

Even my mother, who's only a few marriages shy of beating Elizabeth Taylor's record, hadn't divorced by the time she was my age. She'd been happily married until my father's death when she was thirty-five. Her first divorce wasn't until she was in her forties.

"Better to be divorced at thirty than stuck in a loveless marriage. Were you married young and simply grew apart?"

It's a natural question, one I'd ask myself if I learned a friend of mine had divorced at such a young age.

"Nope. We were married less than a year. I went to surprise him when he was out of town on a business trip. Unfortunately for me, *I* was the one who was surprised when I walked in and found him with a man."

He doesn't say anything for several protracted moments. Simply stares, mouth slightly agape, eyes wide as he processes my unexpected answer. Then he shakes his head, exhaling.

"Damn. That's rough. Not your typical woman scorned story."

"Tell me about it," I quip with a roll of my eyes.

"But the question remains. Why Route 66?"

"I told you. I got divorced and—"

"Yeah, yeah. I heard. You're on a divor-cation. That's more the answer as to *how* you came to drive Route 66. It doesn't answer *why*."

I part my lips, taken aback by his rather astute observation. Everyone else I came across today who asked me why I was driving Route 66 had been satisfied with my story. But not Anderson. He seems to be able to see past the excuse and realize there's more I'm not telling him.

"Does it have something to do with the ashes I noticed you spreading in front of Lincoln's tomb?" His voice is low and timid, unlike the confident tone he's used until now.

"I—" I shake my head, struggling to come up with some explanation. I'd looked around before I sprinkled Hunter's remains. I hadn't seen anyone nearby.

"As well as at the official start of Route 66 in Chicago?" he questions, but he's not smug about it. More curious than anything.

It shouldn't be this difficult to admit the truth. That I lost my fiancé six years ago in a car accident and am now taking the trip we were never able to, spreading his ashes along the way. But this is supposed to be for me. I'm not ready to share Hunter with anyone else.

"It's okay if you don't want to tell me, Nora. Trust me." He levels his gaze on me, a genuine smile curving the corners of his mouth. "I more than understand. Sometimes our reality is too painful and we need a break."

"Is that what you're doing?" I lower my eyes, fidgeting with the hem of my yoga pants. "Why you're also presumably driving Route 66? Taking a break from reality?"

"Actually... No."

I lift my head.

"I'm gay and found out my partner's straight." He winks, his demeanor lighthearted.

"Is that right?"

"Nah."

"Which part? About you being gay. Or your partner being straight."

Swiping the bottle off the ground, he curves toward me. I stiffen as the heat of his breath warms my skin, the addictive scent of muted body wash or shampoo filtering into my nostrils and making my mouth water.

"I think we both know I'm not gay," he growls as he refills my wine.

The last thing I need is to drink even more, especially around Anderson. Regardless, I can't pull myself away from him.

"I wouldn't presume anything," I reply in a sultry voice, my gaze locking on his.

"Trust me. I'm not gay. How can I be when I haven't been able to stop thinking about those plump lips of yours all day?"

I gasp, my pulse skyrocketing, lightheaded, dizzy, and a thousand other sensations I haven't experienced in too long now. That I didn't think I'd ever experience again.

When he pulls back, he regards me with an intensity that causes warmth to spread through me, my skin prickling, insides vibrating.

"You were right." He casually leans against the lounge chair, pretending as if he hadn't just dropped that bomb. But he did, turning my stomach into knots in the span of a heartbeat.

"Excuse me?"

"About taking a break from reality." A darkness crosses his face before he schools his expression. "I guess we're alike in that respect. We both came out here to forget for a minute."

I study him thoughtfully, wondering what his story is. "Want to talk about it?"

"Do you?" He gives me a knowing look, and I subtly shake my head. "Me, either. Talking about it will make it real. I'm not quite there yet."

"So, still in denial." I sip on my wine and settle into the chair, stretching my legs in front of me and crossing them at the ankles. "Wait until you get to the bargaining stage. That's the worst of them all."

"Where are you?"

I offer him a slight smile. "It changes every day."

"Have you ever reached acceptance?"

"I once thought I did." I down the rest of my wine, needing the burn of the alcohol to dull the other pain. "In retrospect, I think I was in denial but ignored the signs."

"That reminds me of something my sister likes to say." There's affection in his voice as he speaks of his family. I may not know much about him other than his name, but it's obvious he has a lot of respect and admiration for his sister.

"What's that?"

"Ignoring the signs is a sure way to end up at the wrong destination." He pauses, then laughs, almost to himself.

"What is it?"

"Nothing." Averting his eyes, he grabs the bottle, splitting the last of the wine between our two cups. "It's just curious is all."

"What is?"

"For the past week, I've been driving around, pretty aimlessly at that, going where my nose takes me."

"Wow. That sounds kind of exciting. And liberating. You don't have any destination in mind?"

"My plan is to make it out to my place in LA eventually, but I had no intention of taking my time and driving Route 66. Until I saw you in that diner and decided to change my original path. And since we keep running into each other…" He trails off.

"What?" I urge him to finish his thought.

He focuses on something in the distance as he worries his bottom lip, seeming to weigh his options. Then he returns his gaze to me, steady and unwavering.

"Maybe the fact we keep running into each other is the universe's way of sending me a message."

"What message would that be?"

"That maybe I was on the wrong path before."

Lifting my cup, I meet his gaze, feeling more in tune with my body and spirit than I've been able to attain in my years of meditating. "To the right destination."

His smile causes my heart to skip a beat. "The right destination."

Chapter Eight

ANDERSON

"HAS NEW YORK always been home?" I ask several hours later as Nora and I finish yet another bottle of wine.

I can't remember the last time I've enjoyed a woman's company as much as I've enjoyed Nora's. Her smile. Her laugh. Her vitality. Yes, a cloud of sadness seems to hover over her, but now and then a ray of sunshine pokes through, allowing me a glimpse of the real Nora.

As the hour crept toward midnight and beyond, we've remained by the pool. She may be acting polite, but I get the feeling she's no more prepared for tonight to end than I am. And to think, if I hadn't been talking to my sister, hadn't walked up to the grimy window in my hotel room at that precise moment, I never would have noticed Nora at the pool. We may never have crossed paths again. We never would have had…*this*. I don't even know what this is, but for the first time since I received my diagnosis, I'm not wallowing, not depressed. I'm smiling, and it's not forced. It's natural. I want more of whatever this is.

"Not always," she answers. Her voice is lazy from the late hour and amount of wine she's consumed. "Grew up in Florida. But *not* that Florida. Nice Florida."

I furrow my brow as I pull the cork out of yet another bottle of wine. "Nice Florida?"

"There are two Floridas," she answers with a wave of her hand. "There's the Florida where news reporters find all the colorful witnesses who are more than eager to give a first-hand account of anything and everything, from hurricanes, to gator wrestling, to my personal favorite, alien abductions."

"Ah. I see. So more like rednecks."

"Exactly." She rolls her eyes. "Then there's the Florida everyone knows. Theme parks and beaches, like where I lived in Pensacola for the first five years of my life. After that…" She shrugs, exhaling deeply. Then, to my surprise, she grabs the wine bottle and drinks straight from it. Some men might find it uncivilized. I don't. It's another piece of her personality coming into focus. "After that, we left. My mom, my brothers, and me."

"Was your father not in the picture?"

"Not anymore."

"Divorce?"

She shakes her head. "Died on deployment."

My shoulders fall as I offer her a sincere look. "I'm sorry."

"It comes with the territory of having a father in the military, I suppose."

"I suppose it does. Doesn't make it any easier, though."

"No. It doesn't."

She smiles a tight-lipped smile, several protracted moments passing as I admire her. I want to know more about her, about why I'm drawn to her when no other woman I've met in recent history has made me feel like this. Like I'd die without her next word, next smile, next laugh.

"After that, my mother couldn't bear being around the constant reminders of my father, so we moved to

Naples in Southern Florida. I stayed there until college."

"Then where did you go?"

"Syracuse."

"What did you study?" I press.

She blows out a sarcastic laugh. "Psychology."

"What? Did you not enjoy it?"

"Actually, I did. Immensely. But I studied it because that's what my mother wanted me to study." She pauses, her eyes narrowed in contemplation. "To put it mildly, my relationship with my mother is…complicated. She's a psychiatrist. After my father died, her new favorite hobby became analyzing everything I did or said. I pretty much grew up under a microscope."

I nod, knowing all too well how that feels, but I don't say so. I can't. As far as she knows, I'm simply Anderson. Not Crown Prince Gabriel Anderson Joseph Xavier Wellingston of Belmont. I prefer it this way. She's able to see me, not the title.

"So, I don't know…" She averts her gaze. "It sounds stupid now, but back then, I saw my course of study as a way to finally earn her approval. It took me a few years to realize I could invent a flying car and shit diamonds, yet it still wouldn't be good enough for her. But that doesn't matter. I've been living in Manhattan for six years now and love it. And the best part about it?" She arches a brow, swiping the bottle off the ground and taking another long pull from it. "My mother lives over a thousand miles away."

"I'll drink to that," I say, taking the bottle from her and sipping from it. I'd be lying if I said a thrill doesn't run through me over the prospect of my lips being where hers just were. Normally, I wouldn't think twice about such a thing, but to have a taste of Nora, even indirectly, makes electricity flow through my veins, reigniting something that's lain dormant for years.

"So, what's your deal, Anderson?" Nora asks, cutting through my thoughts of whether her lips would taste as sweet as the remnants she left on the bottle. I imagine they'd be even more addictive.

"My…deal?"

"Yes. Your deal." She mimics my accent. "I'm guessing you've spent some time in England." Tilting her head, she rakes her gaze over me. "But there's something American about your accent, too."

I study her for a moment, surprised she picked up on that. Most people only hear the British inflection I acquired during my years of prep school outside of London. Not to mention most citizens of our country also speak with a British accent, although it has a slight French influence, as well. The combination of Belmont's location bordering France and across the channel from the United Kingdom has provided our people a beautiful mix of culture. Regardless, no one really picks up on the way the American accent creeped in, thanks to the years I spent here for college and after.

"Well, I've lived in both places. London for prep school. Then the States for university."

I give her the story I developed years ago for my Anderson North identity. Although this is the first time a tiny amount of guilt settles in my stomach over the idea that I'm not being completely honest with her. I remind myself it's for the best. When most people find out who I am, they…change. I can't explain it. It's rare to find someone who can look past the title and see the person. Kendall could. It's why I fell for her so hard, so fast. She treated me like I was normal. I miss being normal.

"Where did you go?"

"Harvard."

"I didn't realize I was in the company of a genius," she jests.

I chuckle, shaking my head. "Certainly no genius. Just…well-connected."

"What did you study?"

"Excuse me," a voice cuts through. We both tear our eyes from each other and toward the pool where a man dressed in khakis and a polo shirt boasting the hotel's insignia stands. "This area closed at ten. You can't be here." He eyes the bottle on the ground between our two chairs. "And glass isn't allowed."

"Well then…" I expel a breath as I stand from the lounge chair, which proves to be slightly difficult, thanks to the hours spent sitting and drinking wine. I fight against a dizzy spell, praying it's not a sign my MS is progressing. But when it passes as soon as it begins, I brush it off, blaming it on the sudden movement and alcohol. "Shall we retire inside?" I play up my accent as I extend my hand toward Nora.

She giggles, her cheeks turning even more pink than they already are. A smile plays on my lips from the beautiful sound. All I can do is stare in wonder. We've only spent a few hours together. Such a short time when you think of the years most people spend on earth. Yet in these few hours, this woman has done what no one has in over half a decade.

She made me smile.

She made me stop thinking about the future.

She made me want to move on from the past.

She reminded me what it's like to live.

And I want more of this.

With careful movements, Nora places her hand in mine. I try to ignore the warmth that fills me from the simple sensation of her skin on mine. I take a moment to admire our joined hands. Mine is rough and large.

Hers is soft and dainty. Two worlds. Two polar opposites. But two people who have somehow found each other.

I help her to her feet, but don't want to let go of her hand. Don't want to do anything to break this bubble. To return to the reality I've all but forgotten about tonight. Ever since my diagnosis, it's been the only thing on my mind. But in these hours with Nora, I've barely thought of it. Instead, I've been consumed by her. Her laugh. Her smile. Doing anything to hear that laugh and relish in her heartwarming smile.

I brush my thumb along her knuckles, watching as her complexion flushes more, her breathing growing uneven under my stare. I know she feels this, too. This spark. This electricity. This unmistakable connection. It hums with urgency between us. Normally I'd brush it off, blame it on the alcohol. But I haven't experienced anything so intense and profound in quite a while. Maybe ever.

A throat clearing cuts through, reminding me we're not alone. I reluctantly drop my hold on Nora's hand and grab the half-empty bottle of wine. Once we're content we have everything we came here with, we head out of the pool area, the hotel clerk following.

After spending all evening under the light of the stars and a few dim streetlamps, the florescent lights of the lobby are blinding. I squint to readjust my eyes to the artificial illumination, silence filling the air as Nora and I walk toward the bank of elevators. It's not uncomfortable. More like neither one of us wants to say anything for fear it will break the magic we just experienced tonight.

And there's no question in my mind. Tonight was magical. At least for me.

I press the call button and the steel doors slide open,

inviting us inside. Glancing at Nora, I gesture for her to walk ahead of me. She hesitates a moment, meeting my gaze. Is she thinking the same thing I am? That she doesn't want this spell to be broken?

She releases a long sigh, then steps into the elevator, but I don't miss the reluctance in her strides. I join her, pressing the button for three, noticing the number two already illuminated.

The doors shut, locking us in this tiny space that seems even smaller with Nora so close. I take a deep breath, smelling lavender and baby powder. It's fresh and comforting. Just like I get the feeling this woman is. I inch closer as we stand in silence, inexplicably drawn to her. Our bodies are two magnets, a force outside our control constantly urging us together.

A ding cuts through the charged atmosphere, the doors opening. Nora slides her eyes up to meet mine, a small smile curving her plump lips that I imagine leaning down to kiss. But I won't. Not with this lie hanging between us. It was a promise I made to myself years ago. If I were to meet a woman while using my Anderson North identity, I wouldn't pursue anything meaningful until I told her the truth. Normally, it's not a problem, as many of the women I've shared a bed with weren't ones I was actually interested in for anything more than some fun and a much-needed release. Either were they.

But I felt it the second I stepped into that diner. The instant my eyes fell on her at Lincoln's tomb. The moment her body rammed into mine by the pool. Nora isn't most women.

She steps out of the elevator, then turns around, meeting my gaze once more. "Well, thank you for the wine, Anderson. And the company. I didn't know how much I needed tonight until you forced yourself on me."

Her eyes widen and she sucks in a breath as her words replay in her mind. "I mean, not like that. You didn't force yourself on me," she flounders, her cheeks turning an even brighter shade of red. "But—"

I take her hand in mine, cutting her off. "I know what you mean. I'm glad I…forced myself on you, too."

She brings her eyes to mine, nodding, but doesn't move. We just stare at each other, her outside the elevator, me within. When it dings, I react quickly, dropping my hold on her and slamming my hand against the closing doors to prevent them from doing so. I refuse to allow them to sever this bond, this connection.

"Want to come up?" I lift the bottle. "Finish this off?"

She inhales sharply, her eyes searching mine.

"Crap. I'm sorry. Now I'm the one with my foot in my mouth. That probably sounds pretty skeevy, right?"

"Actually, it sounds like an invitation I'd love to accept." Her expression falls.

"But?" I arch a brow, sensing there's more.

"But I can't."

I nod, my shoulders falling slightly. "I understand."

She holds my gaze a moment longer, then sighs. "Thanks again."

Turning, she starts toward her room. As I watch her walk away, I fear it will be the last time I'll see her, so I scramble out of the elevator, allowing it to close without me inside it.

"Nora," I whisper-shout, so as to not wake up any guests.

She whirls around, eyes flaming in surprise to see me standing here and not in the elevator on my way up to my room.

I stammer, not having thought this far ahead. All I know is I don't like the idea of watching her walk away without knowing if I'll ever see her again.

"Want to meet up somewhere tomorrow?"

She chews on her bottom lip, hesitating as she shifts her weight from foot to foot. Seemingly torn, she peers over my shoulder, as if hoping the answer is written on the walls. Then she exhales, bringing her gaze back to mine.

"You said you think the fact our paths keep crossing is a sign."

I swallow hard. "I did."

"Then this is your chance to prove it."

"Prove it?" I tilt my head. "I don't—"

"If we're meant to see each other again, the universe will make it so." With a small smile, she spins from me, making her way down the hallway once more.

"So that's it?" I say louder than I intended.

She stops, glancing over her shoulder. "What's it?"

"This." I gesture between our two bodies, stalking toward her. "I have one of the most amazing nights I've had in a long time…a night I was able to forget everything for a minute and enjoy a genuine conversation with a woman I find incredibly fucking attractive…but I'm supposed to be okay with watching you walk away, praying our paths cross again?"

She shrugs. "Have a little faith."

"Faith?"

"Yeah." She smiles contemplatively. "Faith."

I shake my head, running my hand through my hair. I haven't had faith in years. Not since I lost Kendall. Ever since then, it's been impossible for me to put faith in anything. But here's this complete stranger who sparks something inexplicable inside of me asking me to go against everything I believe in, to relinquish the control I've carefully maintained and put it all on faith?

"Maybe this is what you need to restore your faith."

She lifts herself onto her toes and brushes her lips against my cheek. The contact is so slight, I almost question whether it was her lips or simply a breeze. Then she lowers herself, her eyes meeting mine once more. "Good night, Anderson."

I bring my hand up to the place where her lips just hovered, a tingle spreading through me. "Sweet dreams, Nora."

Maybe having a little faith isn't such a bad idea, especially when there's such a sweet reward.

Chapter Nine

NORA

AN INCESSANT BUZZ startles me awake and I groan, fumbling on the nightstand for my phone. I normally don't need an alarm to wake up, but after not getting to bed until after three, I could have slept all morning.

Groggy, I wipe the cobwebs from my eyes, sitting up and stretching. Despite usually never sleeping well in a strange bed, I had a restful night. I could probably thank the copious amount of wine I consumed for that, but I get the feeling it was something else.

Some*one* else.

A warmth fills me as I recall my evening with Anderson. It was surprising to say the least. For a few hours, I could forget everything and just enjoy my time with him. To laugh at his jokes. To relish in the stories of his past. To blush when he flirted with me.

It took every ounce of resolve to turn down his invitation to go up to his room to finish the bottle and our conversation. I didn't come on this trip to hook up with the first attractive man who crossed my path. I came here to close this chapter in my life. I can't start a new one until this one is over.

Looking at the time, I reluctantly pull myself from the comfort of the bed and start getting ready for my day. Within an hour, I'm showered, dressed in a t-shirt and shorts, my makeup applied and hair pulled back from my face. I check my room one last time, making sure I didn't forget anything, then head down the corridor and into a waiting elevator.

It's been six hours, but I can still sense Anderson's presence in here. Can still smell his addictive scent. Can still feel his heat. I wonder what he's doing right now. Is he still in bed, sleeping off all that wine? Or did he get a head start on his day and is already miles ahead of me? A part of me hopes to run into him, but as the doors open to an empty lobby, any chance of seeing him before I leave is dashed. I must simply do what I told Anderson last night. Have faith our paths will cross again if they're meant to.

I wave goodbye to the front desk clerk, then make my way out to the parking lot and my rental car. Popping the trunk, I set my suitcase inside before sliding in behind the steering wheel. I retrieve my phone from my purse and set it into the holder I attached to the dashboard, bringing up the Route 66 app, which will help direct me during today's trip.

Once I'm settled, I press my foot on the brake and push the start button by the steering wheel.

Nothing happens.

I take my foot off the brake, making sure I have the key fob, which I do. Then I try again. Still, the engine refuses to turn over.

"Oh, come on, you piece of shit," I curse under my breath. It's just my luck that I get the rental car with engine troubles. That's what I get for booking this trip last minute.

With a deep inhale, I release the brake, giving the car a second to do whatever it needs in order to work. After sending up a silent prayer to not be forced to end this trip before it even begins, I put my foot back on the brake and press the engine start button yet again. And yet again, nothing happens. There's something dissatisfying about urging an engine to start by pressing a button instead of turning a key in the ignition as far as it will go.

Finally, after an eternity of refusing to take my finger off the button, pushing it as hard as I can, the most incredible sound fills the air. The engine roars to life. Well, I can't really call it a roar. This tiny, compact car doesn't roar. I'm not even sure it purrs. More like sputters.

I close my eyes, issuing a thousand thank yous to whomever made this miracle happen, patting the dashboard as if the car were a dog that had listened to his master and earned a treat. I hope this is simply a fluke. Not a sign of things to come. I've only traveled a little over two hundred miles on a journey that is over two thousand. I need a working car.

Backing out of my spot, I glance out the rear window, then shift into drive. I take one last look at the hotel, a twinge of regret filling me that I hadn't made plans to meet up with Anderson today. Silencing the voice in my head urging me to track him down to see if the spark I felt last night is still here, I navigate the car out of the parking lot, passing the pool on the way. Everything looks different now. Last night, it was…magical, a cocoon where I could admit things I normally don't. But today, it looks just like every other pool at a roadside motel.

I convince myself this is for the best. That in the light of day, whatever I thought I experienced last night would be ordinary and unremarkable, just like this pool.

After checking the directions on my phone, I pull onto the main road, pressing my foot on the gas to pick up speed. But the car doesn't respond, refusing to go faster than twenty-five miles an hour, no matter how much pressure I apply. I drive a few blocks, remaining in the right-hand lane, hoping the car will eventually correct itself. But even after a mile, it's still struggling to pick up any power.

When I come to a stoplight, I consider my options. There's obviously something wrong with this car, despite it only having a little over twenty thousand miles on it. The last thing I need is to be stranded on the side of the road in the middle of nowhere without cell service.

With a groan, I make a U-turn and drive back to the hotel, parking in the same spot I'd just left. After pulling the lever for the hood, I step out of the car and prop it open, leaning over the engine. I'm not sure why I even bother. It's not like I know what I'm looking at. Hell, when I'd picked up the rental car back in Chicago, it was the first time I'd been behind the wheel since moving to Manhattan.

"Car trouble?"

A voice comes out of nowhere, startling me. I straighten, forgetting what I'm doing, and smack my head on the hood, a loud crack seeming to echo around me.

"Fuck," I hiss out as I rub the sore spot.

"Sorry. I didn't mean to scare you, gorgeous."

If the accent weren't a dead giveaway regarding the owner of the voice, the nickname confirms it. Stepping back, my eyes lock onto Anderson's, a sexy smirk on his lips.

He crosses his arms over his chest, his bulging biceps tugging on the fabric of the black t-shirt. His hair is damp from a recent shower, and it takes every ounce of resolve I have to not fantasize about him in the shower. Tonight, I *definitely* need to put that vibrator to use.

"What's wrong with your car?" he asks when I don't respond, too busy ogling him. It's impossible not to. He's the epitome of eye candy.

"It wouldn't start a few minutes ago." I tear my gaze from his. "When it finally did, it wouldn't go over twenty-five miles an hour."

He gestures toward the engine. "Mind if I take a look?"

"You know something about cars?"

"I can get by."

I step away, allowing him to take a look under my hood.

The *car's* hood. Not *my* hood.

He bends down, toying with different parts of the engine. My heart rate increases as I watch him check the oil, grease getting on his hands. There's something oddly erotic about watching a man as handsome as Anderson working on a car, the corded muscles in his forearms straining, his brow creased in confusion.

His broad shoulders pull at the fabric of his shirt, and I'm able to make out the defined muscles of his back. When his t-shirt lifts, it reveals a sliver of olive-toned skin. I wonder if he has that little V at his waist all women seem to lose their minds over. In my fantasy, he most certainly does.

In my fantasy, I even lick the ridges of that V, all the way to his——

"Nothing looks off," he comments, straightening and facing me.

I inhale a sharp breath, his sudden movement taking me by surprise. I attempt to regain my composure and make it appear as if I hadn't been checking him out, but the sly grin and nefarious glint in his eyes tell me he caught me.

"Is that right?" I hold my head high, smoothing a

hand along my hair, making sure it's secure in my low ponytail.

"That's right." His voice oozes with sin as he advances toward me.

With each step he takes, I take one in retreat, my heart pounding in my chest. It's been so long since a man has looked at me with this much heat, this much want, this much hunger. This has to be a dream. This kind of thing doesn't happen in real life. But another part of me doesn't care if it *is* a dream. Because it's the sweetest dream I've had in quite a while, and I don't want to wake up.

When my back hits the side of a midnight blue Jeep Wrangler parked a few spots from mine, I pray the owner doesn't choose this second to need his car. Because I have no desire for this to end any time soon. And for the first time in a long time, that's all I care about. This moment. Not the pain of my past. Not the anxiety of my future. Just right now. Just this ridiculously attractive man looming over me. I told him to have faith we'd run into each other again. Maybe it's time I have that same faith that there's a reason we keep running into each other.

"Nora…," he exhales, angling closer.

I lose myself in his intoxicating scent, a combination of the ocean and fresh rain. "Yes?"

"You…"

"Yes?" I repeat, tilting my chin back.

He draws near, his lips skimming mine. "Need to move."

His words snap me out of my trance, and I stiffen, blinking in bewilderment.

"I need to get into the glove box." He nods at the Jeep behind me. "That's my car."

"Oh. Right." My cheeks burning with

embarrassment, I scramble away from the Jeep and toward my car. "So, what's the verdict? Anything that can be fixed easily?" I study the coils and wires in the engine, needing to focus on something other than the growing desire flowing through my veins.

When I hear the door shut, I glance up, watching as Anderson uses a rag to wipe his hands clean. I even find that ridiculously attractive. Handsome, hot British accent, and he knows a thing or two about cars? It's like someone took a page out of my version of the perfect man and dropped him into my life at the absolute worst time possible just to taunt me. Or perhaps to motivate me to finally get my shit together. To finally let Hunter go. To show me that life *can* go on without him.

"There aren't a lot of miles on it. You usually don't have a problem like this until there is. Then again, it's a rental, so God knows who's been driving it. Sometimes you might have trouble turning the engine over if one of the battery connectors is loose. But that's not the case here. Everything looks intact." With his hands free of grease, he tosses the rag onto the hood of the Wrangler, then leans against it.

"My best guess is it's the transmission, or a clogged fuel filter. Regardless, it's not a quick fix. You'll need a new car."

Great.

Chapter Ten

ANDERSON

Frustration covers Nora's expression, lips pinched, muscles rigid with tension. She digs her fingernails into her hair that, like the last few times I've seen her, is slicked back into a tight ponytail at her nape. Then she closes her eyes and inhales a deep breath, holding it for several long seconds before slowly pushing it out.

When she opens her eyes, she calmly turns to her car and opens the driver's side door.

"What are you doing?"

She retrieves her phone from the dashboard and waves it. "Calling the rental company to have them get me a new car." She heads toward one of the benches in front of the hotel.

I react quickly, darting after her and sitting beside her, the scent of lavender and baby powder overpowering that of the lingering stale cigarette stench coming from the ashtray on top of the garbage bin. She peers at me, arching a manicured brow. Everything about her seems flawless and put together. I wonder if it's all a façade, like it is for me. A show she puts on so everyone thinks her life is the picture of perfection.

"I'll wait with you." I answer the question drawn on her face.

"You don't need to," she whispers, placing her hand

over the phone and pulling it away from her ear. "I'm sure you want to get on the road, too. It could be a while. I'll be fine on my own."

"I don't doubt that." I lean back on the bench, crossing my legs at the ankles and folding my arms over my chest. I'd be lying if I said I didn't do it just to see Nora's reaction. And like every time before, her gaze darts to my biceps. "But I'd be a fool if I didn't jump at the opportunity to spend a little more time with you. Like you encouraged me last night, I had faith. And look what having faith brought me."

"What's that?"

I smile. "You."

She parts her lips, about to respond, when I hear a voice answer the line.

"Thank you for calling Easy Rental Car. This is Tabitha. How can I help you?"

Nora turns away from me, focusing her attention on her phone. "Hi. My name is Nora Tremblay. I rented a car a few days ago, and it's having engine trouble. It won't go over twenty or thirty miles an hour. I'd like to see about getting a replacement."

She flashes me a sweet smile, then answers the agent's request for her reservation number. I take this opportunity to admire her profile, starting at her brilliant eyes, moving to her full, glossy lips that are tinged pink, then appreciating the smattering of freckles across her cheekbones and nose. She has a natural beauty, but there's also something deeper that draws me to her. That makes me think she's something more than just a pretty face. Although her face isn't just pretty. She's stunning, possessing a classic beauty most women spend a fortune to achieve. But for Nora, it comes naturally.

"So you're telling me there are no cars in either St.

Louis or Chicago?" Nora cuts through, and I tear my gaze away from checking out the rest of her body, most notably her legs that are left exposed in a pair of shorts. "How is that even possible?"

"I apologize for the inconvenience," the agent says, her voice muffled. "We're at max capacity for reservations and have had some other cars that had to be taken out of rotation for repairs. What I can do is arrange a tow of your vehicle as well as transportation to Chicago or St. Louis, whichever you'd prefer. We should have a car freed up within a day or two. If one is returned earlier, you'll get priority."

The more the agent speaks, the more I notice Nora's expression turn to one of resignation, her lips turned downward, shoulders slumping. I can only imagine what kind of wrench this has thrown into her plans. I doubt she can just take off for as long as she wants to. Having to wait upwards of two days for a new car may be the nail in the coffin on her trip. A trip I know is important to her. Not just as a divor-cation, but as something bigger.

"I'm on a tight schedule." Her words ooze with desperation, confirming my original suspicions. "I'm driving Route 66 and—"

"Come with me," I blurt out before I have a chance to give the idea the deliberation it deserves.

Her eyes whip toward mine, wide and searching. "What did you say?" She covers her phone's microphone once more.

I straighten my posture, not immediately responding. This is my opportunity to back out, which is what I should do. Creed will lose his mind once he learns I invited a woman, a complete stranger, into my car. I can hear his voice in my head, coming up with every scenario about who she could be, each one more ridiculous than the last. But she encouraged me to have faith our paths would cross again if they were meant to. Now I have faith that there might be some bigger power at play, forcing us together. A bigger plan. A bigger purpose.

"You can come with me," I repeat, not a hint of hesitation in my words.

She peers at me skeptically, her lips parting. I can already hear the refusal that's about to fall from her mouth.

"At least until St. Louis," I interrupt before she can turn me down. "Then you can decide if you want to continue on together or go our separate ways."

"I appreciate the offer, but I don't make a habit of getting into a car with people I don't know." She starts to return her attention to her phone.

"But that's where you're wrong." Sliding off the bench, I crouch in front of her, not allowing her to escape this conversation. "I'm *not* a stranger."

"Excuse me a moment," she says to the woman on the phone before focusing her eyes on me. "We met yesterday, Anderson. I don't know anything about you, other than your name and that you're driving Route 66. And that you spent your younger years in London before coming to the States for college."

"But I make you smile." I waggle my brows. "I bet there are people you've known years who can't even do that. Don't forget we spent… What was it? Seven hours together last night and drank almost three bottles of wine. I'd say that makes us friends."

She shakes her head. I can practically feel the war raging in her brain. The same war as when I went out to the pool and asked if she wanted some wine. The same war that seems to plague her whenever she shows a single ounce of happiness. And she deserves to be happy. Don't we all deserve that?

"You enjoy my company, do you not?"

"I do," she admits, albeit guardedly.

When I take her free hand in mine, she inhales a sharp breath. Just like yesterday, my body comes alive from the innocent contact. A yearning for even more consumes me.

"Then enjoy my company today."

She starts to shake her head, but I interrupt her once more.

"If you have the car company pick you up and take you to St. Louis, you won't be able to see the things on your list between here and there."

I squint, recalling the places on the list I snuck a peek of yesterday at the diner. Then it hits me, two pieces of the puzzle snapping into place. The list… The ashes…

Lowering my voice, I edge closer. "You won't be able to spread those ashes at every place on your list."

She squeezes her eyes shut, shoulders slumping. Sure, she could easily backtrack once she gets a replacement car, but that will only add to the delay.

"Come on, Nora. Have a little faith," I encourage.

She blinks her eyes open, peering at me. "Faith?"

"Yeah." I smile at our role reversal. "You told me to have faith we'd see each other again, and we have. So now I'm asking you to have a little faith in me. Faith that it's okay to step out of your comfort zone. Faith that it's okay to…dare I say it…have some fun. With me."

"Faith…" She turns from me, peering into the distance. The seconds tick by, each one feeling as long as a day as I wait for her reply. Then she smiles, locking her gaze with mine. "Okay."

"Okay?" I repeat, surprise apparent in my tone.

"Yes. Okay. I'll drive with you. But only until St. Louis," she adds sharply, pulling her hand from mine, re-securing whatever mask she wears.

"If that's what you need to tell yourself." I wink. "I have faith you'll change your mind."

Chapter Eleven

ANDERSON

"ARE YOU HUNGRY?" I ask, cutting through the stiff silence that's a complete shift from the easy conversation we shared last night. Then again, wine was involved. Not to mention, we weren't stuck in a small space, unable to escape the tension crackling between us.

"I can eat, if you don't mind stopping."

"I'm in no rush for this day to end," I comment, stealing a glance at her. She bites her bottom lip, trying to subdue her smile, but she can't hide the pink blush blooming on her cheeks.

Putting my indicator on, I turn into the parking lot of a diner and yank on the emergency brake, then hop out. My phone pings relentlessly in my pocket as I run to the other side of the Jeep. But like I've done since I left the hotel after sending a quick text to Creed to inform him of a change in plans, which I'm sure caused him to have a heart attack, I ignore it.

"I can get that for you," I tell Nora when she starts to open her door. I pull it the rest of the way, extending my hand toward her.

"So you're a gentleman then. Is that right?"

"At least in public." I flash her a devious grin, to which she rolls her eyes. Nevertheless, she places her hand in mine, allowing me to help her down from the

Jeep.

Once she has her footing, I rest my hand on the middle of her back, steering her toward the building, reaching for the door before she gets to it. As I stand aside to allow her to enter before me, I notice a familiar black SUV pull into the lot and park beside my Jeep. I knew I wouldn't be able to avoid Creed all day. I just wanted a little more time with Nora before he intervened, reminding me of the protocol I'm supposed to follow. Reminding me my life is far from normal.

"Sit anywhere you'd like," a woman calls out as she speeds past us, four plates balanced between her hands and arms. "I'll be right with you."

"Thanks." I look at Nora. "Booth okay?"

"Sure."

I lead her toward a booth by the front windows and grab two of the menus from the condiment holder, handing one to her. Another awkward silence fills the air as we peruse the menu. I skim the beverages, thinking perhaps a shot of vodka might loosen her up. At the very least, bring back the easy-going atmosphere we enjoyed last night. Unfortunately, the strongest thing they have is espresso, and it's probably not nearly as strong as I prefer.

"Coffee?" the same woman asks, approaching our table and holding up a steaming pot.

"Yes," Nora and I say simultaneously.

The waitress turns over the coffee cup placed down on its saucer and fills it, pushing it toward Nora before repeating the same to mine. "Do y'all need a little more time?"

I glance at Nora, who nods. "Please."

"Take your time. I'll be back to check on y'all in a few minutes." The woman spins around, shoving her order book into the pocket of her apron.

I'm about to return my attention to the menu when the door to the diner opens, Creed's intimidating figure striding inside, looking out of place in his dark jeans and black shirt when everyone else is dressed casually.

When he catches my gaze, he gestures inconspicuously toward the restrooms before heading in that direction.

"Will you excuse me for a minute?"

Nora whips her head up from studying the menu. "Of course."

"Thanks."

With a smile, I slide out of the booth and make my way toward the men's room. As I'm about to disappear down the hallway, I look over my shoulder, watching Nora blow out a long breath and close her eyes, as if meditating again.

This time, I hope she's meditating about me.

Inhaling what I hope to be my own calming breath, I prepare to face Creed, who I'm sure is about to chew me out for what he considers an extremely reckless move.

The second I open the door, my suspicions are confirmed when he whirls around, his dark eyes on fire. He's only an inch taller than my six-four height, but with the muscular physique he's acquired after nearly two decades in the military, first as part of the infantry, then as a member of the Royal Guard, I feel like he dwarfs me immeasurably.

"Are you out of your fucking mind?" he hisses, digging his large fingers through his slick, black hair. "What were you thinking, inviting a woman, a complete stranger, into your car?"

"I was thinking she needed a ride, so I offered her one," I respond nonchalantly, shoving my hands into my pockets. "Her vehicle broke down. The car company offered to send an agent to pick her up and take her to St. Louis, but then she'd miss out on driving Route 66 between here and there."

"So? Not your problem."

"But it's important to her."

He glares at me, studying my expression. "You barely know her."

"I know enough."

"Enough to know she is who she claims to be?" He arches a brow. "She could have recognized you and faked car trouble to get close to you. Perhaps she's a reporter who's wondering why you haven't had any public appearances lately and is hoping for the inside scoop."

I roll my eyes. "That's absurd."

But Creed gets paid to think of every possible scenario that could potentially threaten my safety and, while traveling under this pseudonym, my anonymity.

"It took a lot of convincing on my part to get her to even agree to drive with me just for today. Although I'm hoping she agrees to continue with me once we get to St. Louis."

"Absolutely not. I don't know the first thing about this woman you're sharing such close quarters with. I thought you lost your mind when you decided to buy a Wrangler and drive across the country, but I let it go. I understand this time of year is always difficult for you, what with it being around the time Kendall passed away. But I agreed to follow behind and not drive with you on the promise that you wouldn't do anything stupid. And this?" He shakes his head, spit forming on the corners of his mouth as he whisper-shouts, "This is monumentally stupid. She hasn't had the usual background check done."

"That's what you're focused on?" I lean into him, the

muscles in my neck straining. "That you haven't been able to run a background check on her? Do you realize how fucked up that is?"

He straightens, smoothing his t-shirt. But as I've come to expect from Creed, it's free from any sign of wrinkles or disarray. This man may no longer be in the trenches of the military, having been my chief protection officer for the past seven years, but some of his old habits from his military days will always remain. It wouldn't surprise me if he ironed the sheets of his hotel bed because he noticed a wrinkle.

"It's protocol."

"Fuck protocol," I spit out. "All my damn life I've followed protocol. Did what I was told. And for once, Creed, just one time, I want to make my own decision about someone. Not have you dig into her past to see if there are any skeletons in her closet that may negatively affect me. I don't care about that. I want to learn about the skeletons in her closet for myself. I want to have a normal relationship for once in my life!"

My words seem to echo against the off-colored walls in the restroom, everything else going silent. I almost expect Nora to walk in, having overheard our raised voices. But she doesn't.

"Relationship?" Creed's expression softens as he relaxes his wide stance. "Is that what you're hoping for with this woman?"

"No," I answer quickly, then sigh, scrubbing a hand over my face. "I don't know. But whatever happens, I want it to be normal."

He seems to roll my words over in his head. Creed's been one of my closest friends my entire life. Apart from Esme, he's the only other person I trust with my darkest secrets. Which is why I should tell him about my MS, but once I do, this will all end. He won't risk it. He swore his loyalty to the Royal Family first. To me second, even though I'm a member of the that family. It doesn't matter. When he swore his oath to protect the Royal Family, he did so knowing he may have to protect it from within.

"What is it about her when, for months, you ignored any woman who attempted to get your attention?"

"I don't know." I shake my head, trying to find the words to explain Nora. It's like trying to explain music to a deaf man or the majesty of the Grand Canyon to someone who can't see. Some things in life can only be experienced. And that's Nora. "She's…lost. A mystery. A thunderstorm desperately searching for her place in a world that seems to only want sunshine and rainbows. She's sad. Broken."

"Is that why you're doing this? Because you see her as someone you can fix? A way to make amends for—"

"I don't see her as someone I can fix." I pull my lip between my teeth. "I'm drawn to her. I started out on this road trip looking for something. Maybe she's my Virgil, guiding me out of the depths of the hell I've been living in since I lost Kendall."

I peer at the graffiti on the walls of the bathroom, a sense of clarity washing over me. For months, I've felt lost, more so this past week once I received my diagnosis. But now I feel like I have a purpose again. *She's* given me purpose, and I've only known her twenty-four hours.

"I didn't want to believe it at first, but there had to be a reason our paths kept crossing yesterday. At the diner. Then Lincoln's tomb. Then the hotel." I lick my lips. "Do you want to know what she said to me last night after we got kicked out of the pool area?"

"Which was another stupid idea," he quips.

"Still. I asked if she wanted to meet up some time

today. She told me if our paths were meant to cross again, I needed to have faith."

"Faith?"

"Yeah. Faith. I haven't had faith in years, Creed. So I don't know what's going to happen. Hell, she may follow through on her original plan and ask me to drop her at the airport in St. Louis to continue on her own. But I have faith that what's meant to be will be."

He blinks, mouth agape. "Who are you? What happened to the man who liked to control every little thing about his life? The man who would never put his future in the hands of faith or destiny?"

I blow out a laugh at how ironic his question is, considering there may come a time in the near future when I'll no longer have control over anything in my life, including my own body.

"I think he realized there are some things we can't control."

He expels a long sigh and closes his eyes, pinching the bridge of his nose, the vein in his forehead throbbing. I can see the struggle between being my lifelong friend and the man charged with my security. Normally, his oath to his country wins. But for once, I pray our oath of friendship overpowers it.

"I can lose my job for this," he mumbles, "but fine." He lifts his eyes to mine. "I'll keep this quiet."

"Thank you, Creed."

"But I insist on running a background check on her."

"What? Why?"

"If you want me to leave all mention of this woman out of my reports, it's my one stipulation."

"She's not dangerous."

"I need some sort of peace of mind about that. Let me run the background check. Even if you picked up Mother Teresa, I'd insist on doing the same."

I rub the back of my neck, my fingers digging into my skin. "Do you know how fucked up it is that everyone needs to have a background check before I'm allowed to have any meaningful interactions with them?"

"Your father needs to protect the Royal Family. As do I. And this is how I do it."

I glare at him, not wanting to agree to this. It will defeat the entire purpose.

"It's either you give me the information I need or I join you two."

"Fine," I relent. "Run the check. Nora Tremblay. The only other information I know is that she lives in New York but was born in Pensacola."

"Thank you."

"But do not send me a report," I add vehemently. "I don't want to know her favorite color or what restaurant she prefers. For once, I want to learn about all that myself."

"Agreed. I'll only bring it to your attention if I discover anything…abnormal."

"No. The only thing I want brought to my attention is if she has a criminal record. And not just for smoking some pot before it was legalized. We all did that. I'm talking about serious crimes. Everything else, you keep to yourself. Got it?"

"Got it."

When I hear orders being called out from the kitchen, I check my watch, hoping I haven't left Nora alone for too long.

"Are we done?" I bite out, aggravated I even have to endure this conversation. It's not like I'm a member of the British Royal Family, who is recognized all over the world. Most people forget royalty still exists elsewhere. Although, as Creed often reminds me, ever since Prince Harry was taken off the market, many women's magazines have focused their attention on me, naming me as the world's newest, most eligible prince.

"If Your Highness doesn't need me for anything else," Creed answers, his tone all business, speaking to me as my guard and not my friend.

A twinge of remorse burns at my throat. "I'm sorry, Creed. I'm just…off."

"No apologies necessary, sir. Just doing my job," he reminds me.

With a nod, I turn from him, about to push the door open with my shoulder when I stop, glancing back at him. "Thanks, Creed. I know I'm not the easiest person to deal with, and I'm grateful you put up with me. I can be quite a dolt sometimes."

"Yes, you can. But I'm used to it by now." He winks, my friend returning. "Just don't act like that around Nora or she'll walk away before I can even find out who she is."

"I'll try my best."

Chapter Twelve

NORA

I'VE LOST MY *mind.*

That's the only explanation I can come up with as to why I agreed to join Anderson today. Or he really is some wizard, like Harry Potter, and cast a spell over me, causing me to agree to his proposition. No sane person would willingly get into a car with a stranger, would they?

Well, I suppose that's the whole concept behind Uber and Lyft, but those drivers supposedly undergo background checks. I did no background check on Anderson. I didn't even make sure he had a driver's license. I took his word on faith.

Faith.

That word I encouraged him to have last night that he so coolly threw back at me, asking me to have faith in him. How could I possibly be expected to say no when he put it that way? He may not be a wizard, but he definitely cast a spell over me.

"How about a game?" he says once we're on the road again after I forced him to pull over at a rundown gas station to snoop around.

All day, he's happily stopped wherever I wanted, both at places on my list and not. Much to my surprise, at every stop, he's given me a moment to myself to spread more of Hunter's ashes, not questioning or pushing me to talk about whose remains I carry with me. And I don't ask him about the darkness that seems to fall over his expression once in a while. We're content in our avoidance and denial of reality.

I can almost hear my mother's voice in my head, telling me this arrangement is incredibly unhealthy and detrimental. If anything in my life is unhealthy and detrimental to my wellbeing, it's that woman. A part of me feels like I need this time with Anderson. That it's good for my soul.

"A game?" I peer at Anderson from over the rim of my sunglasses, pausing to appreciate his appearance. He rests one hand casually on the wheel, the other placed on the gear shift. The wind streams through the top of the Wrangler, causing his hair to blow around, everything about him sexy and commanding.

"Yes. A game."

"And what kind of game are you proposing?" I pass him a flirtatious grin.

Although dark sunglasses hide his eyes, I can sense them flare. The ticking of his jaw gives every indication he's no longer thinking about playing an innocent game.

"So many, Nora," he whispers huskily, briefly lowering his sunglasses, confirming my original suspicion about the unyielding desire flaming in his gaze. Then he pushes his shades back on, shifting his attention back to the road. "But for now, how about Would You Rather?"

"Would You Rather? I don't think I'm familiar with that one. Spin the Bottle and Seven Minutes in Heaven, yes. But not Would You Rather."

"Perhaps we can have a little Seven Minutes in Heaven later tonight, although I doubt I'll get my fill after seven minutes." He playfully waggles his brows.

"I doubt you'll be so lucky," I quip. "So, how do we

play?"

"It's exactly how it sounds. One person proposes a scenario between two options, and you answer which you'd rather do. I'll go first so you know what I'm talking about. Unless you want to, of course. Ladies first and all that."

"That's fine. You can go. It'll give me time to come up with something good." I lean against the seat, settling in for our game as we travel along a country road, the afternoon sun beaming down on us. Miles of brilliant blue are interspersed with billowy clouds, so different from the obstructed skyline I'm accustomed to in New York.

I didn't think I'd enjoy being out in the middle of nowhere as much as I do. For years, I've craved the fast pace and overpopulation of Manhattan, preferring to live somewhere no one knew who I was or what I'd lost. But something about the fresh air, chirping birds, and friendly people out here in rural America has me rethinking everything.

"Would you rather lose the ability to see or the ability to hear?" Anderson asks after a moment of contemplation.

"Hmm... That's a tough one," I respond thoughtfully, weighing my options. "Probably my ability to hear."

"Why's that?"

"Is this part of the game?" I tilt my head at him. "An answer *and* an explanation?"

He shrugs. "It allows me to learn more about you."

"How? By finding out if I prefer my eyes or ears?"

"Everything someone does or says teaches me more about them."

"Is that right?" I cross my arms in front of my chest.

"Absolutely. For example, your hair."

I sit upright, uncrossing my arms. "What about my hair?"

"You always wear it back. Pulled away from your face. Not a single strand out of place. A place for everything and everything in its place. I might be wrong, but I get the feeling it's a mask."

"Masks are worn *on* the face," I remind him, trying to hide any unease filling me from his assessment.

"Not all of them. Some people use everything at their disposal to hide who they are. Hair. Makeup. Clothes. It's all a front so people think you're happy when, in reality, nothing could be further from the truth." He arches a single brow, holding my gaze before returning his attention to the road. "So tell me, gorgeous. Why would you rather lose your ability to hear?" he presses on, as if he didn't just admit he's able to peer straight into my soul, into the very fiber of my being.

I gape at him for several long moments, then snap back to the present, answering his question so he won't read into my reluctance to share this with him.

"I'd hate having only my memories to keep me company. After a while, memories fade, and you'll soon forget things you once took for granted. After—" I stop abruptly. "Well, I've learned that life's too short to take anything for granted."

"I couldn't agree more," Anderson responds softly.

After our conversation last night, I sense he's dealing with some sort of loss, too. Now, I'm all but certain he is. He understands how frightening it is when, one day, you try to recall something a loved one said but too much time has passed. So you scramble to hold on to everything that's left, fearful if you don't, you'll dishonor their memory.

I think that's why I attached myself to Jeremy so quickly. He reminded me so much of Hunter, from his appearance, to his love of sports, even to his passion for rock climbing. For the longest time, I was convinced some higher power sent Jeremy to help me heal, that maybe he was the stranger I recognized the psychic told me about all those years ago.

Or maybe I was just desperate to feel loved again that I saw things that weren't really there.

"How about you?" I ask.

"I'd probably choose the same. While not being able to hear someone's voice or listen to music would be difficult, I'd hate being unable to appreciate the beauty surrounding me." He floats his gaze to me, the way he seems to strip me of everything I've held dear invigorating yet frightening at the same time. I've only known this man twenty-four hours, yet he sees me. Like, *really* sees me.

"My turn." I clear my throat, looking away when his stare becomes too intense, too…meaningful. "Would you rather spend the rest of your life living in an extravagant mansion with live-in staff or a tiny home in the middle of nowhere?"

"A tiny home." His answer comes with little deliberation.

"Really?"

"Don't sound so surprised."

"I'm not. I just figured since you're so used to having money—"

"Who said I had money?" His tone is even, giving nothing away.

"You did."

"I did? I don't—"

"You didn't come right out and say it, but it's obvious you're well-off. Like you said, everything a person says and does can tell you something about them." I gesture to his wrist. "People living paycheck to paycheck don't wear Tag Heuer watches."

He follows my line of sight. "I could have stolen it."

"But you didn't."

He doesn't immediately say anything, as if weighing his options. Eventually, he relents. "You're right. I didn't."

"So I guess that's why I assumed you'd go for the extravagant mansion. Figured you'd want to live somewhere with everything you could need to be comfortable. Where you'd be…free."

"Living in an extravagant mansion doesn't mean you'll have everything you need," he says, his voice distant, almost cold. "Money doesn't always equate to happiness. And it certainly doesn't equal freedom. It's more a prison sentence."

His last few words are barely audible. I doubt he intended for me to hear them. He appears to speak from a place of familiarity. It makes me wonder who Anderson North truly is.

Suddenly, a loud chiming cuts through, the sound striking against the silence. Apart from following directions, neither one of us has so much as glanced at our phones. We're back in our bubble where the outside world doesn't exist. My cell ringing is a reminder it does.

"You should answer that," Anderson suggests when I don't immediately reach for my bag. "Might be the car company with good news."

"Of course."

Rummaging through my purse, I find my phone, a number I don't recognize flashing on it. It could be a telemarketer or political call. But my gut tells me it's not.

I touch the screen. "This is Nora."

"Good afternoon, Ms. Tremblay. This is Tabitha from Easy Rental Car. We spoke earlier."

"Yes. I remember." I steal a glimpse at Anderson as

he brings both hands to the steering wheel, straightening his spine. He tightens his grip, seeming to focus on the road ahead, but I can tell his attention is on my phone call.

"I have good news. St. Louis had a car returned early. It's been serviced and is ready for you to pick up."

"That's great." My tone is less than enthusiastic. As much as I want to get on with my journey, my heart deflates at the idea of my time with Anderson coming to an end. Sure, we can plan to meet up along the way, but it won't be the same. We won't have *this*, even though I have no idea what this is. "Thanks for all your help."

"I hope you enjoy the rest of your trip, and thank you for choosing Easy Rental Car for all your travel needs."

"Thank you," I say once more, then end the call.

"They have a car for you," Anderson states after a beat.

I keep my stare forward. "They do."

His Adam's apple bobs up and down in a hard swallow, a forced smile crossing his mouth. "I suppose we should get you to the airport then."

I nod, the motion subtle. "I suppose we should."

An unsettling silence falls over the car now that our time together is nearly over, our game of Would You Rather forgotten. It could be because the app directed us to get onto the interstate, an uneasiness filling the atmosphere, both of us preferring the tranquility and slower pace of the back roads.

But even after we've crossed the Mississippi River into Missouri and Anderson navigates the Wrangler off the interstate once again, the silent tension still permeates us.

"I've got one," Anderson says as he comes to a stop at a light. The Route 66 app on his phone indicates for him to turn left and head south toward the heart of St.

Louis. But a sign for the airport up ahead directs him to get on I-270.

"One…what?" I ask hesitantly.

"Would you rather…"

"Okay…"

"Nora?"

I drift my gaze toward his. He lifts his sunglasses off his face, and I peer into his vibrant blue eyes.

"Would you rather I follow that sign up ahead and drive you to the airport where we'll part ways, perhaps never to see each other again…"

I swallow hard. "Or?"

A smile pulls on his mouth. "Or do I turn left to stay on Route 66, continuing on this journey together. All the way to the end."

I blink, chewing on the inside of my cheek. This is crazy. What woman in her right mind would entertain the thought of driving across the country with a stranger?

But is he a stranger? Or is that just something I keep telling myself so I can maintain my distance, despite the tug I feel toward him?

When the sound of honking surrounds us, I snap my head forward, seeing the light has turned green, but Anderson doesn't move, waiting for my answer.

"Anderson," I warn, glancing over my shoulder before looking back at him.

"I need an answer, Nora."

"Just… Go."

"Not until you tell me which way. Straight or left?"

"I…" I flick my gaze between the sign for the airport and the road to my left.

Hours ago, this would have been an easy decision. I would have taken the path I'd already decided on, nothing able to change my mind.

But spending the day with Anderson has been enjoyable. I haven't been consumed by my past, wishing things had been different. Haven't constantly thought about how Hunter would have loved the rundown drive-in, or the covered bridge in Glenarm, or the talkative waitress who served us breakfast this morning, regaling us with stories from the glory days of the Mother Road. Instead, I've stayed in the moment. With Anderson. Isn't that what this trip is supposed to be about? Not only saying goodbye to Hunter, like I should have years ago, but no longer living in the past?

Horns continue to blare, but Anderson pays them no attention, his sole focus on me.

"Nora?"

I part my lips, still torn. Then I spy a lone penny in the cup holder and grab it, chuckling to myself as I stare at Abraham Lincoln's faded silhouette. I doubt I'll ever think of the sixteenth president again without being reminded of Anderson.

"What are you doing?"

I flash him a smile. "Flipping a coin."

"So that's it? A coin will decide my fate? What happened to having a little faith?"

"Now I'm asking *you* to have faith in *me*. Again."

"But——"

"Heads I stay. Tails I go."

Cars honk as they pass, some of the drivers flipping us off and shouting, but we ignore it, our bubble protecting us. Briefly closing my eyes, I draw in a deep breath, then toss the coin into the air. It only takes a few seconds to fall back into my outstretched hand, but it feels like an eternity.

When I catch it and open my palm to reveal it landed on tails, Anderson's shoulders fall. With a downcast expression, he shifts into first, about to continue straight.

"Take a left."

He whips his eyes to mine, confused. "But the coin… I thought you said if it landed on tails you'd go."

"I did. But I didn't flip the coin so it could decide for me. I flipped the coin to help *me* decide."

He furrows his brow. "I don't understand."

"Someone I used to know told me to flip a coin when you're not sure about something. Because while that coin is in the air, you'll realize what you want." I beam, more certain about this than anything else in my life recently. "And I really want to stay. With you. Continue toward the right destination."

He pushes out a relieved breath. When he returns his gaze to mine, his lips curve in the corners. "To the right destination."

Chapter Thirteen

NORA

"**I**S THIS A good spot to stop for the night?" Anderson asks, pulling into the parking lot of a budget hotel somewhere in Missouri.

Anderson and I made the most out of the rest of our afternoon, checking more items off my list. Chain of Rocks Bridge. Ted Drewes Frozen Custard. And we even toured Meramac Caverns, where I sneakily sprinkled more of Hunter's ashes. He would have been happy if I'd left a part of him by the entrance, which I did, but once we ventured farther into the caverns, I knew Hunter would love the breathtaking view of the natural formations. Anderson sensed it, too, whispering into my ear to leave some there.

"Works for me," I agree, peering at the three-story brick building.

Easily finding a spot near the entrance, Anderson yanks on the parking brake before jumping out to open my door and help me step down, as he's done all day. Once I'm out of the Wrangler, he heads to the back and grabs our luggage, mine feminine, his black. I reach for my suitcase, but he keeps it out of my grasp.

"I *can* carry my bag," I insist, walking alongside him as he strides through the automatic glass doors and into the lobby.

"I know. But as you noticed earlier, I *am* a gentleman.

At least in public."

"And in private?" I flirt, batting my lashes.

His eyes skate over me. "All bets are off, gorgeous."

His seductive tone causes goosebumps to prickle my skin, leaving me a bundle of hormones. All I can do is watch as he walks through the lobby, a debonair smile plastered on his full, kissable lips. This man has serious swagger. I have no idea what his profession is, but I can see him in sales. Or politics. He has this charm that seems to endear everyone to him.

That's endeared me to him.

A young woman behind the reception desk peeks up when Anderson approaches. Her brow furrows as she squints, a flicker of recognition in her eyes as she studies him. She must feel the same way I did when I first saw him. That he looks familiar. We've gotten the same look a few times throughout the day. Some people just have that familiarity about them. He does bear a slight resemblance to Matthew McConaughey with his wayward hair and dazzling smile. But a hot British version.

"Do you have any rooms available?" Anderson asks.

The woman snaps out of her daze, turning her attention to the computer in front of her. "One room?"

"Two rooms," I say urgently, darting toward the desk. "We need two rooms. Two separate rooms. With a wall and everything." I reach into my purse and grab my wallet.

"Yes, ma'am. I'm happy to report all our rooms come with walls," she jokes.

"Do you have any adjoining rooms?" Anderson asks smoothly.

"I believe I do."

"That's not necessary," I insist.

"Why?" He flashes a devious grin as he leans toward

me, his voice a husky whisper. "Worried I might overhear you moan my name in your sleep tonight?"

"Absolutely not!" I hold my head high, smoothing my hands down my shirt. Which I worry only draws attention to my chest, so I adjust how it falls on my shoulders instead. Which only serves to cause it to lift around my midsection, revealing my stomach. When Anderson's stare floats to my exposed skin, I yank down the shirt.

Inhaling a deep breath to settle my nerves, I turn my attention to the clerk, doing my best to ignore Anderson's looming presence beside me.

"I don't want to trouble you any more than necessary."

"It's no trouble at all. If I can get your IDs and a credit card, I'll have you on your way... To your *adjoining* rooms."

We hand over what she needs and, within a few minutes, step into an elevator. But the tight, enclosed space only serves to amplify every single emotion within me. Nervousness. Agitation. Anxiety. Desire. Lust. Holy crap, the lust coursing through me is enough to make me combust. It didn't feel like this last night when we rode in an elevator together. Then again, I wasn't feeling much after drinking all that wine. Not to mention, our rooms weren't adjoining. The idea of sharing a wall with Anderson has me all out of sorts.

Just when I don't think I can bear the fever of his stare anymore, the elevator arrives on our floor. I scramble off, walking purposefully down the long corridor.

"I can take that now," I say once we approach our assigned rooms, reaching for the handle of my suitcase. This time, Anderson allows me to take it.

I bring my keycard up to the door, and it beeps, granting me entry. I turn the knob, then face him, keeping the door propped open with my body.

"Nine o'clock a good time to hit the road tomorrow?" I arch a brow.

"See you then." With a slight nod that almost resembles a bow, he turns, taking the few steps to his room.

"Hey, Anderson?" I say as he brings his keycard up to his door.

He tilts his head. "Yes?"

"Thank you for today. For offering to drive me."

"Thanks for accepting."

I smile, then slip into my room.

"Goddammit!" I scream into the pillow, hoping the aroma of detergent and bleach will cleanse Anderson from my mind.

But it doesn't.

Nothing seems to. And I've tried. I took a shower. Wrote in my journal. Even attempted to meditate him away. But no matter what I do, I can't seem to empty my mind. Every time I close my eyes, I see Anderson's devilish smirk. Inhale the scent of his cologne. Feel the heat of his hands on my skin.

The knowledge he's just on the other side of this wall doesn't help, either.

I doubt anything will.

A ding rips through my breakdown, and I shoot upright, glancing at my phone on the nightstand to see a FaceTime call from Chloe.

"Shit," I curse under my breath.

She's been texting all day, but I haven't returned any of her messages, too lost in the moment with Anderson and not wanting any reminder of the world outside our little bubble.

I click the answer button, her face appearing on the screen.

"Where have you been?" Her eyes are fierce as her words come rapidly. "You promised you'd text last night, but you didn't. Then all my messages today go unanswered. I love you, Nora, but you're a woman traveling alone. It doesn't matter that you can probably take any man by the balls. I still worry about you being out there on your own. The least you can do is answer your texts so I don't wonder if I need to send out a goddamn search party!"

"I'm sorry," I exhale, a ball of guilt settling in the pit of my stomach. "I didn't mean for you to worry. I've been…busy."

This catches her attention, and she arches a thin brow. "Busy? Doing what?"

"Driving Route 66."

She pinches her glossed lips into a tight line, studying me. "And what were you busy doing last night? Surely you're not driving at night, too."

I should have known she'd pick up on my evasive answer. A former celebrity news columnist, not much escapes Chloe's attention. She made a career out of seeing things most people can't. Which is why it's impossible to keep secrets from her for too long. She'll eventually get to the bottom of things. She always does.

"I hung out by the pool."

"The…pool?" She frowns. "At a roadside motel? That's not the first place *I'd* hang out."

"I went out there to meditate. And…"

"Yes?"

I chew on my bottom lip, then blurt out, "I met someone."

At first, she doesn't respond, her expression

unmoving, making me wonder if perhaps our connection froze. Then the background shifts, and I recognize the kitchen in her apartment transition into her home office. I make out the familiar sound of a door clicking closed before she lowers herself behind the desk.

"Who is he?" she asks, as if interviewing me for a piece she's writing for the women's magazine where she now works as the current affairs editor.

"His name is Anderson."

"How did you meet him?"

I almost feel like I should have been read my rights prior to this interrogation. "We first met at a diner yesterday morning. Then at Abraham Lincoln's tomb. When I was rubbing Lincoln's nose, I heard this accented voice."

"I'm going to table my question about rubbing Lincoln's nose for now and focus on the more pressing issue." She leans toward the screen. "He has an accent? What kind? Like Midwestern?"

"It's not overpowering, and it's certainly been Americanized, but…British."

Her mouth drops open. "You met a guy with a British accent?"

"Yes."

She remains in a state of disbelief for several protracted seconds before she exhales, fanning herself. "Damn. You hit the jackpot, Nora."

Chloe has a fascination for all things British, mainly from her coverage of the Royal Family during her time on the gossip column. But you'd have to be deaf not to grow weak in the knees in response to Anderson's smooth voice.

"What does he look like? Is he Prince Harry incarnate?"

"Not everyone who's British looks like Prince Harry,

but he does have some red coloring through his hair, as well as some brown and blond. It's hard to describe, but it's sexy as hell." I giggle, relaxing against the headboard as I gush with my closest friend. "*Everything* about him is sexy as hell."

"What's his body like?"

"From what I've been able to see, he has a nice physique. Tall. Broad shoulders. Hard as a fucking rock."

"So you haven't seen everything?"

I narrow my gaze on her. "No, Chloe. I haven't seen everything. I haven't really seen anything."

"Why not? By that blush on your cheeks, you obviously find this guy attractive."

"I'm not here to hook up. I'm traveling with my dead fiancé's ashes, for crying out loud. A fact Anderson's aware of."

"All the more reason to make the first move. He knows you have Hunter's ashes——"

"Well, not exactly," I interrupt. "I didn't tell him *whose* ashes I was spreading along the road. And as I said, the last thing I need on this trip is——"

"What? An amazing orgasm that's not because of your hand or a vibrator? If you ask me, that's the *first* thing you need."

"Chloe…"

"What? You do. This is supposed to be your 'me' trip. The trip where you make peace with your past and embrace the future. There aren't any rules about how you go about that. Whether it's spreading Hunter's ashes. Or spreading your legs."

"Chloe!" I gasp, but she ignores me.

"The only rules you have to play by are *your* rules. No one else's. I get that this is your version of an *Eat, Pray, Love* trip where you'll come back home with a new outlook and clarity of mind and soul, or some such bullshit. But if I were you, instead of eat, pray, love, I'd kiss, spank, fuck."

"Chloe!" I say again, this time louder. I shoot my gaze to the connecting door, frantically attempting to lower the volume on my phone.

"As your best friend, it is my duty and obligation to point out the obvious."

"Is it? And what obvious thing do you need to point out?"

"That you need to get laid. Like I already said."

"Sex only complicates things."

"Only if you let it. I don't think Hunter would want you to stay in this place you've been."

"Are you seriously trying to talk sense into me by using my deceased fiancé to guilt-trip me?"

She gives me a smug look. "Damn straight. And if it helps you to move on, I'll keep doing it." Her expression softens, her gray eyes shining with sincerity. "I just want you to be happy again." She pauses, then adds, "And I really think a good dicking will help." Her laughter is infectious, and I can't help but join in, grateful for the levity.

That's the thing about Chloe. She always knows when I need to laugh, cry, or smack a piñata likeness of my ex with a bat. She calls it a special gift. I call it being a good person and paying attention.

"Any dicking would make me happy again," I admit through my laughter.

"Damn straight." She flashes a devious smile. "So, tell me about the pool."

"The pool?"

"You said you met someone at the pool last night. I'm assuming it's this same guy. Right?"

I nod.

"Then tell me what happened."

My lips curve up in the corners, warmth filling me as I flash back to last night. "We drank a couple bottles of wine and talked. Really talked. It was refreshing. Before I knew it, it was three in the morning and the hotel manager kicked us out."

"At three in the morning?" She waggles her brows, grinning deviously. "Why do I sense you're not telling me the whole story?"

"That *is* the whole story," I insist, although I'm certainly keeping her in the dark regarding the way my stomach erupts in butterflies every time our skin touches. The way my core tightens with want every time his eyes rake over me, desire swirling in his deep pools of blue. The way the air between us crackles with electricity every time we're in each other's presence.

"You really didn't do anything? Even after drinking wine? You didn't let your inhibitions loose?"

"We really didn't do anything, Chloe."

"Damn… I was hoping to hear what kind of British things he moaned when in the throes of passion. Like, instead of 'Oh god, I'm coming', was he all like 'This is indeed splendid'," she imitates in a British accent. "'Oh heavens. You really know how to butter my crumpets. Tally ho, old sport. My word. That was a good show.'"

Laughter consumes me once more, tears dotting my eyelids, my stomach aching. This is what I needed. A few moments to joke with my oldest friend and be reminded I shouldn't take life so seriously. That I do deserve to be happy. That meeting someone and allowing my heart to open won't dishonor Hunter's memory like I've worried it would.

"I hate you."

"No, you don't. You love me. You'd be lost without me."

"Maybe."

"So that's it?" she states once our laughter dies down.

"What do you mean?"

"You and your British prince. No sex, and now you've gone your separate ways, never to see each other again?"

I cringe, unsure how to explain this so she doesn't think I've lost my mind. Maybe I have. But maybe that's a good thing.

"What is it, Nora?"

"Well, I had car trouble this morning when I was about to leave the hotel. Anderson happened to see me and offered to drive me to St. Louis so I wouldn't have to wait for the rental car company to come pick me up. But once we got close to the city, he convinced me to drive together all the way to California," I blurt out, like ripping off a bandage.

She stares at me, unblinking, mouth agape. "Wow."

"Is that a good wow, or a 'Nora, you've lost your dang mind' wow?"

"It's more of a…processing wow."

I flop back onto the mattress, throwing my arm over my head. "It was a mistake, wasn't it? I should just ask him to drive me back to St. Louis to pick up that rental car."

"Do *you* think it was a mistake?"

"I don't know, Chloe," I sigh. "When we're not together, like now, my brain seems to list all the reasons it was stupid."

"And when you *are* together?"

A rush of adrenaline fills me at the mere idea of being in Anderson's presence. "I can't imagine doing this trip without him." I level my gaze on her. "It's crazy, right?"

"A few years ago, I probably would have said yes and encouraged you to run as far away as possible. But that was before Lincoln. The beginning of our relationship was kind of crazy, too."

I laugh under my breath. "It most certainly was."

"Sometimes we need a little crazy in our life to open our eyes to things we've been blind to for too long. It may not go anywhere. Then again, it may go exactly where you need it to. Stop thinking about what the final destination will be and enjoy the ride. And if that ride happens to be on a hot, British guy, go for it." She winks as a knock echoes in my room.

I snap my head up, staring in the direction of the sound. It didn't come from the main door, but from the connecting one, meaning it could only be one person.

"I'm guessing that knock is Prince Hotty."

"Just because he has a British accent doesn't mean he's a prince, Chloe."

She shrugs. "I know, but I like the fantasy of that. So go. Don't allow your misplaced guilt to make you do something you'll come to regret. After everything, you deserve to be happy. So don't deprive yourself of that."

"Thanks, Chloe. I'll text you later."

"Hopefully you won't be able to." She winks, then the screen goes black.

I push out a breath, staring into the distance, contemplating our conversation. Then the knocking breaks through once more.

Jumping to my feet, I dash toward the scuffed desk in the corner, surveying my reflection in the mirror above it. My hair is still drying from my shower and is much more unruly than I tend to wear it, but I don't have time to straighten it. Instead, I tousle my locks, allowing it to keep its natural wave. Inhaling a steadying breath that does nothing to calm the pounding in my chest, I place my hand on the doorknob and turn, opening the door.

A breathtaking smile greets me, the scent of ocean

breeze surrounding me. Anderson's hair is damp, and he's changed into a plain white t-shirt and a pair of gym shorts.

"Hey," I exhale huskily.

"Hey." He holds up a bottle of what I recognize to be a pinot noir from one of my favorite California vineyards. "Want some company?"

"Trying to drug me with more truth serum so I tell you even more of my secrets than I already have?"

He slowly shakes his head, his pupils dilating. When he closes the distance, I struggle to breathe, every synapse in my body firing. "Like what? Perhaps how you'd like to kiss, spank, and fuck?" he asks, his voice deep, wanton, guttural.

I freeze, gaping at him, trying to come up with some explanation for what he overheard. "I… She… That wasn't me. That was my friend, Chloe. She… Well, she doesn't have much of a brain-to-mouth filter."

He chuckles, the sound a direct line to my starved libido. "Then I already like her."

He arches a single brow, lifting the wine bottle once more. "So what'll it be, gorgeous? Care to join me for a drink? Perhaps the truth serum will work on me and you can find out what I sound like in… How did your friend refer to it? The throes of passion?"

I close my eyes, heat covering my cheeks. "I'm going to kill her the next time I see her."

He steps toward me, no longer waiting for me to invite him into my room. "I'll let you in on a little secret. I don't use the phrase 'butter my crumpets' during sex." He leers at me, licking his lips, desire radiating from every inch of him. "But something tells me with you, Nora, it will most certainly be a damn good show."

As he brushes past me, a shiver runs through me. I remain locked in place, taking a moment to calm my hormones. It was one thing to hang out by the pool with him last night. We were in public. But in my hotel room? There's too much appeal. Too much temptation.

"Hope this is acceptable."

When I hear his voice, I dart my gaze to him, a plastic cup extended toward me.

Pushing down my unease, I smile, taking the cup from him. "It's better than not having any wine."

"I'll drink to that." He raises his cup, and I do the same, his eyes fixated on mine.

I marvel at how blue they are. More picturesque than even the most beautiful ocean. I can get lost in them for hours. But I fear I'll soon reach the point where I won't want to be found.

I clear my throat, looking anywhere but at Anderson. "So, what shall we do?"

"Strip poker?"

I shoot him a playful look of irritation.

"Okay. Okay." He holds up his hands in defense. "Maybe we should save that until we're a little farther down the road. At least until we hit Kansas." He winks before nodding at the laptop on the corner of my bed. "Have any movies on that?"

"I do." Setting my wine on the nightstand, I lower myself to the mattress, opening my laptop and bringing up all my movies.

Anderson walks around the other side of the bed, pausing before sitting down. With a raised brow, he asks, "May I?"

His request is another reminder that, behind all the confidence, he's still a gentleman who won't put me in an uncomfortable position. He reminds me of Hunter that way.

"Of course."

"Thank you." He lowers himself, and I shift the

laptop toward him.

"What are you in the mood for?" I ask.

"What's your favorite movie?" He throws the question back at me.

"I don't think I could pick just one."

"Okay. How about this? What's your rainy-day movie?"

"Rainy-day movie?"

"What movie do you put on whenever you're having a shite day? A movie you've seen hundreds of times, but always go back to."

I don't even have to think about it. There's only one movie that fits that description. One movie I watch whenever I'm feeling down and need to believe that two people who are meant to be together will eventually find their way back to each other, regardless of the passing of time and circumstance.

"*An Affair to Remember.*"

For months after Hunter died, I imagined he hadn't. Imagined our last night together was just us saying goodbye on that ocean liner with plans to see each other again. As unhealthy as it was, it got me through my darkest of days.

"That's one of my favorites, too."

"I doubt that."

"It is," he insists. "Especially now."

"Why now?"

"It just so happens to remind me of another pair of travelers forced together by chance." He waggles his brows.

I roll my eyes as I hit play on the movie, ignoring his insinuation. "Once our journey comes to an end, I can assure you, I have no intention of making any plans with you to meet at the top of the Empire State Building in six months."

"Good." He pauses, then locks his gaze with mine. "Because I fear six months would be far too long for me to wait for you."

Chapter Fourteen

ANDERSON

"D ROP ME OFF at the side of the hotel," I order Creed when he pulls the SUV into the parking lot the following morning.

I'd gotten up early to go in search of coffee. After asking the front desk clerk where the closest Starbuck's was, to which she responded with uncontrollable laughter, she pointed me in the direction of a local spot. Just as I threw my luggage into the Wrangler and was about to duck behind the wheel, Creed pulled up and offered to drive me, like I should have anticipated he would.

The entire ride there and back, I sensed something was on his mind, an unusual edginess about him. I almost asked what was going on, if he'd found something when he ran Nora's background, but decided against it. Like I told him yesterday, I wanted to learn about her myself.

"Got it." Creed follows my directions, slowing to a stop around the corner of the brick building.

He reaches for the handle, about to jump out to get my door for me, as he's trained to do, but I stop him. "No. Not here."

"Of course, Your Highness."

The tray of coffee in one hand, I open the door with the other and step into the chilly air, the smell of wet asphalt heavy. I hadn't noticed it had rained last night. Why would I when I spent the night with Nora? Or most of the night, anyway.

She'd fallen asleep before Cary Grant and Deborah Kerr made their pact to settle their affairs and meet on the top of the Empire State Building. I should have taken it as my cue to go back to my room, but I couldn't find the strength to leave. There was something so peaceful about her as she slept. Gone were the hard edges she'd constructed around herself. In that moment, her body nestled against mine, she looked infinitely more calm and in tune with herself than she ever had the few times I'd seen her meditate.

"Any idea of your final destination tonight?" Creed asks.

"Not sure. We'll probably make it into Oklahoma before stopping."

He nods. "Let me know once you have a better idea."

"Will do." I start to close the door.

"Anders."

I stop, the sound of the name I've gone by in private catching me off guard. He normally refuses to call me anything other than Your Highness or sir. Rarely Anderson. Never Anders. At least not in years.

"What's wrong?"

"I…" He shakes his head, the turmoil heavy. "I found out something about Nora. She—"

I shoot up my hand. "I told you, Creed. Unless she has a criminal record as a violent offender, I'm not interested. *Does* she have a record as a violent offender?"

He gives me a pleading look. Then he pushes out a long sigh, his shoulders falling. "No."

"Then I don't want to know."

"I understand your reasoning, but—"

"No. This is important to me, Creed. I want a few

more days of being normal. When this journey ends, you can tell me everything you found out about her. Until then, keep it to yourself. I don't want to ruin this."

"But what *is* this? What's going on?" He repeats his same line of inquiry from yesterday.

I shake my head. "I have no idea. But I want to find out. On my own."

Creed peers at me through worried eyes, then eventually relents. "Yes, sir. Safe travels today."

A part of me wants to ask him what he discovered about Nora, what could have him so concerned. To say I've been intrigued about this woman from the moment I laid eyes on her is an understatement. If I know Creed, he put together a thorough background check, leaving no stone unturned. Hell, he could probably even tell Nora a few things about her she doesn't know.

But I want to feel normal. There's nothing normal about having a background check run on anyone you hope to have a meaningful relationship with. So, instead of pressing for more information, I say goodbye to Creed, then close the door to the SUV and continue through the parking lot. When I walk into the hotel's lobby, I offer a smile of thanks to the front desk clerk, raising the tray to let her know I found the coffee shop she'd recommended.

The corridor is silent as I step off the elevator and make my way toward Nora's room. A thrill of excitement fills me over the prospect of seeing her again. It's a strange reaction for me, one I didn't think I'd experience again.

Balancing the tray with one hand, I bring my other up to the door, about to knock, when it flies open. I freeze, as does Nora the instant she notices me standing there.

As opposed to last night when she was fresh from a

shower, her face bare and hair tousled, her appearance this morning is as impeccable and perfect as it was when I first saw her. Makeup covers her face, hiding any mark she deems an imperfection. Her hair no longer sports the messy waves, now straightened and pulled into a tight ponytail at her nape, not a single strand out of place.

She's stunning. She always is. But I miss the other Nora, the one from last night. I doubt many people get to see that version of her. I doubt she *wants* people to see that version of her. The messy, wild Nora. The one who doesn't pretend to have her shit together.

"I thought we were going to meet in the lobby at nine." Her voice pulls me back to the present.

"I got up early and found some decent coffee." I remove a cup from the tray, handing it to her. "Wasn't sure what you preferred, so I took a guess," I tell her as she takes a sip, appreciation covering her expression.

"Americano. One of my favorites. Lucky guess."

I shrug. "Perhaps. I like to call it more of an…educated guess."

"Educated? How so?"

"Based on your personality. You seem the type of woman who prefers her coffee like she prefers her men." I take the handle of her suitcase from her, rolling it down the hallway and toward the elevator, pressing the call button.

She leans against the wall, folding an arm over her stomach, using her other hand to bring her coffee back to her lips. "And how do you *think* I prefer my men?"

I erase the distance between us, her delicious scent of lavender and baby powder filtering into my nostrils. The same scent that covered my t-shirt last night when I returned to my room. The same scent that surrounded me as I slept in that t-shirt, refusing to take it off, although I'm usually more comfortable sleeping shirtless.

"Strong and bold."

The vein in her neck throbs, drawing my attention to it. What I wouldn't give to flick my tongue against it and find out if her skin tastes as delicious as I imagine it does. If she were anyone else, I would. I'd have my fun, then walk away. But something tells me Nora isn't the type of girl you throw away. Something about her makes me think she could give me everything she has and it still wouldn't be enough. I'd still want more. That's the kind of power this woman holds over me, even after only a few days. Creed was right. This woman *is* dangerous. Just not in the way he thinks.

"At least that's how I *hope* you like your men. I consider myself strong and bold. Don't you?" I straighten slightly, meeting her eyes with a single brow cocked.

A loud ding rips through the silence, and she pushes against me, walking into the waiting elevator. "I'm not sure I'd use those words."

"Humor me then. How *would* you describe me?" I press the button for the lobby and the doors close, the elevator lurching to a start.

"Are you sure you want to know?"

My gaze unwavering, I slowly nod. "I'm on pins and needles, gorgeous."

"Well then, I'd be more inclined to classify you as…an acquired taste."

My free hand flies to my heart, feigning pain. "Ouch. You wound me, m'lady."

A brilliant smile lights up her face, her giggles infiltrating me as the elevator doors open to the lobby.

"Sometimes that's a good thing," she comments as she waves a polite goodbye to the front desk clerk before we step outside. "It's better than being referred to as the chicken of the gene pool. Don't you think?"

"The chicken of the gene pool?" I repeat.

"Exactly. No one gets excited about chicken. It's what you make for dinner when you're not sure what else to eat. It's the standby. When you go out to eat, do you ever order chicken?" She looks at me as she approaches the passenger side of the Wrangler. I open the door for her, helping her in.

"Not unless I'm in the south and it's fried. I'd argue if you're in the south and *don't* have fried chicken, you're missing out." I close the door, then place her suitcase next to mine in the rear compartment before jumping behind the wheel.

"Chicken isn't an acquired taste. It's not unusual. There was never a time you *didn't* like chicken, right?"

"Not that I can think of."

"Well, how about caviar? Or sushi?" Her eyes become intense, an urgency about her. "Please tell me you like sushi."

"I love sushi." Although I'm technically not supposed to eat it.

"Phew." She brushes a hand over her brow. "Otherwise, I'd have to find some other schmuck to cart my ass across the country." She winks as I crank the ignition and put the Wrangler into first, steering toward the main road. "Sushi is an acquired taste. Not something you like as a child. It grows on you. At first, you don't think you'll ever enjoy it. That, on its surface, it doesn't appeal to you."

"I'm not sure I like where this is heading. Are you trying to tell me that on the surface, you don't find me appealing?"

She squints, her brows wrinkling in contemplation as she chews on her bottom lip. "I guess what I'm trying to say is the last thing I wanted was to meet someone new. All I wanted was to have some time to myself. To take this journey on my own." On a long inhale, she tilts her eyes toward mine. "But the more time I spend with you, the more you grow on me."

Heat radiates through me, a wide smile covering my expression.

"But don't gloat or let that go to your head," she snaps. "It was either I suffer driving with you or be stuck in St. Louis." She shrugs dismissively. "It was a no-brainer."

"Oh, come on." I drape my arm around her shoulders, brushing my fingers along her exposed skin. A visible shiver rolls through her, her face becoming flushed. She lowers her sunglasses over her eyes to hide her reaction, but she can't hide from me. "You're glad I'm here."

"Maybe."

When I remove my arm from her to shift into fourth, I notice her expression fall slightly.

"I'll take maybe. Who knows? By the time we reach California, I might be able to turn that maybe into a yes."

"I wouldn't count on it," she snips playfully.

I flash her a devious grin. "Is that a challenge?"

"And if it is?"

I lean toward her as we come to a stop at a red light. "Then I should warn you." My eyes skate over her face, settling on her plump lips, my tone becoming more sensual. "I love a challenge."

Chapter Fifteen

NORA

"WHERE ARE WE?"

Grabbing the Route 66 guidebook out of my bag, I flip through it, trying to figure out what landmark this could be. I glance out my window, looking for something I'd recognize. Instead, all I see is a chain-link fence with a "No Trespassing" sign on it.

"Thought we could use a little break." With a wink, Anderson jumps out of the Jeep, hurrying around to open my door.

"Break? We're in the middle of nowhere." I take his hand, allowing him to help me out.

"Only if you don't think there's anything worthwhile around."

"What's worthwhile about this spot? Don't you see the 'No Trespassing' sign? Or did they not teach you how to read at that hoity-toity London prep school of yours?"

"They taught me how to read…" He levels his gaze on me as he cracks open the rear half-door of the Jeep, retrieving a black backpack and slinging it over one shoulder. "And a few other things, too." He slams the door shut, then heads toward the fence, grabbing onto it and scaling it.

"What are you doing?" I whisper-shout, looking around, worried we're about to get caught.

"What does it look like? I'm jumping the fence."

"Why? To check out an empty field? I'm sure we can find plenty of other empty fields that don't have 'No Trespassing' signs posted. Getting shot is not on my list."

"You won't get shot," he assures me, then stops short. "At least I don't think you will." He winks before hoisting himself over the top of the fence and jumping to the ground. Dusting off his shorts, he turns around to face me. "Okay. Your turn."

I gesture to my sundress. "Sorry. I didn't exactly wear fence-scaling clothes."

"I know." He waggles his brows mischievously.

"Is that why you're doing this? Are you so desperate to catch a glimpse of women's panties you have to come up with some elaborate scheme to do so?"

He steps toward the fence, his blue orbs darkening, raw hunger dripping from every inch of him. His powerful stare makes my knees weaken, goosebumps prickling my skin.

"Trust me, gorgeous. I've seen more than my fair share of women's knickers. Some crotchless."

My eyes bulge, but I shouldn't be surprised at how shameless he is. He's proven he can be quite the flirt at times. At others, he seems as lost and tormented as me. I never know which version of Anderson North I'll get. Truthfully, it doesn't matter. I find each one endearing.

"I'm sorry to report I don't own any crotchless panties… Or *knickers*, as you call them," I imitate in a horrific British accent. "You'll have to settle for my granny panties."

He leans down, his mouth practically even with mine through the links in the fence. "I don't believe for a second you're wearing granny panties."

"What makes you say that? I didn't come on this trip

with an eye toward getting laid."

Hooking my fingers into the links, I carefully scale the fence to the best of my ability. At least I'd traded the flip-flops I almost wore for my Egyptian sandals that lace up my calves, mainly to draw Anderson's attention to my legs. Now I'm drawing his attention to a lot more than my legs.

"Because I know for a fact that's not the case." He steps back, crossing his arms over his chest. It takes everything I have to focus on what I'm doing, not the way his muscles stretch the fabric of his t-shirt.

"Care to explain how?" I ask, approaching the top.

"Because…" He smirks. "You left your suitcase open last night."

I freeze, gripping the chain link with so much force my knuckles turn white. All I can think about is the gift my friends got me for my road trip — the Mercedes Benz of all vibrators.

"Don't worry. I'm not about to ask about the vibrator, although I'm certainly intrigued."

I close my eyes, wishing a freak storm would roll in, causing lightning to strike me dead right now.

"But that's how I know you're not wearing granny panties. My guess is you chose the pale pink knickers today. Girly and feminine. Like that dress." His gaze dances with amusement as it skates over me before his expression turns serious once more.

"Now, here's where it gets tricky. You'll need to hoist yourself up over the top, then push off." He holds out his arms. "I'll break your fall."

I follow his instructions, although I'm surprised to learn I don't need them. Granted, it's been years since my brothers taught me to scale a fence when I was a teenager, but it's like riding a bike. You never forget. Muscle memory kicking in, I angle away from Anderson and push off the fence, dismounting with ease, just to prove a point.

"Like that?"

He stares at me, dumbfounded. "Exactly like that."

I start to brush past him, but pause, leaning into him. "And you're wrong," I murmur seductively, my lips skimming his neck. "They're yellow today."

Every muscle in his body hardens, his breathing growing ragged and uneven. I linger near him, drawing it out until he's on the verge of breaking. Then I retreat, swaying my hips. I can feel the greed in his stare from several yards away.

"So, care to tell me what we're doing here?" I ask when he manages to catch up to me after taking a moment to compose himself.

"Doing something different." He grabs my hand, pulling me deeper into the field.

When a large, tattered, white screen comes into view, the remnants of what was once a drive-in movie theater, he drops his hold on me, setting his backpack on the ground. He kneels and unzips it, revealing what appears to be a professional camera. At least it looks much more professional than any camera I've ever used.

I watch in awe as he pulls out a lens and twists it onto the body of the camera. After fiddling with it, he brings it up to his eye, making a few adjustments before the sound of the shutter echoes around us.

"So you like photography," I state.

He looks up from the camera, contemplating a response. "Used to. I kind of got away from it for a while."

"What made you pick it up again?"

He pulls his bottom lip between his teeth. "Regret." His answer hangs heavy in the air between us until he returns his attention to the camera.

I turn from him, taking this opportunity to meander through the tall grass and weeds. Rays of sun shine between the clouds, illuminating patches of the overgrown field. Butterflies flit by in the distance, birds swooping from tree to tree.

I can almost picture what this place was like back in the day. Back before the interstate cut off Route 66. Weary travelers stopped here for a break from reality for a few hours after driving all day. Now, the only vestiges of the past are the ripped and battered screen, the projection house covered in graffiti, and a few of the old speakers customers had to hang inside their car to have sound.

"How old do you think this place is?" I ask.

"My guess is fairly old."

I glance over my shoulder, my breath hitching when I notice Anderson's attention no longer focused on his camera, but is on me instead. There's something in his gaze that leaves me breathless. It's not the carnal want that covered his expression minutes ago. It's different. Respect. Veneration. Longing.

The air crackles with intensity as I fully face him, a gravitational pull beckoning me closer.

"Stop," he orders in a gruff voice.

I halt abruptly. Then he raises the camera and snaps a picture.

"What are you doing?"

"Taking your photo."

"Why?"

"Because you're beautiful, Nora. Especially now that you're starting to relax around me and let me see the real you." He takes a few more photos, checking them before clicking several more.

"You've always seen the real me," I insist, although my voice lacks conviction.

His mouth curves into a smile. "I find that hard to believe."

"Why? You barely know me."

"True, but I know me."

I swallow hard. "And?"

"And you and I are a lot alike. We've both been hurt. We've both done everything to piece our lives back together. We've put up a wall so no one can see how fucked up we really are. We've become masters at fooling everyone around us. I'd even go so far as to say we've even fooled ourselves."

I blink away the tears forming in the corners of my eyes, wondering how this man, this *stranger*, can see through me with such clarity. We've known each other less than forty-eight hours. Yet he seems to know me on a deeper level than anyone else.

Maybe he's right. Maybe we are alike. Maybe that was why I felt this strange camaraderie toward him before I even knew his name.

"But you make me want to stop lying to myself. Make me want to be real again." He furrows his brow, as if his words surprise him. "You make me want to know the real you, too."

I lift my gaze to his, losing myself in him as he stands a breath away. "I don't even know who that is anymore," I whisper.

"Then let me help you find her."

When he reaches for me, I tilt my head back, every torturously long second causing the thundering in my heart to increase. The way he focuses on my lips, I expect him to grip my cheeks and pull me toward him, sealing his mouth over mine. And despite my reservations yesterday, I won't stop him.

Instead, he tugs on the band securing my ponytail in place, freeing my hair from its binding.

"We'll start with this."

"My…hair?"

"Yes. You need to let your hair down. Literally. Life is messy. Your hair should reflect that." He burrows his fingers into my locks, tousling them, then steps back to admire his work.

A wind blows through, whipping my hair in front of my face. I attempt to smooth it behind my ears, but Anderson's voice stops me.

"Don't. Don't move."

His demanding tone hits me deep in my core and I drop my hands, barely breathing as he raises his camera, feverishly snapping my photo from a variety of angles.

"I thought you came out here to take photos of an old drive-in," I comment, every click of the shutter ratcheting up my anxiety. "I'm sure that's a much more worthy subject."

"Not a chance in hell. I can't think of a more worthy subject than showing you how beautiful you are, scars and all."

"Did you study photography in college or something?" I inquire in an attempt to distract myself from posing as Anderson's unexpected model.

"Took a few classes. But my main course of study was history and economics."

"Hence your uncanny knowledge of President Lincoln."

"I suppose."

"Then how did you get into photography?"

He pauses for a moment, peering into the distance. "My therapist suggested it as a coping mechanism. A distraction. A way to channel my anger into something positive."

I nod, not pressing him any further. I know how difficult it is to talk about loss. To relive the darkest moments of your life.

"At first, she proposed art." He chuckles, his eyes gleaming with nostalgia. "Let's just say Disney won't be hiring me as an animator anytime soon. I can draw maybe three things. A tree with a single branch and a swing. A flower. And Rufus' face."

"Rufus?"

"My sister's cat when we were kids." He brings his camera back to his face. But this time when he snaps photo after photo, the sound of the shutter isn't as jarring. Now that we're talking, I'm not as uneasy about being on display for him to find every imperfection.

"So instead of drawing happy little clouds, you learned to take pictures."

"There's still art involved. It's not as easy as grabbing a camera, then just pointing and shooting. There's a difference between a photographer and someone with a camera. A big difference."

"And that is?"

"A photographer is trained to find the beauty in the mundane and ordinary."

"Like an empty field and rundown drive-in that's seen much better days?"

He grins. "Exactly."

"Will you show me?" I ask after a few more clicks of the camera.

"Show you?"

"Yeah. Show me how to do what you do. See what you see." I soften my voice. "How you're able to find beauty even in something that's worn and broken."

Anderson lowers the camera, closing the distance between us until our bodies are only a breath away. When he pushes a tendril of hair out of my eyes, his fingers graze the contours of my face, sending a jolt of electricity through me, his touch the most potent drug.

He cups my cheeks, his expression filled with understanding and compassion. "Even broken things deserve love."

Chapter Sixteen

ANDERSON

"Photography isn't something you can learn overnight."

I step away from Nora, my subconscious reminding me I'm the last thing she needs in her life right now. She's just been through a divorce. And there's still the mystery of the ashes. I refuse to cause her any more pain, and that's exactly what I'd do. There is no future between us. How can there be?

She takes a moment to regain her composure, smoothing her hair behind her ear. "I don't expect to." She flashes me a grin that causes my insides to tighten and skin to heat. "But perhaps daily lessons while we're on the road could be beneficial."

My lips quirk into a smile, spontaneous yet refreshing. Just like everything about my time with Nora.

"Here. Take this." I hand her the camera.

She squints, an adorable look of confusion crossing her expression as she stares at the screen and buttons. I walk behind her, peering over her shoulder. Her hair blowing in the breeze tickles my face and I inhale, her scent like a natural aphrodisiac. This is only our second day together, but I can already tell I'll miss that aroma when I return to the real world at the end of this journey.

Leaning over her, I point out the button on the top

right of the camera. "This is your shutter. It's what you'll use to focus and take your photos."

"It doesn't do it automatically? Like on a phone?"

"It can." I touch her shoulder, and she faces me. "But trusting the camera to automatically focus on exactly what you want it to doesn't always work well. There have been some incredible advancements over the years, but it still can't do all the thinking for you. Why would you want it to? I prefer a more advanced kind of autofocus."

"And what's that?"

"Well, there are two. Single-servo and continuous-servo."

"What's the difference?"

"It's in single-servo mode right now. It's great if you don't have a moving subject." I help her raise the camera back up. "You press down the shutter halfway, like this."

I adjust my body so I'm flush behind her, pointing the camera at a tire in the distance. My finger hovers over where hers is set on the shutter and add a bit of pressure, but don't press all the way. Then I pan back and forth over the tire, keeping it in frame but changing the view.

"See. The camera already focused on that tire. As long as I keep this slight pressure on the shutter, I can move the camera and it will still only focus on that tire, even if it's almost out of frame. It won't focus on anything else until I take my finger off the shutter." I remove my finger, nudging the camera toward the tattered movie screen before pressing the shutter halfway once more. This time, it focuses on a rip in the screen.

"And if I want to take a picture of that?"

"Then you press the shutter the rest of the way down." I fully press the button, and it clicks, capturing the image.

"What about the other way to focus? Continuous-servo was it?"

"That's good if you have a moving target. Like if you're on a photoshoot with models and want them to keep moving without having to set up each individual pose."

"You've shot models?" She waggles her brows, her playful side coming out.

"I have."

A wry smile crosses her face. "Lucky girls."

"You can pose for me. You won't hear any complaints."

She bats her lashes, passing me a demure look. "Maybe I'll take you up on that offer."

My pulse skyrockets, the idea of Nora posing seductively causing an inferno to burn inside me. She won't be the first woman I've taken risqué pictures of. But something about the thought of snapping photos of her, giving her direction on how to pose, has my imagination working on overdrive, every muscle in my body hardening.

"So, continuous-servo?" her voice cuts through.

"Right." I tear my gaze back to her. "Like I said, it's good for moving targets." I grab the camera from her and make a few adjustments to the mode before returning it. "Now the camera will continue to focus on an object whenever the camera or subject is moving. Remember the tire before?"

She nods, her attention glued to the viewfinder.

"Now look."

I cover her hands with mine, directing the lens at the tire. When it comes into view, I press the shutter halfway, the camera focusing on it. But this time when I move the camera, the tire doesn't stay in focus.

Instead, it tries to focus on the next large object it comes across, which happens to be a rusted speaker.

"See? As long as I press the shutter halfway and move the camera, it will keep trying to focus on something else."

"And a moving target?"

"Well, if you focus on a moving target, the camera will keep refocusing as that target moves. Instead of like in single-servo where if a subject moves, you'd have to manually refocus, in continuous-servo, the camera will continually refocus on the moving target."

She nods. "I get it."

I drop my hold on her, albeit reluctantly, allowing her to play around with the camera.

"Don't get too overwhelmed with the technical aspect. The different types of focusing are just instruments to make it easier for you to come up with that finished product." I lick my lips, trying to figure out a way to explain it so she'll understand. "Think of it like an artist's paintbrush or charcoal pencil."

"That makes sense." Squinting, she lifts the camera and snaps a few photos, her face lighting up with excitement when she checks her work on the viewfinder. Then she faces me. "Thank you for showing me this. For letting me know this side of you." She laughs under her breath. "I never would have taken you for the artsy type, or someone interested in photography."

"Is that right? Then what *did* you think when you first saw me?"

"That you were a pompous ass who tried to impress me with his useless knowledge of Abraham Lincoln."

"Really?"

"Well… No." She bites her lower lip, holding back her smile. God, I love when she does that. Makes me want to bite her lip, too. Makes me want to do a lot more than just bite her lip.

"Tell me." I widen my stance, crossing my arms over my chest.

She looks up at me, her eyes searching mine. She opens her mouth, but is cut off by a gruff voice.

"Hey! What are you two doing here? Didn't you see the sign?"

She stiffens, and we tear our gaze toward a wooded area in the distance, a heavily bearded man stalking toward us. Then she flings her wide expression back to mine, looking to me for instruction.

I grab the camera from her and shove it into my backpack. "Let's go."

Taking her hand, I drag her back through the field, our pace almost a run. By the time we reach the fence, our laughter is infectious, filling my heart with feelings I didn't think I'd experience again. Maybe my diagnosis isn't the death knell I'd originally thought. Maybe it doesn't have to dash all my hopes, plans, dreams. Maybe I can still have it all. Maybe I still deserve to have it all.

I drop her hand as we approach the fence, looking at her to ask if she'll be able to do it again, but she's already climbing.

"For someone who seemed hesitant to break a few rules, you sure know how to scale a fence." I make my way up the links, then leap onto the other side, landing with little effort.

I glance toward the field, grateful when I notice the man retreating to wherever he came from. Creed's probably having a heart attack that I trespassed on private property. If we'd gotten arrested, he would have lost his mind. Not to mention, Nora would find out I've been lying to her about who I am.

"What can I say?" She shoots me a mischievous grin

as her feet hit the ground, forcing my eyes back to her. "Maybe you've brought out a side of me I'd forgotten about." She approaches the passenger side of the Wrangler and I follow. But unlike all the other times, she doesn't step out of the way to allow me to open her door. Instead, she draws her body closer, her eyes not straying from mine.

"Is that right?" My voice is husky, my breathing heavy.

"That's right."

My heart skitters to a stop when she lifts herself onto her toes and curves toward me. But instead of pressing her lips to mine, she turns at the last second, kissing my cheek before lowering herself. A tingle spreads through me, emanating from my cheek and flowing out to the rest of my body.

"Thanks for that, Anderson. It's exactly what I needed today."

I reach for her, and she leans into my hand, closing her eyes. As I admire her with her hair tumbling around her face, I'm struck with an unsettling sensation of déjà vu, knocking the breath from me. My ears ring as flashes of that night all those years ago play before me like it was yesterday.

The doctors telling me Kendall didn't make it, that there was nothing they could do. The heart-crushing truth that she was gone. Forcing Creed to give me the keys to the SUV, needing to get as far away from that hospital as possible so I could breathe. I barely remember anything after that, until I found myself darting from the car and sprinting down an embankment toward a smoking SUV, the front end smashed into an overgrown tree. In my mind, if I couldn't save Kendall, at least I could save someone else.

Again, it wasn't enough.

"Are you okay?" Nora's voice cuts through.

I rip my unfocused gaze toward her, blinking repeatedly, shaking off the memory of the worst night of my life.

"Yeah." I clear my throat, breaking the connection. "Just having a déjà vu moment."

She gives me a flirtatious grin. If she notices my changed demeanor, she doesn't mention it, turning back toward the door. I grab the handle and open it for her, placing my hand on her elbow to help her up. I peer at her as she sits in the passenger seat, trying to remember the image of the woman I pulled from that car. But I can't see her anymore. It's gone, something in my brain protecting me from it.

"I seem to have a few of those when I'm with you, too. Maybe we knew each other in another life."

I smile, but it doesn't reach my eyes. "Maybe."

Chapter Seventeen

NORA

"OKAY, OKAY. I have one," I announce as we make our way through the Texas panhandle toward Amarillo, where we plan to stop for the night.

The past few days have been exactly what I needed, even if it bears little resemblance to the trip I originally imagined. Instead of spending my nights meditating or doing yoga, Anderson and I watch a movie while drinking wine out of plastic cups. I usually fall asleep before the movie's over, and when I wake up, he's tucked me into my bed and left water and a few aspirin on my nightstand.

Around nine every morning, he knocks on my door, greeting me with a cup of coffee and a panty-dropping smile. Then we hit the road, where we pass the time playing Would You Rather between making stops on my list so I can spread more of Hunter's ashes. But I'm no longer only leaving them in places on the list. I'm also leaving them in other spots we discover. Ones I think Hunter would appreciate.

Anderson still hasn't pushed to find out whose ashes I've been spreading across the country. I can tell he's curious, but that's as far as it's gone, allowing me to keep this to myself. Just like I haven't pressed him to talk about the weight I can see burdening him.

"If you were reincarnated into an animal based on

your personality, what do you think you would come back as?" I push a strand of hair behind my ear.

Ever since Anderson loosened my ponytail in the field the other day, I haven't put as much effort into my appearance as normal. It hasn't been without a struggle, though. It's difficult to break habits. Not to mention, every time I look into the mirror and see my wavy hair and the smattering of freckles across my nose that Hunter adored, it reminds me of the girl who lost everything. I've hidden that girl beneath layers of makeup and perfectly straight hair for years, pretending she didn't exist. In my mind, if I didn't look like that Nora anymore, I wasn't her. But maybe it's okay to be that Nora again.

"That's a good one." Anderson pulls his bottom lip between his teeth, drawing his brows together in contemplation. "What do *you* think I'd come back as?"

"You know the rules. You need to answer first."

"Fine," he huffs, feigning annoyance.

He peers forward at the terrain that's become less green over the miles, signaling the fact we're nearing the desert regions of New Mexico and Arizona. Then onto California and the end of the road, something I don't want to think about. When I started this journey, I looked forward to reaching California and having this trip behind me. Now, I hate the idea of everything I've experienced with Anderson ending. Of walking away and never seeing him again.

"I think I'd go with a cheetah."

"Is this solely based on your affinity for Cheetos?" I joke, having grown familiar with his preference in junk food.

He chuckles slightly, his eyes wrinkling behind his dark sunglasses. "We share certain characteristics. The cheetah is active with a sense of adventure. They're in tune with their surroundings and are able to react quickly to any perceived threat. I've been known to be manipulative to get my way."

"Oh really?" I respond sarcastically, all too familiar with his ability to get what he wants. After all, it was his unique powers of persuasion that convinced me to agree to his ridiculous proposal that we drive together across the country. "I never would have guessed that about you."

He flashes me a devilish smirk before looking back at the two-lane road in front of us. "I'm also loyal to those I care about. Sometimes to a fault. I'll fight for you, despite the personal cost to myself." He peers at me over the rim of his sunglasses so I can see the honesty in his words. "Not to mention, I find cheetahs to be charismatic as hell. And that certainly describes me to a T." He winks.

"I can't argue with that." I pause, then add, "Except about that charismatic part. I personally find you dull and boring." I force my lips into a straight line to fight the grin threatening to break free.

"Dull and boring?"

"I'd probably have more fun scrubbing tile grout for days on end than I've had with you on this trip."

"If that's the case, I can make a detour to the airport in Amarillo." He puts on the blinker as we approach a highway on-ramp. "I'm sure you'll find a rental car there."

"No!" I shout, placing my hand on his arm.

"That's what I thought." With a sly grin, he turns off his signal. "Your turn, gorgeous. What animal would you come back as?"

"A horse."

"And why would that be?"

"They're reluctant to trust, but once they do, they're

loyal. They're dependable and strive to have peace and harmony in their world. Like me."

"Hmm…" His brows pull together in concentration.

"What?"

Anderson waves me off. "Nothing."

"It's not nothing. What are you thinking?"

"I don't think you're horse material. Not yet, anyway."

"Oh no? Then tell me. What animal do you think I'd come back as?"

"A deer."

"Great." I roll my eyes. "You want me to come back as roadkill."

"You don't scream horse to me," he argues as a large truck rumbles past us, the scent of wildflowers and exhaust filling the Jeep through the open top and windows. "I see you as someone who cares so much about the people you let into your life that you'll do anything for them. But you don't let in just anyone. You're selective, hiding in the bushes until you're sure you can trust someone. So in my mind, you're more like a deer. You'll protect those you let into your circle, but you're not going to let anyone in. Which makes me wonder why you let me in."

"Who says I have?"

"You have," he responds with certainty, but his statement lacks any hint of arrogance. "And I like that you're giving me a glimpse of the real Nora." He reaches for a lock of my hair, twirling it around one of his fingers.

On a hard swallow, I shift my gaze to his. I want to tell him he's the reason I've allowed myself to remove the mask I've worn since losing Hunter. Tell him I can't remember the last time I've been this carefree, this laid-back, this…happy. But I don't. Instead, I clear my throat and peer out my window at the dusty terrain, the trucks and cars on the interstate visible in the distance.

"It's your turn," I say softly.

The heat of his stare burns my skin as he studies me, the questions he doesn't ask screaming loudly in the silence. Then he sighs, untangling his finger from my hair.

"If you were to be listed in the *Guinness Book of World Records*, what would be your claim to fame?"

I breathe a sigh of relief, grateful his question isn't nearly as deep as my last one, although I didn't think it would be that way when I first posed it. I thought it was a fun topic where he'd tell me he was most like a wolf because of his ability to mold any woman he looks at into putty, and I'd accuse him of being cocky and arrogant. But as I've begun to learn, beneath Anderson's flirtatious exterior lies layers and layers of who he really is. I have a feeling I've barely scratched the surface.

"Longest human gorilla crawl," I answer confidently.

"Gorilla crawl?" he repeats, a combination of intrigue and confusion in his tone.

"I'm double-jointed in my elbows." I extend my arms in front of me, then hyper-extend them backward so they bend beyond what most people can do. "Because of that, I can crawl around like a gorilla. That, and certain yoga poses come incredibly easy."

"Anywhere else you're *extra* flexible?" He waggles his brows.

I playfully punch him in the bicep, and he feigns pain. "Too bad you'll never find out."

"That is too bad."

"What would you be known for? What strange skill do you possess?" I ask in an effort to shift our conversation away from anything to do with sex.

"That's easy." He smirks. "Best road trip partner." He puts on his blinker and pulls into a dirt lot.

"That's debatable."

"Even you admitted I'm growing on you."

"As much as a tumor can grow on you." Flashing him a smile, I open the door and slide out, slinging my bag over my shoulder.

"You're really doing a number on my already fragile male ego."

I snort out a laugh. "I may not know much about you, but I get the feeling there is absolutely nothing fragile about that supposed ego of yours. It'll take a lot more than some harsh words to dampen your confidence."

"Trust me, gorgeous…" He takes my hand in his, leading us away from the Jeep and toward a series of Cadillacs buried nose down in an art exhibit that's become the Western Wall to all Route 66 travelers — Cadillac Ranch. "You know me better than most people in my life. Traveling across the country together will have that effect, wouldn't you agree?"

"I suppose you're right."

The wind whistles along the flat terrain, the sun high in the sky warming us. But it's not unbearable. It's comfortable. All week, the weather has been perfect, apart from a few rainy spots. But even the little rain was welcome.

We approach the line of cars, taking in the unique sight. A cacophony of colors adorns each of the ten Cadillacs, their tailfins sticking out of the sand at the same angle. Cans of spray paint are scattered along the dusty ground for those who didn't bring their own, an invitation to leave your mark. I wonder how many coats of paint these cars have seen over the years. I can't even fathom a guess.

"This is the place that started our idea for Route 66,"

I say in a small voice as I approach one of the cars, running my hand along it. It's rusted over, the windows and engine long gone, leaving just the shell.

"*Our* idea?" Anderson asks softly.

"Yeah." I glance over my shoulder, smiling, but don't embellish. Based on the look of understanding crossing his face, he knows I'm referring to whomever is now reduced to the ashes I've been carrying.

"Did you ever drive Route 66 together?"

I slowly shake my head, returning my attention to the cars. "No. But he would have loved this. He loved kitschy Americana. When we drove down to Florida once, he made us stop at South of the Border. Do you know what that is?"

He chuckles, nodding. "The tourist trap between the Carolina borders."

"It's so cheesy and dirty, but he loved stuff like that. That's why I know he would have loved every second of this trip."

"What you're doing is a good thing," Anderson says after a protracted pause. "Giving him one last adventure." A shadow creeps over his face. "It's a beautiful gesture."

I smile through the lump in my throat. This was the spot I'd dreaded visiting the most. After all, it was Cadillac Ranch that sparked Hunter's idea we drive Route 66, one last adventure before we started an even crazier adventure as parents.

An adventure we never got to realize.

But as I stare at the Cadillacs, each representing a different year, it's not nearly as overwhelming as I thought it would be. I imagined myself breaking down, yelling furiously at Hunter for leaving me. But somewhere between that Chicago diner and the dusty Texas plains, I've let go of my anger and resentment.

I'm no longer wishing things were different. That Hunter were still here and we were living the life we'd planned for us and our daughter. I'm not sure I've reached that pinnacle of acceptance. But now I understand. And maybe that's all we can hope for — understanding.

Digging into my bag, I grab the canister that's decreased in weight with every mile. A lightness in my heart, I sprinkle some of the ashes on the ground in front of the Cadillac, then return the container to my purse.

A breeze picks up, and I close my eyes. I know it's simply nature, that environmental forces caused the pressure in the air that resulted in the wind, but I'd like to think it's Hunter's soul wrapping around me, telling me he's okay. That it's time for me to move on.

I open my eyes and look toward Anderson standing several feet away, allowing me this moment for myself. He arches a brow, silently asking if I'm okay. When I nod, he approaches.

"Shall we leave our mark?" Bending down, he grabs a can of spray paint, shakes it, then hands it to me.

"I'm not even sure what to leave as a mark."

He surveys the cars. "It seems names and initials seem popular. Better than 'For a good time, call Debbie'."

"Why is it always Debbie?" I joke, grateful for the break in tension. "I've known a few Debbies, and they've all been good people."

"Shall we put 'For a good time, call Frank'? Give Debbie a break?"

I laugh. "Perhaps we leave Debbie out of this altogether and put our names and the date."

"I like that." He steps behind me, taking me by surprise when he places his hand over mine, holding the paint can. "Is this okay?" he asks in a throaty voice.

A shiver rolls down my spine, his breath warm on my

neck as he leans close. Days ago, I never would have done something like this, not wanting to dishonor Hunter's memory. But that's not what I'm doing. I'm starting to understand my old way of thinking has been anything but healthy. I've allowed a ghost to dictate my life, to prevent me from chasing what truly made me happy. From now on, that's what I need to do. Chase my own happiness. Even if that happiness is with a man I may not have any future with.

"Yes," I whimper.

"Good."

I hold my breath as Anderson raises our joined hands and presses against my finger. My chest rises and falls in a quicker pattern, electricity coursing through my veins. On its face, there's nothing erotic about what we're doing — two adults on a road trip spray-painting our names on one of the cars at Cadillac Ranch. It's something thousands of travelers before us have done. Something thousands of road warriors after us will do for years to come.

But I can't ignore the crackling spark igniting between us, Anderson's body flush with mine, his large hand covering my delicate one. It has all the tiny hairs on my body standing on end, making me want to spin around and have a taste of what I've been fantasizing about since the first time I heard him speak, met his eyes, felt his soul.

I relax my muscles and fuse into him, a puppet who is more than happy to allow him to pull every single one of my strings. A stream of blue sprays onto the car, Anderson's motions slow and deliberate. After he adds the month and year, he lowers my arm to my side, then gradually removes his hand. But he doesn't increase the distance, both of us standing flush with each other, his front to my back as the paint can falls to the ground with a clatter.

"They look good together, don't they?" he comments in a low voice as we stare at our names — *Anderson + Nora*.

"They do," I murmur, my body humming from his proximity.

When he runs his hands down my arms, I quiver, anticipation coiling through me, making me devoid of reason. Nothing matters. Not the fact that I barely know this man. Or that we only have a few more days together. Or the secrets we're both keeping in order to protect our hearts. I don't care about any of that. When I'm with Anderson, I'm able to forget about my past. And the future doesn't matter. All that does is right now. And right now, I just want to be near him. To drown in his waters. To burn in his flames.

His breath scorches my nape as he pushes my hair over my shoulder, exposing my skin. When his strong hands land on my hips, every inch of my body comes to life and my pulse skyrockets. In one quick move, he spins me around, our gazes locking as if it's the first time. In them is my redemption. My atonement. My salvation.

His lips part, his gaze raking over my face, settling on my mouth. His Adam's apple bobs in his throat, breaths increasing. He wants to kiss me. I can see it in the way he looks at me, the way his eyes never stray from me, the way he holds me so possessively, as if worried I'll disappear if he lets go. But something holds him back, causing him to retreat instead of advance. I don't want him to hold back anymore. Don't want him to think he has to keep his distance out of respect. He deserves to know what I want. And I want him.

With all the confidence I can muster, I clutch his face in my hands, not allowing him to escape. Then my lips are on his, stealing what I've deprived myself of since our first meeting. He stiffens, but doesn't push me away. Not yet. He stays in this place, unsure if he should cross the invisible line we've drawn between us.

"Please," I beg, sliding my tongue along the seam of his lips. "I need to feel. I need to feel you."

My pleading tone is all it takes for him to snake an arm around my back, yanking me against him. The sudden movement catches me off guard and I gasp, not expecting him to be so dominant, so powerful, although I should have.

Anderson takes advantage of my open mouth, his tongue plunging inside. Synapses fire. Fingers ache. Legs quiver. All from this man's kiss.

He guides me against the Cadillac where we just made our mark, pressing his body to mine, thrusting, pulsing, wanting, showing me how much he craves me. A moan falls uninhibited from my throat and I dig my fingers through his hair, clawing, pulling. This isn't a soft and gentle kiss, not like my first kiss with Hunter was. It's bruising, an exchange of years of pent-up pain, each of us giving and taking everything we can until all that's left is a shell of the person we pretended to be. This kiss is a baptism. An awakening. A rebirth.

A sudden jolt startles me. I fling my eyes open, watching Anderson jump from me, wiping the pink stain of my gloss off his swollen lips.

Bewildered, I blink repeatedly, attempting to make sense of this abrupt shift. One second, he kissed me in a way that made me think he had a direct line to my soul, the very essence of who I was. The next, he pushed me away like I held some contagious disease.

"Nora, I'm sorry," he pants, his chest heaving as he struggles to catch his breath. "I..." Running a hand through his thick locks, he lifts his remorse-filled gaze to mine. "I can't do this with you."

"Oh." I swallow hard, embarrassment burning my cheeks. "I see." I push off the Cadillac, keeping my head lowered as I brush past him, his fresh scent kicking up.

What was I thinking? Why did I think it was a good idea to kiss him? Just because I'm coming to terms with my past doesn't mean he is. Based on the little I've learned about him, he's just as messed up as I am. Maybe even more.

I thought he'd try to stop me before I reached the Wrangler, but he doesn't. Instead, he acts as if nothing unusual happened as he helps me into the passenger seat, like he always does.

When he closes the door, leaving me alone for a moment, I blow out a held breath, silently berating myself for making the first move. For taking a risk. I was overcome with the moment. It was a mistake. One I don't plan on repeating.

Anderson opens his door, stealing a glance at me as he slides behind the wheel. I hate the apologetic smile on his face. Hate the pity I see. Hate the rejection in his gaze.

I wrap my arms around my stomach, shrinking into myself as I stare out the window, watching the Cadillacs grow smaller as we drive away.

"It's not that I didn't want to kiss you, Nora." Anderson's voice cuts through the strained silence several moments later. "I just—"

"Don't worry." I straighten my spine, rebuilding the pieces of the wall Anderson was able to blast through. "It was only a kiss."

"That's the thing… It wasn't only a kiss. Not to me." The passion in his voice forces my eyes to his, and he burns me with his stare, allowing me to see the truth in his words. Then he looks forward once more, navigating the few miles to our hotel for the evening. "But that still doesn't change who we are to each other. Who *I* am."

"And who are you?" I inquire, even though my gut tells me to drop it.

Turmoil covers his expression, as if he's weighing which response to give me. Then he blows out a sigh, his face sobering. "I wish I knew."

Chapter Eighteen

ANDERSON

To say the tension in the Wrangler has been thick today would be a gross understatement. It's suffocating, making me hyper-aware of every sound, every movement, every shaky inhale. Being so close to Nora, knowing how her lips feel, how she tastes, has been the cruelest form of torture.

All week, I've fought my growing attraction to her. Convinced myself I don't deserve someone like her. Convinced myself I can't hurt her any more than she's already been hurt. And that's exactly what I would do. Hurt her. Shatter her. Obliterate the life she has left after suffering so much heartache. I've lied to her from the beginning when she's been nothing but honest. Even if she understands why I lied and shows me the compassion she seems to show everyone, I can't sentence her to a future with me when my own future is uncertain. She's already lost too much. I can't add to that.

But that knowledge hasn't made today any easier. Every inch of me yearns to touch her. A hunger made even more intense thanks to the short, flowing skirt and cut-off shirt she's wearing. Every time a wind breezes past, blowing her skirt, revealing even more of her toned legs that I'd give anything to feel wrapped around me, my heart skips a beat. Every time she raises her arms above her head, causing her shirt to lift and reveal a narrow sliver of her torso, making my mouth water with what the skin would taste like, an intense craving threatens to undo me. To destroy the self-control I've struggled with all day. Hell, struggled with since I first saw her.

"We should be getting close." Nora's sultry voice enters my subconscious. The sound seems foreign against the song filling the void in the Jeep.

There were no games of Would You Rather today. No flirtatious comments that bordered on inappropriate. No secrets shared or truths revealed. We've both resorted to the people we were when we first met at that diner in Chicago. Nora even straightened her hair again, slicking it back into a neat ponytail. I hate it. Hate that I'm the reason for it. I wish I weren't. I wish I could convince her to let her hair loose and enjoy the moment again. But at what cost?

A few more silent minutes pass, then we approach civilization again after miles of nothing. We've made it to Tucumcari, New Mexico, our stopping point for the night and another item on Nora's list.

"Wow," she breathes, giving voice to my exact thoughts as we drive on a road that looks like it could have been pulled straight from a postcard. Motels with oversized signs that light up with neon once the sun sets. Teepee-shaped buildings advertising curios and other roadside non-essentials. Casual restaurants specializing in local fare to give tourists a taste of the region. "This is what I imagined whenever I pictured driving Route 66."

"It is a bit like stepping back in time, isn't it?"

"It is." She keeps her gaze trained forward. This time, it's not out of nerves or awkwardness. It's out of awe. And perhaps excitement.

When our destination comes into view, I turn the Jeep into the parking lot of the roadside motel that's been in operation since before the interstate made Route 66 practically obsolete. For the most part, Nora hasn't had much of an opinion regarding where we stay. Except tonight. After all, spending the night here is on her list, a huge star beside it. I can see why. Just like spray-painting your name on one of the cars at Cadillac Ranch is a rite of passage, so is staying at the famous Blue Swallow Motel.

The second I yank on the parking brake and kill the engine, Nora jumps out of the Jeep, not giving me a chance to open her door. She's been doing that all day, which has only added to the edginess between us. I react quickly, scrambling out and hurrying toward the main office, catching up to her in time to open the door for her. If she won't allow me to help her out of the car, at least I can do this for her.

"Welcome to the Blue Swallow," a woman with graying hair and kind eyes greets us when we step inside the air-conditioned building. Vintage photographs of the motel cover the walls, like a timeline of it through the years. It's not a large space. Just big enough to house the registration desk and a small merchandise area, boasting t-shirts and other Blue Swallow or Route 66 memorabilia. "How can I help you?"

"My name is Nora Tremblay. I have a reservation."

I fling my gaze to hers. "You do?"

She peers at me like the idea of not having a reservation here is preposterous. "Don't you?"

"Well… No. We've been sort of winging it."

"Yes, but I told you yesterday that this was the plan for today."

I cringe inwardly, wondering how many more times I'm going to disappoint Nora. Then I face the woman behind the desk. "Do you have any rooms available?"

Her expression falls. "I'm sorry, sir. We're booked solid tonight. There are a handful of other options nearby. Mostly budget-friendly chains."

I nod at her in thanks, then turn back to Nora, her expression difficult to read. Almost like annoyance mixed with relief.

"I'll go check in somewhere else. You get settled in, then maybe we can grab dinner or something. If you're up for it." I give her a pleading look.

The last thing I want is for her to turn me down. Hell, the last thing I want is to stay in a different hotel. I fear it will only widen the divide between us.

"That's not necessary," Nora states.

I half-smile in understanding. "I guess we can both use some time to ourselves tonight. If you change your mind, the offer for dinner still stands." I'm about to turn and go to the Jeep to grab her things when her voice stops me.

"Not dinner. That's not what I meant."

I stop, facing her. "It's not?"

She draws in a deep breath. "It's not necessary for you to stay somewhere else. You can just stay here."

"But—"

"With me." She worries her bottom lip, tilting her head to gauge my reaction.

"Are you sure?" I ask, recalling the multiple times in the past several hours she intentionally went out of her way to avoid my touch. How will she avoid me if we're sharing a room? "I don't mind. I—"

"It's fine." She squares her shoulders, her tone and expression akin to that of a businesswoman negotiating a deal, not a young woman offering to share her room with me. "Hell, most nights I fall asleep while you're in my room anyway. This won't be any different."

Maybe if I were a better man, I'd thank her for the invite but decline, especially after the awkwardness that permeated everything we did today. But I'm not a better man. I'm a man who knows his time with this woman is a ticking bomb, nearing closer and closer to detonation.

"If you're certain…"

"I am." Except her words sound anything but. She turns back to the clerk. "Do you have anything with two beds?"

"I'm sorry. We don't."

"Do you have a king bed?" I interject.

She cringes. "Our rooms are on the smaller side. King beds would take up the entire space, and then some." She laughs to herself. "The best I can offer is a room with a queen bed."

Nora taps her fingernails against the counter, the idea of sharing a room seeming to lose its appeal with the knowledge that not only is there just one queen-sized bed, but that the rooms are too small to accommodate anything bigger. I'm about to voice my original offer of staying elsewhere when she straightens, nodding curtly, resolved.

"A queen bed is fine." She reaches into her purse, pulling out her wallet, but I step in front of her.

"Allow me." I pull my wallet out of my back pocket, placing my credit card on the counter. Or, rather, Anderson North's company card.

"I made the reservation. I should pay."

"But you're letting me stay. Doesn't seem fair for you to pay for a room you're now stuck sharing with me."

"I'm not *stuck* sharing it. I offered. I didn't have to do that."

"I know." I place my finger on her credit card, pushing it back toward her. "Which is why I should pay. As a token of my gratitude."

She glares at me, then her lips twitch into a hint at a smile. It's the first break in the tension all day. I didn't think I'd miss Nora's smile as much as I have. Sure, we shared a few lighter moments as we continued checking items off her list and spreading the ashes along the way — the midpoint of Route 66 in Adrian, the Vega Motel in Vega, the ghost town in Glenrio right on the Texas/New Mexico border. But I haven't seen her smile and actually feel it. They've all been forced and stilted, like a smile you'd give an old acquaintance you wished you hadn't run into at the local pub. The authentic smile slowly building on her face fills me with hope that we'll be able to cut through this tension and go back to the way things were before I screwed it all up.

"Why do I get the feeling that even if I refuse to let you pay, you'll find a way to do so anyway?"

"Because you know how persistent I can be." I step toward her, narrowing my gaze. A blush blooms on her cheeks under my stare. "When I want something, I don't stop until I get it."

She chews on her bottom lip, fighting a grin, but there's no hiding the amusement dancing in her eyes.

"Fine." She huffs in feigned annoyance as she grabs her card and returns it to her wallet. "But I'm paying for all the road snacks the rest of our trip."

My mouth curves up into a small smile, relief filling me. The confirmation she wants to stay with me until the end gives me the boost I've needed all day.

"We'll see about that." I nod at my card, indicating for the clerk to run it, which she does.

After I sign the slip, she turns to a board behind her, a few keys hanging off the four rows of pegs. I can't remember the last time I've stayed at a hotel where they gave you actual keys instead of an electronic card.

She's about to hand me a set, then stops. "Can I say something?"

Nora and I share a look before returning our attention to her.

"Sure…," I reply in a drawn-out voice.

"I've seen all types of people walk through that door." She gestures past our shoulders at the glass door. "I've seen all types of *couples* walk through that door. Honeymooners. High school sweethearts. Older couples. Road companions." She gives us a knowing look.

"It may not be my place to say, and maybe I'm misreading the signs, but I get a feeling about you two. You say you're merely friends on a road trip, and you've probably even tried to convince yourself of that, but trust me…" She rests her elbows on the counter, leaning toward us. "There are some people whose souls are too inexplicably intertwined to ever be just friends." She straightens. "And that's what I see when I look at you two. Your souls are intertwined." She studies us, the intensity causing goosebumps to prickle my skin.

I've never been one to believe in psychics or fortune-tellers, have always considered them frauds, swindling people out of their hard-earned money by offering them vague statements that could apply to anyone. But as this woman grabs Nora's and my hand in each of hers, a chill washes over me. My insides vibrate with a connection I can't explain.

"There are secrets between you." She directs her steely gaze on me. "You've caused her pain. Or maybe you're afraid of causing her pain." She pauses, briefly closing her eyes, as if trying to see something in the recesses of her brain. When she returns her eyes to mine, they're peaceful, determined, confident. "But you're also her salvation. You saved her."

I yank my hand from hers. "That's preposterous. I—"

"And you." She ignores my outburst, focusing on Nora, who seems intrigued, albeit skeptical. "There's pain inside you."

"Of course you'd say that, especially if you claim I've caused her pain."

The woman lifts her free hand, silencing me, then closes her eyes, bringing a single finger to her temple. This entire situation unnerves me, makes me antsy. Not because the idea of anyone being able to see things buried in a person's subconscious is crazy, but because a part of me wants to believe she can. Wants to believe that maybe I can be Nora's salvation. And maybe she can be mine, too.

"You're still clinging to the past when your future is right in front of you," the woman finally says.

"My…future?" Nora repeats.

"Yes. It's time to let go of the past. To live again. If you don't, you won't have a future." She turns Nora's hand over, studying her palm. "It won't be easy. I still see more pain, more heartache."

I lean toward Nora, peering over her shoulder as the woman analyzes the lines on her palm. Her gaze narrows, as if attempting to read the fine print. Then she points to a line that's been cut short by a scar.

"There's a point where your past and future will collide unexpectedly. You'll want to run. Return to what's familiar. Want to return to that time in your life when you thought you had everything. But you'll soon realize what's important."

"And what's that?" Nora asks hesitantly.

The clerk smiles, looking between the two of us. "Love." She covers Nora's hand with hers, squeezing it. "In the end, love is the only thing that matters. And you'll find that love in a familiar stranger."

Nora's breath hitches, surprise covering her expression. "What did you say?" she asks frantically.

"It's what I see. You'll find your soul mate in a kindred spirit. A stranger your heart will recognize."

"Oh, jeez," a voice bellows.

Nora and I both jump, snapping our heads toward the door as a burly man walks through, carrying a black motorcycle helmet.

"Are you telling your fortunes again?" He rolls his eyes in playful annoyance as he approaches. "Miriam here fancies herself a 'clairvoyant' or something," he explains in a subtle drawl. "Says she can sense things about people."

"And I can." She places her hands on her hips. "I sensed you were a giant pain in the ass, yet I married you anyway."

"And I'm glad you did. Now if you could 'sense' the winning lottery numbers, maybe I'd stop teasing you." He winks, slinging an arm around his wife's shoulders and kissing her temple. Based on the affection between them, I can tell he appreciates his wife's "gift", whether he believes in any of it or not.

"Well, thank you." I swipe the keys from the counter. If we stay any longer, I worry about what else Miriam will "see".

"Hope you enjoy your stay," the man says. "If you need anything, just holler. Oh, and if you can park outside of the carport next to your room, we'd appreciate it. Visitors like to stop by here to look at all the murals painted in them. They light up at night, what with all the neon."

"Will do." I turn to Nora. "Ready?"

"Of course." She forces a smile onto her face, giving extra care to keep her distance yet again as we make our way out of the office and toward the Wrangler.

If I thought the tension throughout the day was thick, it's practically impenetrable now, thanks to Miriam's psychic reading.

Tonight is going to be very interesting.

Chapter Nineteen

NORA

ANDERSON'S PRESENCE PERMEATES our room for the night, my pulse increasing when I observe how small it is. It doesn't help that Miriam's words seem to play on repeat.

In the end, love is the only thing that matters. And you'll find that love in a familiar stranger.

I try to ignore it, tell myself it's only vague ramblings that could apply to anyone. But I can't ignore the fact her premonition is nearly identical to the vision that psychic shared with me all those years ago. That I'd find my soul mate in a stranger I recognize. Could she have been talking about Anderson? He's a stranger. But is he one I recognize? I can't discount that I've always found something familiar about him.

"Where would you like me to put your suitcase?"

When I hear Anderson's voice, I snap out of my thoughts, waving my hand around. "Wherever you can find space."

He heads toward the front corner beside a small window facing the parking lot and main road. "This okay?"

"Sure," I reply nervously.

The room has been lovingly restored, boasting all the charm one would expect in a roadside motel back in the heyday of Route 66. Instead of a plush duvet covering the bed, there's a handmade quilt with a pair of blue swallows on it. The walls are a dull yellow, framed prints of famous Route 66 landmarks adorning them. A queen bed takes up most of the room, along with a small recliner in an alcove by the bathroom. Other than that, there's not much space to move. Miriam wasn't lying when she said a king bed wouldn't fit. A queen barely does.

Anderson sets down my suitcase and turns, both of us doing an uncoordinated dance to get out of each other's way. But every time I step right, he follows, the awkward factor increasing exponentially, this already compact space getting tighter by the second.

"Sorry." The flush along his brow gives the impression he's as rattled as me.

Grabbing my biceps, he forces me to stop, the warmth of his hands on me sending a current from my arms straight to my core, my insides humming. It's the first time he's touched me since our kiss yesterday. I've kept my distance, probably obsessively so. The last thing I wanted was a reminder that even an innocent touch has the ability to light my body on fire. Now I can't avoid it, his flames engulfing me.

When his eyes lock on mine, the blue hue darkens, his chest rising and falling in a faster pattern. With an unwavering gaze, he maneuvers our bodies, turning us like two teenagers dancing for the first time. Once he's free from the tight corner by the bed, he drops his hold on me and scoots to the opposite end of the room.

Anxious to focus on something, *anything* other than Anderson, I open my suitcase and shift through its contents, finding my toiletry bag and a change of clothes. Careful to keep my vibrator hidden, I glance at him.

"Mind if I use the bathroom first to freshen up?" I ask shakily.

"Not at all."

With a nod, I hurry toward the rear of the room, keeping my head lowered until I duck inside the bathroom. Leaning against the door, I take a moment to calm my nerves, blowing out a breath, thankful for the temporary reprieve from Anderson's larger-than-life presence. What was I thinking when I offered for him to stay with me? Apparently, I wasn't. How the hell am I going to keep any distance between us when we're supposed to share a bed that may as well be a twin for all I care?

I push off the door and turn on the shower. Like the rest of the room, the bathroom is small, containing only a pedestal sink, toilet, and a shower stall. I wrap my hair in a towel, so I don't have to go through the lengthy process of straightening it, then step under the water, washing the day off me.

After a longer than normal shower, mainly so I can avoid Anderson and the way he has me tied in knots, I dry off before pulling on a breezy sundress. Then I apply a hint of makeup and re-secure my strawberry blonde hair that's more blonde than strawberry these days, thanks to the hours spent with the top down on the Wrangler.

Content with my appearance, I step into the bedroom and make a beeline toward my suitcase, avoiding Anderson's eyes once more, as if not meeting his gaze will make him disappear.

"Are you all set in there, or…"

"It's all yours," I answer quickly.

"Thanks."

He grabs his own toiletry bag and steps into the bathroom. Only a second or two passes before I hear the shower start. I flop onto the bed, grateful to have a little longer to myself. I'm probably making a bigger deal out of this than necessary. We're two grown adults. Just because we're sharing a room doesn't mean anything. I've fallen asleep beside him in my bed every night this past week. Well, *almost* every night. Every night except for last night. Still, this is no different. Right?

God, I hope so.

I'm so consumed by unease that I don't notice when the shower turns off. It's not until the door creaks open that I snap out of my thoughts, watching Anderson stroll out of the bathroom…wearing nothing but a towel.

For the love of all that's holy.

I can't help but stare at the strong panes of his abs. The broad muscles of his shoulders. The surprising tattoo of a compass over his heart, something vaguely familiar about it. Droplets of water continue to fall from his mussed-up hair that seems to be a cacophony of shades, from dark brown, to auburn, to blond at the ends. I've never seen anything like it. I doubt I will again.

When I manage to lift my eyes to his, I notice he's smirking at me.

"Sorry." I jump to my feet and head toward the small window.

He chuckles. "What are you sorry for?"

"Nothing. You just, well… You're in a towel."

"So I've noticed." His voice is amused, the cocky man I met a week ago returning.

"And you're not wearing a shirt."

"Does that bother you?"

I hear the rustling of clothes followed by the telltale thump of a wet towel dropping to the hardwood floor. All it would take is a slight movement of my head to either side and I'd catch a glimpse of Anderson in all his glory. Based on our kiss yesterday when he had me pinned against the car and circled his hips against me, I know I won't be disappointed.

"It's not like I walked out with nothing on at all."

"I know. I just…"

"What is it?"

"I don't know…" I shake my head, struggling to find the words to explain what's going through my mind, to make Anderson understand why I'm jittery around him. Why these past twenty-four hours have been a perpetual see-saw. How one minute, I don't want to do anything that would tarnish Hunter's memory. Then the next, I'm convinced Hunter would want me to move on, to be happy, to take a risk. And that maybe I should take a risk on Anderson. But didn't I do that? Look how that worked out.

"Okay. That's it."

A hand on my bicep forces me around. I gasp, the sudden movement taking me by surprise. Thankfully, Anderson is now fully clothed in a pair of khakis and a white linen shirt, the rolled-up sleeves revealing his corded forearms.

"What do you mean? I—"

"This." He gestures between our two bodies. "It's…stupid."

I scrunch my brow, my heart pounding in my chest at the magnitude with which he stares at me, the muscles in his face strained, the vein in his neck throbbing.

"What is?"

He throws up his hands. "This tension. This awkwardness. It's been driving me crazy all bloody day. So we're leaving."

My eyes widen. "But I wanted to stay here. I'm not—"

"We're still staying here. But we're going out. We're

going to walk to a little Mexican place a few blocks away, and the first thing we'll do is take a shot of tequila so you'll stop feeling so goddamn on edge around me. I fucking hate it. You're supposed to be on this amazing journey, having the time of your life. So if I'm interfering with that—"

"I'm glad we ran into each other," I assure him, the words leaving my mouth before I have a chance to stop them. It's true, though. Despite yesterday's setback, I can't imagine doing this trip without him.

His lips curve into a sweet smile, his expression and voice softening. "And there's nowhere I'd rather be right now than with you. But we need to do something to cut through the obvious unease. And in my experience, a shot of tequila is the best medicine for awkward tension." He winks.

"So is a glass of wine."

"True. But I think the best thing we can do is get out of this room, not barricade ourselves inside." He extends his hand toward me. "So, are you in?"

I expel a breath. Getting drunk on tequila and beer is the last thing I need, considering I'll be sharing a room with Anderson tonight. But he's right. Today has been ridiculous. We need to put last night and today behind us. And there's no better way to forget than several shots of tequila.

Linking my fingers with his, I revel in his warmth and familiarity. "I'm in."

Chapter Twenty

ANDERSON

"**Y**OU WANT TO play what?" Nora asks as we sit across from each other in a booth hidden in the corner of a dark bar a few blocks from our motel.

We'd gone out for Mexican food and, as I'd hoped, the tequila and beer relaxed us both, Nora finally letting her hair down again. But I still wasn't ready to go back to the room. Not yet. Instead, I dragged her to a bar where the music is loud and the drinks strong. The perfect spot for two people to get reacquainted after a setback.

"Truth or Drink."

"I'm not familiar," she says with a slight slur as she takes a pull from her beer bottle.

"You're familiar with Truth or Dare, though, aren't you?"

She passes me a flirtatious grin as she pops a tortilla chip into her mouth. "I am. I didn't think they'd play that in jolly ol' England," she jokes, trying to mimic my accent.

"I'm fairly certain where there are adolescent teenagers, there will be Truth or Dare. This is similar, with a minor variation. A person asks you a question and you can either answer it truthfully or drink. No dares to make out in a closet or crank call the object of your affection."

Our waitress approaches and drops off the shots I'd ordered, her timing impeccable.

"Sounds reasonable enough."

"I should warn you, if you drink, it's not a sip from your beer." I nod at the row of shot glasses in front of us. "It's a shot of tequila."

"If I didn't know better, I'd say you were trying to get me drunk." She playfully bats her lashes, drawing my attention to her large, blue-lilac eyes that shine even in the dim lighting of the bar.

"No. Simply trying to give you an incentive to open up instead of hide behind your mask. Or tequila, as it were." I grin. "So, what do you say? You up for a game?" With a single brow arched, I tilt my bottle toward hers, waiting for her agreement.

Her gaze flickers between me and the shot glasses as she weighs her options. Then she shrugs, lifting her beer and clinking the bottle against mine. "Let the games begin."

We each take a sip, sealing the deal, our eyes never straying from each other.

"As always, ladies first." I gesture toward her. "Ask me anything your little heart desires."

Her plump lips curve into a charming smirk that causes my pulse to kick up a bit. "Are you sure about that? My mind can be a twisted place."

Placing my forearms on the table, I lean closer. "That's what I'm counting on, gorgeous."

Desire seeps from my words and I pause, admiring her reaction. Her mouth parts, breathing growing more uneven as her cheeks turn pink.

"Now, ask away." I sit back, watching as she takes a moment to collect herself, expelling a long breath. Then she squares her shoulders, her eyes resolute and steadfast.

"Okay then. What's your favorite sexual position?"

"Not beating around the bush, are you?"

"I figure it's best to take a more…direct approach with you."

"You won't hear any complaints from me."

I bring up my leg, resting my calf on the opposite thigh, making it appear as if I'm about to answer her question. Nora's expression lights up with intrigue. Then I grab one of the shot glasses. She frowns.

"Sorry, doll. As much as I'd love to tell you all about my favorite sexual position, I'd rather wait to show you." I throw back the shot, the liquid burning slightly as it travels down my throat and into my stomach. "My turn." I slam the glass down, ignoring Nora's wide eyes at my admission, her jaw dropping. "That vibrator I noticed in your suitcase."

"What about it?" she asks cautiously.

"Have you used it since we met?"

Several protracted moments pass as she looks between me and the line of shots, weighing her options.

"I have." A sly smile crawls across her mouth.

I harden, my grip on the beer bottle tightening from the mere notion. God, this woman will be my undoing. I'm trying so hard to keep my head around her, but I can't deny the way I crave her.

"Did you think about anyone in particular while you got off?" I ask gruffly, my eyes intense as they lock with hers.

She folds a leg underneath her and slowly pushes herself up, closing the distance. My heart thunders in my chest, the air between us no longer thick with awkward tension but with raw desire. She licks her lips, drawing my attention to them.

"I believe that's another question," she breathes, then adds, "gorgeous." With a smirk, she lowers herself back to the booth.

"Now I know what my next question will be. Although I already know the answer."

"Don't be so sure. No one likes cockiness." The instant the word leaves her lips, her eyes widen and she slaps a hand over her mouth. "I mean——"

"I'm willing to bet money that you'd quite like my cock…iness."

Her face turning a shade of red that would rival that of the salsa on our table, she grabs a chip and chucks it at me. "Shut up. That's not what I meant."

"I think it was, darling," I tease, laughing.

She averts her gaze, but can't stop the smile from forming on her mouth. Soon, she joins in my laughter, the sound like music to my ears after the past twenty-four hours. This is what we needed. Good food. Strong drinks. And a reminder that life shouldn't be taken so seriously.

And for the next several hours, we don't take life too seriously. We laugh. We share stories from our past. I learn Nora is the youngest of four and has three older brothers. And I tell her all about my family, apart from the whole royalty thing, although I'm finding myself more and more eager to share that part of my life with her, too.

Nora's the first person I've met in a long time who I want to know all of me, who I feel like I can trust with that. Most of my life, people only wanted to be around me because of the notoriety and fame that comes with dating the Crown Prince of Belmont. It wasn't until I met Kendall, who had no idea who I was, that I knew what it felt like to be with someone who wanted to be with me for me. I didn't think I'd ever experience that again… Until now. And like with Kendall, I know it won't change how Nora feels about me.

"Okay. Okay. Here's one." Nora takes a large gulp of her ice water. "And it's something I've been curious about since I met you."

"And that is?" I ask with an arched brow.

"What the hell kind of work do you do that you get to take off all this time?" She brings the straw back toward her mouth. My eyes are drawn to the way her lips wrap around it, making it difficult to focus. The alcohol hasn't helped, either. "I thought I was lucky being able to take off for two weeks. But you…" She waves her arm around, her motions slow, speech lazy. "You've been on the road for what? Over a month?"

I nod. "More or less," I answer, not wanting to go into the specifics of my recent travels.

"So what do you do?"

"That's your question? What I do for work?"

"It is."

"I was quite hoping you'd ask the weirdest place I've had sex."

"Nope. Not going to happen. You're not going to distract me with learning about you and sex." She maintains a straight face, albeit with difficulty.

One thing I've learned about Nora is that she's a happy drunk. And slightly amorous, too, which I won't complain about. I've missed the subtle brush of her skin against mine, each touch causing me to want more.

"So tell me, Anderson North…" She leans toward me, her breath intoxicatingly sweet, "what do you do for work?"

I study her, weighing my options. I could easily give her the standard response I give everyone when I travel under my pseudonym. But I proposed this game so we could learn more about each other. So we would stop keeping secrets. So we'd start opening up to one another, at least to the extent we're comfortable. And I *do* want Nora to know this part of me. I want to erase the lies between us.

"I'm the Crown Prince of Belmont."

She bursts out laughing, the sound drawing the attention of nearly everyone in the bar. "Nice try, but if you didn't want to tell me, you could have taken a shot. Or can't you handle your liquor anymore?"

I keep my expression calm as I level my gaze on her, wanting her to see I'm not joking.

"I can handle my liquor perfectly fine." To prove it, I grab the last shot glass and throw it back. The tequila stings a little, but I manage to push down the burn. "I understand why you'd think I wasn't being honest, but it's true. I'm the Crown Prince of the Nation of Belmont, heir to the throne when my father, King Gabriel Maxwell Luther Hamilton Wellingston, either passes away or steps down from his position. Go ahead and Google me." I slide her phone toward her. "Crown Prince Gabriel Anderson Joseph Xavier Wellingston of Belmont."

She studies me for a moment, seemingly torn between brushing off my answer as a joke and believing me. Her curiosity eventually gets the better of her, and she swipes her cell off the table.

"Think I can just type in Prince Gabriel? That's a lot of fucking names to remember."

I chuckle. "You're telling me."

A few moments pass. I assume she stumbled on the Wiki article about me, which is usually the first result. Squinting, she reads out loud.

"Prince Gabriel (born Gabriel Anderson Joseph Xavier on February 27, 1985) is the oldest son of King Gabriel and Princess Grace, who passed away from complications due to Multiple Sclerosis in 1995. He is

the Crown Prince and will ascend to the throne when his father passes away or voluntarily resigns. He has one sister, Esme Louisa Victoria Grace, the Princess Royal."

Her brow crinkles, and I can see the recognition as she reads Esme's name. Then she straightens.

"This still doesn't prove anything. I'll admit, you do bear a slight resemblance to him." She turns her cell to me, and I see a photo from an event several years ago, my hair styled back, face shaven. A complete shift from my current appearance.

"You're right. It doesn't. But this might change your mind." I grab her phone and type a new search term into the browser and click on the first link, handing it back to her.

"What's this?" she asks warily.

"Some reporters don't have anything better to do than gossip about a member of the Royal Family getting a tattoo." I watch as she enlarges the photo in the article, then inhales sharply, her eyes widening.

She runs her finger over the image, unable to deny it now, not when she saw that same tattoo on my chest mere hours ago. "The compass...," she breathes.

"My father lost his bloody head when he found out." I chuckle at the memory, although it didn't seem amusing at the time. "That's one of the pitfalls about being born into a family with notoriety. You can't get away with lying to your father. If you fuck up or break the rules, chances are someone was there to witness it."

She shakes her head. "But—"

"I don't want you to think I lied to you," I interrupt. "In my inner circle, I've always gone by Anderson. My father's Gabriel. I did spend my younger years at school in London. When it was time to go to university, I didn't want to get preferential treatment because of who I was, so I enrolled under an alias the Royal Guard developed for me. And whenever I want to disappear and be normal, that's the name I travel under. Anderson North. I may not have told you about my title, but everything else has been true, Nora. The person you've gotten to know this past week *is* me."

She takes a few more seconds to process this, my admission having sobered her. Then she brings her eyes back to mine. "You really are a prince?"

"I really am a prince."

She peers out over the dance floor at several of the patrons who have started to dance to the live band. I stare at her, feeling like a man accused of a heinous crime he didn't commit awaiting the verdict. For some reason, I'm desperate for Nora to accept this.

When she finally looks at me, I hold my breath, praying she's not about to walk away. Then she bursts into a fit of giggles. "What the fuck are you doing here with me then?"

Tension rolls off my shoulders, and I exhale deeply. "That's another question. But I will tell you this…" I clutch her hand, running my thumb along her knuckles. "There's no place I'd rather be than in this dive bar with you."

"Even though I'm completely ordinary?"

"That's where you're wrong." I lean across the table, my voice low. "You're not ordinary. Not in my eyes. I find you exceptional. A breath of fresh air in a world that usually only sees me as a way to climb the social ladder. Which is why I normally don't share this with people I meet, at least not when I'm traveling on personal business, like now. I value my anonymity."

"Then why did you tell me?"

"For some strange reason I can't even begin to

understand, I wanted you to know this about me. Wanted you to know the truth. And I was right."

She tilts her head. "About what?"

"That it hasn't changed the way you see me." I smile as I run my fingers over her skin. "You still look at me the same way."

"I'm not sure I'll ever see you as a prince, even if you're in front of me wearing a crown and sitting on a throne. To me, you'll always be Anderson North."

I exhale a sigh of relief, her response exactly what I'd hoped. "That's all I ever want you to see me as. For you to look past the crown and see the man sitting beneath it. Nothing else."

Chapter Twenty-One

NORA

I BLINK AWAY my shock, still trying to wrap my head around this unexpected turn of events. Chloe would lose her mind if she knew, considering she once worked as a celebrity news columnist and penned a few stories about Prince Gabriel. Hell, since Prince Harry was taken off the market, she'd named him the most eligible prince. But just like Anderson doesn't want me to only see a prince when I look at him, I don't want any inside information Chloe may possess to color my opinion, either.

I'm not sure I want to share him with Chloe yet anyway. We had a slight rip in our bubble today. I like to think we've repaired it, that we're back in our cocoon where it's just us. No one else. I fear sharing this with Chloe will destroy our bubble.

"Okay. My turn." Anderson's voice enters my thoughts.

I bring my eyes to meet his. Now that I know the truth, I do see the resemblance, although I must admit, I like this version of Anderson much better than his public persona, with the slicked-back hair and clean-shaven jawline. He's still attractive like that, but I like my Anderson a little rough around the edges. Like he is now.

"I'm not sure how to follow that one. I'm not really a

princess or anything," I joke.

"True. But you still have valuable secrets I'd love to crack."

"Not as earth-shattering as that."

"Maybe not to you, because you already know everything there is to know about yourself. I don't. I feel like I've only scratched the surface about who you are."

"Well, then… Ask away." I raise my beer up to my lips, then add, "Your Majesty."

He chuckles. "Technically, that's my father."

"What are you then? I'm new to all this royalty stuff." I wave my hand around. "I must have skipped Royalty Etiquette 101 in college."

"And we'll keep skipping it. As far as you're concerned, I'm just Anderson. No title."

"I know. I'm just curious how people are supposed to address you. Like when you're at an official event, what do they call you?"

"Your Highness. Or Your Royal Highness." He pauses, then inches toward me, lowering his voice. "Can I tell you a secret?" His question is barely audible over the sound of the band playing a Tom Petty tune.

It brings to mind my first day on Route 66, how I didn't even know Anderson's name. It's remarkable how much can change in a week's time.

"What's that?"

"I bloody hate it."

"What?"

"Being addressed as Your Highness." He blows out a relieved sigh. "It drives me crazy."

When he returns his eyes to mine, there's a lightness about him, as if a giant weight has been lifted. Like the burden that's caused him to keep his distance from me has disappeared and he can breathe again. Like the truth has set him free.

"God, it feels good to tell someone that."

"What else do you hate?" My expression dances with excitement. I love learning about this part of him. Not because I'm impressed by his notoriety, but because he's finally peeled back the mask and allowed me a glimpse at another layer.

"The rules. Everything is so structured." He takes a pull from his bottle, then holds it up. "Case in point, this beer."

"What about it?" I edge closer, eager to hear what rules his family has about beer. The only rule my mother had about beer was not to drink it before I was twenty-one, which I broke my first day of college.

"I'm only allowed to drink bottled beer. Never draft."

"Why?"

"Less risk of being poisoned. Same thing goes for wine. I'm only permitted to drink wine that a member of my security detail has witnessed being opened. And this water?" He lifts the glass in front of him that he hasn't touched. "Forbidden." Then, with a sly smile, he brings it up to his lips and takes a sip.

"You bad boy, you."

"Oh, gorgeous…" He closes the distance, his azure orbs alight with mischief. "You have no idea how bad I can be."

Desire, hot and intense, coils inside me. All evidence of the awkward tension that plagued us last night and today has disappeared. In its place is this new level of comfort. Perhaps this is what we should have done from the beginning. But I don't think it would have been as effective. We needed to experience each other's scars before we realized they're simply one part of what makes us, well…us.

"I could always go online. I'm sure there are some informative articles about that. I'd rather find out on my own, though."

"That certainly gives *me* something to look forward to." He winks, then clears his throat. "Now that I shared my big secret, it's only right you do the same."

"Okay…," I say in a drawn-out voice. "What big secret of mine do you want to know?"

"The ashes," he states without a second of deliberation. "Who do they belong to?"

I freeze, the light atmosphere shifting.

He quickly grabs my hands in his. "It's okay if it's still too raw."

I dart my stare to our linked fingers, a warmth filling me as he affectionately brushes my knuckles with his thumbs. Such a simple gesture, yet it gives me what I need right now. What I've needed for years but never found. Understanding. Hope. Comfort. He's shared a huge piece of himself with me. It's time I do the same.

"My fiancé," I blurt out. "Well, *former* fiancé, I suppose. Hunter."

"I'm assuming this was several years ago, correct? You *did* recently get divorced, or was that only a story?"

I shake my head. "No. I did just get divorced. I've realized Jeremy was a cover for losing Hunter, though."

"How do you mean?"

"Hunter passed away about six years ago. Met Jeremy three years ago. He was supposed to be a no-strings-attached hookup. I guess I have my mother and Jameson to thank for things getting as out of hand as they did."

"Your mother and Jameson? Like the whiskey?"

I nod, blowing out a laugh. "I already told you how my mother's a psychiatrist. Well, she constantly put my life under a microscope. The woman hadn't paid any attention to me in years, but the second I have a dead fiancé, I became her new favorite project. She loved calling me up, telling me everything I was doing wrong, why I was a failure."

"Jesus. And that's your mother?"

"Yup. She's a fucking piece of work. So when I met Jeremy… I don't know… He was really sweet, and there were quite a few things about him that reminded me of Hunter. I thought I could fake it till I make it, more or less."

"And the Jameson?"

"I'm not proud of it, but it was St. Patrick's Day. In New York, it's a big deal. Drinking all day. And all night. So Jeremy and I got pretty wasted. One thing led to another, and we left one of the bars and went to the Diamond District. The next morning, I woke up with a ring on my finger. I think we both regretted it but refused to say anything. A part of me liked the idea of marrying Jeremy. Figured I could kill two birds with one stone. Could get my mother to leave me alone, as well as make everyone else around me believe I'd moved on from losing Hunter, even if I hadn't."

"I don't think we ever truly move on after losing a loved one." His gaze flickers with the experience of someone who knows what he's talking about. Someone who understands this level of loss. "We simply learn to acclimate to a new normal. Doesn't mean you're a horrible person or are dishonoring their memory. You just decide to swim instead of sink."

Silence falls over the table as Anderson continues running his thumb along my knuckles. Earlier today, the silence between us drove me crazy, but it's no longer awkward. So much is said in this silence. A thousand apologies. A thousand words of understanding. A thousand promises of hope. It warms my heart and brings a smile to my face when normally nothing about discussing Hunter's death would make me smile.

"How did he die?" Anderson asks hesitantly.

"Car accident." I swallow hard. I'm about to tell him I was also in the car, that the baby I'd been carrying for six months also died that night, but don't. He only asked about the ashes. So that's all I share. I can now manage the pain of losing Hunter. The pain of losing our baby is a different story. "We were about to move out to California. Drive Route 66 and everything."

"That's why you're spreading his ashes."

I nod. "After his memorial, his mother gave them to me, insisted I take the trip. So that's what I'm doing." I lift my beer, gulping down a large swallow. "Going on one last adventure with my fiancé."

"Well…" Anderson's tone is bright, a change from the solemn air. He raises his beer bottle to me. "Here's to one last adventure. Thank you for including me in it." His gaze is awash with sincerity and veneration. "I'm truly honored."

"It's not like I had a choice." I laugh nervously to cut through the tension. "My car broke down."

"No." He shakes his head, licking his lips. "You had a choice. So thank you for choosing me." The corners of his mouth quirk up, peace washing over his face in gentle waves, appreciation and reverence swirling in his profound eyes.

No one's looked at me this way in so long, like they can't continue breathing unless I'm in their universe. I can't recall Hunter admiring me this way. The old Nora would beat herself up over the idea of allowing my memories of Hunter to fade. But I'm no longer holding onto them with all my strength, praying they don't slip away. I can appreciate that time in my life for what it was, for what it taught me. I'm finally ready to make new memories.

I *deserve* to make new memories.

A loud cheer cuts through the bar as the band plays the familiar opening measures of Chuck Berry's "Route 66". I turn from Anderson, watching as dozens of patrons swarm the dance floor, everyone moving to what's obviously akin to this place's National Anthem.

The energy infusing me, I jump to my feet and grab Anderson's hands, pulling him up with me.

"What are you doing?" he asks, eyeing me with curiosity.

"What does it look like? Making you dance with me."

"Dance? I don't—"

"Don't even try to tell me you don't dance. I'm sure you had to take plenty of dance lessons so you didn't make a fool out of yourself at public functions. Am I right?"

He hints at a devilish grin. "Maybe."

"Then let's dance." I yank him into the center of the dance floor. "What other time will we be able to dance to 'Route 66' *on* Route 66?"

"Probably never."

"Exactly. When in Rome…" I pass him a devilish grin as I move in time with the slow, bluesy beat. When a hand clutches my hip, another sliding up my arm and wrapping around my fingers, I dart my gaze to Anderson, a silent question within.

"And I'm sure you took dance lessons for your wedding. Correct?"

"Why do you think that?"

He shrugs. "Just a hunch. But based on what you've told me and what I've figured out for myself, you probably put on quite the show at your wedding to make people believe you were actually in love. And I'm sure that included some carefully orchestrated dance numbers."

My lack of response is the only answer he needs.

"And you probably know how to swing dance."

"I knew how even before my wedding. My mother insisted I take dance all throughout my childhood and into my teenage years."

"Perfect."

At the downbeat, he squeezes my hand, steering my body with ease. At first, my motions are stiff and disjointed, considering it's been close to a year since I've danced like this. Soon, muscle memory kicks in and my moves become more fluid and natural. It helps that Anderson's a born leader, in more ways than one. And boy, does he know his way around a dance floor.

The more we dance, the more confident I become, the more difficult moves Anderson tries. This isn't a fast song, so I'm able to keep up easily, my motions relaxed. He squeezes my hand again and drops his hold on my hip, twirling me in a spin before yanking my body back into his.

Cheers and applause erupt, taking me by surprise. I momentarily falter as my attention strays from Anderson for the first time, noticing that everyone's assembled in a circle on the edge of the floor, enjoying the show we're giving them.

"Stay with me, Nora," Anderson murmurs.

I return my gaze to him, falling back into step, smiling and tuning out everyone else. At my wedding, I was more nervous about dancing with Jeremy in front of all those people than I was about saying my vows. It was why I forced him to take every dance class I could find. I didn't want to look like I didn't know what I was doing. Didn't want people to look at us dancing and realize how awkward we were together.

But with Anderson, even knowing all these people are watching, I'm comfortable. He makes this so effortless. So easy. So uncomplicated. Everything with him seems uncomplicated. Like life should be.

The song ends, and the audience cheers for the band, as well as our impromptu performance. Anderson steps away from me, keeping my hand clasped in his, nodding in acknowledgment at the crowd. My cheeks heat, but Anderson acts as if the attention is nothing. To him, it probably *is* nothing. What's a few dozen people clapping for you when he's used to hundreds, even thousands?

When the band starts a slower number, I break from his hold and head back to our table, but only make it a few steps before Anderson grabs my elbow and pulls me into his hard, firm body. I jerk my gaze up to his, the sudden motion catching me off guard.

"Where are you going?" A grin teases on his mouth.

"I thought—"

"We're not done yet," he croons, his tone dripping with sin and seduction.

All I can do is nod and drape my free arm over his shoulder, everything about this moment rendering me mute as "Fading Into You" plays around us. The title of this song is more than appropriate, because right now, I'm fading into this man. Into his body. His heart. His soul. It's consuming and electrifying.

I sway with the rhythm Anderson sets. This time, there's no complex footwork to concentrate on. There's no respectful distance separating our bodies. There's no lighthearted atmosphere. There's just this intense connection sizzling to life.

I toy with a few of the curls that fall past his collar, and he briefly closes his eyes. His grip on me tightens, his jaw clenching, nostrils flaring. He can deny it all he wants, but his body doesn't lie. I felt it yesterday. And I feel it now. He wants me. I'm desperate to ask him why he pushed me away yesterday, if it was because of the secret he was keeping. But I don't want to ruin this moment. Don't want anything to come between one of the most erotic things I've experienced in all my thirty years, something I didn't think possible fully dressed. But even a flimsy sundress can't prevent Anderson from stripping me bare. As his eyes sear into mine, that's precisely what he does. He strips me bare. Obliterates every single one of my fears and trepidations. Makes me only see what matters.

Makes me only see him.

His hands go to my face and he cups my cheeks. We stop swaying to the music, tuning out the world. In this moment, nothing else exists. There is no past. And the future is out of our control. There's only the present. Only us. Only this unyielding craving that I'm done fighting.

That I hope he's done fighting, too.

My breathing increases with every inch he erases. His fingers dig into my hair, his grip on me tightening as his lips descend toward mine, barely a whisper away. But that breath between us may as well be a football field. It's still not close enough. Desperation courses through me, making me blind to anything other than having this man capture me, claim me, consume me.

But as much as I need to feel him, I won't make the final move. Not again. He needs to make this decision. Needs to scale that wall and free himself.

A growl rips from his throat, his lips poised over mine. I exhale, bracing myself for his kiss. Suddenly, he's jostled and stumbles, breaking our connection. I fling my eyes open, disoriented at first. Then I see a tall man dressed in black hovering nearby, a rocks glass in his hand.

"Oh, I'm so sorry," the man says in a heavy Texas drawl. "I forgot what I was doing for a second."

I look between the man and Anderson, something about the way they stare each other down striking me as odd. Almost like they're having a conversation without uttering a single word. I sometimes do that with Chloe, but she's not a stranger like this man is.

The man glares at him as he walks away, making my hackles rise. I'm about to ask Anderson if he knows him when he grabs my hand and pulls me across the dance floor, bodies moving and bumping into us in time with the fast, driving beat of a different song.

"Let's get some air."

I nod, following him without protest, unsure if we're leaving to have more privacy or because he's worried he almost crossed a line he doesn't want to.

Chapter Twenty-Two

NORA

FRESH AIR GREETS us when we step outside, and I inhale. It's soothing after a night of drinking, the lower temperatures cooling my flushed complexion from a combination of alcohol and Anderson's presence.

I pull my denim jacket tighter around me and start in the direction of the motel when Anderson wraps his hand around my bicep in a firm grip and hauls me into the alley between the bar and auto repair shop next door. His labored breaths echo against the stillness of night, his chest heaving as he peers down at me with unwavering lust and need.

"What are you doing?" I squeak out, my heart caught in my throat.

"What I've been wanting to do all damn day."

With a firm grasp on my hips, he slams his mouth against mine, his tongue plunging inside, leaving me no room to protest.

At first, I'm taken by surprise, his kiss bruising and biting, making it impossible for me to draw in a single breath. Sensing my confusion, especially after his previous rejection, he pulls back. His wild eyes rake over mine, the same tormented expression from yesterday making an appearance. But it disappears just as quickly, his stare intensifying.

"Kiss me back," he growls, his demand causing my skin to heat, my knees to buckle, my core to tighten.

"Is that what you want?" I ask huskily.

"More than you can imagine, Nora."

Cupping the back of his head, I burrow my fingers into his hair and drag him toward me. This time when his lips cover mine, I do as he begged and kiss him back.

A groan wrenched from his throat, he kisses me with wild abandon, the assault causing my heart to thump madly in my chest with such intensity I'm convinced it's about to burst through my ribcage. Desire spirals like a tornado, crawling over my skin and settling in my aching fingers. I draw him closer, a bomb detonating inside me when he thrusts his hard length against my stomach.

I whimper. I exhale. Then I feast on him again, grinding and groping in the temperate New Mexico air. The faint sound of the music within the bar makes its way out to us, but it doesn't distract me from this. From Anderson.

He tears away, his facial hair scraping against my flesh as he moves to my neck, licking and tasting as he goes. His hand trails from my hip and lands on my ass with a harsh squeeze. I yelp, then moan, throwing my head back, hooking a leg around his waist, pulsing against the erection straining his pants.

"Are you wet for me, love?" he murmurs. When he nibbles on my earlobe, a shudder rolls through me.

I've fantasized about Anderson's bedroom voice. How could I not when his accent as he speaks of normal things causes goosebumps to dot my flesh? But right now, his voice dripping of sin goads me to drop every single one of my inhibitions and be free. With him.

His hand glides from my ass, a slow journey before it lands on my thigh, squeezing harshly enough for me to know there will be marks there tomorrow.

"If I move my fingers slightly and rub against your knickers, what will I find? Will they be soaked for me?"

Locking my eyes on his, I summon all the confidence that's been missing from my life lately. "Why don't you find out for yourself?"

"You're a naughty girl, aren't you?"

Clutching his face, I pull him toward me, but he resists. "You have no idea how naughty I can be."

"Not yet. But I plan to find out."

His mouth captures mine, his tongue swirling and tempting me. It's not enough. No matter how deeply he kisses me, how breathless he makes me, how much pleasure he fills me with, it's not enough.

Sensing my appetite growing with each passing second, he drifts his hand from my thigh and up toward my panties. The closer he gets, the more ragged my breathing, the more desperation threatens to unravel me.

When his thumb ghosts against my center, I can't stop the moan from escaping my throat. Anderson sucks in a breath, his eyes darkening at the slight contact. He shifts my panties aside, exposing me to him in this alley where anyone can interrupt us. But neither of us seems to care. We're in our bubble again. It's just us, finally succumbing to the desire we've been skirting around all week.

"Jesus, Nora," he rumbles, his fingers deftly exploring and teasing. "You're so fucking wet."

I tighten my grip on his nape, circling against him, trying to extinguish the fire he lit. If this is how I react to a tease of his fingers, I can't imagine what would happen if he pushed one inside me. Hell, if he pushed himself inside. The mere thought causes another jolt of desire to pool between my legs.

"I need more," I pant, thrusting against him.

"More?"

"Yes."

He crashes his lips against mine as he slips a finger inside. I mewl, quaking under his expert touch. I'm in another place, another time, another dimension. This seems too good to be true. It *feels* too good to be true.

"God, you're so tight, love. So warm. So damn perfect."

I lose myself in his words, in his scent, in his everything, climbing higher and higher. The euphoria washing over me is unlike any I've experienced. It's a rush, the high more addictive than the most potent drug.

"I can't wait to have my cock buried deep inside you, watching as you come all over me harder and more violently than you ever have."

"Anderson," I moan, my breathing growing more uneven. My thrusts become more desperate and unhinged, my greed threatening to swallow both of us. I squeeze my eyes shut, focusing only on that peak growing closer and more vibrant the faster and harder Anderson thrusts his fingers inside me.

"Come on, gorgeous. Let go. I want to see how beautiful you are when you come. When *I* make you come. Let me have it."

He touches his thumb against my clit and, like a hair trigger, detonates the desire that's been locked inside for too long. I start to cry out, but Anderson clamps his mouth over mine, swallowing my screams of ecstasy as waves of bliss wash over me, each one more abrasive and earth-shattering than the former. I clench and tumble, constrict and uncoil, my body quivering and tingling as my skin dances with the heat of a thousand tiny fires.

I reach for his belt and pull at it, desperate to unbuckle it, but he stops me, removing his fingers from me and stepping back. At first, I'm bewildered, wondering if I'd imagined what just happened, if he *regrets* what just happened. Then a sly smile lights up his darkened expression and he kisses me.

"Not here," he murmurs against my mouth. "Not with the things I want to do to you." He rests his forehead on mine as he fights to catch his breath. "I hadn't exactly planned to finger fuck you in this alley. I seem to struggle sticking to my plans around you. Nevertheless, you deserve better than a dirty alley with beer cans and used condoms around. Truthfully, you deserve better than a tiny motel room, too, but I need you, Nora. I can't wait any longer. I can't deprive myself any longer. Say I can have you."

I dig my fingers into his hair, forcing his lips back to mine. "I'm all yours."

* * *

A fluttery sensation erupts in my stomach as I stare at the queen bed in our room. We practically ran the few blocks from the bar, hands clutched, silence riddled with anticipation stretching between us. A twinge of guilt fills me for not having any second thoughts about this. A week ago, I wouldn't have even entertained the idea of sleeping with a man on this trip, thinking I had to devote my entire journey to Hunter and his memory.

But this trip isn't for Hunter. It's for me. It took Anderson to make me realize that.

A warmth approaches from behind. I close my eyes as Anderson pushes my hair off my nape, smoothing it to one side. When he feathers soft kisses along my shoulder blade, my nerve endings stir, arousing me even more.

Splaying his hand on my stomach, he draws me into him, circling his hips. "Do you feel what you do to me, love?"

"Yes," I moan, a tidal wave of lust careening over me as his lips continue their torturous journey, settling on that spot where my neck meets my shoulders.

"I love the way you feel." He yanks me harder into him. "Love the way you smell." He inhales a deep breath, shuddering on the exhale. "But mostly, I fucking love the way you taste."

He wraps my hair around his fist and, in one quick motion, jerks my head to the side, clamping his teeth on my strained and exposed neck. My shocked yelp turns into a moan, the pain mixed with pleasure electrifying me.

I've never been with someone who exuded this much dominance in the bedroom. Hunter and I were so young when we were together that we never fully explored our sexuality. And sex with Jeremy was only moderately satisfying when we were drunk.

But Anderson...

His touch intoxicates me.

His sensual tone seduces me.

And his body tempts me to crave everything I've denied myself for too long.

"Harder," I plead, unsure if I can handle any more, but dammit, I want to find out.

He tears away and spins me around, glowering at me with dangerous eyes. "Is that how you want it?"

I swallow hard, but nod vehemently. "I want to feel everything you can give me. I want to feel alive." I bring my lips to him. "You make me feel alive. Give me all of you."

He deepens the kiss, steering me the few steps toward

the bed. Once the back of my legs hit the mattress, he pulls away. Stepping back, he crosses his arms in front of his chest, an air of absolute superiority and control about him.

"Strip."

Fuck.

My heart rate spikes, making me lightheaded. But I do as he orders, tugging on the tie keeping my halter dress in place. With unhurried movements, I allow the fabric to slide down my body, leaving me in a strapless bra and panties. Anderson's eyes flame, and I want to pinch myself. I still struggle to believe that I'm here, that I'm about to sleep with a prince. An actual, real-life prince. But like I told him earlier, I don't see a title when I look at him. I just see Anderson.

The room throbs with sexual craving as I reach behind me and unclasp my bra. When it joins my dress on the floor, Anderson's jaw clenches, his hands forming tight fists. I'd love nothing more than to strip us of our clothes and feel him sink deep inside me. But for all the want flickering in his wild eyes, I can tell he's enjoying the show. I am, too, the way he hungers for me boosting my confidence even more.

Hooking my fingers into my panties, I push them down and kick them off. Emboldened, I turn from him and crawl onto the bed. Lying on my back, I prop my legs up, exposing myself to him. Then I leisurely run my hand along my collarbone, over a breast, and down my stomach, not looking away from Anderson's gaze as I lower it past my waist.

"Come have me," I demand as I toy with myself.

That's all the invitation he needs. He reaches me in one long stride, his body settling over mine, his mouth covering mine. His kiss is untamed, yet controlled. Bruising, yet comforting. Harsh, yet humane.

"You have the heart of a saint." His breathing is labored as he pulls away, slinking down my frame. He takes a nipple into his mouth, his teeth biting and tongue caressing at the same time. I grip the sheets below me, writhing and jerking. "But your body…" He leans back, running a hand from my throat, between my breasts, pausing before reaching my center. "You have the body of a sinner."

I hold my breath as he inches closer to my apex, the seconds stretching. It doesn't matter it's been less than ten minutes since he last touched me. I need him again, my addiction to this man unmatched.

He hovers over me, his lips skimming mine. "And baby, I really want to sin with you." He cups my sex, plunging two fingers inside, stretching and stimulating my already sensitive flesh. But it does nothing to persuade my body to back down. It only makes me crave him with more intensity, more fervor, more thirst.

He snakes down my torso, kissing and sucking every inch, every freckle, every slight imperfection. When he settles between my legs, he removes his fingers, placing his hands on my thighs and spreading them. I prop myself up on my elbows, our eyes connecting through the lust-filled haze.

Slowly, he brings his mouth to me. When he makes contact, I fall back onto the mattress, the ache returning with more determination and vengeance.

"So good," I groan as I move in time with his ministrations. Reaching down, I run my fingers in his hair, my nails digging into his scalp. "So fucking good."

"You taste incredible, love," he comments, slipping a finger back into me, his tongue never straying too far, the combination of his warmth on me and fingers inside pushing me higher. "I could feast on you for hours and never get my fill."

"That can be arranged," I exhale breathily, my mind in a daze, my body a slave to the sensation.

He increases his motions, determined to make me come again. But I don't want to. Not like this.

"Anderson," I moan.

"Yeah, baby."

"I need you inside me. Now."

"My fingers are inside you."

I vehemently shake my head, then sit up, scooting away so he has no choice but to stop. My body shivering and tightening with the promise of an orgasm, I kneel on the bed, tugging his belt. This time, he doesn't prevent me from unbuckling it. He keeps his razor-sharp stare on me, jaw ticking and chest heaving.

Once his pants are unzipped, I shove them, along with his briefs, down his legs, relishing in the tight muscles of his ass and thighs. Kicking off his flip-flops, he steps out of his khakis, but doesn't make a move to remove his shirt, allowing me the pleasure. And when I unfasten each button and push it down his arms, I see that the pleasure is most certainly mine.

When I saw him without a shirt on earlier, I was too rattled and on edge to fully admire it, but my god, it is truly a sight to behold. Vast shoulders give way to the rigid lines of his chest, his stomach toned and firm. And this time, I run my hands along each hard pane, soaking in every inch of him. I pause my perusal when I reach his waist, confirming what I'd pictured earlier.

"Touch me," he whispers huskily.

Our shoulders rise and fall in time with each other as I trail my hand down the grooves of his stomach and wrap my fingers around his girth. A hiss escapes as he tilts his head back, ecstasy covering the lines of his face. Then he shifts his eyes forward, nostrils flaring, muscles clenching.

Grabbing my wrist, he forces me to loosen my hold. With deft motions, he grips my waist and tosses me onto the mattress, my body springing with the impact. He strides to his suitcase, rummaging through it and finding a condom. Like a beast untamed, he crawls on top of me like I'm his captured prey on the brink of being devoured. Using his teeth, he tears open the packet, then flings the wrapper aside, rolling on the condom.

When he lifts his erection up to me, I wrap my legs around his waist, pulling him toward me. Neither one of us makes a sound as he slowly pushes inside, filling me until I can no longer take any more of him. He stills, remaining at the point of absolute fullness before retreating and inching back in once more.

I rock with his rhythm, unhurried at first, wanting to remember every miraculous sensation, every caress, every flutter, every quiver. He buries his head in the crook of my neck, his beard raw yet invigorating.

"I always knew you'd feel good. I never thought you'd feel this incredible."

"I really know how to butter your crumpets, don't I?" I breathe, recalling the conversation he'd overheard between myself and Chloe our first night as travel companions.

He stills, staring down at me. Then we both erupt in laughter, the sound echoing in our tiny room. "This may be the first time I've ever laughed during sex." A shadow crosses his expression, as if he flipped the switch from playful and flirtatious Anderson to dark and dangerous Anderson. "Get on your hands and knees."

A thrill washes over me like an avalanche. As if I weren't already soaked with my desire for him, another surge of moisture pools between my thighs.

He pulls out and helps me flip over. I spread my legs, putting my weight onto my elbows before glancing over my shoulder. Anderson runs a hand down my spine as he brings himself up to me.

"Any reason you wanted a change of position?"

"In my experience, it's easier to make you come like this."

"Is that right?"

He chews his lower lip and nods. Teasing me with his erection, he inches inside once more. "That's right. And based on how wet you are, I give it maybe another minute. Max."

"A little confident of your abilities, aren't you?"

"Not confident. I can just read your body, Nora. Your flushed complexion." He leans over me, running his hands down my arms and intertwining our fingers. "Your uneven breathing." His tongue traces a circle along my neck, his own breathing ragged. He releases his hold on my hands, one hand going to my hip, holding me in place as he increases his pace. I throw my head back, moaning at the pleasure twisting within me, begging for release. "How you squirm with every touch." He brings his free hand to my center, rubbing my clit as he slams into me with a fury and intensity I hadn't expected.

"Fuck!" I scream as I bury my head in the pillow, clutching onto the sheets.

His motions are relentless, each drive inside and pinch outside pummeling me closer to the edge until I have no choice but to give him what he wants. I cry out his name, unleashing all the pent-up yearnings I've locked away for years, too scared to repeat the past to give them life. But I don't care about that anymore. I want to feel again. I need to feel Anderson again. And again. And again.

"So good," he pants, his voice strained and tense. "So. Fucking. Good," he emphasizes, each word accompanied by another thrust, each one deeper and more punishing than the previous. "I love how your pussy clenches around me. Love how you feel around me. Love how you mold to me."

He removes his finger from my clit, gripping my hips tightly with both hands. He stops his motions as he covers my body with his, taking my earlobe between his teeth.

"This is going to be hard and fast. Is that okay?"

My mind reels. Harder and faster than he's already fucked me? I didn't think it was possible.

"Yes."

"That's my girl."

My heart warms at his words, but I don't have long to bask in his affection before he straightens. He briefly pulls out of me, spreading my juices around once more. Anticipation swirls in me, my pulse skyrocketing, every hair standing on end.

When he thrusts back inside, he's merciless, fingers digging into my hips, each thrust impaling me to the point where I'm convinced I'm on the precipice of breaking in half. I pant. I moan. I scream. But at the same time, I indulge. I crave. I ignite, until he stills with a strangled cry, jerking and lashing through his release.

He drops his hold on me, both of us collapsing onto the bed. I can only imagine what the people in the next room must be thinking right now.

"My word, that was a good show," he jokes in a forced, proper British tone after several moments of our heavy breathing.

It's silent at first, then laughter cuts through. I roll onto my side, playfully pinching Anderson. He swats my hand away, a smile lighting up his eyes as he lies facing me. Sated, he runs a lithe finger up and down my body, the gesture at odds with the way he just fucked me.

"Do you regret it?" he asks after a beat, worry evident in his expression. I can't blame him for wondering.

"Not even a little bit. I needed this." I touch my lips to his. "Needed you."

He kisses me deeper, breathing into me. "And I needed you. More than I realized," he adds as an afterthought. "Now, get some sleep. I plan to wake you up multiple times throughout the night to do that again."

He throws the sheet over our bodies and pulls me into his embrace, kissing the top of my head. I inhale a comforting breath, content to finally be in this place with Anderson.

"You won't hear any complaints out of me."

"Good."

Chapter Twenty-Three

ANDERSON

SIX YEARS AGO

I STARED AT the white wall, blinking repeatedly, everything seeming like it was happening in slow motion. The stench of cleaning supplies and stale coffee permeated this place of death and sorrow. I tried to react, my brain telling me to respond to the man in green scrubs standing in front of me. But I couldn't. That would make this real. It would give credence to what he'd just told me.

It would mean Kendall was gone.

How? How was that possible? I'd just seen her this morning. Felt her in my arms. Lost myself in her love. How could an active twenty-seven-year-old have a heart attack and die? All I heard were words like underlying, undiagnosed, and hypertrophic cardiomyopathy.

"Anders."

Creed's voice entered my subconscious as a firm hand landed on my shoulder. I slowly turned to my oldest friend and the man I'd recently brought on as my chief protection officer, his eyes narrowed in worry. At least he knew not to use any formalities with me right now. There were times I needed him to put our friendship above the job, and this was one of those moments. "Do you understand what he said?"

"Understand?" I managed to squeak out.

A thousand razor-sharp knives poked at my throat, making it excruciating to speak. Making it excruciating to breathe.

To live.

"How can I possibly be expected to understand that Kendall died from a heart attack?"

This wasn't supposed to happen. She was supposed to participate in a huge beach volleyball tournament today. Then she was supposed to meet with a coach who was interested in bringing her on to a two-person team in the hopes of reaching the Olympics. Now, all those dreams were gone.

Kendall was gone.

"I can understand what a shock this is," the doctor stated firmly, yet still with compassion. How many times did this man stand in this exact spot and deliver the same news to a different family? "Sudden death is a very real consequence for those who suffer from this condition."

"But how did it go undiagnosed for so long?" I choked out.

"It's hard to say." His sympathetic eyes fell on me. "There *are* warning signs. Fatigue. Shortness of breath. Lightheadedness. But in my experience, young people tend to shrug off these symptoms as being caused by stress."

I scrubbed my hand over my face, acid churning in my stomach. Kendall *had* complained about feeling tired and lightheaded this morning. I'd told her she was probably just nervous about the tournament. I'd brushed off the warning signs. Downplayed them. Minimized them. Because of that, Kendall was gone.

The truth hit me like a freight train, knocking the wind out of me and forcing me to stumble back. The heat of dozens of eyes glared at me, studied me... *Blamed* me.

I blamed myself.

Unable to breathe, I tugged at the collar of my t-shirt, feeling like it was suffocating me, blocking me from getting any oxygen. The world spun, the walls closing in. I couldn't be here. Couldn't be in this place where Kendall's lifeless body lay. It couldn't be true. I *refused* to believe it was true. This was simply some cruel joke, some sadistic prank, some god-awful nightmare. If I drove back to the hotel, I'd prove it. See her smile, feel her lips, drown in her love.

Abruptly spinning from the doctor and Creed, I stormed out of the hospital and into the humid night air. I scanned the frantic atmosphere outside the emergency room entrance — ambulances offloading people on stretchers, worried family members hurrying in behind them. All I wanted was to get out of this place, and I couldn't even do that without a car of my own.

"Anders!" Creed shouted, rushing through the automatic doors and toward me. "You can't—"

"Give me the keys," I demanded, cutting him off.

He stilled, eyeing me with a mixture of confusion and concern, brows wrinkling. "The keys?"

"Yes." I closed the distance between us, getting in his face. "The bloody keys, Creed." I held out my hand. "To the car. I'm taking it."

"I don't think that's a smart idea." His voice was soothing, expression calm. But I didn't want to be placated. I wanted to drive, to have some control over one thing in my life when it felt like it was spiraling out of control.

"I don't give a fuck what you think," I roared, heat rising in my body. Spittle formed in the corners of my lips, the cords of my neck straining. I'd probably regret my behavior tomorrow, but I couldn't do this right now. I needed to get out of here. "Give me the goddamn keys, Creed!"

"Like I said…," Creed continued in the same tone, completely unperturbed by my anger, "that's not a smart idea. You're not in the right frame of mind. It's my job to ensure your safety. I don't think it's safe for you to drive right now."

Frustration choking me like a noose, I advanced on him. I took him by surprise when I gripped the collar of his button-down shirt, tightening it around his neck.

"The keys," I ordered through a clenched jaw. "Now." I noticed a few security guards begin in our direction. "Or I'll make a scene and you can explain to my father why both his son and CPO were arrested."

Creed's eyes flamed. I could tell it took all his resolve not to reel back and land a hard blow to my jaw or a quick knee in my groin. I wasn't naïve. His military training far surpassed mine. But I'd give him a run for his money, especially with the amount of anger-fueled adrenaline that had replaced the blood in my veins.

"Last chance, Creed. Give…me…the…keys."

He held his resolve for another moment, then sighed, reaching into his pocket and reluctantly handing them over. "Here," he strained out.

I released my hold on him, and he stumbled backward a few steps. I started toward where the black SUV was parked.

"But I'm coming with you."

I spun toward Creed, glowering.

"It's either you let me come with you or I tackle you to the ground and make sure you can't hurt yourself, even if that means zip-tying your ass and throwing you into the back of the damn car."

"You wouldn't do that." I brushed him off.

"Try me," he growled.

My last chief protection officer wouldn't have been as bold as to threaten me like this, but he also wasn't a friend. Creed had absolutely no problem standing up to me and bringing me down a few pegs when I acted like an "entitled little prick", as he often called me. I supposed I was acting like an entitled little prick now, too, but I was angry. Bitter. Defeated.

"Fine," I finally relented. "But no backseat driving. I need to have some sort of fucking control in my life right now. Not a reminder that I don't have any."

"As you wish," he stated, following me toward the parking garage.

I pushed him aside when he tried to open the door for me, as he'd been trained to do. Instead, I jumped into the SUV and cranked the engine, a small sliver of relief filtering through me when I put the car into reverse. I hadn't driven myself anywhere in what felt like an eternity. It may not have seemed like a big deal to many, but it was everything to me. Was everything I needed right now.

I ignored Creed's glare when I peeled out of the parking lot, speeding along the roads and parkways, not really sure where I was going. Creed tried to direct me toward the hotel, but I didn't pay attention. I just wanted to drive. Just wanted to stay in this moment where I felt some control, regardless of how fleeting it was.

As I drove along a winding road through a wooded area, an intense pain shot through my eyes, blinding me. I momentarily squeezed them shut, pinching the bridge of my nose. I should have expected this. I tended to suffer from migraines, especially during times of high stress.

"Sir."

Creed's voice filtered into my brain, but just as I'd been doing since I got behind the wheel, I didn't respond.

"Sir," he repeated, more urgently. Yet again, I didn't acknowledge him, my brain unable to tell my muscles to move and look at him. My skin tingled, but I ignored it, adrenaline fueling me.

"*Anders!*" he bellowed.

"What?" I finally managed to turn my head toward him as a bang reverberated.

I slammed on the brakes, and the SUV skidded to a stop. I studied my surroundings, making sure the loud crash didn't come from us. When I glanced into the rearview mirror, I noticed smoke coming from down an embankment on the other side. Instinct kicking in, I flung open the door and dashed down the street to see if I could help.

As I approached, I observed a small SUV down a steep hill, the front end crumpled against a large tree. Smoke billowed from what remained of the engine, the smell of gasoline overpowering. I coughed, struggling to breathe, but it didn't make me retreat. If anything, it encouraged me forward to help anyone who may be stuck in that car.

I *needed* to help them.

I bolted down the embankment, branches and twigs scratching my exposed legs, but there was no pain. Only the thought that I needed to make up for failing Kendall.

"Anders! Stop!"

Hearing my name, I paused, looking up to see Creed rushing toward me, expression wild.

"What are you doing?"

"Helping!"

The odor of gasoline getting stronger, I darted toward

the demolished car, trying to figure out a way inside. The driver's side door was crushed to the point it was impossible to open. But the passenger side hadn't been. I hoped.

I ignored Creed's pleas to keep my distance and ran to the passenger side, yanking at the door. After a few tugs, it finally opened. A young woman sat in the passenger seat, eyes closed, a gash across her forehead.

"Give me your knife!" I bellowed at Creed as he approached.

"What?"

"Your knife! Give it to me!"

Without a moment's hesitation, he reached for his ankle, withdrawing the blade he'd always kept hidden. I stabbed the airbag holding the woman hostage. It deflated in a cloud of dust, revealing the woman's rounded stomach.

"Shit. She's pregnant!" I looked around her body to make sure there weren't any other injuries, noticing a pool of blood between her legs. "And bleeding. Call for an ambulance!"

"Already done, sir," Creed said from behind me.

I returned my attention to the woman and managed to unbuckle her from the seat belt. Unsure of any hidden injuries she may have, I carefully lifted her into my arms, doing my best to not jostle her any more than necessary.

As I pulled her from the car, I heard a slight jingling. I looked down to see a necklace fall from her neck and land on the seat. I grabbed it, along with what I presumed to be her engagement ring attached to it, and shoved it into my pocket for safekeeping.

"Hunter," she groaned, her eyes narrow slits, breathing shallow.

I glanced across the center console at the young man

behind the wheel before looking back at Creed. I didn't have to say a word for him to know what I wanted.

"We'll get him, too," I promised, carrying her up the hill.

"I don't feel well," she whimpered, her voice barely audible.

Reaching the road, I strode toward the SUV and set her into the back seat. Sirens blared in the distance, but they still seemed so far away.

I grabbed her hand and squeezed it. "Just stay with me, okay? Don't close your eyes. Fight it, okay?"

"Okay."

"Anders!" Creed bellowed.

I looked up to see him frantically run up the hill and toward the SUV, eyes panicked. Seconds later, the car burst into flames. I flinched, the heat of the fire reaching us, even up here.

"What was that?" the woman asked weakly. "Was that the car?"

I peered back at her, fighting the tears welling in my eyes. This must have been how the doctor felt minutes ago when he had to deliver the news about Kendall to me. Just like the doctor didn't sugarcoat it, I couldn't, either. Couldn't lie to her.

When I nodded sadly, she released a soul-crushing wail that clouded the night air, as tumultuous and violent as a summer thunderstorm. Her entire body trembled through her sobs, the injuries she suffered in the crash now doubled as she fought to breathe through the excruciating pain in her heart.

"It hurts," she struggled to say. Her grip on my hand weakened, her eyes closing.

"No, no, no. Don't do that," I pled urgently, desperately. "You have to stay with me." The sirens grew near, but still weren't close enough. "Paramedics are almost here. I need you to fight. For yourself and your baby." I glanced down at the sticky blood staining her dress between her thighs, refusing to believe this poor woman would not only lose the man I assumed to be her fiancé or husband, but also their baby.

"I'm so cold." She shivered, the bright lights of the ambulance rounding the bend. "I can't—"

"Yes, you can. Just keep talking. Just focus on my eyes. Tell me your name."

"Nora," she said as the ambulance screeched to a stop behind the SUV. "My name is Nora."

Chapter Twenty-Four

ANDERSON

PRESENT DAY

I BOLT UPRIGHT, a cold sweat dotting my skin, breathing uneven. My heart pounds, every inch of me on edge. I run my hand through my hair, telling myself it's just a dream. It's not even the first time I've had that particular dream. For months following that night, it played on repeat whenever I closed my eyes.

But up until now, I thought she'd told me her name was Laura. Not Nora.

My mind reels as I steal a glance at the woman sleeping peacefully beside me. Her chest rises and falls with her relaxed breathing, lips curved up slightly, as if whatever she's dreaming about makes her smile.

There's a slight glow in the room with the dawning of day, bringing attention to our discarded clothing thrown on the floor in our haste to finally succumb to our desires. From the moment I saw her, I felt drawn to this woman. Could this be why?

I scrub a hand over my face, putting the notion out of my head. It's just my brain playing tricks on me. That's the only explanation. So what if Nora lost her fiancé in a car wreck? So what if she told me his name was Hunter, the same name I'd heard the poor woman cry out in my dreams? If it *were* Nora, wouldn't she have mentioned she was also in the car? That she was pregnant? That she was pulled from the wreckage? But she hadn't.

I pinch my eyes shut, trying to rewind to the night I lost everything. I fight to remember the woman's face, her eyes, her hair. *Anything* that could put myself at ease, but nothing comes, the woman no more than the faceless ghost she's been the past six years.

I settle back onto the bed, doing everything to convince myself she's not that woman, that I'd have a better chance of winning the lottery, the probability of it so low it shouldn't even register in my subconscious.

But it does.

That morning earlier in the week comes rushing back. Creed had wanted to tell me something he found in Nora's background check, but I refused to listen. Could this have been it? Been why he bumped into me at the bar last night when I was about to kiss her? To stop me from doing something he knew I'd eventually come to regret?

My curiosity getting the better of me, I swipe my phone off the nightstand and, after glancing over my shoulder to make sure Nora is still asleep, type her name into the search bar of my browser.

As expected, the first few hits are her social media profiles, as well as a website for her yoga studio in the Village. I resist the temptation to click any of those links, steadfast in my resolve to learn about her from her alone.

Except in regards to the possibility that she may be the woman I pulled from the crash.

I tap on the search bar once more, adding "Hunter" and "car accident" to Nora's name.

This time, the first link that pops up is for an obituary of a man named Hunter Allen Copeland.

A voice in my head warns me against clicking on it, my stomach churning with acid at the premonition I won't like what I learn. But I have to know. I have to do this.

With a heavy heart, I click on the link and read all about Nora's fiancé. About his happy childhood. About his love of sports. About his academic achievements. About his recent job offer as a sports therapist for the Lakers, a lifelong dream realized. How he was excited about starting this new chapter with his fiancée at his side.

Then I read all about his death as the result of a single car accident that occurred in North Harbor on the same day Kendall died.

My shoulders curl forward and I squeeze my eyes shut, as if that would make the truth disappear. But it won't. Nothing can make this information go away.

I sit up, digging my fingers through my hair, my lungs struggling to breathe as I do everything to process this unexpected turn of events. Throat aching, I glance at Nora as she sleeps, the morning light filtering in behind her making her appear ethereal. Like an angel.

What am I supposed to do? What am I supposed to tell her? Do I share that I know she was in that wreck? That I was the Good Samaritan who pulled her from the car?

That I failed to save her fiancé?

In this moment, I wish I'd followed up on what happened to the woman I'd pulled from that wreck, but I hadn't, too overwrought with Kendall's death and the aftermath of mourning my girlfriend with cameras capturing my every move.

Slipping out of bed, I yank on my shorts, shirt, and shoes, then grab my wallet before heading outside. The second I step into the fresh air, I feel like I can breathe again. I start toward the Wrangler, thinking a drive might help me process everything. But when I notice the dark SUV parked in a distant spot, I change direction, storming toward it, my footsteps echoing in the quiet morning air.

As I approach, Creed jumps out of the driver's side, looking polished and put-together, despite the early hour. I ignore him when he opens the back door and slide into the front passenger seat instead.

"Where to, sir?" he asks tentatively as he slips back behind the wheel.

"Just bloody drive."

"Yes, Your Highness." He puts the car into gear and pulls onto the main street.

Not many cars are on the road yet, the sleepy Route 66 town just starting to come to life. The sun slowly rises over the desert horizon, bathing everything in light, not a cloud in sight. Tumbleweeds roll with the wind, birds swooping into distant fields in search of food.

After a few silent moments, Creed pulls into the parking lot of a Mexican bakery and heads inside. I take this time to collect my thoughts, try to think rationally about this. But all rationale left me once I learned the truth.

When Creed returns to the car, he hands me a tray with two coffees, one for me and one for Nora, as well as a box filled with what I assume are pastries. I still don't speak, so he starts the car and navigates the few blocks back to the hotel, parking beside the Wrangler and turning off the ignition.

A silence stretches between us as I stare straight ahead, my jaw clenching, wanting to scream.

"This is what you found out about her, isn't it?" I say finally. "That she's..." I trail off, struggling to finish my thought.

"Nora Tremblay was in a car accident on Long Island six years ago. Her fiancé, Hunter Copeland, didn't survive. Nora was pulled from the vehicle by a mysterious Good Samaritan—"

"I'm fucking aware of that, Creed," I bite out.

"And rushed to the hospital," he continues, despite my outburst, "where she was listed in stable condition with a mild concussion. Unfortunately, the baby she was carrying didn't survive."

I'm not sure what I wanted him to tell me. A small part of me held out hope it was just a coincidence. That there was another car wreck that same night with another man named Hunter. But now I know.

"You slept with her, didn't you?" Creed asks when I don't immediately say anything.

I slowly lift my gaze to his, neither confirming nor denying. I don't have to. We've been friends for years. He knows when I'm happy. When I'm depressed. When I've gotten laid.

He shakes his head, the vein in his neck pulsing as he tightens his grip on the steering wheel. "I knew she looked familiar. Knew her name *sounded* familiar. It's why I insisted on the background check. Why I tried to tell you days ago. I feared this might happen, but—"

"Feared *what* might happen?" I ask, my hackles rising.

"That you might put the pieces together. It's why I tried to dissuade you from continuing on this journey. Worried of what memories it might—"

"What? That it would remind me of Kendall?"

"No." He jerks his head toward me. "I was worried *she* might remember. And she can*not* know about your involvement."

"Why? Don't you think she deserves that? If it were me and I'd been pulled from a car seconds before it burst into flames, I'd want to know who saved my life."

He pinches the bridge of his nose, conflicted. Then he heaves a long sigh as he looks through the sunroof before bringing his gaze back to mine.

"Because you didn't just save her life, Anders. You caused that car wreck."

Chapter Twenty-Five

ANDERSON

CREED'S WORDS ARE like a punch to the gut. A chill sweeps over me as I process this shock. How is that possible? I would have remembered something like that. Sure, I'd been upset that night, but if I'd caused a wreck, the SUV I'd been driving would have suffered some damage. But it hadn't. All I knew was one minute I was driving, ignoring Creed as I fought through a blinding headache, my body seemingly frozen. The next, a crash stole my attention.

Shit… The headache.

I'd closed my eyes for what I thought was a millisecond to ease the pain. Had it been longer? I mentally rewind to the night I've tried to leave in my past for years now, but it's like a fog has settled, the memories unclear and hazy.

"Explain," I grind out through a clenched jaw. "Now!"

"You rounded a curve and swerved into the other lane," he answers in an even tone, as if giving a report to his superior. In a way, I suppose he is. "I thought you'd correct yourself. Remember you were in the States, not back home. But you never did. I tried to get your attention, but you ignored me. When I saw a car coming straight for us, I shouted. Needing to act quickly, I yanked the steering wheel to pull you back to the correct lane." He exhales deeply. "But it was too late. The other car lost control and skidded down the embankment."

"I don't remember any of this. I—"

I swallow hard and shake my head. As if it weren't a shock to my system to learn that Nora was the woman I pulled from that wreck, now I have to face the fact that I caused that accident. That I killed her fiancé. That *I'm* the reason she lost her baby. And that my father probably covered it up so as to not paint the Royal Family in a negative light. It's too much, my emotions yanked in every direction.

"Why the fuck didn't you tell me?" I roar. "Why is this the first I'm hearing about it?" My ears pound, nostrils flare, adrenaline rushing through my body.

"You were in a really dark place after Kendall's death, Anders," Creed responds calmly, trying to pacify me. But nothing can pacify me now. Not after this. "After learning that the lone survivor..." He clears his throat. "That Nora had been asleep until the crash, it was decided not to mention what I'd witnessed regarding your somewhat erratic driving."

"It was decided?" I repeat, my voice rising in pitch. "By whom?"

He opens his mouth, but hesitates.

"By...whom?" I say again, getting in his face.

"Your father, upon the advice of your psychiatrist. He was of the opinion that telling you would only add to the mental duress you were under. You already blamed yourself for Kendall's death. They worried if you learned the truth, you wouldn't be able to carry that weight and would break. So, for your safety, I was ordered to keep the truth from you."

I stare at him, struggling to make sense of the

excruciating new world I find myself in. I wish I could rewind the clock, return to bed with Nora, ignorant of who she is. But I can't. And now I'm faced with the cruel reality that I've fallen for the woman whose life I destroyed. There is no happy ending here. Only tragedy.

"But you're my friend, Creed," I whisper.

His Adam's apple bobs up and down in a hard swallow, a flicker of emotion passing over his face before he schools his expression, returning to the trained officer he is.

"When I agreed to be your CPO, I told you there may be times I have to put the job above our friendship. This was one of those times."

"I should have known," I spit out. "You had no problem putting the *job* ahead of my sister. You'd surely have no qualms doing it with me, either."

"I didn't have a choice. This is my job," he reminds me.

"Yeah? Well, consider yourself fired, at least from this post."

Heat flaming my face, I throw open the door, grabbing the coffee and pastries before slamming it.

My behavior is juvenile, but my world's been turned upside down in the past few minutes. I need someone to feel the same agony and heartache threatening to rip me apart. It's not the first time Creed and I have gotten into a heated argument. But he's never kept something of this magnitude from me before. He's always been one of the few people in this world I can trust. Now I question everything.

"You're firing me?" Creed scrambles from the SUV and runs in front of me, forcing me to stop. "Why? So you can get a piece of ass from Nora, then toss her aside, just like you've done with every other woman since

Kendall?"

His words hit me hard and I lean into him. "She is *nothing* like those women, and you know it. She's so much more than a piece of ass, so don't you *dare* speak about her that way." I move around him, but he calls out before I can make it more than a few steps.

"What do you expect me to tell your father?"

I pause, slowly facing him.

"If I go home without you, he'll ask why. He'll want to know what happened. *Everything* that's happened."

"What do I care? You're going to tell him what you want anyway. What the *job* requires. So go. Leave. And so help me, if I notice you trailing me, I'll make sure the only post you'll ever get again is checking bags of tourists visiting the palace."

I spin from him, heading across the parking lot and toward my motel room. I do my best to make as little noise as possible as I slip inside and close the door, blocking the outside world from infiltrating our bubble. But it's already too late for that.

My vision blurs as I pause to admire Nora's sleeping form in the same position she was in when I left her less than a half-hour ago. I wish I could return to that time. Wish I'd stayed in bed. Wish she didn't have to learn the horrific truth that she gave her body, her heart, to a devil.

As if sensing my gaze on her, her eyelids flutter open, a smile building on her mouth when she sees me standing at the edge of the bed.

"Morning," she murmurs in a husky voice.

I peer into the same eyes that begged me to save her fiancé all those years ago. Pressure builds in my chest, making everything uncomfortable. Every motion. Every breath. Every heartbeat. My conscience is torn in a thousand directions, splintering me.

I want to wrap my arms around her, then kneel before her to beg forgiveness.

I want to surround myself with her affection, then lay prostrate before her so she can punish me like I deserve.

I want to bury myself inside her, then sacrifice myself for her own peace of mind.

Noticing something's off, she props herself up, not doing anything to cover her exposed breast.

"Anderson, what is it?"

I part my lips, struggling to come up with the words I need. All the education I'd received in my formative years about what syllables formed which words and how to string words into a sentence has vanished, rendering me mute.

Leaving the tray of coffee and pastries on the desk, I walk to the bed and crawl on top of her. Overwhelmed with misery and desperation, I capture her mouth in a deep, burning kiss.

Last night, every kiss was lust-filled and wanton, our need to succumb to our desires driving everything we did. This kiss, however, is nothing like those. It's riddled with anguish and vulnerability. With heartache and guilt. With torment and hopelessness.

"I need you," I breathe.

This will only make things more complicated, but I'm desperate to extinguish the torturous flames threatening to engulf me. I need Nora. Her compassion. Her kindness. Her mercy. Please, God, let her show me some mercy.

"Have me," she murmurs, just like she did last night.

I don't move from her as I clumsily push down my shorts and kick them to the floor. Ripping my t-shirt over my head, I settle between her legs and thrust into her, no barrier between us, breaking the rule that was ingrained into me the second I became interested in girls. I no longer care about the goddamn rules. No longer care about following protocol. All I care about is feeling something other than the crushing weight threatening to destroy me. Nora's the only one who makes me forget. And I need to forget.

I bury my face in the crook of her neck, inhaling her scent. I pull my bottom lip between my teeth, now knowing why her perfume seemed so familiar. Why *she* seemed so familiar. Because she was.

She wraps her legs around me, her fingers threading through my hair. Unlike last night, there are no statements of desire, no loud moans, no carnal biting. It's just two broken souls desperately trying to find solace in a world that's devoured us and spit us out.

I frame her face in my hands, moving my mouth to hers, giving her everything I have as I continue thrusting inside her. Even when I break away to catch my breath, I keep my lips poised on hers, our eyes locked, remaining in this place until we both cross that point of no return.

And that's what I've done by sleeping with her knowing the truth. Crossed the point of no return. There's no going back now. There's no trying to make things right.

There's only serving the sentence karma has bestowed on me for my sins.

Chapter Twenty-Six

NORA

"**W**HAT'S THIS PLACE?" I ask when Anderson pulls into a dirt parking lot late in the afternoon. The desert sun shines high in the sky, heading toward the west, casting a pinkish glow over the terrain. Or perhaps it's all the clay buildings that seem to tint everything red.

"San Miguel Mission." He puts the Wrangler into park. "Oldest church in the United States."

"We're at a…church?" I peer at the traditional pueblo-style building that seems to dominate the architecture of this area. But this place looks much older, lacking any flair one would expect in modern construction.

"It's a historic landmark. Built in the early 1600s, it was damaged during the Pueblo Revolt of 1680, then rebuilt in the early 1700s."

"Did you read all this in my guidebook?" I joke.

He smiles, but it doesn't light up his expression as it normally would.

All day, something about him has seemed off. I can't quite put my finger on what. He's been affectionate. Even pulled the Wrangler off the side of the road and made me straddle him after I'd teased the bulge in his pants to the point of desperation. Despite the physical connection, there was something missing. Since this morning, sex has been…different. Almost like he's using it to make him forget whatever's ailing him. I should know. I once did the same thing. But I don't want to use Anderson to forget. And I don't want him to use me to forget, either.

"No." He briefly shifts his attention to the steeple, appreciating the craftsmanship, before looking back at me. "I just really like history. But you already know this about me." He grabs my hand and leads me toward the building. "Let's go look around."

"Are you sure we're allowed to just…go in? Don't churches have rules or something?"

"What are you so scared of?"

"Organized religion," I mutter under my breath, which makes him chuckle.

"Not big on attending church, I take it."

"I never grew up around it. Why?" I tilt my head. "Are you religious?"

He pauses outside the entrance, pulling his lips between his teeth as he contemplates. "I don't know if you could call me religious, so to speak." He chuckles to himself. "I'm certainly no stranger to sin."

"Nothing wrong with a little sin," I murmur in a husky voice as I rub my body against his, the subtle contact awakening his erection. Despite his reaction, a vacancy still looms in his eyes, turmoil swirling like a hurricane. "Sinning makes life interesting. Wouldn't you agree?"

"You're bad, you know that?" He pulls me along with him, discreetly adjusting his shorts.

"I didn't hear you complaining last night."

"Certainly not," he whispers once we cross the threshold, serenity engulfing us. And there's something else in the air, too. Something more potent than history.

Grace.

Forgiveness.

Absolution.

As one would expect from a church constructed centuries ago, the building is small and smells of dust and decades of stories. The stark, white stucco walls contrast with the ornate wood beams crossing the ceiling, perhaps a dozen rows of pews beneath it. The décor has a Mexican influence, a few splashes of turquoise and blue making it stand out from any other church I've been to, which isn't many.

Anderson and I walk toward the altar, both of us silently taking in the solemnity of the space. Out of the corner of my eye, I notice an elderly woman clutching a rosary, her hand pressed against a clay carving on the wall. Glancing around, I see there are over a dozen more carvings.

"The stations of the cross," Anderson whispers, answering the question clearly evident in my expression. "It's big in the Catholic religion. Tells the story leading up to Jesus' death and subsequent resurrection."

I try to follow along, although the words he speaks may as well be a foreign language for all I'm concerned.

"Here. Look at this." He points to a panel of glass by the wooden stairs leading up to the altar. I join him, squinting at several adobe bricks contained within. "The original steps."

"Wow."

I've never been infatuated with history, at least not like Anderson is. Nevertheless, there's something humbling about standing in a building that's been around for centuries. About seeing pieces that have survived war and the passing of hundreds of years. It puts things into perspective. No matter what life throws at you, it's important to carry on. To find the strength to rebuild. To repair.

"Incredible, isn't it?"

I meet his enthusiastic grin. "It is."

We walk around for a while longer, soaking in the history contained within these hallowed walls, admiring the architecture and stunning craftsmanship. A few other tourists snap pictures to memorialize their visit, but other than the occasional clicking of a shutter, it's quiet. Subdued. Reflective.

As we approach a table to the left of the altar holding dozens of small votives filled with red candles, Anderson grabs a long match. When he strikes it, a flame erupts, and he brings it toward a candle, lighting it.

My curiosity getting the better of me, I sidle up next to him. "What's that for?" I ask in a hushed tone.

"It's a tradition in the Catholic religion to light a candle for a loved one who has passed."

I admire the three tiers of candles set on the antique wooden table, a cross hanging above. A few candles are already lit, but the majority aren't. I don't press him to talk about it. Loss is one of those things you can't pressure someone to discuss, regardless of whether it's recent or in the distant past. We never truly get over the loss. We simply learn to adapt to life without that person.

Like I've finally done with Hunter…with Anderson's help.

"Her name was Kendall."

"I know."

Now that I'm aware of *who* Anderson is, my knowledge of him has increased. I haven't looked at tabloid articles, but everyone knew about his relationship with Kendall Davies. Everyone expected to see an engagement announcement any day. Unfortunately, she passed away from a heart attack before that happened, shocking the world.

"She's the reason I got the tattoo." He brings his hand to his heart, covering it briefly. "She said my alter-ego was fitting. That I was her compass, her true north." He pauses for a beat before turning his impassioned eyes on me. "So I understand what it's like to lose someone so unexpectedly. Understand how much it can mess with you, keep you tethered to the past. Make you feel like you're doing a disservice to their memory by moving on."

I nod, swallowing through the tightness in my throat. Feeling compelled by Anderson's actions, I grab a match and light two candles. He doesn't press me for details. Just wordlessly acknowledges my own gesture.

Several moments pass as we stare at the flames dancing in front of us, representing three lives cut too short. Representing loss. Representing a moment in time we'll never be able to return to.

But in this moment, I feel a connection to this man, stronger than I have all week. In our heartache, we've become bonded, our lives intertwined.

"I was in the car," I admit softly.

Anderson brings his gaze to mine. He doesn't appear surprised, just processing.

"When Hunter crashed. I was six months pregnant."

He closes his eyes, hanging his head as he draws in a deep breath.

"Ember." I say the name I haven't been able to in years. "That was going to be our baby's name." I look back at the candles, a heaviness settling in my heart.

"Nora…" His gaze glosses over with unshed tears. "I am so sorry."

I swipe at my cheeks. "And you know the truly awful part? Not only did I lose my fiancé and baby in the accident, but I had to continue carrying her. She didn't have a heartbeat, but the staff at the hospital didn't give me an option, didn't tell me I could stay and be induced right then. They made it sound like I had to wait until either I went into labor naturally or the baby posed a risk to my health. I was in my third trimester, so I just assumed that was why. For two weeks, I had to carry my baby. My *dead* baby. I had to go out in public where people would ask me when my baby was due. If it was a girl or boy. If I was excited." My words become louder and more incensed, thinking back to the injustice of it all.

Maybe if I weren't dealing with the aftermath of the accident that took my fiancé's life, I would have known to fight harder. To insist they induce me before leaving the hospital. But I wasn't thinking clearly. All I could think about was everything I'd lost. How I could possibly keep living without Hunter and Ember.

"I had to go on with my life as if nothing had changed. And I blamed myself."

Anderson whips his eyes to mine, his gaze intense and powerful. "What? Why?"

"How could I not? I'd convinced myself it was my punishment."

"Punishment for what?"

My chin quivers as I struggle to admit the awful truth. "Because it's my fault he crashed. We were on our way to a going away party. I'd intended to take a nap that afternoon so I wouldn't be tired, but I never did. So I took a little nap in the car. If I had just stayed awake——"

"No."

Anderson clutches my cheeks in his hands, his grip painful yet invigorating at the same time, making me forget about the ache of being responsible for Hunter's and Ember's deaths. I blink, the passion and magnitude in his gaze stealing my breath.

"Don't you dare say that." His voice echoes in the

now empty space. "Don't you dare blame yourself."

"But if I hadn't—"

"No," he interrupts. "I've been living with regret for years now, too. *Years*, Nora. Believe me when I say you have no blame in what happened. Nothing you did or didn't do made any difference. I *need* you to believe me." He brings my head closer to his, his mouth a breath away again. "Say you believe me."

"I believe you," I whimper, the words falling from my mouth of their own volition.

He expels a long sigh, tension rolling off him in waves. He rests my head against his body, pressing a soft kiss to my forehead. We remain in this position, the candles flickering before us, his arms wrapped around me, my head buried in his chest as I inhale his familiar scent. In the past few days, this place has become my solace, my serenity…my salvation.

He clears his throat, releasing his hold on me and stepping back. "We should probably get going." He extends his arm, allowing me to walk in front of him.

I start toward the exit, glancing over my shoulder when I don't immediately sense him beside me. I watch as he stares at the large cross in the center of the altar. Then he bows his head and murmurs, "God, forgive me."

It could mean nothing, just a man of faith seeking forgiveness for recent sins. But I can't shake the unsettling feeling in my stomach that there's another reason for it.

Chapter Twenty-Seven

NORA

SANTA FE IS vastly different from where we stayed last night. Where Tucumcari was on the kitschy side and overflowing with Route 66 nostalgia, this place is more steeped in history while staying current at the same time. A trendy downtown area boasts eclectic food options, boutique shops, and even several art galleries. It draws into focus the difference between Hunter and Anderson, too. Hunter loved Americana. The quirkier the better. While Anderson appreciates the history behind many of these tackier tourist attractions we've stopped at, he has a more refined taste. And that's what Santa Fe is. Refined history.

Luxury surrounds us as Anderson leads me into the lobby of a hotel a few blocks away from San Miguel Mission. Just like everything else in this city, the pueblo influence is strong in the architecture. My sandals slide against the clay tile beneath them, fragrant desert flowers filling the air with a refreshing scent.

"Good evening," a woman in a black business suit greets from behind the reception desk. "Do you have a reservation?"

"I do," Anderson answers proudly.

I whip my head toward him, furrowing my brows. "You do?"

He shrugs, reaching into his wallet and pulling out his

ID and credit card. "I wanted to make up for last night's mix-up." He hands his cards to the clerk, who smiles, then types on her keyboard to pull up his reservation.

"I think you've already made up for it." I wink, hoping to get a laugh out of him, but he's still distant.

"Here it is," the clerk says. "The two-bedroom vista suite. Beautiful accommodations."

Normally, I'd be thrilled to find out that not only had Anderson thought ahead to book a room at what appears to be a lavish hotel, but he also reserved us a suite. Instead, all I hear is that it's a two-bedroom. I try not to read too much into it. Maybe he didn't want to presume anything. But after his somewhat cool and aloof demeanor today, I can't stop that tight ball of dejection from forming in my stomach.

"Here you go." She hands Anderson his ID and credit card, as well as two keycards. "Just head out those doors and through the courtyard. You're in the next building. The Mesa. Elevators will be on your left when you enter. Take them up to the third floor. If you need anything else to make your stay more comfortable, or any local information, don't hesitate to call."

"Will do," Anderson says politely, then places his hand on my back, steering me out of the main building and through the courtyard.

But this isn't like any courtyard I've ever seen. We're in the desert, yet this looks like a lush rainforest, oversized green leaves interspersed with vibrant pink and yellow blooms. An Aztec-tiled fountain sits in the middle, wrought-iron benches surrounding it. Overgrown trees provide shade on the lawn, the perfect spot to relax and read a book. If I had more time here, that's exactly what I'd do.

We follow the directions the clerk provided and, within a few minutes, find our room. Anderson unlocks the door and holds it open for me, allowing me to walk ahead of him. When we first arrived here, I knew it would be nothing like the motel from last night. As I step across the threshold and onto the hardwood flooring, I confirm that fact.

Southwestern-style tapestries adorn the furniture and floor. It's not overdone, just a subtle nod to the culture of this city. A traditional New Mexican kiva fireplace hugs the far corner of the living room, a faint aroma of burning wood wafting through the air.

With wide eyes, I continue into the suite, checking out the master bedroom. An enormous four-poster bed sits in the center, everything about the room oozing romance. The bathroom is just as posh. Large, marble-tiled shower with several showerheads. Jetted tub that beckons me. Lush robes sporting the hotel's insignia. There are even fluffy slippers.

Once I finish my inspection, I head back into the living room, Anderson hovering near the doorway to the second bedroom.

"What do you—"

"I'm going to go for a quick walk," he interrupts before I can finish my question about our sleeping arrangements tonight, something I didn't think I had to discuss with him. Maybe I was wrong.

Averting his gaze, he spins from me, bolting to the door.

"Do you want any company?" I call after him, feeling like I'm losing him. Then again, he's not really mine to lose.

As he's about to turn the knob, he pauses, glancing over his shoulder. "I'm sorry. I just... I need to be alone for a minute." He looks past me. "Remembering Kendall can sometimes be—"

"Say no more." I force a smile, pushing down the

uneasy feeling building inside me. "I understand. Go do what you need to."

He nods slightly before opening the door and disappearing through it.

I don't move for several moments, a part of me holding out hope that he'll come back, apologize for being daft, as he'd call it, then we'd have hot, crazy, four-poster-bed sex.

But he doesn't. Not after a minute. Hell, not even after five minutes.

Trying not to overanalyze his behavior, I shuffle into the master bedroom and flop onto the mattress. I can't help but notice that this would be the perfect bed frame to be tied to. And I can't even appreciate that fact. All I can think of is Anderson's strange demeanor, and this premonition in the pit of my stomach that something's wrong. If there were a time I wish my girl gang was here with me, it's now. But if they can't be here with me physically, at least I can have the next best thing.

Grabbing my phone, I find Chloe's contact and start a FaceTime session. It only rings once before her face pops up.

"So you *are* alive."

"Yes, Chloe," I groan playfully. "I'm alive."

"Is it true you picked up a hitchhiker?" Evie interjects, grabbing Chloe's phone from her, walking around what I recognize to be Izzy's Gramercy Park townhouse. I imagine Chloe and Evie are keeping her company while her boyfriend, Asher, is out touring the world, melting thousands of hearts with his music every night.

"I didn't pick up a hitchhiker."

"I may have exaggerated a little when I told them about your British prince," Chloe shouts.

I wince. When I first told Chloe about him, I laughed when she called him a prince. Then again, she calls anyone who's hot and British a prince. It's remarkable how accurate her description turned out to be.

Izzy squeezes her face next to Evie's, noticing my reaction. "What is it?" She pushes a strand of her dark hair behind her ear, and a sparkle catches my eye.

"Wait a second!" I shoot straight up. "Do that again."

"Do what again?" Izzy asks.

"Let me see your hand."

Fighting the grin crawling on her lips, she raises her hand, revealing a stunning diamond on a very important finger.

"You're engaged!" I shriek.

"I am," she answers excitedly.

"When did this happen?"

"The night before you left on your trip. I'm sorry I didn't tell you sooner. I wanted to wait until you came home. Let you focus on your journey. So let's do that. What's going on? Who's this British prince, as Chloe calls him?"

"Yeah. Spill it." Chloe swipes the phone from Izzy and heads over to the couch, setting it on the coffee table. "I want the dirt." She sits in the middle, Izzy and Evie flanking her, leaning close so I can see everyone.

"Before I say anything, I want both of you to promise this stays between us." I point toward Chloe and Evie, since they both work for the magazine and this information is most certainly newsworthy. "This is off the record. For your ears only. No one else."

"You got it," Evie agrees.

"We'd never do anything to break your trust. You know that," Chloe reminds me.

Content in their guarantees, I draw in a deep breath, unsure whether I should do this. But to get my friends' advice, they need to understand. And learning about Anderson is all part of that.

"So my British prince… Turns out, he's not actually British. He's from Belmont, which is right across the channel from the UK. Hence the accent. He did go to prep school in London, though."

"Oh, Belmont." Chloe waggles her brows. "Talk about another hottie prince." She fans herself. "He's taken the number one spot since Prince Harry got hitched."

"Chloe, you're married," Evie reminds her.

"I can still look. You guys can't sit here and tell me that Prince Gabriel isn't sin in a perfectly tailored suit."

My cheeks heat at how accurate her analysis is. Based on the photo I saw last night when Anderson had me Google him, he certainly does look amazing in a suit. But I like his casual look, too. And towel look. And naked look.

"Holy shit." Chloe's voice cuts through my growing inappropriate thoughts. I dart my gaze back to the screen to see my friends peering at me curiously. "Why are you all flushed? And why do you have this look on your face like you just got caught with your hand in a cookie jar? But instead of a cookie jar, it's some guy's pants."

I straighten my spine, steeling myself for what I'm about to do, wondering if they'll believe me. I still have trouble believing me.

"Actually, Prince Gabriel prefers to go by his middle name."

They all blink simultaneously.

"Anderson."

It's silent for a moment as they stare at me, mouths agape.

"You're shitting me," Izzy states.

"No fucking way," Evie adds.

"Are you saying what I think you are?" Chloe asks,

practically bouncing off the couch.

"I didn't believe it myself at first."

My friends share a look, then return their attention to me.

"Photos," Evie orders.

"Now," Chloe adds.

I navigate out of FaceTime and bring up my photos. Finding a selfie we'd taken outside a mural wall in Kansas that reminded me of the movie *Cars*, I send it to our group chat. I hear the pinging of my incoming text sound in the background of the FaceTime call. Evie grabs her phone and brings up the message, showing it to Chloe and Izzy. The three of them scream, and I wince, lowering the volume.

"You met a fucking prince!" Evie exclaims.

"This is unbelievable," Izzy adds.

"Only you would meet a guy who'd end up being a prince," Chloe remarks.

"Did you not recognize him?" Evie asks.

"Well… No. It's not like he walks around in his royal uniform or whatever and people bow before him," I say in my defense. "Plus, his hair is longer and a lot messier than he wears it during public events. And he's sporting a really sexy goatee and mustache."

"I can see how you wouldn't recognize him," Chloe states, studying the photo I'd sent.

"But the eyes," Izzy coos. "They're so…"

"Soulful," Chloe finishes.

"They sure are." I blush, the memories of getting lost in those soulful eyes last night returning, which only causes my heart to squeeze.

"When did you figure out who he was?" Izzy asks, my three friends hanging onto my every word.

"I didn't. He told me. Last night. We went out drinking because yesterday was so awkward after I kissed him the day before and—"

"Wait a hot second." Evie holds up her hand. "You kissed him?"

"I'm hoping she did more than just kiss him," Chloe mutters.

"Yes, I kissed him," I admit, my gaze focused on Evie before shifting to Chloe. "And last night we did more than kiss. And again this morning. And again on the side of the road."

The girls hoot and whistle, as I knew they would. Then Chloe returns her analytical stare to me, scrutinizing me. "But there's something bothering you, isn't there?"

I blow out a breath. "Last night was hot. Hotter than hot." My skin burns from the memory of how he slammed me up against the exterior wall of the bar. How he made me come right there where anyone could see. How no one had ever brought me so much pleasure.

"But?" Chloe urges.

"But he's been…off all day."

"How?" Evie scrunches a brow. "You just said you had sex this morning. How is that being off?"

"More like getting off," Izzy deadpans.

"It's hard to explain. He was with me last night. Well, obviously he was with me, but he was *with* me, you know? Like totally in the moment. The intensity in the way his eyes speared through me—"

"As well as his cock," Chloe mutters under her breath.

I roll my eyes, unable to stop the smile from tugging on my mouth. She's not far from the truth.

"He was there. He was present. He was only thinking of me and nothing else." I worry my bottom lip, considering my words. "But this morning, he was…different."

"How do you mean?" Evie inquires.

"I heard him walk back into the room after fetching us coffee, so I stirred in the bed. He just stared at me for a while, this haunted look about him. I can't explain it better than that. Then, with barely a word, he came to me, like he physically needed me to breathe. And the sex was incredible."

I chew on the inside of my cheek, deciding to leave out that we didn't use a condom. It was a lapse of judgment on both our parts, one I hadn't even thought about at the time. All I could think about was the agony I felt coming off Anderson's body.

"But he wasn't *with* me," I continue. "He's distant. I don't want to waste the rest of my trip obsessing over what he wants. I'm not stupid. I know there's no chance of a future between us."

"Why not?" Chloe asks.

"A lot of reasons. Mainly because he lives a world away."

"So?" She shrugs nonchalantly. "In my experience, if two people are meant to be together, they'll find a way, regardless of any obstacle."

She would know. She and Lincoln had to overcome more than their fair share of obstacles. But they made it work.

"True, but I'm not going to let what might or might not be control what I do right now." As the words leave my mouth, I'm hit with a realization I hadn't considered before. "Do you think that's what *he's* doing? Do you think he's keeping his distance because he knows nothing will ever come from this?"

"That's not for us to say," Izzy responds. "We can't tell you what's in his head. Only he can. So you need to talk to him. Not let this fester between you."

"Lay it all on the line," Evie suggests. "Tell him

everything you told us. And give him a reminder of everything he'll miss out on if he keeps pushing you away."

"And then when you come home, you can tell us all about hot, royal sex." Chloe leans toward the screen. "It *is* hot, right?" She clasps her hands in front of her in prayer.

"Hot enough to make those California wildfires burn for quite a few decades."

They all whistle and cheer once more.

"Then why are you talking to us?" Chloe jests. "Go get some of that hot sex. And don't come home until he's made up for the lack of good sex you've endured these past three years."

Chapter Twenty-Eight

ANDERSON

I DON'T EVEN know where I'm going. I just had to get out of that room to stop staring at a constant reminder of what a horrible person I am. I was on the brink of confessing the truth to Nora so many times today, but at the last minute, I changed course, too much of a coward to say the words. And that's what I am. A coward. A fraud. A bastard undeserving of her affections and respect.

I want to tell Nora everything, but I hate the idea of her seeing me as a heartless prick. I want to walk away, but I'm drawn to her, this connection only growing stronger the more time we spend together.

Which is why I needed to go for a walk. Clear my mind. Do something to break free from the spell she seems to have cast over me.

The sidewalks of downtown Santa Fe teem with people checking out one of the many local galleries or shops, or perhaps looking for a place to stop for a drink and bite to eat. They all seem so happy. Families exploring this historic Southwestern city. Couples in love stealing kisses. I envy their blissful, simple lives. My life has never been simple.

As I stand at a crosswalk, I glance over my shoulder, noting the dark SUV lingering in a nearby parking lot, keeping me in its sights.

Creed.

It didn't escape my notice that he's been following us all day, even after my threat this morning. I considered reminding him of it, but I haven't. Truth be told, I'm not even upset he's still here. I expected nothing less. I've lost count of the number of times I've fired Creed, especially in the months immediately following Kendall's death when I tried to drown myself in a bottle and he'd cut me off.

But that didn't violate the trust I put in him. Not like this did.

In just twelve hours, my entire world has been tilted on its axis. It was one thing to blame myself for Kendall's death, to blame myself for failing to see the signs that something was wrong with her. It's a completely different thing to learn that my carelessness caused another car to careen off the road and into a tree, resulting in the loss of two lives.

Needing to speak to a voice of reason in a world that seems to lack any, I cross the street toward a public park and find a bench beneath the shade of a giant tree. I lower myself onto it and grab my phone out of my pocket, hitting my sister's contact.

Children play in the distance, squealing with joy when their parents hand them an ice cream cone they'd just purchased from a street vendor. I wish I could go back to that time. To when I could find happiness in something as mundane as ice cream.

"Hey, Anders." Esme's groggy voice comes over the line.

"Sorry for waking you."

"It's okay." She heaves a sigh. "I was expecting your call."

"You were?"

"I spoke with Creed earlier."

"Oh." I pause, then ask, "What did he tell you?"

"Everything."

"Everything?"

"Yes, Anders. Everything. About who this woman you've been traveling with truly is. About the car wreck." A silence falls before she asks, "How are you holding up?"

I blow out a mirthless laugh, running my hand through my hair. "How do you think I'm holding up?"

"I can't even imagine." Her words are laced with all the sincerity and compassion I've come to expect from her. "It was the MS that caused it, wasn't it?"

I hang my head, nodding, even though she can't see me. Once Creed told me about what happened, it all clicked. Based on what my neurologist told me when I snuck off earlier to call him, all the symptoms I experienced the night of the crash could very well have been a flareup. But I refuse to blame it on my MS. I still got behind the wheel and drove carelessly enough to force a completely innocent person off the road.

"I'm so fucking confused, Esme," I admit through the frustration in my throat. "I want to tell her, but I can't seem to summon the words. Then I convince myself the best thing is to leave, but my legs refuse to walk away. It's like I'm stuck in purgatory. I'm tormented by the fires of hell all while having a taste of heaven." I pinch the bridge of my nose, my stomach knotting. "This all could have been avoided if Creed had told me about this years ago. Do you realize how fucked up it is that my own friend kept it from me? I think that's what hurts the most. That he kept me in the dark."

"He was just doing his job," Esme reminds me, catching me off guard.

Normally, she takes my side. Living as we do, every decision is made for us. What we wear. Where we go.

Whom we date. Being born into a powerful family doesn't give you *carte blanche* to do whatever you want. Instead, every day is carefully scheduled, your behavior dictated to you. After a while, it becomes grueling. I may have grown up in a luxurious palace, but it was always more like a prison.

"Why aren't you more upset about this? About everything? He kept a huge secret from me for six years, Esme. Six. *Fucking*. Years." When a few passing tourists glance my way, I lower my voice. "How have you remained so close to him after he betrayed you?"

"He didn't betray me, Anders," she responds calmly. "I may have felt deceived at first. Angry. Like I wasn't enough. It hurt that he chose his job over me. But when I stopped to consider everything, I realized I'd known all along how it would end between us, despite the hope I held onto. Creed was always going to be a member of the Royal Guard. It's his legacy. Just like mine is to be Princess Royal. Nothing will ever change that."

"Yet you stayed with him right up until his induction. Why?"

I've never delved into her history with my best friend. They kept their relationship private from the public eye. Hell, they'd even kept it from me in the beginning. But Esme can't hide much from me, so she eventually revealed they'd been seeing each other in secret. At least until he was inducted into the Royal Guard at the age of twenty-six after serving the required eight years in the military.

"Because I'd rather know what it's like to fly than to imagine it from the safety of the ground," Esme breathes dreamily.

"You didn't push him away to protect yourself from the inevitable heartache?"

I have no doubt she knows I'm no longer asking

because I'm a good brother. I'm doing it for myself, my own peace of mind. Learning the truth of who Nora is and what I did has turned everything on its head. In a way, this is worse than losing Kendall. When she passed, I had no warning. I wasn't forced to count down the minutes I spent in her presence, knowing each ticking of the clock would be one less second I'd have with her.

"I'm not going to tell you what you should or shouldn't do here," Esme states. "Our situations are vastly different. Yes, I knew my relationship with Creed would eventually come to an end. And I can't pretend to understand what you must be thinking about your role in the car wreck that took not only Nora's fiancé, but also her baby—"

"If you're trying to make me feel like even more of a complete bastard, you're doing a great fucking job."

"But I don't want you to have any regrets, Anders," she soothes, ignoring my outburst. "You asked why I stayed with Creed when I knew there was no future. It's because I didn't think about it. I understand it's nearly impossible not to look toward the future. Not only are you constantly reminded of yours as next in line for the crown, but now you face the added pressure of your MS diagnosis. But you, more than anyone, should know that the future is uncertain. It's not guaranteed. Right now is the only thing that is. This moment. Do you want to walk away from Nora and always wonder what if? That's why I stayed with Creed. I didn't want to have any regrets."

"And do you?"

I can hear the smile in her tone when she responds. "Not for a second. Every tear shed, every ache in my heart was worth it to know how it feels to fly. To be loved."

I pinch my lips together, processing her words. I'm

still conflicted, considering every time I selfishly steal a kiss from Nora, I feel like I'm deceiving her. When we first met, I wanted her to get to know the real me. Now I want nothing more than to keep that person locked away.

"Thanks, Esme. For everything. For always listening. For smacking some sense into me, even from thousands of miles away."

"That's what I'm here for. Now go. Why are you talking to me when there's a beautiful woman who deserves your attention?"

"You know why. I—"

"You can't go back and change what's happened in your past. But maybe you can do something today to change the future. Maybe it won't work out, like you say. But maybe seeing if it does will be the exact adventure you need to remind you what it's like to fly. That's what Creed was to me. An adventure. That's what Nora can be to you. Don't let her become your biggest regret."

"I think it may be too late for that," I murmur, but the line's already gone dead.

Chapter Twenty-Nine

ANDERSON

As I MAKE my way back to the hotel, all I can do is hope I haven't completely ruined things with Nora. No matter what she did to pull me out of my slump — the jokes she told, the way she tried to distract me by jerking me off, the kisses she'd coaxed from me to make me return from my thoughts — all I could think about was the night I took everything from her.

Isn't that what I'm doing by staying with her? Taking everything from her again?

Or am I just using that an excuse for the real reason I've been withdrawn all day?

That the last time I felt this way about another woman, it ended in disaster.

That I'm not sure I can put myself through that again.

That I'm scared.

Approaching the door to our room, a buzz fills me at the knowledge Nora's just on the other side. A wall separates us, but I can feel her energy. Her vibrancy. Her devotion. I picture her lying on the bed, a book in her hand. Or maybe she's meditating in front of the fireplace. Or perhaps she opted for a relaxing soak in the jetted tub.

But when I open the door and step inside, I learn every scenario I imagined is wrong.

She bolts up from the couch, not giving me a second

to greet her before she rushes toward me, eyes wild, expression frantic.

"Why are you pushing me away?" she demands, sounding agitated.

"I—"

"Because I am trying so hard to wrap my head around it," she cuts me off, pacing in front of me, tugging at her hair. Then she whirls toward me once more. "Did you not enjoy last night?"

"What?" My gaze widens, her question catching me off guard. "Of course I did. You know I did."

"Right." She turns, pacing again. "I did, too. I *really* fucking did. But then today…" Pausing, she peers into the distance, turmoil covering every inch of her. "Today was different." Her eyes lock with mine, her frustration turning more to understanding. "I get it. I've been where you are. I *am* where you are."

She takes my hand in hers, rubbing her thumb along my knuckles, like I so often do to her. It's a simple touch, but it sends a warmth through me, offering me comfort when I need it the most. I wish it didn't feel like a lie, like I'm undeserving of this gesture.

"We've both lost someone we cared about. We've both suffered the worst kind of heartbreak imaginable. So instead of risking it and enduring that again, we've kept our hearts locked up. Pushed people away. All to *protect* ourselves."

I try to open my mouth and tell her that's only part of it, but words don't come. All I can do is lose myself in her eyes. We're back in the bubble where nothing else matters. Where the future is just an abstract idea. There's only here. Only now. Only us.

"I know you're scared. I am absolutely petrified, too. These feelings…" She licks her lips. "I haven't felt this way about anyone since Hunter." Pulling away, she treads a path in front of me once more. "I get how fucked up this situation is. I'm out here spreading my dead fiancé's ashes, for crying out loud!" She stops pacing, standing a breath away but not touching me.

"I don't care about that anymore. Don't care that the probability of anything coming from this is so minuscule it's laughable. Don't care that in just a week, I'll say goodbye to you and hope my heart manages to heal. I am so fucking scared that when I walk away, I'll never feel this again. That I'll go back to my life and nothing will be the same. Flowers won't be as fragrant. Colors won't be as vibrant. And the wine certainly won't taste the same."

A smile tugs on my lips. We've known each other for such a short time, but in that time, she's opened my eyes, lifted the fog I've lived in since I received my diagnosis. Hell, probably since I'd lost Kendall.

"I'm so scared of this, Anderson," she chokes out. "But for the first time in years, I *want* to be scared… With you."

The passion and fervor in her voice reminds me exactly why I was drawn to her in the first place. Why I proposed she join me when her car broke down. Why I couldn't keep my distance from her, even if I wanted to. There's a fire in her. A spirit. A life.

I want more of that.

I want more of *her*, to hell with the consequences.

"You're right," I begin, my voice uneasy in the stark silence. "I am scared. So much about you absolutely petrifies me, Nora. The way I feel…" I shake my head. "I can't describe it apart from feeling like I'm…flying. Like I'm about to jump out of a plane without a parachute, and it is one of the most frightening things I've done in my life. But I'm not going to let that stop me." I grip her face, passion and want dripping from my fingertips. She inhales a sharp breath, surprised by my sudden movement.

"You scare the shit out of me, love. But there's no one I'd rather be scared with."

Before she can utter a single syllable, I crush my lips to hers, kissing her with the same ardor and fury with which she just poured her heart out to me. She wraps her arms around my neck, deepening the exchange, pressing her body as close to mine as possible. The distance I forged between us today is gone, and she's desperate to reconnect as we did last night. Her hunger is insatiable, her confidence doing things to my own desire. But as much as I'm also anxious to feel her again, I need to do this right.

When she palms my erection and squeezes, about to lower my zipper, I grab her wrist, stepping out of her reach. Chest heaving, she peers at me through bewildered eyes.

"I don't want to fuck right now, Nora."

"Excuse me?" Her confusion is written in her furrowed brow and downturned lips.

Hooking an arm around her slim waist, I pull her body against mine. "I want to go slow."

I circle my hips, hitting that spot I know she's desperate for me to touch. Her eyelids flutter closed, mouth parting just slightly. God, I love this look on her, this expression of unyielding ecstasy. There's no bigger turn-on for me than to know I do this to her. That I push her to the edge of all reason. Because this woman has pushed me beyond reason.

I pepper kisses down her neck to her collarbone, savoring the taste of her skin. "I want to seduce you. Your mind. Your body. Your heart." I force her lips back to mine. "I want your heart more than anything, Nora."

My tongue traces the seam of her mouth, begging for entry. She opens for me, answering my demand, our tongues tangling in a controlled kiss. Unlike last night, we're not desperately trying to remove our clothes in an attempt to experience each other for the first time. We're taking our time, savoring this feeling neither one of us thought we'd experience again.

Swooping her into my embrace, I carry her into the master bedroom, ignoring her demands that I put her down. I don't want to ever put this woman down.

Maybe Esme's right. Maybe it won't work out. But maybe this next week with Nora is exactly the adventure I need in my life. After all, isn't that why I stayed in the States after my diagnosis instead of heading home to break the news to my father? I wanted one last big adventure.

Maybe Nora *is* my adventure.

I carefully place her on the luxurious bed, then step back and kick off my flip-flops before shrugging out of my t-shirt. Nora props herself up and reaches for the hem of her sundress, but I stop her.

"Not yet," I whisper with a soft kiss. "I want to undress you."

Her cheeks flush, unable to hide the effect I have on her. But she's never been able to. Even when she fought her attraction to me in those early days, I could feel the desire building inside her. This isn't the type of thing that happens every day. We share a connection that goes beyond meeting in a Chicago diner. That goes beyond that fateful night when both our worlds were turned upside down. And hopefully, when the time comes, Nora will see that, too.

"There's something so…intimate about undressing a woman," I continue, snaking down this body I've become quite familiar with yet still have a lot of exploring to do. "It's like a present. A present wrapped up just for me to open. To touch." I run my hands down her midsection, and she arches her back, her heavy breaths echoing around us. Meeting her gaze as she peers down at me with yearning, I bunch the hem of her sundress around her waist, revealing her yellow panties. "To taste."

I press my mouth to her center, tasting her through the silken fabric. A moan falls from her throat, her fingers digging into my scalp to a point it's almost painful. But I don't tell her to stop.

I ease her underwear to the side, floating my gaze toward hers. "Do you want more?" I ask, circling her with my thumb.

She squeezes her eyes shut, succumbing to the sensations, words seeming to escape her. Grinning, I return to her, swiping my tongue against her before pulling away. Her breathing only increases, hips thrusting, thighs clenching.

"More?" I ask again.

"Yes, Anderson," she pants. "More."

I hook my fingers into her briefs and drag them down her legs, dropping them on the floor. I take her foot in my hands, my motions languid as I kiss my way up her leg, not wanting to miss a single inch, single dip, single freckle.

When I reach her apex, I steal a glance at her, the anticipation driving her wild with need. I'm ready to fall apart, too. But not yet. Our remaining time together is limited. I'm not going to waste a single second. Not anymore.

I move from one thigh to the other, completely ignoring her center, then kiss my way back down her opposite leg. When I reach her foot, I rest her leg back on the mattress, then kneel in front of her on the bed, pulling her into a kneeling position with me.

Her eyes don't waver from mine as I lift the flowing, cotton dress over her head. When I reach behind her body to unclasp her bra, she remains motionless, allowing me to slide the straps down her arms, leaving her completely bared to me.

My hand splayed on her lower back and the other digging into her hair, I pull her toward me, our mouths colliding in a wanton and revealing kiss. For the first time, I actually feel like I'm kissing Nora. I finally know all her scars, all her fears. And she's willing to face all of them for me.

A small voice reminds me I'm only making matters worse by continuing on with this charade. That every second I spend with her and don't tell her the truth is another lie I'm saddling her with. But this woman is a drug. I need just one more hit, despite the devastation I'll leave in my wake.

Curving toward her, I delicately ease her onto her back, my lips never straying from hers. I revel in the sensation of her lustrous skin beneath my hands. Skin I have no right to touch, but I can't stop. Can't pull myself away. I doubt I'll ever be able to, even when this ends. Even when the truth rains down on us.

Gripping her thigh, I hook her leg around my waist, gently thrusting against her.

"Anderson," she moans into our kiss, my name coming out as a cross between a prayer and a plea.

With torturously slow movements, I skate my hand along her waist, her breathing increasing the closer I get to her sex. As I slide my finger along her clit, she releases a noiseless gasp.

"I need you inside me," she murmurs against my mouth. "I need you to make love to me."

I lift myself from the bed, pushing down my shorts in

one swift movement before returning to her. Kneeling between her legs, I take a moment to admire her beauty, brushing her hair out of her face.

Whenever I peered at Nora today, I saw the woman I pulled from the wreck. Saw her desperate eyes. Heard her anguished cries. But right now, I don't see any of that. In this moment in time, that's not part of our story. At some point, we'll have no choice but to make it part of the fabric of who we are, but right now, I see the Nora who decided to meditate in a busy Chicago diner. Who made me stop at every rundown gas station between Chicago and here. Who's given me the adventure of a lifetime, one I'll always cherish, despite the inevitable end.

"I know it's kind of late to be asking you this, considering we've already had unprotected sex, but are you on birth control?"

"It *is* kind of late." She smirks. "But yes, I'm on the pill. After Hunter and Ember, well… It kind of ruined me for wanting kids."

I drape my body over hers, pressing my lips to hers, wanting to take away the memory of everything she lost. "Not here," I whisper. "Not now. It's just us."

She melts into my kiss. "Just us."

I reach down and ease my way inside her, slowly at first, reacquainting myself with this woman I've grown to know so well, even in such a short period of time. I keep her head held tightly in my hands as I continue moving inside her, our eyes never straying from each other, the tether binding us unbreakable.

The sex last night was incredible. Watching her let loose with me and release all her inhibitions was truly a sight to behold. But this moment is so much bigger than that.

We don't need the distraction of heavy breathing and

loud moans. Not here. All we need is to lose ourselves in each other. To bare ourselves to each other. To be scared with each other. To fall into each other.

And I have fallen. Hopelessly. Mercilessly. Impossibly. This woman walked straight into my life and possessed my heart, like she always owned it. She tore through the walls I've hidden behind and breathed air back into my lungs.

Our lives may not fit together. Our story may end tragically. But for now, I find comfort in the fact that our hearts beat as one, even if for only a passing moment.

Chapter Thirty

NORA

SUNLIGHT SEEPS THROUGH the plantation shutters, and I release a contented sigh. For once, I'm at peace. I'm exactly where I need to be. *Anderson* is exactly where I need to be.

Once we were able to keep our hands off each other for more than a few seconds last night, we ordered room service, not wanting to leave this suite for anything, not even food. But shortly after we finished our dinner of lamb and paella, Anderson got dressed and told me he needed to take care of something. It made me nervous, worried he was pushing me away again.

But he returned a few minutes later, knocking on the door, despite having a key. When I opened it and saw the bottle in his hand, I realized he was keeping with the tradition we started at the beginning of this adventure. Knocking on my door with a smile and bottle of wine, hoping to spend more time together.

All throughout the evening, as we savored our wine and I lay snuggled against Anderson's firm chest, the love story between Terry McKay and Nickie Ferrante playing before us, I couldn't help but reflect back to the first night we'd watched *An Affair to Remember*. Anderson had remarked on the similarities between their story and ours. At the time, I thought the only similarity was that we'd both formed a friendship while away from home.

That's no longer the case.

Now I understand all too well the heartache the characters must have experienced when the boat arrived in New York City and they were tugged in two separate directions, the only shining light their promise to meet again in six months. I hate the idea of being away from Anderson for more than six days. I doubt I'd survive six months.

A supple mouth feathers against my shoulder blade, and I sigh as Anderson tightens his arm around me, pulling me closer. He pushes my messy locks over my shoulder, moving his lips toward my neck, shivers rolling down my spine.

"This is what I've been fantasizing about," I murmur, my voice scratchy from sleep.

"What?" He playfully circles his hips against me, making his need for me known. "Morning sex? Pretty sure we checked that off our list yesterday."

"No. Not morning sex. Although I'm certainly looking forward to that." I wiggle against him, and he grips my hip with hungry fingers.

"Then what have you been fantasizing about?"

I roll over, brushing his hair out of his face. The more I look at him, the more I see Prince Gabriel in his features. His eyes. His dimples. His wicked smile. But I also still see Anderson North. *My* Anderson.

"This is the first morning you're beside me when I wake up. Every other morning, I've woken up alone. Even yesterday. Sure, you were in the room, but you weren't with me. I like that you're finally with me."

"There's no place I'd rather be than with you, Nora."

He captures my lips in a teasing kiss before he retreats, propping himself up on an elbow. He runs a delicate finger along my ribs as a thoughtful expression crosses his face, brows pulled in, mouth pinched. Then he peers down at me. "How much wiggle room do we have in your schedule?"

It's a little thing, but my chest expands at his use of the word "we", like we're finally on this journey together, instead of two people on their own trajectory who crossed paths for a few days. We may have to go our separate ways when this comes to an end, but for now, this is our journey. *Our* adventure.

"Why?"

"Instead of hitting the road, what do you think about staying here another night? Explore Santa Fe. Go to some art galleries." He waggles his brows. "Stop for some food where I'll get under the table and make it impossible for you to talk."

Feigning indignation, I playfully slap him, although I like the idea of him making it impossible for me to talk.

His chuckles fade, expression becoming serious once more. "What do you say? Let's spend the day together."

"We spend every day together," I remind him.

It's barely noticeable, and if I blinked, I wouldn't have seen it, but I catch Anderson's eyes flick to the desk where I'd placed the canister containing Hunter's ashes.

My heart falls, my stomach churning. "Oh."

I can't imagine what's going through Anderson's head. No wonder he was so distant yesterday. Why hadn't I realized it before now? Of course he'd be aloof. We slept together, yet the instant we were back on the road, my focus was on Hunter and spreading his ashes at every spot on the list without a single regard for how it must make Anderson feel. If I were in his shoes, I'd question things, too, keep my heart guarded, wonder if there will always be a ghost between us.

Rolling away from him, I slip out of bed and pad across the floor, the hardwood cool on my feet.

"It's okay if you don't, Nora. I just…" He trails off as

he watches me grab the ashes from the desk.

As I flash him a slight smile, I walk toward the bed. Confusion flashes on his face before I turn to the ottoman where my suitcase sits. Unzipping it, I do something I've refused to do since I started on this journey. I bury the reminder of Hunter, placing the canister in my suitcase, hiding it beneath my clothes.

His stare traces my motions as I rejoin him underneath the duvet. Caressing his mouth with mine, I kiss him fully before pulling back. I cup his cheek in my hand, relishing in the scratching of his facial hair against my skin.

"Anderson, I'd love nothing more than to spend the day with you…"

I push him onto his back and straddle him, his pupils dilating as I circle my hips, reawakening his desire. He groans as I rub his arousal against me, then ease him inside. Leaning down, I breathe into him.

"And only you."

* * *

Anderson's fingers intertwine with mine as we stroll along the streets of downtown Santa Fe later that afternoon. I've never seen anything quite as remarkable as this city. The pueblo architecture. The bright colors. The art. It makes me wish I had more time here.

"Guilty pleasure?" Anderson asks, glancing at me.

Throughout the afternoon, we've taken the opportunity to learn more about each other. Our upbringing. Our families. Our fears. All things I've gotten a taste of, but we never discussed in detail. It's refreshing to share these things and not hide behind a mask. Everything's out in the open. For both of us.

"Sex with a hot prince," I answer without a moment's

hesitation.

Lust in his eyes, he pulls me to a stop and leans toward me, his breath warming my neck. "Glad you think I'm pleasurable." His finger grazes a sliver of exposed skin along my hipbone, fanning the flames of my desire. Then he retreats. "But I hope you don't feel guilty about this."

I raise myself onto my toes, brushing my lips against his. "I don't. Do you?"

He shakes his head. "Not for a second." He kisses me again, then grabs my hand, leading me along the busy street that's overflowing with tourists enjoying the beautiful weather. The sun is shining. Birds are chirping. And I have a hot guy beside me. Could life get any better?

"How about you? What's your guilty pleasure?"

He smirks. "Sex with a beautiful American woman."

I playfully pinch him in the side. "You stole my answer."

"No. You said your guilty pleasure was sex with a hot prince, not a beautiful American woman. Although I'm willing to accommodate if you're into that."

Yanking his hand, I pull him toward a clay building. I lean my back against it, forcing his body against mine. "Are you telling me I don't satisfy you on my own?" I rub against him. "Doesn't feel that way to me."

"Oh, gorgeous, you do more than satisfy me. You drive me wild." His tone is gruff, sending a thrill through me. "The mere notion of being deep inside you has me hungry for another taste." He nuzzles my neck, running his tongue along the length.

I no longer care that we're in public on a very busy street with dozens of people sidestepping us. A few give him a second glance, most likely finding his appearance familiar. But as has been the case throughout our journey, they brush it off, probably thinking he's simply some celebrity doppelgänger.

"Makes me want to lift this skirt and fuck you right here."

"Bad boy," I tease in a breathy voice.

"Only with you." He pulls back, the fire in his depths transforming into something more meaningful, but still as vivid and intense. "You make me want to break all my rules, Nora. Hell, you make me want to set the rule book aflame and start over again from the beginning. With you."

His words cause my heart to swell, the hairs on my nape standing on end. "Some things are worth breaking the rules for," I murmur.

"And I get the feeling you're *more* than worth breaking my rules for." He seals his mouth over mine, his kiss gentle, like that first snowfall of the year. Innocent, beautiful, serene.

He gradually releases his hold on me and links our fingers, resuming our leisurely stroll. Neither one of us speaks for several minutes. There's something magical about not polluting the silence with words. I don't have to focus on what comes out of his mouth, listening to his body's distinct language instead.

"Let's go in here," I suggest when we come upon an art gallery.

We've passed quite a few, but this one catches my attention. The display window in front showcases a large photo split between three canvases of a Native American woman overlooking the plains. The lower saturation and vibrancy of the colors make it appear haunting in its simplicity, reminding me of some of the images I've seen Anderson export onto his laptop and tweak.

"Sure."

We walk into the large, open gallery, more images of Native Americans hanging on the plain white walls. I read a placard explaining the exhibit is to showcase the connection between Native American traditions and modern society. The photographer certainly captured it. There's an image of a young man in traditional Native American headdress standing between the shelves at what appears to be a college library. Two women holding hands, draped in cloaks with tribal markings, their son between them. A teenager wearing Indian-inspired jewelry, as well as a sash declaring her the winner of a beauty pageant. A clash of two distinct cultures.

"Have you ever considered showing your work?" I ask Anderson quietly as we study a young man in war paint, a cell phone visible in his outstretched hands.

"Nah," he responds, brushing it off, averting his gaze.

"Why not? I've seen some of the stuff you've shot. It's really good." I nod at the image in front of us. "Just as thought-provoking as this."

He turns from me, grabbing my hand and continuing through the gallery, admiring antique Native American jewelry on display in the center of the room. "I *have* considered it before," he admits. "In fact, I once had an exhibit booked." A nostalgic smile lights up his face. "Kendall actually encouraged me to do it. To step outside my comfort zone."

"What kind of exhibit?"

He looks forward, keeping my hand clutched in his as we head into another room. "In my…position, I do a bit of traveling."

"I imagine."

"I started a foundation years ago," he continues, his voice barely more than a whisper. "A clean water initiative. We both grew up in countries where clean water generally isn't a problem. But it is for so many. And without clean water, health complications abound. Every so often, I travel to one of the places where my foundation hopes to provide locals with resources to deliver clean water. The people always fascinate me. They have nothing, Nora. Absolutely nothing."

The more he speaks, the more impassioned he becomes. I can tell this isn't simply a charity he slaps his name onto for the positive publicity, but something he genuinely cares about. Another piece of the Prince Gabriel Anderson puzzle.

"But they're always so happy. They invite me into their village, prepare this huge feast. Even slaughter the pig they've been raising for years. Just to feed me."

"It sounds like a very rewarding venture."

"It is. Anytime I want to complain about something in my life, I remember their generosity."

I nod, a beat passing before speaking again. "So you've photographed them?"

"Yes. With their permission, of course."

"Naturally."

"This was years ago now, but I wanted people to see what I do when I visit these villages. Wanted to instill the same humility I experience. I wanted to show these places where a family of ten lives in a hut no bigger than this room…" He gestures around the space, which is probably only ten by fifteen feet. "But they're happy. They don't need material things. Don't need the latest game system or iPhone. They have each other. In my eyes, that's what makes them wealthy beyond measure."

"And the exhibit?"

He worries his lower lip, the excitement draining from his expression. "Kendall died a few weeks before it was supposed to premier. After that, I couldn't stand the thought of going through with it. Of being surrounded by the memories of her, considering it was her encouragement and motivation that made it happen."

"Maybe that's exactly *why* you should do it. You have unfinished business."

"I don't—"

"You do, Anderson. Trust me. I get it. It took me six years to take this trip Hunter and I had planned. I was so scared of what it would mean. I avoided this because I didn't want to let go of the one thing of Hunter I had left. Just like your exhibit. The one thing you have left with Kendall."

He closes his eyes, his silence the only confirmation I need that I'm right.

"And if I'm being honest, I wish I'd taken this trip sooner. It would have saved me from a lot of bad decisions and a marriage to a gay man," I add in an attempt to get a laugh out of him.

Instead, he brings his hand to my face, cupping my cheek. I melt into his touch, inhaling his calming scent of ocean breeze and something else that is quintessentially Anderson. His lips skim mine in a simple kiss that lights my soul on fire.

"For what it's worth, I'm glad you didn't take this trip until now."

"I am, too."

Chapter Thirty-One

ANDERSON

I STEAL A glance at Nora as we sit at yet another stoplight. Over the course of the past several hours, we've watched the sparsely populated areas that make up most of Route 66 transition into more heavily developed towns. Now we're almost at the finish line. Just another ten miles or so until our adventure is over.

What I wouldn't give to turn this car around and start this journey again. To stay in this bubble.

The last few days have been some of the best of my life. They were certainly the most satisfying and fulfilling since I lost Kendall. An easygoing atmosphere had settled between Nora and I as we traveled through New Mexico and into Arizona before navigating through Sitgreaves Pass and entering California.

We posed with a giant jackrabbit at the Jackrabbit Trading Post in Joseph City. We stood on a corner in Winslow, Arizona, that was complete with a red flatbed Ford, an homage to the classic Eagles tune. We had to navigate around burros roaming the streets in Oatman. And we marveled at the majesty of nature as we admired the Grand Canyon, having taken a detour to visit since we were so close.

In each place, Nora left more of Hunter's remains. Instead of it being a solemn event as she was forced to say goodbye to another piece of him, it seemed to lighten her load. She was no longer filled with sorrow, thinking how much Hunter would enjoy the kitschy shops in Seligman, Arizona, or the giant rooms in the shape of teepees at the Wigwam Hotel in Holbrook. With each throw of his ashes, she cut another tether keeping her bound to her past.

Sensing my eyes on her, Nora looks at me, offering me a smile, but I can tell it's contrived. She's as twisted up inside as me.

"You doing okay?" I ask.

The light turns green, and I shift into first, creeping along Sunset Boulevard in Hollywood. My left leg aches from the constant stop and go of traffic, requiring me to use the clutch more than I have the entire trip. I try not to focus on it. Try to tell myself it's not my body giving up on me. That I'd be sore even if I didn't have MS.

"Of course." She quickly nods, her voice more high-pitched than normal.

"It's okay if you're not. This is your final goodbye."

She brings her gaze to mine. "It's not today's goodbye I'm dreading."

I nod, swallowing through the pain, the vice-like grip on my heart threatening to undo me. I grab her hand and bring it to my lips, brushing her knuckles, trying to offer her the comfort she needs. That *I* need.

Like Nora, I've been apprehensive about reaching the end of the road. Not just because I'll have to say goodbye, but because I have to decide what to tell her. Do I let her go home without knowing the truth, her feelings for me still intact? Or do I tell her about my involvement in the night her life was ruined, forcing her to see me for what I really am?

After another hour of navigating heavy traffic through Hollywood, Beverly Hills, and Brentwood, we hit Ocean Avenue in Santa Monica and turn left, no longer able to continue West any farther.

I drive south along the coastal road, joggers and cyclists getting exercise in the park to our right, tourists filling the sidewalks and stopping for food at the restaurants lining the street to our left. The bright sun glimmers on the ocean, surfers cresting on the waves. When I first decided to drive across the country, since I wasn't sure how much longer I'd be able to do something like this, I looked forward to reaching California. To have some time here to decompress before needing to return home and address my diagnosis.

Now, I'd give anything to have more time on the road, crappy motel rooms and all.

When we reach Santa Monica Pier, I turn onto the wooden structure and navigate toward the parking area. Even after I kill the ignition and yank on the brake, neither one of us makes a move to get out. Seagulls squawk overhead as the occasional thunder of the rollercoaster booms around us. But it's muted, our bubble blocking the outside world.

Nora lifts her sad eyes, swallowing hard. "I don't want to open the door."

I bring my hand to her face, and she melts into my touch. "Either do I. But we came this far. We have to see this through to the end." I glance at the brightly colored buildings on the pier, the Ferris wheel turning a slow circle beneath the picturesque backdrop of the California coast. "And that's the end right there. It's within your grasp. Time to close this chapter."

She squeezes her eyes shut and pulls in a deep breath. On a long exhale, she returns her gaze to mine and nods. "Okay. Let's turn that page."

I leave a tender kiss on her nose, then jump out of the Jeep, rushing to help her. She places her hand in mine and I squeeze, leading her up toward the frivolity and carnival atmosphere of what's become the point of celebration for most Route 66 travelers. But for us, it marks the ceremonial end of the adventure we'd give anything to continue.

The smell of fry oil and sugar, mixed with briny, ocean air, greets us as we maneuver through hordes of people walking in every direction, the wood groaning beneath our feet. Bells ding from the myriad of carnival games as excited children run past us, their parents hurriedly trying to catch up. I notice Nora touch her stomach, probably thinking that could have been her.

If it weren't for me.

As we make our way past the rollercoaster and Ferris wheel, the crowd thins substantially, the only people out this far a few couples strolling hand-in-hand as the sun inches closer to the horizon.

We come to a stop at the end of the pier and stare into the distance. The wind whips Nora's hair in front of her, but she does nothing to smooth it back. It's a complete contrast to the woman I first met nearly two weeks ago. Hair impeccable. Makeup covering her face like a mask. The picture of perfection. Now she's content to be a little messy. Life *is* messy. We're both living proof of that.

"At least the wind isn't blowing straight at us," I joke, cutting through the tension. "Otherwise, I fear this scene would be reminiscent of *The Big Lebowski*."

"Goddammit, Walter!" Nora laughs, quoting what Jeff Bridges' iconic character said when he'd attempted to spread their friend's remains, a typical California wind blowing them back on both men.

With a calming inhale, she reaches into her bag, withdrawing the canister for the last time. A bittersweet smile pulls on her mouth as she stares at it, a single tear cascading down her cheek.

"Do you want to say anything?" I encourage, not wanting her to feel like she shouldn't make a big deal out of this for my sake.

"I didn't plan on it. Do you think I should?"

"If you want." I start to step away, giving the moment the deference it deserves, but she grabs my wrist, preventing me from doing so, an unspoken request. I nod, remaining at her side, although I feel like an intruder being here.

She takes a second to collect her thoughts, peering at the miles and miles of ocean in front of us. I can faintly make out the outline of Catalina Island toward the southwest. Other than that, there's nothing but sparkling water.

"I'll never forget the day my cell buzzed with an incoming text from a number I didn't recognize," she begins after several long moments, smiling through the nostalgic tears brimming behind her lids. "I almost didn't respond. It was obviously a wrong number. I would have remembered going out for drinks the night before with a guy who sounded as endearing as you. Your words made it seem that you liked whomever you thought you were texting. If I were in your shoes, I would have wanted to know my affections were being wasted.

"Turned out, your affections *were* being wasted, that she intentionally gave you the wrong number. I'm just lucky she gave you mine. For weeks, we exchanged texts. Shared parts of ourselves with each other. Parts I never shared with anyone. It was so refreshing to talk to someone I could just be myself around with no judgment." She chuckles, rolling her eyes. "You know how my mother can be.

"The night we agreed to meet after months of

exchanging messages and late-night phone calls, I almost turned around a dozen times. I was so worried it would change what I felt in my heart. Worried that the playful banter and flirtatious jokes wouldn't be the same once we met in person. But it was. In fact, it was better." She smiles, swiping away at her tears, the moment overwhelming her.

"You were my first serious relationship. My first love." She chokes out a sob. "And my first heartbreak. After you died, I didn't think I'd ever be able to move on, that I'd ever find what I had with you." She gradually tilts her head, her gaze locking on mine. "Up until two weeks ago, that was the case." Her lips tease at a grin. "But now I know it's okay to live my life again. To allow you to live on, but only in my memories."

With a shaky breath, she slowly turns over the canister, dumping the final remnants of Hunter's ashes into the ocean below us. We both watch as the sea takes him, spreading him along its waves and crests.

"Take care of Ember," she strains to say. "All little girls need their daddies. I'm glad she has hers, that she's not alone. That *you're* not alone. I love you, Hunter, with all my heart. But it's time I let you go."

I reach for her hand and squeeze it, giving her the encouragement she needs. Then she looks at me, her mouth curving up in the corners, serenity crossing her expression.

"Because I found someone worth letting you go for. And he deserves all of me, not just the broken pieces."

I no longer care what's appropriate and what's overstepping my bounds during this personal moment. One she wanted to share with me. To let me know she's relinquishing the ghost that's been between us since the beginning. That she's ready for it to be just us.

Her cheeks clutched in my hands, I press my lips to

hers, my kiss respectful but still greedy at the same time. I breathe into her, my grip tight, my admiration for this woman growing with every second, every swipe of her tongue, every heartbeat.

Because with every second, every swipe of her tongue, every heartbeat, my time with her grows shorter and shorter. I no longer want that to be the case. Not now that she's finally free, finally let go of Hunter. Now I want nothing more than to run away with her where we can have a future of our own. Free from our past. Free from my future. And free from the truth that will inevitably be our undoing.

I pull back, peering down into her eyes I'd give anything to wake up to every morning. "Come on. Time to write the next chapter of your life."

"I like the sound of that." She links her fingers with mine, and I lead her away, her steps light and shoulders no longer carrying the weight of her grief.

Chapter Thirty-Two

NORA

"WHAT IS THIS place?" I squint as I peer up at the high-rise building a mile or so north of Santa Monica Pier. The glass panes glimmer in the late afternoon sun, fractals of light bouncing off it.

"You'll see." Anderson smirks as both our doors are opened simultaneously by men in shorts and a polo shirt, obviously valet attendants.

"Afternoon, Ms. Tremblay," the man who opened my door greets, smiling as he helps me out of the Wrangler.

"Welcome back, Your Highness," the attendant at Anderson's side states.

I pause in my tracks, his acknowledgment striking me, leaving me momentarily stunned. It's the first time I've heard anyone address Anderson that way. I'm not sure how to process it. I still struggle to see him as royalty. To me, he's just the cocky man who offered to help when I needed it most. Who had faith we'd see each other again, and that faith brought us back together.

"I trust you had a pleasant journey," the valet continues, following him toward the back of the Wrangler.

"It was the adventure of a lifetime," Anderson answers in a formal tone I'm not used to hearing from him. It's lacking the ease and familiarity I've grown accustomed to. I imagine this is his Prince Gabriel voice. "You'll see that our bags are brought up?"

"Certainly, Your Highness."

Anderson removes several large bills from his wallet and hands one to each of the attendants before placing his hand on my lower back, ushering me, wide-eyed and bewildered, into the building.

Everything in the cavernous lobby is marble and crystal, the aroma of fresh-cut flowers and ocean breeze filtering into my senses. Leather couches and reading chairs are arranged in small groupings, but it's not densely furnished.

We only make it a few steps before a man hurries out of one of the few offices located off the lobby. His dark hair is impeccable and slicked back, his eggplant-colored tie perfectly straight, not a single wrinkle to be found on his navy blue suit or light purple shirt.

"Your Highness," he exclaims jovially, approaching us with a wide smile. "So wonderful to see you again."

"It's good to be back in LA, if for only a few days."

I note that the man doesn't extend his hand toward Anderson, at least not right away. He waits until Anderson offers his for a shake before taking it. I wonder if that's some sort of protocol. I imagine it must be.

"As always, we hope to make it as difficult for you to leave as possible," he says with a flourish, leading us past a round table in the center of the room, a crystal chandelier overhead. An arrangement of white lilies and irises overflows from a large vase.

When we approach the elevator bank, the man presses the button, barely even stealing a glance in my direction, as if pretending I don't exist. Able to sense my thoughts, Anderson pulls me closer, wordlessly reminding me that I do.

"Everything has been prepared as requested. The

kitchen is stocked, as is the wine cellar. Is there anything else you require?"

"This is only a short stay."

The man finally looks my way, giving me a once-over before returning his attention to Anderson. "Yes. Of course." The elevator dings, steel doors opening to invite us inside.

"Thank you for your assistance," Anderson offers with authority, effectively dismissing him.

"It's my pleasure." The man reaches into his pocket and holds a business card toward Anderson, who takes it. "If you have any additional requirements, do not hesitate to reach out, no matter the hour."

He simply nods, then ushers me into the elevator. After he punches a code into the keypad, he hits the button for PH1, which I can only assume is for the first floor of the penthouse. The second the doors close, we both expel a breath. But it does nothing to push aside the unease coiling in the pit of my stomach. The way that man looked at me made me feel like I was just another woman Anderson brought here for a few days. It's probably irrational, but I always thought I was different. He always made me *feel* like I was different. What if I'm not? What if he's not on the same page as I am. Do I even know what page we're on?

"Are you okay?"

"Is this what it's always like for you?" I blurt out.

"What do you mean?" he pushes, sensing there's more behind my question than simply wondering if he's always waited on like this when people know who he is.

"Do people always fawn over you, then look at whatever girl you're with like they have no idea how she caught your eye? Because, believe me, I have no idea how it happened and still question it—"

He cups my cheeks, cutting me off. "Don't." His gruff

voice is filled with emotion. "Don't ever question why I'm with you. Your soul spoke to me the second I felt it. This is why I didn't tell you who I was. Why I normally don't tell anyone until I…"

"Until you?" I urge when he pauses.

His expression softens. "Until I know it's real. And I knew from the very beginning this was real. It just took a little while for my head to catch up to my heart."

The door slides open and he winks, grabbing my hand and leading me out of the elevator and into one of the most glamorous places I've ever seen. It even edges out Julian and Evie's penthouse apartment overlooking Columbus Circle, albeit on a smaller scale.

I pull away from Anderson, taking in my surroundings. Everything is rich wood, neutral tones, and iron accents. Natural light saturates the space, thanks to the floor-to-ceiling windows filling several of the walls. I move past the more formal sitting area, through an open-concept kitchen, and into another sitting area, walking up to the large glass doors. Anderson follows, pressing a button on the adjacent wall, the doors sliding open.

Mesmerized by the view of the setting sun, I step onto the balcony. A breeze blows around me, causing a chill to trickle down my spine, and I shiver. Anderson wraps his arms around me, pulling me back against him.

"This is stunning," I exhale.

"If you're into that sort of thing."

I spin in his embrace, but he doesn't release his hold. "You can't stand there and say you don't find this view spectacular."

With strenuous patience, he gradually erases the space separating our mouths, covering mine in a soft kiss.

"Now I do."

He increases the pressure, swiping his tongue along my lips. I part them, his kiss caressing, entwining, enticing. He pulls back, framing my face in his large hands.

"The view right here is much more spectacular than any boring sunset." Then he returns his attention to the miles of ocean, turning me around, keeping me in his arms. "But the sunset's not too bad to look at, either."

"No, it's not."

We watch the remnants of the day disappear over the horizon, the sky now a purple hue as night descends. I struggle to swallow through the lump building in my throat over the thought that we only have one more sunset together.

"Come on." He links his fingers with mine and pulls me back inside, leading me toward a staircase off the entryway. "I'll give you the grand tour. Then I'll cook you dinner."

"You…cook?"

"Don't sound so surprised. I quite enjoy cooking. It relaxes me."

"You won't hear any complaints out of me. It'll be nice to have a home-cooked meal after these past few weeks of eating mostly diner food."

"And to stay somewhere with soundproof walls." He pulls me into a master bedroom that's bigger than my entire apartment. A king-sized bed sits in the middle, a fireplace and sitting area tucked into the corner. As I fantasize about all the fun we'll have on that bed, he leans toward me. "No one will be able to hear your screams."

I whirl around, crossing my arms, and give him a playful look of disapproval. "That's something serial killers say. How do I know this isn't some five-star torture chamber?"

His eyes flame with desire as he drags me into his arms, pushing his arousal against me. "Oh, gorgeous, the only thing I plan on torturing you with is orgasm after orgasm." Feather-light kisses fall along my neckline, causing my pulse to increase.

"Well, then, lock me up and throw away the key."

With quick motions, he grabs both of my wrists and hoists them over my head. Holding them in one hand, he uses the other to lead me toward the bed. "That can be arranged." He lowers me to the surface, covering my body with his.

"What happened to dinner?" I pant as he snakes down my frame, lifting the hem of my dress and yanking my panties off.

"I figured we could both enjoy a little *amuse-bouche* beforehand." He licks his lips, his sinful eyes locking with mine. "A little something to whet our appetites."

When he flicks his tongue against my clit, I moan, threading my fingers into his hair as I succumb to his touch, forgetting about Hunter's ashes that now lay scattered across the country. About the uncertainty of what tomorrow may bring.

Our journey may be over, but I can't shake the feeling that our adventure together is just beginning.

Chapter Thirty-Three

ANDERSON

THE EARLY MORNING glow filters into the room as the sun slowly creeps over the mountains, bathing LA with light. My thoughts are all jumbled, as seems to be the case with Nora. Maybe if I didn't have this huge secret eating away at me, I'd be able to enjoy these last precious hours we have.

I should have stopped this charade days ago. But I couldn't find the wherewithal to come clean and walk away, like she deserves. Now I've backed myself into a corner of my own making. There must be some way I can tell her the truth and keep the girl, too. And I have twenty-four hours to figure out how.

The clicking of the shutter echoes against the gentle sounds of Nora's breathing, as well as the subtle ocean waves that can be heard through the crack in the sliding glass door, even a dozen stories up. I check the focus on the image in my viewfinder, then snap several more photos in quick succession.

Peace surrounds me as I admire Nora's sleeping form. Her back toward me, her hair sprawled on the pillow comforting her. The white down comforter sits a breath below her waist, revealing a hint of her ass. That's not what drove my need to photograph her from this angle, though. It's the line of her spine and the way the rising sun casts a beam along her face. So serene. So tranquil.

So beautiful.

She moans, rolling over, as if I'm the sun and she's a flower, constantly seeking me out. Her eyelids flutter open, her gaze falling on me. "What are you doing?"

"Taking your photo," I answer in a soft voice, not wanting to break the mood.

"Perv," she jokes.

"No." I shake my head, remaining in my reading chair. "I'm simply appreciating the masterpiece in front of me. Your body is a work of art, Nora, worthy of being admired and revered by all who see it." I pause, smirking. "But I want to be the only one who's lucky enough to do so."

"You have free admission to the Museum of Nora any time you'd like."

"I'll hold you to that." I smile, although it doesn't reach my eyes. Once she learns the truth, she'll retract that offer.

I tentatively return to taking her photo, waiting for her to tell me to stop, but she doesn't. Her eyes lock with mine through the lens.

"How do you want me?" she murmurs seductively.

My pulse skyrockets, my dick hardening. When Nora steals a glance below my waist and grins, I know she notices how much she turns me on. She always has. But this… The idea of photographing her like this makes me ache for her even more.

I stand, not trying to hide my erection straining against my gym shorts, and walk to her. I push her hair out of her face, smoothing it behind her ear.

"Can I pose you?"

Stare trained on mine, she nods.

Silence fills the room as I place her the way I want, her body pliant and agreeable to my desires. I keep her on her side facing me, but take the arm beneath her and extend it, resting her head on it. When I pull the duvet off, she doesn't protest, baring herself to me. I set one leg on top of the other, bending her knees slightly. Then I place her other arm along the silhouette of her body, encouraging it to mold to her hourglass figure.

I step back, admiring her frame in the tranquil light. I make a few minor adjustments to some angles before returning to my chair and checking the focus.

"You sure?"

She doesn't say anything, only nods.

I continue snapping away, concentrating on different parts of her body with each frame, starting at her peaceful expression, making my way down to her supple breasts, the curve of her waist, her stunning legs.

"You can move now if you want."

"Move?"

"Or we can stop. Whatever you're comfortable with. I'll follow your lead. Sometimes the best shots happen when you let the model do what she wants."

Her pupils darken as she props herself up. "Do whatever I want?"

My pulse increases at the sensuality in her tone. I swallow hard. "Anything. No limits."

"No limits," she repeats, closing her eyes and returning to the same position I'd posed her in, remaining motionless for several moments.

Then the hand resting along her silhouette moves, slowly, gradually, tentatively. It travels along her waist, caressing her stomach, before continuing up to her breast. When she squeezes, my breathing increases, echoing in the stillness of the room.

She levels her gaze on mine, a devilish glint within. "Shouldn't you be snapping photos?"

I return my camera to my face and feverishly click away. When she rolls onto her back, I stand, skirting around the bed to shoot from a better angle.

A few weeks ago, I doubt Nora would have done anything like this, still trapped in whatever cage she'd locked herself in years ago. Hell, she probably wouldn't have done this a few *days* ago. But I saw it the instant she dumped those ashes into the ocean. She's finally free. And I want nothing more than to keep feeding this newfound freedom.

I squat at the end of the bed, shooting her from this low angle, the camera capturing how addictive her curves are, how beautiful she looks as she explores her own body, comfortable enough with me to do so in my presence.

She bends her knees, propping up her legs and spreading them, revealing herself to me. My jaw tenses, every inch of me frozen in place. I'm unable to move, to breathe, to think. This may be one of the most erotic moments of my life.

"Go ahead," she whispers, her hand continuing its tortuously slow journey down her body. "Take your photos. These better not end up on the wall of some gallery, though."

"Not a chance in hell am I sharing you like this," I respond in a gruff tone. "These are for my own personal collection to jack-off to."

"Glad to know I'm spank-bank material."

"Oh, gorgeous, you're more than spank-bank material," I assure her.

She keeps her gaze trained on me for several protracted moments, the atmosphere shifting from light and playful to thick with sexual tension. Chewing on her bottom lip, she slides her hand past her waist.

When she toys with her folds, spreading her wetness around, it takes everything I have to not throw the camera to the side and bury my face in her, to be the one giving her the pleasure building on her expression as she rubs her clit. But even though I'm not touching her, I'm still the reason her breathing is ragged, her complexion flushed.

I raise myself to my full height, snapping a few photos of her from above, one hand squeezing her breast, the other between her legs as she pleasures herself.

"Pull your nipple," I demand through a clenched jaw.

She focuses her eyes on mine before closing them once more and following my command. I hiss out a breath, struggling not to touch her. But this is infinitely more erotic. More…intimate.

Her chest heaves as she teases herself, pulling on her nipple and slipping a finger inside her sex. When a tiny moan escapes, I can no longer control myself. I toss the camera onto the bed and free my erection from my shorts. Noticing the lack of a constant shutter clicking, Nora looks at me, watching me stroke my cock.

Spreading her legs wider, she removes her fingers, giving me permission to take their place, but I shake my head.

"No. Like this." I continue pumping my dick with my hand. "I want us to get off like this."

A shiver visibly rolls through her and she returns her fingers to where they were, her breathing becoming more erratic and uneven, matching my own.

"I won't last much longer," she warns.

"Trust me, gorgeous. Watching you like this? I won't last long, period. You're so fucking hot. So fucking beautiful. So fucking mine."

With each word, her whimpers grow louder as she pulses her hips against her hand, desperately seeking release, until her body spasms, her cries reverberating against the walls.

"Fuck," I grunt, increasing my motions. I step closer

to her, running my free hand along her waist, then disappearing between her thighs, taking the place of her fingers. Her wet and greedy body pushes me closer to the edge. "I'm about to come."

"Okay," she breathes.

I look around for a towel, anything, but she grabs my forearm.

"On me."

Fuck.

I kneel on the mattress, slipping my fingers back between her thighs, pumping my cock feverishly until I can't control myself anymore and release onto her stomach, my body convulsing.

Unable to go another minute without feeling her lips against mine, I hover over her, slamming my mouth to hers, my tongue caressing, tangling, taking.

"Goddamn, baby," I exhale when I pull back. "That may have been one of the hottest things I've ever seen in my life. You make it difficult for a man to walk away from you."

"Good." She captures my kiss once more as my phone chimes on the nightstand.

But I ignore it, kissing her deeper.

"Aren't you going to get that?"

"It's not even seven in the morning," I answer.

"Exactly. Might be important."

I groan, reluctantly tearing my lips from hers. Glancing at the screen, I see my sister's name. Normally, I'd let it go to voicemail, but I *did* call her in the middle of the night, desperate to talk to her about what to do now that I'm mere hours away from leaving Nora.

I place one last kiss on Nora's mouth before standing. "I need a minute, then I'll bring you some coffee."

Grabbing my cell, I dash to the bathroom, retrieving

a towel and handing it to Nora as I raise my phone up to my ear and tug on a pair of shorts.

"Hey, Esme." I steal one more glance at Nora before disappearing out of the master bedroom, heading up to the office on the third floor, needing to have this conversation in private.

"Anders. I'm sorry I missed your call."

"It's okay. It was… What? Four in the morning your time when I called?"

"Something like that." It's silent while I close the door and sit behind the desk. "So how are you?"

I release a long sigh, scrubbing a hand over my face, unsure how to answer her question. This is my last full day with Nora. Tomorrow, we'll board my plane and fly to JFK, where we'll go our separate ways. I'm just grateful I finally convinced her to cancel her coach seat on a commercial flight. Regardless, I still don't know what I plan to tell her when we land. What kind of promises I'll make. What kind of secrets I'll reveal.

"That good, huh?" she retorts with a laugh.

"How can you tell?"

"Because I know you better than anyone. You may be thousands of miles away, but I can feel your turmoil. You're caught between having a clear conscience and a broken heart."

I don't know how she does it, but Esme's always had an uncanny ability to analyze things and boil them down to the most simplistic terms. This situation I've found myself in is as complex and convoluted as they come. But she's right. What it all comes down to is deciding between leaving my conscience or my heart intact.

"All along I've said she deserves the truth."

"I agree." She pauses before continuing. "But I doubt she would have been ready to hear the truth a week ago, do you?"

I heave a sigh, reflecting back to who Nora was mere days ago. The nuts and bolts are still there, but the woman who just bared her body and soul to me, relinquishing her control and vulnerability, only remotely resembles the woman I first ran across in Chicago. She's free, while my chains only grow heavier with every touch, every kiss, every devoted whisper.

"She needed to complete this journey," I remark.

"But now the journey's over, yet you're no closer to figuring out what to do than you were when you realized the truth," Esme states, reading me like a book.

"She deserves to know," I say through the lump in my throat. "The truth about that night was kept from me for years. I can't keep it from her, too. But doing so——"

"Destroys everything you've built with her," she completes my thought.

"Even though it was all built on a foundation of lies."

Esme's quiet for a moment, and I sense her brain spinning. "That's not entirely true. I think you'd built a strong foundation before you ever learned the truth. It may have rattled things a little, but I like to think it can still survive. This is merely an earthquake."

"A 7.2 magnitude earthquake."

"It's a tragedy, Anders. I'm not trying to downplay it. I'm simply trying to give you hope."

"Hope?"

"Maybe if you show her you have the courage to let her go, she'll find the strength to look past the biggest regret of your life. I think we both know there's no other option here. Your conscience won't allow you to say goodbye without telling her the truth."

I bow my head. "You're right."

"No matter what happens, just know you're doing the right thing." Her voice wavers. "Mom would be proud."

I squeeze my eyes shut. If there were a time I wished my mother were still alive, it's now. She always had a way of giving us confidence when it was lacking. She never used her MS as an excuse for why she couldn't do something. And I'm not going to do that now, either.

"Thanks, Esme."

"Anytime. Just promise me one thing."

"What's that?"

"That you'll take that girl out tonight. Spoil her to the point where nothing else will matter. Maybe in the end, nothing else will."

"Not even the finest jewels will make her overlook this…" I trail off.

The finest jewels…

"What is it?" Esme asks.

"Nothing." I jump to my feet. "I have to go. I'll phone you later."

I end the call, then walk toward the wall safe. After inputting my code, I press my thumb against the scanner. The door clicks open and I pull it back, pushing aside boxes containing various necklaces and earrings I'd purchased for Kendall during our relationship. All worth a small fortune, but the memories of their previous owner make them priceless.

As I rummage through, I don't immediately find what I'm looking for. When my hand skims against an envelope hidden toward the back of the safe, I grab it, pulling it out. My heart rate increases as I dump its contents into my palm.

For weeks after losing Kendall, I'd fallen asleep with this silver chain and simple diamond engagement ring clutched tightly in my hand. It was a talisman of sorts, offering me comfort when my world felt like it had turned upside down. I'd come back to Los Angeles after her death, to this penthouse where I first saw her on the sand across the street playing volleyball. A part of me held out hope she'd still be here.

But she wasn't.

So I held onto the one memory I had of our last day together. This necklace.

At one point, I vowed to return the chain and ring to its rightful owner.

I never could have expected she'd find me instead.

I wrap my fingers around it, drawing in a deep breath as I summon the magic this jewelry once held for me all those years ago.

I just pray, once she learns the truth, it can offer Nora that same comfort.

Chapter Thirty-Four

NORA

"Wow," I MURMUR as I peer at my reflection in the mirror, barely recognizing myself.

Earlier today, Anderson had arranged for me to go out with a personal shopper to find a dress for dinner, after which I was treated to an afternoon at the spa, complete with massage, manicure, and a pedicure before having my hair styled and makeup done. Now that I'm back home, or at Anderson's place, and have slipped into the dress I procured, I can't help but feel like a princess.

My hair is pinned back on the right side with pristine waves reminiscent of the way Hollywood starlets wore their hair in the forties. My makeup is clean and not overdone, apart from the bright red hue covering my lips, which contrasts with my fair skin. The sleek, black dress, with its off-the-shoulder sleeves and sweetheart neckline, a string of pearls falling just above it, makes me look like a modern-day Grace Kelly.

Another woman who'd fallen for a prince.

Electricity buzzes through my veins as my mind wanders to how Anderson will react to this version of me. I haven't seen him since the personal shopper whisked me away from the penthouse earlier. It's the longest we've been away from each other since we met, and I hated every minute, despite all the pampering.

I don't know how I'll survive once we part ways. I'd wanted to raise the subject on more than one occasion as we made our way to California, but it wasn't fair to have that discussion with Anderson while Hunter was with me. Now I've let him go. Let my past go. Yet I still can't seem to bring up our future. Maybe because, somewhere in the recesses of my brain, I know there *is* no future with us. That he was brought into my life to serve a purpose — to help me finally accept Hunter's death. His job is done.

But I don't want it to be.

Checking the time, I grab my clutch that almost caused me to have a heart attack when I saw the price tag. However, my personal shopper assured me it didn't matter. Anderson had instructed her to get me whatever I wanted, regardless of the cost. He said he planned to spoil me today. He most certainly did.

On Jimmy Choo-clad feet, I carefully make my way from the master bedroom, holding onto the iron railing as I descend the stairs into the open living area. My heels click against the hardwood flooring, announcing my arrival, and Anderson whirls around from the kitchen island, the champagne cork flying out of his hands and zooming past my head, making me flinch.

"Shit." He rushes to place the bottle on the island, hurrying toward me and pulling me into his arms. "Are you okay?"

I burst into a fit of giggles. "Having trouble controlling your…cork?" I joke flirtatiously.

"Only when you're around, gorgeous." He nuzzles my neck, inhaling. "*Always* when you're around." He remains in my embrace for a moment before pulling back. "Now, let me get a look at you." He takes my hand in his and spins me around.

I smile demurely, allowing him to take in the full

package. I've never felt so beautiful, but it's not because of the dress, or the makeup, or the jewelry, or even the sexy lingerie I'd purchased to surprise him with later. It's because of the way Anderson's eyes flame with a mixture of desire and adoration.

He yanks my body to his. "You're stunning, Nora. You look so much like Grace Kelly."

I giggle nervously, his words mirroring my own thoughts. "I *feel* a little like Grace Kelly. Like I'm living a fairy tale."

Except ours won't end with a happily ever after.

His lips curve as he admires me, but it doesn't reach his eyes, isn't as carefree as it has been.

"Anderson, I—"

"No," he cuts me off, his voice pained. "Not right now. Let's pretend we're two people going out on our first date."

"A first date?" I waggle my brows. "Is that what this is?"

He shrugs. "I guess so. I never had a chance to take you out while we were driving Route 66."

"We went out for drinks and dinner. Most nights, actually."

"And while I enjoyed every second, you deserve better. So that's what I'm giving you tonight. Better."

I place my hands on the lapels of his dark suit that he kept casual with just a black t-shirt. It's simple, yet oozes sex appeal and sophistication.

"You could cook me Ramen noodles and open a cheap bottle of wine, and it would still be…better."

"And that's what I lo—" He stops short, catching himself before finishing, "admire about you. But I have the means to treat you like a princess. And a princess you shall be."

"Be careful. A girl could get used to this."

"Good." He winks, then steps back, steering me toward the island.

I watch as he expertly pours the champagne into two flutes, then hands one to me, raising his. "To broken-down rental cars, abandoned drive-in theaters, and Cadillacs turned into art."

I lift my glass to his. "To Truth or Drink, cheap motels, and dancing beneath the stars," I squeak past the lump in my throat.

"All wonderful moments. But may I confess something?"

I swallow hard, my heart hammering in my chest at what he's about to reveal.

"My favorite moment is you."

Tears well behind my lids. This might be the sweetest and most honest thing he's ever said to me. That *anyone's* ever said to me.

"My favorite moment is you, too," I admit as he tips his glass toward mine.

"Although sneaking a peek of your knickers as you scaled that fence comes in a very close second," he adds, his eyes alight with mischief.

I playfully punch him. "And watching you nearly hit a burro when we drove through Oatman is a close second for me."

"That thing came out of nowhere!" he huffs. "And why were donkeys wandering around without a single care for the vehicles on the road?"

"Simple." I bring my glass to my lips. "They were there first."

"I suppose."

Just as he takes another sip of his champagne, the elevator doors slide open, surprising me. I thought we were the only ones who had access to his penthouse.

A tall man with an even more impressive physique

than Anderson's steps into the foyer. I squint, the dark-haired man seeming familiar, but I can't quite place how I know him.

"Good evening, Your Highness. Are you ready?"

"Hey, Creed," Anderson answers casually. "Yes. We're ready. And for the thousandth time, stop with the Your Highness bullshit already."

"And for the thousandth time, as long as I serve as your CPO, I will only refer to you as Your Highness or sir."

"You had no problem calling me some choice words the other day. What was it? A daft prick who you were grateful finally pulled his head out of his arse?"

"You *did* fire me. I called you a daft prick and an arse before you officially rehired me. I took the opportunity while I could." He winks at me, and I sense a strong bond between the two men, one that transcends that of employer and employee. "Creed Lawson." He extends his hand toward me.

"Nora Tremblay," I respond, placing mine in his.

He chuckles. "I know."

"Creed and I have known each other our entire lives," Anderson explains when Creed releases my hand. "We grew up together. His dad is my father's CPO."

I furrow my brow. "CPO?"

"Chief protection officer. So his mum and mine became close. They were both pregnant at the same time. So we've always been good mates. He knows everything about me."

"Is that right?" My expression lights up.

"Yes, ma'am," Creed answers.

"Then I'm coming to you to get the inside scoop on what a pain in the — what did you call it — *arse* he was as a kid."

Creed laughs, wrinkles forming around his eyes. "I

certainly have some stories."

I turn to Anderson. "So he's your friend, but now works for you?"

"He's *assigned* to me. Technically, he works for the Nation of Belmont as a member of the Royal Guard."

"Really?" I scrunch my nose. "But you're dressed, well...normally."

Creed's deep chuckle echoes in the room as he looks down at his clothes. "How did you expect me to dress?"

"Shouldn't members of the Royal Guard be dressed in ornate red jackets, white tights, and fuzzy black hats?"

His and Anderson's laughter increases, echoing against the high ceilings.

"We're not the British Royal Family," Creed explains. "Although if you were to come tour the Royal Palace, the members of the Guard there will be in costume. Not as over-the-top as the British Royal Guard, but in costume, nonetheless."

"Right. So where's your costume now?" I press.

"As you know, I often travel under an alias," Anderson explains. "But even when I do, my CPO is still nearby, and he can't draw attention to himself."

I inhale sharply. "You mean..."

Anderson nods. "Yes. He followed closely throughout our journey."

"That night!" I gasp, realizing why he looks familiar. "In the bar in Tucumcari when we were dancing and about to..."

"Yeah." Anderson scrapes a hand through his hair. "Creed often acts as my conscience, too. He's like my own bloody Jiminy Cricket."

I look at Creed, intrigued. "You didn't want us to kiss?"

My question catching him off guard, he opens his mouth, but no words come.

"He didn't realize I'd already told you who I was," Anderson answers for him. "He didn't want me to lead you on, that's all."

The two men exchange a look, and I can't shake the feeling that's not the entire story. After I laid it all out on the line in Santa Fe, I thought we were past keeping secrets. I told him everything about me. About Hunter. About Ember. Is he *still* keeping something from me?

"We should get going," Creed says, clearing his throat before I can question Anderson. "Traffic is light, but it will still take about fifteen minutes."

"Right." Anderson grabs my glass from me and sets both on the island, then places his hand on my lower back, leading me away from the kitchen.

"Where are we going?"

"Dinner. Then I have a bit of a…surprise up my sleeve."

"Surprise? What kind of surprise?"

He stops, turning toward me. Creed walks ahead of us, allowing us some semblance of privacy.

Anderson tugs me against him, his lips poised over mine. "Be a good girl and you'll find out."

A touch. A kiss. Words laced with desire. That's all it takes for any unease to disappear.

"Didn't you learn this morning?" I counter.

"Learn what?"

I nibble on his earlobe. "Sometimes I like being bad."

His breath hitches as I step out of his grasp, swaying my hips a little more than usual as I walk toward the elevator waiting to whisk me away to a night of romance I have a feeling will be unlike any I've experienced before.

Chapter Thirty-Five

ANDERSON

"Tell me about your sister," Nora says later that evening as Creed drives us away from one of the premier restaurants in LA.

While I was initially hesitant to take her out for dinner, not wanting tonight to be like every other night, I had to remind myself it wouldn't be. Not to her.

This has been my life for so long, I forget that being catered to by a team of waitstaff at a five-star restaurant isn't an everyday experience for most people. Hell, most people don't even get to do this once in their lives, let alone as often as I do. Nora deserves to be spoiled, deserves one day of absolute happiness, of feeling how much I care about her before I turn her world upside down. It's not what I want, but like Esme observed… I'm torn between having a clear conscience or a broken heart. I need to break my heart to keep my conscience clear.

"She's my best friend. Next to Creed, of course." I meet his eyes in the rearview mirror, and he nods.

Thankfully, he wasn't too upset with me when I finally apologized to him. After all, I've only carried the guilt of that night for a few days. He's carried it for years, knowing two lives may have been saved had he done as he threatened and tackled me to the ground in the hospital parking lot, preventing me from driving. He

293

apologized for keeping the truth from me. And I told him about my MS diagnosis. He reacted worse than I did when I first received the news. Then he did what Creed's always done throughout our friendship. Offered his unyielding support.

"Of course," Nora states with a smile as she leans back against the leather seat of the SUV, her fingers interlocking with mine. The only time I haven't had my hand on some part of her body all night was while we ate. Even then, I'd stolen a brush here, a squeeze there, needing to feel her to know she's still with me. That it's not over yet.

"Esme's only a year younger, so we've always been inseparable. I tell her everything."

"Everything?"

I nod. "She was the first person I told about you." A smile teases on my lips. "Well, actually, I guess that would be Creed, but I didn't exactly *tell* him about you. He just kind of...found out, considering he was following me."

"Do you ever get tired of it?" Nora asks softly. "Of constantly being on display? Never being alone?"

"Why do you think I took this trip? I'd been in the Hamptons, after which I'd planned to fly out to LA and spend a while here to decompress. This time of year is always difficult, what with Kendall's death and all. It's why I always tend to disappear for a bit."

She squeezes my hand, offering me a reassuring look.

"Instead, I decided to take the opportunity and drive across the country. No rules. Only me and the road. Oh, and Creed. But I refused to let him chauffeur me this time." I glance at him. "No offense, Creed."

"None taken, sir. I'm used to you being a giant pain in the arse, with all due respect." He finds Nora's gaze through the mirror and winks. Despite all his warnings,

I sense he likes her, that he thinks she's good for me. I wish I could be good for her, too.

"So... What? You went and bought a car to drive across the country?" She laughs under her breath. "You can probably do that, can't you?"

I nod subtly.

"So, Esme?"

"Right." I straighten. "Esme's brilliant. I've told her repeatedly that I think she should have been born first."

"Why's that?"

"Because she'd be Crown Princess, heir to the throne."

"You don't want to be king?"

"It's not that I don't want to. I simply believe Esme would do a better job." I force a smile.

"How so?"

"She's very passionate," I answer without a moment's hesitation. "The Royal Family is notoriously non-political."

"Even though you're the head of your executive branch," she states.

"You've done your research, I see."

She shrugs. "I was curious how it all worked."

"Then you know that, while the king *is* the head of the executive branch, there's also the Executive Council that's elected by the people that must approve of each of the executive's decisions. It was written into the Constitution in the 1800s. A check against executive powers, so to speak. Like your government's checks and balances. We have them, as well."

"So you don't have free rein to do whatever you want."

"No." I chuckle. "We don't, and it's always been believed to be in the Royal Family's best interests to remain neutral."

"But your sister doesn't."

I roll my eyes. "That may be the understatement of the year. She's a huge champion for racial and gender equality, worker's rights, immigration."

"I don't see anything wrong with that."

"There isn't, but like I said, we were brought up to remain neutral and simply execute the laws as we believe will best benefit our constituents, not those that will benefit individual politicians or large corporations."

"That's not a bad thing. Look at our messed-up political system."

"I'd rather not." I grimace, then straighten my expression. "But despite Esme's tendency to be quite vocal, people would love her as queen. She has the tenacity and drive to propel our country into this century, when so many other countries seem to be reverting."

"No kidding," Nora quips. "Can't you just abdicate your throne or something?"

I pause, on the brink of telling her I may soon not have a choice. That once I return home and inform my father about my MS diagnosis, he'll most likely request the Executive Council to approve a new line of succession. That's the hardest thing about this. Not only will I possibly lose the ability to walk, but the one thing I've spent my life preparing for could also be taken away. Yes, I truly believe Esme will make an incredible queen, that our people will admire and respect her. But that doesn't make it any easier to give up my position. To be relegated to the sidelines and hidden away when I can no longer walk without assistance.

"We're here, sir," Creed says, saving me from having to explain all this to Nora. He steps out of the SUV and runs around to open the rear door. I slide out first, then extend my hand to Nora, helping her.

"Where are we?" She surveys the industrial-looking parking lot, rows and rows of prop cars filling the spots, ranging from antique Model A's to more modern muscle cars, and everything in between.

"Picking up our transportation for the next part of the evening."

"Transportation?" She looks back at the SUV. "But I thought—"

"Figured you might like to go for a little drive." I gesture toward a light blue 1954 Chevy Bel-Air convertible Creed procured for the evening. While I hate throwing my title around, sometimes it does have its benefits. Like now, when I see the excitement brimming in Nora's expression.

"We're going for a drive in that?" she exclaims, bouncing on her feet.

"We sure are."

I'd seen her admiring all the vintage cars along Route 66 and thought this would be the perfect way to end our adventure together. Plus, I've always wanted to drive one.

I place my hand on the small of her back and lead her toward it, helping her onto the front bench seat. Once she's situated, I walk around to the driver's side and give Creed a wave. He returns a slight salute, then drives off.

"He's leaving?" Nora asks when I slide behind the wheel.

"Under extreme protest, but yes. It's our last night. I don't want to share it with anyone." Edging toward her, I capture her mouth in a soft kiss.

As much as I crave our soul-crushing kisses as we devour each other, hungry for more, I love these simple ones, too. The light touch of our mouths as we breathe into each other feels more intimate, exposing our vulnerabilities.

Pulling back, I turn the key in the ignition and the engine roars. We both grin like giddy teenagers who are about to go on their first date without a chaperone. In a sense, it kind of is for me. All throughout my life, I've always been flanked by some kind of security. They may not be right beside me, but they're still close, ready to jump into action at a moment's notice. Creed normally would have insisted he follow and remain nearby, but I begged him for this one taste of freedom before it all ends.

The temperature is perfect for an evening drive with the top down as I navigate toward our final destination. Neither one of us speaks, simply enjoying the moment and the scenery of Los Angeles at night. Our last night together.

When I slow the car and pull up to a bolted chain-link fence twenty minutes later, Nora passes me a mischievous look.

"Trying to get me to scale another fence?" she jokes. "I'm *definitely* not dressed for that." She gestures to her dress-clad body.

"No scaling fences tonight." I reach into my pocket. "This time, I have a key." I dangle it in front of her, then hop out of the car and head toward the fence, unlocking the chain securing it. After opening the gate, I get back behind the wheel, driving the car inside before locking the gate behind us.

"Should I be worried that you're locking me…" She waves her hand around, "wherever we are."

"Dammit. You've discovered my master plan." I chuckle, easing down the gas, driving at a slow speed along the dimly lit pathway. "Abduct you to a field in the middle of nowhere and have my way with you." I waggle my brows. "But as enticing as that sounds, I opted for something else instead." I grin as we round the corner and a large, drive-in movie screen comes into view.

She gasps, a hand flying to her mouth. Throughout our journey, she'd kept mentioning how she wished we could actually watch a movie at a drive-in. It never worked out. While we visited plenty of rundown drive-ins along the route, there were never any functioning theaters near where we stopped for the night. I'm grateful I could finally give this to her.

"A real drive-in?"

"A real drive-in," I confirm. "I did have to bribe them to reopen. They'd closed for the season after Labor Day, but I persuaded them to let us rent it out."

I park in the center of the darkened dirt field, the only light coming off the screen and the moon shining overhead. The screen flickers, and I turn to the correct FM radio station just as the opening credits play.

"*An Affair to Remember*?" Nora says in awe, her eyes brimming with tears.

"Thought you'd enjoy it."

She unbuckles her seat belt and slides over the bench seat into my outstretched arm. "It's perfect." She tilts her head back to meet my gaze. "The perfect end to this journey."

I brush my lips against hers, our kiss soft at first before I clutch her face in my hands and deepen the exchange, telling her with my body everything words can never relay.

Will this be the last time I hold her like this as we watch Nicki Ferrante and Terry McKay meet for the first time? The last time I squeeze her tighter when Terry excitedly crosses the street to meet Nicki at the top of the Empire State Building after their six-month separation, only to be struck by a car? The last time I kiss her when Nicki discovers the true reason Terry never showed up that night?

But I can't focus on that, as difficult as it may be. Nora and I made a pledge to only think about the present, to live in the moment. So instead of dreading what tomorrow will bring, I stay in the moment with Nora.

It's the only place I want to be.

Chapter Thirty-Six

ANDERSON

IN MY TWENTIES, I used to see my share of sunrises, usually because I hadn't yet gone to bed. I never thought much of them, other than it being a sign that it was time to stop drinking.

But now, as I watch the glow slowly filter into the bedroom, I know this is one sunrise I'll never forget. There's a quiet solitude when it's no longer night but still not quite morning. It's in this place that I want to keep Nora. Last night is over, but the day when we must say goodbye, when she'll learn the truth, is not quite upon us. We're still us. Still here. Still together.

"You okay?" Nora's husky voice cuts through, as if able to sense my turmoil.

All day yesterday, I put on a smile, acted as if I wasn't hours away from losing everything, all because of something I didn't even know about until a week ago. A part of me wishes Creed had never told me. But where would that leave Nora? She blames herself. I refuse to allow her to do that, not when I hold the key to finally setting her free.

I push her onto her back, meeting her eyes so she can see the truth in my words.

"No. I'm not."

Her chin quivers as she runs her fingers through my hair. She pulls my lips toward hers.

"We'll find a way." Her breath warms my mouth, the contact light and soft at first. "We'll find a way," she repeats as she drags my body closer, deepening the exchange.

I lose myself in the hypnotic spell she casts over me, not able to form the words to tell her there *is* no way. I can't say them. It would make it real. I just want to pretend for a little while longer.

A vice squeezing my heart to the point of agony, I do the only thing that's erased the pain these past few days. Moving my hand down her frame, I clutch her hip and roll onto my back, yanking her on top of me. Her lips never leave mine, her hair framing our faces, enclosing us in a cocoon. In this moment, the outside world doesn't exist. The day is not on the verge of dawning. My heart isn't on the brink of shattering.

She circles her hips against me, her warmth causing an ache to stir low in my stomach.

"One more time," I murmur against her.

Any other time, she'd joke that I was a fiend or that I'd told her one more time a half-dozen times ago. But she knows this really is our last opportunity. The end of our road.

"One more time," she repeats, lifting herself before gradually lowering back onto me, taking every inch of me inside her.

We close our eyes, neither one of us moving, reveling in this sensation of fullness. Of being one. Of being complete.

I fear I'll never have this again. Never find this again. And maybe that's the penance I deserve to pay for my sins. To have a taste of heaven, then wander the flames of hell.

I delicately pulse against her, urging her to move with the rhythm I set. Her gaze trained on me, she covers my body with hers. I move my hands from her hips to her face, keeping her locked in place as I say goodbye the only way I can.

With my body.
With my heart.
With my love.

Chapter Thirty-Seven

NORA

THE GLITTERING SKYLINE of Manhattan at dusk comes into view below me as I lean against the window of the airplane. It seems like it was yesterday when I'd boarded a plane and set off on my mission to say goodbye to Hunter. I never expected to not only have to let go of Hunter, but also to have found someone who fills me with hope.

"Happy to almost be home?" Anderson asks from beside me.

I pull my eyes toward his, forcing a smile. "I am," I barely squeak out through the ache in my throat.

"We're about five minutes from wheels down," the pilot comes on the intercom. "Please stay seated for the remainder of the flight."

An attendant appears in the aisle. "Is there anything else I can get you two before we land?" she asks in an accent similar to Creed's — British with a barely discernible French inflection on certain syllables.

"No, thank you," Anderson answers with authority, reaching for the straps of his seat belt and securing it. He looks to me. "Do you need anything?"

I shake my head.

"We'll be on the ground shortly. Captain has scheduled a half-hour to refuel before taking off again."

"Thank you."

"Certainly, Your Highness." With a smile, she turns from us, disappearing from the passenger cabin, leaving us alone with Creed, who sits toward the front, his head buried in a file, while we remain in the rear.

I steal a glance at Anderson, his hands gripping the armrests at his side, a nervousness about him. Normally, I'd assume he was scared of flying, but I know he's not. He told me he loves to fly, that he has his pilot's license. Something else must have him in knots. Could it be our impending departure? But why would he be nervous about that? Depressed or somber, sure. But nervous?

Before I can ask him about it, the plane jostles us, the wheels hitting the ground at a high rate of speed. The engines roar as the flaps come up on the wings, causing the plane to slow to a crawl toward the end of the runway.

"Welcome to New York," the flight attendant says over the intercom. "And welcome home, Ms. Tremblay."

I look out the window as the airplane taxies, the silhouette of New York City rising in the distance. I've lived in Manhattan since I lost Hunter. But now, as I look at the familiar buildings, it no longer feels like home.

Home is a dingy motel room.

Home is a rundown gas station.

Home is a Jeep Wrangler.

Home is Anderson North.

The plane jerks to a stop, and a flurry of activity commences as the flight attendants unlock the cabin door, lowering the steps. I unlatch my seat belt and am about to stand when Anderson grasps my hand, squeezing it.

"Wait."

I nod, watching as the flight crew and Creed exit the

cabin. Once we're alone, Anderson clutches my cheeks with a desperate grip, his mouth covering mine in a soul-crushing, impassioned kiss. The way he holds me, the way he breathes into me, the way he devours me makes me feel like this is the last time he ever will.

But I don't want that.

I want a thousand more kisses. A thousand more touches. A thousand more sunrises.

A thousand more adventures.

He pulls away, the sound of our frantic breathing filling the luxurious cabin.

"There's so much I want to say," he pants, hands still framing my face. I swallow hard, tears welling in my eyes when I see his are glassed over. "The past several hours, I've tried to formulate my thoughts." Licking his lips, he shakes his head. "Tried to think of the best way to say this, but no matter what words I conjure, it doesn't seem enough."

"I know how you feel," I admit with a quiver.

This isn't just a fling. This was never just a fling. Our souls are intertwined. Some higher power saw fit to bring us into each other's lives. I've never been as sure of anything in my life as I am that we belong together. That after all the heartbreak and loss we've suffered, we deserve each other.

We deserve to be happy.

On a long inhale, Anderson reluctantly drops his hold on me and reaches into the inner pocket of his suit jacket, pulling out a narrow, black velvet box, a red ribbon wrapped around it. He peers at it for several long moments, as if contemplating what to do. Then he hands it to me.

"This is yours."

His statement catches me off guard, something about the forlorn expression he wears making me think it's not just your run-of-the mill necklace or bracelet.

My pulse steadily increases as I tug on the bow and crack open the box. The instant my eyes land on the contents, I gasp, barely able to see through the kaleidoscope of tears. I pull my bottom lip between my teeth to stop my chin from trembling, carefully removing the simple silver chain and diamond ring.

"Where did you find this?" I breathe, unable to believe I'm finally holding it. I can't fathom what Anderson had to do to not only locate this, but then get it sent to him. "For years, I've searched in every pawn shop in the Tri-State area. Even called all the diamond dealers and asked them to keep an eye out for the serial number on the stone, but nothing ever turned up."

I bring the ring closer, able to make out the faint inscription. *My favorite wrong number.*

"How did you—"

"It's been in my possession over six years," he says solemnly, squeezing his eyes shut.

I furrow my brow and straighten my spine, not understanding how that could be possible. Then it hits me. I never told him about this necklace. There's only one way he would know about it.

"I meant to give it to the paramedics." He gradually lifts his gaze to meet mine. "But everything happened so fast and—"

"What are you saying?" Heat washes over me, my heart thundering. My grip on the ring tightens, knuckles turning white.

"I was there that night," he admits after a pause. "I was the one who pulled you from that wreck."

I inhale a sharp breath, struggling to process this. For years, I'd searched for any clue about who my mystery Good Samaritan was. But the police had no way of finding out his identity. Hunter's parents had even put out a reward, hoping they could thank the person who'd helped me.

"You saved my life," I exhale, running my fingers over the diamond.

He slowly shakes his head, pure anguish covering his expression. His eyes are pinched, muscles strained, lips tight. "No, I didn't."

"But you said—"

"I'm the reason Hunter died."

"You tried to save him." I grab his hands in mine, knowing all too well what he's going through. "You did something so incredibly selfless, something most people wouldn't. You put yourself in harm's way to pull me from that car. You could have waited for the paramedics to arrive, but you didn't. You saw that time wasn't on our side and you acted." I touch my hand to his face. "I don't know how I'll ever be able to repay you."

"No, Nora. Please," he begs, his Adam's apple bobbing up and down. He looks to the ceiling, swallowing a pained breath, before returning his attention to me. The seconds stretch as I await his next words. But nothing could have prepared me for them. "It's my fault he lost control of the car in the first place."

His statement sucks the air from my lungs, and I straighten, withdrawing my hands from him and setting them in my lap. I blink, attempting to make sense out of his statement, but it doesn't seem to register in my brain. I heard it. I know what each individual word means. But strung together like that? I can't wrap my head around it.

"That crash was the same night Kendall died," he continues when I remain silent. "I still can't remember much. I was driving from the hospital and toward our hotel in North Harbor, convinced it was a terrible dream and I'd walk into the room to find her there. But as I drove, I had this blinding headache. The pain was excruciating. It was unlike anything I'd ever experienced. My body was frozen, this weird pins-and-needles sensation crawling over my skin. Then I heard a loud bang and slammed on my brakes. Thought maybe something happened to my car. When I saw smoke billowing in my rearview mirror, I ran to help."

He hangs his head, digging his fingers through his hair, tugging at it. "I've done everything to put the pieces of that night together, but I can't. It's all a blur. All I know is that I swerved into the wrong lane and forced your car off the road."

His confession hangs heavy in the air as I stare into space for what feels like an eternity, but is only a matter of seconds. Not saying a word, I gingerly stand and brush past him. I walk a few feet up the narrow aisle, surrounded by money and luxury. The same things that probably allowed Anderson to keep his involvement in this hidden for years. The police said there was no evidence of foul play, that Hunter had probably swerved to avoid hitting a deer, as was often the case in that area. I never could have imagined he'd swerved and lost control of his car because of another reason.

"When did you figure out who I was?" I face him, crossing my arms in front of my chest. "Did you know from the beginning?"

He jumps to his feet. "No. I had *no* idea. Hell, in my nightmares about pulling you from the crash, your name was Laura. Not Nora. I'm not lying when I say I have absolutely no memory of ever swerving. I *don't*. If I did..."

"What? You wouldn't have fucked me?" My voice rises in pitch.

"I—"

"How long have you known who I was?" I demand, my nostrils flaring, jaw clenched.

"Nora, please…" He steps toward me, hands clasped together.

I shoot up my hand, stopping him from getting any closer. "How. Long?" I ask, my words coming out like bullets.

His expression falls, shoulders drooping. He doesn't have to utter a single syllable for me to know I won't like the response.

"Tucumcari," he answers, his voice lacking all the confidence and swagger it had the first time he spoke to me. Then again, it wasn't the first time he spoke to me. That was six years ago. He was the mysterious hero who rescued me, who begged me to stay with him, to not succumb to unconsciousness.

But he's not a hero. Not anymore.

He's certainly not *my* hero.

My stomach churns, acid burning my throat. I search his eyes, hoping to find some sign that this is just a cruel joke. But I can't stand to peer into them anymore. Those blue eyes I once thought were my salvation are now nothing more than a reminder of the biggest mistake of my life.

"If I'd known earlier, I never would have initiated anything with you. Creed tried to warn me, but I refused to listen. Refused to allow him to tell me anything he found out about you. All my life, every single woman I've dated or was interested in had to be approved. For once, I wanted to learn about someone from them, not because of some background check. When you told me about Hunter, I still didn't think anything of it. But after that night in Tucumcari, there was this nagging voice in my head, so I decided to Google you and the car accident. To my absolute horror, I learned you were the woman I pulled from that wreck, which Creed confirmed. You have to believe me when I say I had no idea who you were until then."

"How can I believe you when you've kept this from me all along?" I choke out. "When every touch was a goddamn lie?"

"Because it's the truth."

"Truth?" I lean into him, my eyes on fire. "Truth? *Now* you're interested in telling me the truth when this entire time, you had no problem fucking me, knowing you're the reason I lost everything? *Everything*, Anderson. Do you have any idea how hard it's been to not only lose the man I planned to spend my life with, but our baby, too?"

My blood heats in my veins, adrenaline coursing through me. I've tried to keep calm, to not completely lose control, but that time has passed. This man needs to know exactly what he's done, what his negligence destroyed.

"To have to carry that baby for two long weeks after the doctors told me the fetus didn't have a heartbeat? And that's what they called her at the hospital. She was no longer a baby. No longer Ember. No longer a person. She was a *fetus*. Then to endure over twenty hours of labor with no one at my side, knowing when it was all over I'd go home empty-handed. Do you have any idea how much that fucked with my mind?"

"I can't even begin to imagine," he says, cautiously stepping toward me, testing the waters. "And that's why I knew I had to come clean and tell you the truth. Because you deserve to know." He pauses, drawing in a shaky breath. "Because I love you enough to lose you, Nora."

"You have—" I snap my mouth shut, his statement finally registering. "What did you say?" I hiss.

He shows no reaction to my demeanor, remaining calm. "I love you."

I squeeze my eyes closed, swiping away the tears falling down my cheeks. An excruciating ache settles in my chest, a vice squeezing every last ounce of life out of my heart. A part of me had hoped he loved me, that we would find a way to make it work, but I never imagined that love would come like this, wrapped up with lies and sugarcoated in deception.

"And you think that's supposed to make me forgive you?"

"I don't expect you to forgive me. I don't deserve it. But you deserve to feel loved. That's all."

I part my lips, struggling to come up with any response. But I can't. Can't bear to be in this man's presence any longer.

I spin on my heels, dashing off the plane and into the cool October evening air before Anderson can stop me. As if anticipating this turn of events, Creed stands beside a dark SUV and quickly opens the rear passenger door when he sees me. A motion from the airplane catches my attention, and I look up to see Anderson standing in the doorway holding my purse and laptop bag, which I'd left on the plane.

Creed is quick to retrieve them. My resolve momentarily cracks when I see the streaks of tears on Anderson's face, making me second-guess whether I did the right thing. But how could this *not* be the right thing? That man took Hunter and Ember from me. And he knew about it, yet kept it to himself.

"Would you like these with you?" Creed asks in a strained voice as he approaches the idling SUV once more. "Your suitcase is already in the back."

Nodding, I take the small bags from him and turn forward, buckling my seat belt. I can only imagine what the driver they hired to take me home must think. I imagine they paid him a substantial tip to keep to himself.

Creed's about to close the door when he stops. He reaches into his suit jacket and pulls out a handkerchief. I almost turn it down when I notice the royal insignia on it, but don't. I take it as a reminder of what can happen when you put your heart on the line. When you allow yourself to become vulnerable, to be taken advantage of.

"For what it's worth, Nora," Creed begins, his tone lacking the serious quality I'd heard last evening and all throughout the flight. He sounds...friendly. "Anders didn't know until a few days ago. When you first...got together, he was unaware he'd caused that wreck. I told him. Disobeyed orders to do so, but I realized he deserved the truth. Just like *he* realized *you* deserved the truth."

"How is that possible?" I lean closer, my voice low so no one can overhear. "How could he not know he killed two innocent people?"

Creed steals a worried glance at the driver, then schools his expression, turning back into Crown Prince Gabriel's chief protection officer. "I'm not at liberty to say, ma'am."

"Then I'm not at liberty to forgive him."

Chapter Thirty-Eight

NORA

THE TELEVISION SCREEN flickers as I gorge on ice cream, sneering at Meg Ryan. How could she forgive Tom Hanks so fucking easily? He lied to her about who he was. Manipulated her into thinking he was just some guy she met online, not someone she already knew. Someone who destroyed her career, caused her bookstore to shutter its doors. I once loved *You've Got Mail.*

Now it hits too close to home.

Just as I'm about to shout at Meg Ryan's character to leave the bastard and find someone who won't deceive her, the door to my apartment flings open. I dart my eyes toward the foyer, Chloe, Evie, and Izzy filing in, each of them wearing a costume. Is it already Halloween? How is that possible?

I glance at my phone. October 31st. I've wallowed in misery for two long weeks. I can only imagine what my mother would say about this. It's probably a good thing I've ignored her phone calls. Otherwise, she would have been on the first flight from Miami to psychoanalyze every aspect of my life and tell me it's *my* fault Hunter was killed in that crash. *My* fault Anderson drove recklessly that night. *My* fault he lied to me.

"Oh, my god! Is that a…rom com?" Chloe asks, her voice heavy with disgust.

"And ice cream?" Izzy adds.

Evie sniffs like a dog. "And when's the last time you showered?" She meets Chloe's and Izzy's eyes. "I told you it might be too late. Look." She drops her voice to a whisper. "She's reached the Meg Ryan stage. There may be no saving her."

"But we have to try," Chloe says, turning her attention to me and tossing a shopping bag at me. "Put this on. We're going out. It's Halloween."

"I'm not in the mood."

I shove another spoonful of ice cream into my mouth, chasing it with wine straight from the bottle, to my friends' absolute horror. Evie covers her open mouth. Chloe scrunches her nose. And Izzy makes a fake gagging sound.

"What?" I lift the ice cream carton and wine bottle. "Red wine and dark chocolate go great together."

The girls all share another look, then rush toward me simultaneously.

"This is much worse than I thought." Evie pries the ice cream and wine from my hands.

"At least her hair isn't a rat's nest." Izzy yanks my locks free from the ponytail holder.

"I've dealt with worse," Chloe states with authority as she grabs my arms and pulls me off the couch. "Go shower and get ready. You've had more than enough time to get over your not-so-Prince Charming."

"Ooh," Evie squeals. "I like that one. I've been calling him Prince Prick."

"Prince Asswipe for me," Izzy adds.

I try to fight my smile, but can't.

When I'd returned home a mess, struggling to come to terms with Anderson's lies and the fact he's the reason I lost everything, they've been at my side every step of the way, not once questioning whether I made the right decision. Not asking what I thought Creed could have meant when he mentioned there was an explanation for Anderson having lost control of the car. Not ooh-ing and ahh-ing over the extravagant bouquets of flowers he sent every day, each one containing a note about yet another one of his favorite moments on the road.

> *The first time I heard you laugh at the pool in Springfield.*

> *The way you rested your bare feet on the dashboard of the Wrangler.*

> *The look of awe on your face when we saw the Grand Canyon.*

Instead, they've done everything they can to help me forget Anderson.

But it's been impossible. The fact he's a public figure doesn't help, which is why I've avoided all social media and the news, not wanting to stumble across any mention of him, even if by accident. The last thing I need is a reminder of the biggest mistake of my life. Of the man who destroyed everything.

"Thanks, girls. I don't know what I'd do without you."

"You'd risk reaching the Nicholas Sparks level of post-breakup depression," Chloe states. "And I'm sorry. Even my professional abilities can't bring you back if you've gone down *The Notebook* rabbit hole."

I burst out laughing, the sound feeling foreign after so long. Reaching into the bag, I pull out the costume they chose for me. "The Queen of Hearts?" Although this dress is much sexier than anything I've ever seen depicted in any of the remakes of *Alice in Wonderland*.

"I figure it's fitting." Chloe beams as she gestures to

Evie and Izzy. "We've all chosen costumes that are a good representation of who we are."

I take in her Harley Quinn costume, the ends of her blonde pigtails dyed red and blue, respectively. When I see her t-shirt says "Daddy's Little Monster", I can't help but shake my head in amusement. From the stories she's told me of her childhood, it's not far from the truth.

"Okay. I get Harley Quinn and the nurse." I nod at Izzy's chosen costume, although this version is a lot more risqué than the scrubs I've seen her wear. "But a hooker?" I squint at Evie, who's dressed as Vivian from *Pretty Woman*, but as prostitute Viv, complete with thigh-high black boots and a cheap blonde wig covering her red hair. "I'm surprised Julian let you leave the house dressed like that."

"I promised I'd keep on the boots and wig when I got home later." She winks, licking her lips.

"Did I miss your stint as a prostitute?"

"No, but even you have to admit the way I met Julian was a lot like how Vivian met Edward. We also made a business arrangement, but ended up falling for each other."

She doesn't have to utter a word for me to know what she's thinking. That her story isn't that different from mine and Anderson's, either. We had an agreement to drive to Los Angeles together on Route 66, then walk away. And just like Julian and Evie, we fell for each other. But that's where the similarities end. She didn't learn Julian was responsible for destroying her life.

"Enough stalling. Go get ready," Chloe orders. "Under no circumstances are we going to allow you to continue to wallow and become every romantic comedy cliché out there."

"But I like being a cliché," I whine, then add, "I like knowing I'm not alone."

Chloe drapes her arm along my shoulders and pulls me into her slim body. "And you're not."

"You have us." Evie joins us, Izzy right behind her.

"Lean on us," Izzy encourages, then steals a glance at the television. "Not on Meg Ryan."

We erupt in a fit of giggles at the ridiculousness of this situation. That's the mark of a true friend. They don't kick you when you're down. Don't whisper behind your back about your broken heart. They lift you up. And these women have always lifted me up, no matter the weight.

* * *

Strobe lights flicker around me, sweat beading on my neck and brow as I move with the hypnotic beat of the club music. Over the past few hours, I've danced away my heartache with my three best girls. I've tried not to focus on the diamond adorning each of their ring fingers. I never thought much of them before. But that was when I still wore Jeremy's ring, despite the fact it was given in a drunken haze.

Now I find myself back to square one, wondering if I'll ever find the same happiness I had with Hunter.

And with Anderson.

I clutch the silver chain around my neck where Hunter's engagement ring dangles. I almost sold it when I first returned home. Every time I looked at it, I was reminded of Anderson and his deception. But this is the last piece of Hunter I have left. Anderson stole every other memory. I refuse to let him steal this, too.

"Break?" Chloe shouts over the music after the DJ transitions from Michael Jackson's "Thriller" to a more modern tune.

"Yes!" I shout back, and we all squeeze our way

through the crowded dance floor and toward the VIP section. After smiling at the bouncer manning the rope, we're permitted access, thanks to Izzy's rockstar fiancé, Asher, who was not only able to get us into this exclusive club, but also a table in the VIP area.

My feet screaming, I'm about to collapse into our booth when Evie grabs my forearm. "Come to the bathroom with me. I'll help you reapply your makeup."

I don't have a chance to protest as she drags me through the VIP section and toward the private ladies' room. It's probably not a bad thing. I have been drinking all night. And sweating under those bright lights. I can only imagine what the makeup Evie painstakingly applied looks like right now.

And when we step into the bathroom, my reflection staring back at me from the mirror, I see it's worse than I thought. The red hearts painted on both my cheeks are smudged, and the red heart in the center of my lips needs a little help.

"Let's pee, then I'll get you all fixed up."

I nod, and we both go about our business. Once we've washed our hands, Evie drags me toward the vanity area in the bathroom and sits me down in one of the cushioned stools before lowering herself onto the one beside me. I open my clutch, removing the costume makeup she'd used on me earlier, and allow her to get to work.

Several moments pass as she works on cleaning up my cheeks, the only sound that of the occasional toilet flushing and the muted chorus of "Monster Mash".

"So, how are you holding up?" Evie asks nonchalantly as she outlines a heart.

"Fine," I answer, ignoring her insinuation. "Just a little hot."

She pinches her lips. "That's not what I'm talking

about, and you know it. I'll ask again." She lowers her voice, her eyes filled with sincerity. "How are you?"

I swallow hard, trying my best to keep my emotions in check, as I've done these past few weeks. I shouldn't even give Anderson a moment's thought. Yet I can't stop thinking about what Creed told me before closing the SUV door. That Anderson didn't know the truth of that night until that week. I want to believe him. But at the same time, I don't.

"I'm so fucking confused," I blurt out, the words leaving me like a tidal wave, fast and cathartic.

Evie takes my hand in hers and squeezes. "Your brain tells you that you should be angry he lied to you, deceived you."

I nod. "But my heart wants to overlook all that and only remember the good stuff."

"Exactly," Evie says, knowing all too well what I'm feeling. She's probably the only one who can even begin to comprehend the mixed-up emotions plaguing me every hour of the day. The constant push and pull. The tumultuous game of tug-of-war being waged in my heart. After all, she went through something similar with Julian, although the secret he kept didn't come remotely close to being this earth-shattering.

"I should just forget him."

"You should. That's what all reason tells you to do." She touches my chin, tilting my head to the opposite side so she can fix up my other cheek. "But you can't forget someone who still owns a piece of your heart."

Does Anderson still own a piece of my heart? I've tried to convince myself he didn't, that he didn't deserve to even be a thought. But he's still on my mind. His kisses still tingle on my lips. And his hold still maintains a grip on my heart, no matter what I do to free myself.

"How did you forgive Julian after he lied to you about

who he was?"

She meets my eyes. "I finally realized the truth."

"The truth?"

"Yes, Nora. The truth. I was like you. For weeks, I only focused on the lie. On the deception. I thought it tainted everything. I was convinced our entire relationship was based on that lie. Nothing else. I was so blinded by it that I ignored what had been glaring at me from the beginning."

"And what's that?"

"That he saved me."

I straighten. "Saved you?"

"Maybe not like Anderson saved you, but Julian saved me, nonetheless. He saved me from myself. Taught me what true love feels like. And there's no question in my mind that Anderson loves you."

"Because I told you he said he does."

She shakes her head. "No. Because he did something extremely selfless. He didn't have to tell you the truth. He could have kept it from you for the rest of your life and you never would have been the wiser. But he thought you deserved to know." She takes my hands in hers. "He told you about that night fully aware there was a possibility you would never speak to him again. There's no more selfless act of love than sacrificing your needs for someone else." She pulls her hands from mine and stands, checking her reflection in the mirror and readjusting her wig.

"You're right to be angry, Nora. You have every right to be hurt, deceived, betrayed. But at some point, you'll need to let go of that anger. You need to ask yourself what you want your life to look like when the smoke clears. Do you want to cling to a ghost of what will never be? Or do you want to finally live again? Finally love again?"

I stare into space, contemplating her words, unsure of the correct answer. There isn't one. How can there be? If I admit I still harbor intense feelings for Anderson, that's a slap in the face to Hunter's legacy.

"And maybe you'll find your answer as to why you're wearing Hunter's ring around your neck."

My eyes darting back to Evie's, I clasp the necklace, drawing in the comfort it seems to provide me. "What do you—"

"Are you wearing it to honor Hunter's memory?" She narrows her gaze. "Or for another reason?"

Chapter Thirty-Nine

ANDERSON

"ARE YOU DOING okay?" Esme's voice cuts through my thoughts as I stare out a window in one of the palace's private sitting rooms, waiting to be told it's time for our formal entrance at the gala commemorating the country's birthday.

I normally look forward to today, since it marks the beginning of the winter holiday season. But this year, more than ever, it's a reminder that I'll be spending yet another holiday season alone. Even the snow falling does nothing to warm my heart. I doubt anything will again.

It's been nearly two months since I returned home to a place that doesn't feel like home anymore. Two months of neurologist appointments, meetings with nutritionists, and MRIs. Two months of jumping whenever my Anderson North cell phone rang.

Two months without Nora.

For the first few weeks, I'd sent her flowers every day, even Sundays. Each bouquet was accompanied by another memory of her I cherished. I knew the chances of winning her over were slim, but a part of me held out hope she'd realize we were stronger than my failings.

But starting the first of November, all the bouquets I sent were returned. I had my courier keep trying, but after a week of refused deliveries, I took the hint. Nora wanted nothing to do with me. I can't fault her. Doesn't make it hurt any less, though.

At least I can have some sort of peace of mind that I reached out to Hunter's parents. Told them who I was and what really happened that night. Then I donated a sizable sum of money to the foundation they'd set up in his name, which offered a small scholarship to one high school graduate who showed promise in the area of sports medicine. It won't bring Hunter back, won't erase the past, but I can find solace in the fact that I owned up to my involvement in his death. I'd expected them to go to the media with the story. But they didn't. They thanked me profusely for my "generosity". It made me feel even more guilty about the role I played in taking their son from them.

"I'm great." I flash Esme the fake smile I've spent years mastering. Too bad she's done the same, allowing her to see through me.

"Sure you are." She glides across the room, her champagne-colored gown flowing behind her, which brings out the gold tones in her blonde hair. "Like I'm Mrs. Claus."

I lean in to kiss her cheek, then pass her a mischievous grin. "Is there something you're not telling me? Are you having an affair with Father Christmas? I knew you had a thing for older men, but I—"

The door swings open, a member of the Royal Guard interrupting our conversation upon his entrance. "His Majesty, the King," the man announces, then steps aside as my father walks into the room, wearing the ceremonial military attire required at all formal events. His gray hair is slicked back, his face clean-shaven, but I expect nothing less.

It's one of the antiquated rules I abhor — short, trimmed hair, no mustache or beard allowed. Out of respect for the occasion, I shaved and cut my hair short again, but it will be the last time. Soon, I'll no longer be subjected to any requirement to adhere to these strange rules that have been passed down for generations.

Creed and Zoey, Esme's lady-in-waiting, jump to their feet. Creed stands at attention, his arms locked at his sides, while Zoey is less rigid, her hands clasped together in front of her, head bowed slightly.

"Gabriel. Esme." My father's greeting is proper, as if we're his employees, not his children.

In a way, I suppose we *are* employees. I've never felt much love from this man. After he split from our mum, we were raised by our nannies, only seeing our father during formal events or perhaps a few minutes before bedtime. It was in these days that Esme and I mastered the art of putting on an act. Our entire lives have been one big show of pretending we came from a loving, doting father. Nothing could be further from the truth.

"Your Majesty," I say in greeting.

"Father," Esme acknowledges, refusing to call him anything else, as she's prone to do.

He glances beyond us at Creed and Zoey, who bow and curtsey respectively.

"Your Majesty," they say in unison.

"Would you please wait outside? There's something I must discuss with the Crown Prince in private."

"Certainly, Your Majesty," Creed says curtly.

Esme nods at Zoey, wordlessly telling her to follow. Then she steals a glimpse at Creed. His stoic expression softens for a moment as their gazes lock. I notice his hand twitch, as if about to place it on her back, but he remembers their roles, keeping his arms at his sides as he walks behind her out of the room, Zoey following.

Once the elaborate double doors close with an echoing click, my father relaxes his posture and exhales a breath. "Are you serious about abdicating?" His tone lacks the formality it contained mere seconds ago.

I blink repeatedly, my mind reeling. How could he know? I've only mentioned this to one person, and only because it directly affects her.

"Esme," I exhale, pinching the bridge of my nose. "She couldn't keep her mouth shut, could she?"

"You two have always been close. Two peas in a pod, really." My father chuckles, the sound as odd as a thunderstorm on a sunny day. I can't remember the last time I heard him laugh. I didn't think he was capable.

Who is this man, and what has he done with my father? The man who never reminisced about the past. Who was notoriously stoic and unemotional.

Then again, wasn't I trained to be like that, too? To smile when expected but never show too much emotion.

"And while she typically keeps all your secrets, she also knows some secrets are too important to be remain quiet." Stepping toward me, he levels his gaze on me, his eyes nearly even with mine. "Think about what you're doing, Anderson," he says, dropping all the formalities of using my given first name, opting for the one I've always gone by in my inner circle. "This diagnosis must have been a punch to the gut. It was to me when you finally shared it with me. Making such a life-changing decision while dealing with the psychological effects of everything? I can't help but think you may be acting irrationally."

"I thought you'd be relieved," I counter. "Then you wouldn't have to go over my head and give the crown to Esme anyway."

He shakes his head, his expression pained. "Why would you think I'd do that?"

I lean into him, my eyes on fire. "Because of the way you tossed out Mum!"

He stares at me for several long moments, then sighs, walking past me and lowering himself onto the divan in the sitting area. Etiquette dictates I should also sit, since no one should stand taller than the crown. But that's the least of my concerns right now.

"I never tossed out your mother. She left." He gradually lifts his eyes to mine.

All I can do is blink. He's wrong. Has it been so long that he's forgotten the truth? Has he convinced himself of the veracity of these claims to help him sleep better at night?

"No, she didn't. She—"

"Do you think I enjoyed watching her self-destruct? Think I enjoyed watching her push everyone away?" His distressed voice echoes in the room before he lowers it. "Do you think I enjoy watching *you* do the same thing?"

I've witnessed my father give more than his fair share of performances in the public eye. Like Esme can always tell when I'm faking it, I can detect when my father is. And right now, these emotions are…genuine.

"I'm begging you to believe me," he implores. "I did everything to get her to stay. Told her it didn't matter what happened. That I'd love her even if she were bound to a wheelchair for the rest of her life."

Tears well in his eyes, his chin quivering, showing me a side of this man I didn't think existed. Vulnerable. Defenseless. Weak.

"Nothing I said or did mattered. She was already battling depression. She never really acclimated to the pressures and scrutiny of royal life. The MS diagnosis only worsened it. She refused treatment. Refused everyone who tried to help. Then, she refused to live," he chokes out.

"What are you saying?" I ask guardedly, stepping

toward him.

He pinches his lips together, not immediately responding, as if doing so will give the truth wings and make it real. "I'm saying your mother didn't die from MS." He slowly lifts his gaze to mine, defeat crawling in his features. "She died from an intentional overdose, Anderson."

I exhale deeply, running my hands through my hair as I pace along the marble floor.

"Mum…killed herself?" I can barely get the words out. It seems so absurd. Like something he made up, not something my mother would do.

A vice squeezes my heart as I relive the pain of a ten-year-old boy who was forced to mourn his mother in front of the public's eye. Now I'm the thirty-five-year-old man who struggles to believe the woman he idolized would ever take her life. Then again, when I received my diagnosis, I considered the same thing. More than once. If I hadn't met Nora, there's a strong probability I may have done the same thing my mum did. Take one too many pills one night and never wake up.

"Why didn't you tell us the truth?"

"You and Esme were both so young, Anders. It was difficult enough trying to explain to a nine- and ten-year-old their mother was gone and wouldn't be coming back. To tell you she *chose* to end her life?" He shakes his head. "I couldn't do it."

"Couldn't do it? Even when I accused you of abandoning her? Of kicking her out because you didn't want to be married to someone who no longer appeared perfect?"

He shrugs, something I don't think I've ever seen him do. "I made the decision years ago. I'd rather you hate me than your mother. That's why I didn't say anything."

"Why are you finally saying something now?"

"Because, son, your mother gave up. Stopped fighting for everything she once held dear. Granted, her MS was severe, her decline rapid, unlike yours. Still, I don't want that to be you." He stands, striding toward me with determined steps and taking my hands in his.

"I should have fought harder for your mother, but I didn't. I won't make the same mistake with you. I'm not perfect. I've never purported to be. And I certainly regret some of the decisions I've made, especially where you're concerned. But every decision has been with one goal in mind. Protecting you and Esme."

I close my eyes, another puzzle piece snapping into place. "The accident. That's why you didn't tell me about the role I played." I slowly face him. "Is that right?"

"You were in such a dark place after Kendall's death. I was worried the truth would send you over the edge. Wanted to wait until you were in a better place mentally. Didn't want a repeat of…" He trails off, then returns his gaze to mine. "I had every intention of eventually telling you. I just never found the right time."

I stare at the cream-colored walls surrounding me, crown molding framing them, making everything appear pristine and perfect. But as I've learned throughout my life, appearances can be deceiving. You may think you know the full story, but there are always truths hidden beneath the surface that can shatter your world.

Like my truth shattered Nora's world.

"Listen to me, Anderson." My dad's firm voice forces my gaze back to him. "I don't want you to give all this up because you think your future is uncertain. I'll let you in on a little secret. *All* our futures are uncertain. I could die tomorrow. But I'm not going to let my fear of the future control my decisions in the present. And you shouldn't, either."

He places his hands on my biceps, offering me a reassuring smile. "I understand you haven't gone public with your diagnosis yet, and I won't tell you what to do, when to share it. You must decide that for yourself. But I *can* tell you that you're in a unique position. You can give a voice to this illness. You can give hope to other people with MS." He takes my hand in his once more, squeezing hard, his voice filled with passion and intensity. "You *will* have a future, Anderson. You *will* live a long life. And you *will* find the happiness your mother didn't think she'd ever have. You can still have it all. Including the crown."

I shift my eyes forward, wishing I could summon the hope and confidence he seems to have about the situation. I may still be able to have the crown, but I'll never have it all.

Not anymore.

Chapter Forty

NORA

"I HAD A great time tonight," I say as I come to a stop outside the door to my building, smiling up at James.

After Halloween, I realized I couldn't continue to wallow in my pit of despair, wishing things had ended differently between Anderson and me. If I've learned anything from all the curveballs life has thrown at me, it's that I can't change the past. But I can make decisions today to have a better future. So that's what I've been doing.

Or at least *attempting* to do.

But nothing seems to work. Nothing seems to have the power to erase Anderson from my memory.

James is nice enough. Handsome. Successful. A complete gentleman. He's the type of guy any woman would fall over themselves to date. And a few waitresses at the restaurants he's taken me to on our handful of outings have done precisely that.

But it's missing that spark. That something I can't explain. That sensation of my soul connecting with another person.

I fear I'll never experience that again.

Then again, a part of me doesn't want to experience that again, especially when the fall from so high can be debilitating.

"I did, too." He leans his arm against the wall behind me and curves toward me, his lips brushing mine.

I close my eyes, desperate to feel something, *anything* when his tongue swipes with mine, his hand grasps my hip, his arousal presses against my stomach. But I'm empty, going through the motions expected to make everyone around me think I'm okay. That I've moved on.

Like I did with Jeremy.

Is James my new Jeremy? Will I keep pretending until things spiral out of control, then the next thing I know, I'm marrying a man I don't love, hoping it will mend my broken heart?

We repeat what we don't repair.

Chloe's words from all those months ago echo in my subconscious, coming out of nowhere, knocking the wind from me. Is that what I'm doing? Am I simply repeating the same mistakes I made instead of trying to repair my shattered heart? But how can I even attempt to repair that? How can I mend something that's missing a huge piece?

"Invite me upstairs," James begs before diving in for another impassioned kiss. "Can't you feel how desperate I am for you?"

He pulses against me, moving his lips from mine, traveling along my neckline, but it doesn't excite me. His clean-shaven jaw does nothing for me, except make me long for Anderson's goatee and wandering hands.

"James," I whimper, but not out of pleasure. It's more apologetic. Contrite. Remorseful.

He hears it, too, and stops, pulling back. Then he sighs. "You're breaking it off, aren't you?"

I hesitate, parting my lips. Then I nod. "I'm sorry. It's not you. You're great. And I want to like you. I really do. I wish…" I look up at the December sky, Christmas decorations lighting up the city. This is normally my favorite time of year, especially in Manhattan. It always feels so magical.

This year, I can't help but feel like part of my soul is missing.

"I wish I weren't still clinging to the past," I admit, surprising myself with my confession of the truth I've fought to hide.

"I wish you weren't, too." He grabs my glove-covered hand and brings it to his mouth, leaving a light kiss on it before releasing his hold on me and stepping away. "Whoever he is, I hope he realizes how special you are." He holds my gaze for a protracted moment. Then he turns and disappears around the corner.

"I think he did." I smile wistfully as a tiny snowflake lands on my eyelash.

Hunter once told me it was good luck, that I should make a wish. I always told him there was no such thing as luck, that everything in life happened for a reason. But something in the air tonight tells me that maybe a little good luck is precisely what I need right now. So, instead of brushing off the snowflake, I pause for a moment and make a wish.

It doesn't matter if I know it will never come true. For the first time in months, a slight twinge of hope flutters in my stomach. I pray this will be a sign of good things to come, of finally starting the next stage of my life.

Of finally starting this next chapter.

I trudge up to my apartment, shaking off the winter chill as I step inside, my heart flying into my throat when a voice greets me.

"How was the date?" Chloe asks, lounging on my couch as if she lives here.

I take a minute to steady my breathing, my hand covering my chest. She should know better than to startle me like this. I'm a single woman living by myself in New York City. It's not exactly the safest.

"Please, make yourself at home," I quip once my pulse has gone back to normal.

"I did." She raises a glass of wine off the coffee table. "So, how was it?"

I shrug out of my coat and hang it over one of the stools by the kitchen island before heading into the living area and flopping onto the couch beside her. "I ended things."

"I had a feeling."

I snap my eyes toward her. "Why do you say that?"

"This was date five." She sips her wine. "You seem to have a five date max lately."

"At least I'm dating," I remind her.

"That's true." She pauses. "But are you dating for the right reasons?"

"What do you mean?"

She blows out an exaggerated sigh. "You know what I mean. Are you dating because you want to meet someone? Or are you doing it to *forget* someone?"

My silence is the only answer she needs. I wish I could tell her I'm genuinely interested in forming a connection with another human, but the truth remains. There's only one person I want that with. Even though I should never trust him again. My heart is still at war with my brain. I fear it always will be.

"Okay. That's it." Chloe shoots to her feet. "I thought you'd eventually come to your senses and realize what's important, but apparently that was wishful thinking."

I give her a sideways glance. "Come to my senses about what?"

"What you walked away from."

"Walked away?" I stand, although my five-four height doesn't intimidate her short, five-two stature. What

Chloe lacks in height, she makes up for in tenacity.

"Prince Gabriel! Anderson! Whatever you call him."

"Did you forget he's the reason Hunter died? That I lost the baby? That he knew who I was when he fucked me but kept me in the dark?"

"I didn't forget. You won't *let* me forget. You remind me at every turn."

"So what? You think I should forgive him? How the hell can I do that? Better yet, how can I respect Hunter's legacy when I'm in love with the man who killed him?" I exclaim, the words spilling from my lips like lava as I say everything I've kept to myself for weeks. "Can you please tell me how I'm supposed to come to terms with that? Because I would fucking love to know!" My voice reverberates against the walls of my apartment, tears streaming down my cheeks. I can only imagine what my neighbors must think of me right now. These walls aren't exactly soundproof.

"That's what it all boils down to, isn't it? This is still about Hunter."

"No. I…," I stammer, struggling to find the words I need to make Chloe understand. I'm not even sure *I* understand. Could she be right? Is this still about Hunter? I thought I'd let him go. His ashes no longer sit on my dresser, but I still wear the necklace with his engagement ring, refusing to take it off. Did I trade one crutch for another?

"You are so goddamn stubborn sometimes," she groans. "Let me put this in terms you'll understand. Your favorite movie. *An Affair to Remember*. Every time we watch it, you yell at the screen during a certain scene. Which one?"

I swallow hard, my face heating. "The theater scene," I answer timidly. "When Nicki Ferrante sees Terry McKay." I release a long sigh as I lower myself back to the couch. "I always scream at him to open his eyes. To realize that she doesn't stand. To figure out the truth."

"Exactly." She sits beside me and pushes what appears to be the January edition of her magazine toward me. "Consider this me screaming at you to open *your* eyes."

A knot forms in my throat as I stare at the cover, Anderson's soulful blue eyes staring back at me. But there's something missing. The spark I once saw every time he peered at me.

I lift the magazine and flip it open to where Chloe placed a sticky note, reading the headline and tagline.

An Exclusive with Prince Gabriel: Heavy is the Head That Wears the Crown

The Bachelor Prince opens up about his recent Multiple Sclerosis diagnosis, and what it means for the future

Inhaling a sharp breath, my chin quivers as I lift my eyes to Chloe's. "He has MS?"

She nods. "His publicist reached out to me a few days after you returned home from your trip. At first, I told her I wasn't interested in writing any story about the fuckhead who broke my friend's heart."

I blow out a laugh. I can picture her saying that.

"But then I started thinking. In my initial dealings with his publicist, she mentioned Prince Gabriel — Anderson — had been diagnosed with MS back in September, but had been displaying symptoms and having flareups as far back as ten years ago." She pauses. "So I looked into what an MS flareup *is*. Do you know what I found out?"

I stare forward, remaining silent.

"Pins-and-needles sensation. Muscle weakness or numbness. Blurred vision. Sometimes blindness in one eye."

"What he described happened the night of the wreck."

Chloe places her hand on my bicep in a reassuring manner. "He refused to come right out and say it, but it appears that's what happened."

"That must be what Creed was talking about," I breathe, then glance at her. "When I learned the truth, I'd asked his chief protection officer how Anderson could have no memory of forcing Hunter's car off the road. He said he wasn't at liberty to say. He must have known about the MS."

"It's not that he couldn't remember. He just couldn't *see*. Couple that with the trauma of losing Kendall Davies, and it's no wonder his brain tried to protect him from the truth. Just like yours did."

I stare straight ahead, processing this, wondering why Anderson didn't tell me. But would it have made a difference?

For months after I lost Hunter and Ember, I was desperate to find someone to blame for what happened. So I put that blame on me. If I hadn't been late getting ready, hadn't selfishly wanted to rest my eyes, maybe I would have seen the car driving toward us and could have prevented what happened.

But once Anderson came clean, I could stop blaming myself. I had someone else I could blame.

If I forgive him, who will I blame?

"I won't pretend this is an easy decision," Chloe soothes, cutting through my thoughts. "You have to do what's best for *you*. No one else." Her gaze catches on my necklace before returning to me. "So you need to ask yourself…"

Standing, she reaches into her pocket. Then she sets a penny on the open magazine next to a paragraph in the article announcing the opening of Anderson's photography exhibit in the Village titled *Faith. Hope. Perseverance.*

When I jerk my head up, she gives me a sly smile, wordlessly answering my question about where she could have gotten this exact penny. One with the same blemishes as the one I flipped on Route 66. She got it from Anderson himself.

"What do *you* want?" She allows her question to linger before turning and leaving me alone.

I shift my attention back to the penny and the article, studying Anderson's smile. But it's not the same one I remember. The one that greeted me good morning. The one that beamed at me when I agreed to travel along Route 66 with him. The one that curled into a smirk when he shamelessly flirted with me.

Swallowing hard, I grab the penny off the table, the weight of the coin feeling much heavier than normal. Probably because of the truth it holds in its rigid edges and tarnished face. The truth it held all those weeks ago, too. And like all those weeks ago, I know how to solve this predicament.

"Heads I stay. Tails I go."

I briefly close my eyes, then toss the coin, watching as it flips and topples until it clatters on the magazine. I don't even bother looking to see how it landed.

Like I told Anderson back on Route 66, I already figured out what I truly wanted while that coin was in the air.

Chapter Forty-One

ANDERSON

SOFT JAZZ MUSIC plays, creating an upscale and trendy ambience as people float around me in the open space that's reminiscent of a refurbished warehouse. Every so often, someone takes a break from mingling with other New York socialites to congratulate me on my photography, as well as my latest venture of founding an organization, the main purpose of which is to encourage those with disabilities to persevere through them, to not limit themselves. I still have a great deal of work to do, but I hope to have an annual sporting event featuring only children and adults who are less abled than most people. Kendall used to volunteer with a similar charity here in the States, teaching them how to play volleyball while sitting on the ground. I'm happy I can now follow in her legacy.

"It appears people are enjoying it." Esme sidles up next to me, handing me a glass of champagne, which surprises me.

Ever since I returned home, she's been adamant that I control my diet, since the research she'd done demonstrated that some of my symptoms can be managed with diet. That meant giving up alcohol and coffee, along with a few of my other guilty pleasures. If it allows me to remain active one day longer, though, I'll do it. It's a stark contrast to what I thought when I was first diagnosed. It took meeting Nora to help me realize that life is still worth living, even if from a wheelchair. For that, I'll always be grateful.

"I hope so."

"Well, if this whole king thing doesn't work out, at least you know you can always fall back on being a professional photographer." She draws in an excited breath. "You could shoot weddings! Bet you could meet some nice single girls in the bridal party."

I roll my eyes. "I'm not king yet. And hopefully that won't happen anytime soon. But at least now I know it's what I want."

She loops her arm through mine, steering me away from the makeshift bar and toward part of the exhibit I've avoided most of the night. "Probably a good thing you have no desire to take up professional photography. You really have no eye when it comes to beauty, do you?"

She stops in front of a series of photographs that make up the "faith" component of tonight's exhibition. Some people probably expected to see images of churches or other religious establishments, but that's not faith to me. I'd lost my faith in everything. In love. In hope. In living. It wasn't until I met Nora I learned to have faith again.

I smile as I admire the collection of photos I chose to show *my* version of faith. It's an innate response whenever I look at Nora, even if only in a photograph. Esme was just joking, but there's a hint of truth to her statement. These images truly don't do Nora's beauty justice.

I pull away from Esme, getting lost in the photos. Each one causes a memory to rush forward. Of scaling a fence and dragging Nora into that abandoned drive-in. Of spray-painting our names on a Cadillac in Texas. Of eating greasy diner food and feeling not a single ounce of remorse. Of laughing. Of living. Of loving.

I approach the image I'd taken that morning in Santa Monica as she slept. I run a finger along the silhouette of her frame, only the shadow of her body visible in the dark light. What I wouldn't give to touch the real thing. But that ship has sailed. A part of me had hoped Nora might show up tonight, especially when her friend, Chloe, had agreed to write an exclusive piece about my MS diagnosis. But it's nearly eleven o'clock. Nora's not coming.

With a sigh, I reluctantly drop my hand, taking one last chance to appreciate Nora's beauty, even if it's in the form of a photograph. "My favorite moment is you," I murmur to no one.

The sound of a gentle clanging catches my attention. I look down, my brow furrowing when I notice a penny between my feet.

But not just any penny.

I whirl around, surprised when my sister no longer lingers a few feet away. In her place stands Nora. *My* Nora. Wearing the same gorgeous dress she did on our last night together.

My heart ricochets to my throat, my breathing increasing as I stare at her. I want to reach out, make sure I'm not dreaming, that this isn't some flareup and I'm hallucinating, although I don't think that's possible. Still, I didn't actually think *this* was possible, either. That she'd actually show up.

I start toward her, but she holds up a hand, preventing me from taking another step.

"I'm going to ask you this once, and I need you to tell me the truth."

All I can do is nod.

"That night," she begins with a quiver as she clutches the necklace around her throat. I recognize that chain.

The same one I kept in my possession for years. My talisman. My good luck charm. She toys with the diamond ring, rolling it around her fingers. "When you swerved into the wrong lane…" She brings her eyes to mine, pain filling her expression. "Was it because of the MS?"

"You read Chloe's article?" I arch a single brow, to which she nods. Then I expel a breath. "At the time of the crash, I didn't know I had MS. Since my diagnosis, all the doctors I've spoken with have agreed the symptoms I experienced that night indicate it was most likely a flareup."

She peers beyond me at the photos adorning the walls as she absorbs my response. Then she returns her gaze to mine. There's still not a single hint of emotion within. Her demeanor is calm and even, like she's asking me the time of day or my favorite color, not about the details of the night that ruined her life.

"And when you told me about your involvement, you already knew about your MS." It's not a question.

"That was why I was driving across the country. I'd just been diagnosed. I knew it was a very real possibility I'd lose the ability to drive at some point, so I wanted to take advantage of it while I still could."

"Oh." Unease registers on her face.

I step toward her, but still keep a respectful distance between us. "At no point were you in danger," I explain hurriedly. "The doc told me what warning signs to look for, and I didn't have a single flareup or relapse while we were together. I have a type of MS called remitting-relapsing, and mine hasn't progressed that much yet. I'm now on a course of treatment to help control it, as well."

"So you knew you had MS when we said goodbye. And you knew the MS caused the wreck."

Her tone is akin to an attorney cross-examining a witness. And that's what I feel like. The accused on the witness stand pleading for my life.

"Yes."

"Yet you didn't say anything?"

Finally, there's a quiver in her voice, indicating she's not just an unfeeling robot. That despite the passing of over two months since we last saw each other, she still feels this same connection, same electricity, same love.

"Would it have mattered?" I ask, my words coming out strong. "Would you have felt any differently if I told you the truth? It still doesn't change anything. Still doesn't erase what happened. And… I don't know…"

I exhale a breath as I shake my head, running a hand through my hair.

"There was this tiny part of me that hoped you *would* forgive me. That you *would* be able to see past the biggest mistake of my life. That you'd soon realize that yes, while what happened was a goddamn tragedy, I was also the person who saved you. Who ran toward a smoking car to pull you from it, completely ignorant of the fact that I caused it. That I ran toward it because, deep down, I *am* a good person. A good person who made a horrible fucking mistake, but a good person, nonetheless."

My voice seems to ring out around us, my breathing labored. For months, I thought about what I'd say to her if I got the opportunity. I didn't think I ever would. But based on the blank expression on her face, I fear it's not enough. That nothing will make her see the guilt that plagues me. That guilt I've sworn to carry with me the rest of my life.

On a long sigh, Nora turns from me, stooping to grab the penny from the floor. "I flipped it."

"Excuse me?"

"Tonight. Chloe brought over a copy of the magazine. And left a penny." She brings up the coin. "*This* penny, which I assume she got from you."

I nod subtly.

"Do you know I can't even look at a goddamn penny without being reminded of you? That every time I do, all I think about is some arrogant bastard who tried to impress me with his knowledge about the plan to steal Lincoln's body."

A smile teases my lips. "Sounds like a complete arse."

"You have no idea." Her eyes shine with unshed tears as she closes the space between us. "I should hate you. I shouldn't be able to stand being in your presence."

"But you don't," I manage to say. It's a mixture of a statement and question. When she doesn't respond, I press further. "Why did you flip the coin?"

"To help me decide."

"Help you decide what?"

Her chin trembles. "About you."

"And what did it tell you to do about me?"

Tears well as she shakes her head. "I didn't need it to tell me what I've known all along." She takes my hand in hers, the warmth of her fingers interlocking with mine for the first time in months sending electricity humming through my veins. I swallow hard, doing my best not to get my hopes up. It doesn't mean anything. She's here, but Hunter's ring still hangs from her neck.

"And what's that?"

"That you may have pulled me from that wreck all those years ago, but it wasn't until you struck up a conversation with me in Chicago that you truly saved my life."

She moves her hands to my cheeks, clutching them tightly as her lips inch toward mine. Her breath kisses my skin, a tingle of anticipation filling me. My pulse increases, my mouth growing dry.

When she's about to erase the final space between us, sealing her declaration with a kiss, I stop her, pressing a finger to her lips. It kills me to have to do this right here, right now, but things are different. I'm no longer Anderson North, some guy who slightly resembles Prince Gabriel of Belmont. I'm here *as* Prince Gabriel of Belmont. She needs to understand what she's getting into.

"What is it?" she asks, gaze searching mine. "I thought this was what you wanted. I—"

"It is," I answer quickly, my jaw clenching with need. "God, you have no idea how much I want this." I glance over my shoulder at a few members of the media, their brows knitted in curiosity, obviously realizing the woman in my embrace is the same woman from the photographs providing the backsplash to our reunion.

"There are reporters here. If we do this, there's no going back. You'll officially be Prince Gabriel of Belmont's girlfriend. So I want you to really think about that. To really consider if you're ready for this."

She stares at me for what feels like an eternity. Blinks. Contemplates. Then smiles. Reaching up, she tousles my hair, messing it up. I can't help but marvel at how our roles have reversed. All those months ago, I was the one encouraging Nora to finally let down her hair and live. Now she's doing the same thing for me.

"I fell in love with Anderson North." She pushes a few tendrils of hair out of my face. "In my eyes, that's who you'll always be. My Anderson North."

She crushes her lips against mine, her kiss fevered and frantic as we reconnect. But this kiss is so much more addictive, so much more heated, so much more intimate than any of our previous exchanges. Because, for the first time, we're sharing this personal moment with every part of each other. With every piece of our minds, our souls, our hearts. We've bared ourselves to each other, put ourselves at risk, praying the other keeps us safe.

My chest heaving through my labored breaths, I manage to pull away. I faintly make out a few whistles and cheers, accompanied by the familiar clicking of camera shutters, but I don't care about any of that. I have this amazing, incredible woman in my arms. We're back in our bubble. The only place I want to be.

"Say it again," I murmur against her.

I feel her mouth quirk up into a smile. "You'll always be Anderson North to me."

"No. The other thing."

She pulls back, peering at me with a furrowed brow. Then understanding tugs on her expression, peace washing over her. Bringing her lips to mine, she whispers those three words I didn't think I'd ever hear.

"I love you."

I push out a relieved breath, my heart expanding. "And I love you." I cover her mouth with mine once more, drinking in everything this woman is. Everything she has been. Everything she's yet to be.

Our love story may be unconventional, but at the end of the day, it's just that. A love story. A story of perseverance. Of strength. But mostly, of the power of forgiveness.

Never in a million years did I expect Nora to forgive me after everything I took from her. I'm still not sure I deserve it. But I plan to do everything in my power to earn that forgiveness every day for the rest of my life.

And I have every intention of living a very long life with this woman by my side.

Chapter Forty-Two

NORA

SEVEN MONTHS LATER

THE SUN WARMS my skin as I sit on the pool deck of Evie and Julian's new home in Rye, just outside the city. I never thought they'd leave their proverbial castle in the sky, the penthouse apartment overlooking Columbus Circle, but with a baby on the way, they decided it was time to move in order to raise their daughter somewhere more family friendly.

As did Chloe and Lincoln, who also have a baby due the same month as Evie and Julian. Based on their due dates this fall, it seems both couples got busy around Valentine's Day.

"Okay, girls. Now that it's just us, it's time to open your *real* gifts," I say, reaching underneath the table by the pool and retrieving two identical gift bags, handing them across the table to today's guests of honor — Evie and Chloe.

I didn't think I'd ever see the day Chloe would be pregnant. Until she met Lincoln, she was vehemently anti-relationship. I guess all it takes is meeting the right person to change your mind, to convince you that you can have everything.

I glance over my shoulder at Anderson, who sits around a table at the other end of the pool, chatting animatedly with Julian, Lincoln, and Asher. It warms my heart to see all the men in our lives get along as well as we girls do. It gives me hope that nothing will ever stand between our friendship. Not misunderstandings. Not children. Not even an ocean…which, in just a few days, will separate us.

"We told you," Chloe begins, rubbing her stomach. She's only six months along, but because of her short and slender body, it looks like she's ready to pop at any second. "You didn't need to get us anything. You two threw us this Baby-Q." She waves her hand around the remnants of today's event. Since Chloe's and Evie's due dates are so close, Izzy and I made the decision to throw a joint "shower" for both of them. It was easier than having to do this twice.

"And we told you that you were crazy," Izzy states. "It's not every day two of your friends get knocked up."

"Yay for sex!" Evie jokes, giggling, readjusting herself in her chair, finding it difficult to get comfortable.

A hint of nostalgia fills me. I hadn't been much further along than my two friends when I lost Ember and Hunter. A year ago, it would have been difficult for me to be around Evie and Chloe, watch them bring life into the world, knowing I lost that opportunity. But I no longer feel that way. Anderson has given me hope I *can* have all that again.

"Go ahead," I encourage, nodding at the bags. "But you each need to do it at the same time. The gifts are identical."

Evie and Chloe share a look, then dig into the bags, pulling out the item on top. When they fold back the tissue, they burst out laughing at the oversized wine glasses decorated with the words "Mommy's Sippy Cup".

"This will definitely come in handy," Chloe jokes. "But I'm not sure I'll use it. I'll probably drink straight from the bottle." She playfully rolls her eyes, but I can tell she doesn't mean it. She's never been a big drinker, too worried she'll follow in her mother's alcoholic footsteps, especially now that she's on the brink of becoming a mother herself.

"Nothing wrong with drinking straight from the bottle once in a while." I wink. "Keep going."

The girls reach back into their bags and pull out a red box that looks like a first-aid kit.

"Open it," Izzy instructs, both of us sharing a satisfied smile.

Evie and Chloe unlatch their kits and laugh once more. Instead of containing bandages and medical supplies as one would expect, it's filled with mini liquor bottles, all of them relabeled. "For poop-splosions." "Drink when the baby's been up all night crying." "For parental use during teething."

"This is perfect," Evie says through her giggles, closing the lid on the kit and returning her attention to the bag, both of them pulling out the final item.

When they push back the tissue, they gasp, the lighthearted atmosphere shifting to one that's more meaningful and poignant. Tears dot their eyes, their gazes trained on the dust jacket of the thin, hardcover book. It's a cartoon likeness of younger versions of the four of us, our arms wrapped around each other.

"How did—"

"We went behind your backs and got help from a few of the graphic designers at the magazine," Izzy explains. "They did all these illustrations for us."

"If you flip through, you'll see they even included the guys in there, too."

Evie opens to the first page and reads the text Izzy and I worked on, which was a feat considering we're not the writers amongst our circle of friends. Evie and Chloe are.

"Life is full of ups and downs, happy moments and sad moments, beginnings and endings," she reads with a quivering voice. *"But with the right friends, your downs won't seem so bad. Your sad times won't be so tough. And the endings will still have a glimmer of hope."* She looks back to us, her tears now streaming steadily down her face.

"This is incredible," Chloe remarks through her own gentle sobs. One thing is certain. Pregnancy certainly softened her. Although I've always known she has a soft side. She just doesn't allow many people to see it. "You two did this all on your own?"

"Your two best friends only have their first baby once," Izzy says. "You deserve something to commemorate it. To commemorate us."

And that's exactly what this book is. Yes, it's written for children as a way to offer advice to help them through all the ups and downs they'll navigate throughout their life. But it was also to commemorate what we've been through as friends. That no matter what life has thrown at each of us, we've found our strength through each other.

"I love you girls," Evie states, wiping her tears. Izzy and I get up and skirt to the other side of the table, all of us wrapping our arms around each other.

A thickness forms in my throat over the fact that I'll no longer have this amazing support group mere miles away. But our bond is too strong. Regardless of what the future brings, of how many miles separate us, we'll survive. We'll teach our children the meaning of true friendship, and one day, they'll be just as inseparable and devoted to each other as we are.

There are friends.

There is family.

Then there are friends who become family.

These three women are my family. They always will be.

***

"How are you holding up?" Anderson asks later that evening as we lay in the bed in the Upper West Side townhouse he'd purchased so I'd have somewhere to call home in New York.

I told him we could keep the lease on my place, but he insisted I deserved something better than a tiny apartment where the pipes creaked and the walls were paper thin. Not to mention the security was questionable, which is something I still have trouble taking into account.

"Good," I say.

"Are you sure about this?" He touches my chin, drawing my eyes to his.

"Why? Are *you* having second thoughts?"

He brushes his lips against mine. "Waking up with you beside me every day? Being able to have you as an *amuse-bouche* before dinner?" he jokes, considering that's how we ended up naked in this bed before seven at night. "Not a chance in hell."

"Me, either."

While I was initially apprehensive about taking this next step with Anderson, it's the right thing to do. I'd be lying if I said I didn't feel a slight bit of vindication when I told my mother I would be moving to Belmont, proving her wrong when she'd told me Anderson was using me as a cheap piece of ass before moving on to something better. I can't wait for her to ask to come visit, only for me to refuse her request.

Regardless, it's time to start this next chapter. With Anderson. He hasn't popped *the* question yet, but we've discussed it. Not like a normal couple would. Instead, he warned me about everything I'd have to give up once I'm his wife. My privacy. My career.

If he was trying to scare me, it didn't work. I knew what I'd give up once I entered into this relationship. And my career isn't really a career. Merely something I did to get over Hunter. I don't need it anymore, considering most of my free time is devoted to Anderson's charitable foundation. He's all I need now. I no longer dwell on the past. My last reminder of Hunter, the ring he proposed with, is now kept safe in my box of memories. Where he belongs. In my memories. Not in my present. In its place is a new necklace Anderson had made for me — a charm with the penny that changed everything for us. That will always remind me of the best adventure of my life.

"You're not going to miss your friends so much that you change your mind?"

"We'll be back here enough. We'll need to get your money's worth out of this amazing apartment. And this bed."

"I can get on board with that." He buries his face in my neck, his scruff causing a tingling to stir in my core, regardless of the fact he just treated me to yet another incredible orgasm. But I doubt I'll ever have my fill of this man. Every day, I find myself falling in love with him all over again. With his heart. With his soul. With his devotion.

"I knew you would. But seriously…" I prop myself on my side, resting my head in my hand as Anderson traces the curve of my body. "An ocean can't sever our friendship." I draw my bottom lip between my teeth, hesitating, before adding, "Although in a few months, travel may become difficult."

He frowns, brows drawing in. "Why?"

I leisurely lower my free hand to my stomach, resting it where a tiny life grows.

Anderson's expression grows wide at my insinuation. "Are you…"

I beam. "I am."

Excitement overwhelms him as he drags me into his arms, his mouth covering mine in an impassioned kiss, consuming, enthralling, loving.

When he pulls back, he frames my face in his hands, his gaze full of wonder. "How?"

"Well…" I smirk. "When a boy likes a girl, they—"

He growls playfully. "I know *how*. But I thought you were on birth control."

"I am. Apparently, they're not lying when they say it's not a hundred percent effective." I frown. "You're not upset, are you?"

"God no." He pulls me back into his embrace, kissing the top of my head. "I never thought this would happen. After you learned the truth, I didn't think you'd *want* to have kids, especially with me."

"I don't care about the past. I told you that."

"No. Not about that. But…" He licks his lips, collecting his thoughts. "I may not always be like this, Nora. I may not always be physically able."

I release a small sigh as I bring my lips to his. "I love you. All of you. Even if you have to use a wheelchair one day, I'll still love you. My love comes without conditions. Always has. Always will."

He presses his mouth back to mine, a groan escaping. "Marry me," he murmurs.

"You're only saying that because you're my baby daddy," I laugh.

I expect his eyes to be alight with amusement, but they're not.

"I'm serious, Nora. I want to marry you." He briefly

releases his hold on me, reaching across the mattress to open the drawer on the nightstand before returning to me, holding a velvet box.

I shoot to sitting, bringing up the duvet to cover my exposed chest, as if that will help me feel any less vulnerable than I do. He leans against the headboard, full of the same confidence I remember from our very first meeting.

"I've been trying to figure out the best time to ask you, thinking I needed to have this elaborate thing planned. But now that I think about it, that's not what you need. If I've learned anything from our time together, it's that the only thing that matters is now. The present. This moment."

When he flips open the box, I gasp, my attention drawn to the stunning diamond ring. It has a vintage flair to it. The breathtaking stone is flanked by rows of smaller glittering diamonds along the band.

"Nora Jean Tremblay, you are the most incredible, selfless, compassionate woman I know. When I saw you sitting in that diner in Chicago, I physically *felt* you. I hadn't experienced anything like that in so long. I didn't know anything about you. Your name. Your smile. Your voice. Regardless, in that moment, you saved me. Before then, I was in a dark place. I didn't think life was worth it anymore. But you reminded me what it felt like to live. To laugh." He cups my cheek, swiping the tears off my face. "To love. So, please, be my wife. Be my partner. Be my lifelong road trip companion." He poises his lips on mine. "Be my greatest adventure."

I can barely breathe through the lump in my throat, but manage to squeak out a tiny, "Yes."

He crushes his mouth against mine, tugging my body to his. Grabbing my left hand, he slips the ring onto my finger. The instant it slides into place, a warmth fills me.

This is now the third time a man has proposed to me. But it never felt like this, even with Hunter. Like a puzzle piece finally snapping into place.

My mother once told me that falling in love is a lot like giving someone a loaded gun pointed at your heart and trusting them not to pull the trigger. I always thought it was a cynical way of looking at love. That allowing yourself to fall in love was giving someone the power to destroy you.

For the longest time, that was how I looked at love. As something that could destroy, not uplift. Something that could break, not mend. Something that should be feared, not revered.

She was wrong.

I no longer look at love as something to be wary of. No longer keep my heart locked tight for fear that someone will destroy it. We can't control what happens in the future. But we can control what happens right now. In this moment.

And right now, I have never been more in love with Anderson North.

All little girls dream of finding their own Prince Charming.

I finally found mine.

The End

Tangled Games

It's not over yet...

Nora and Anderson's next chapter is coming in early 2021.

Every girl dreams of becoming a princess. But this is no fairy tale.

When I met Anderson North, I fell in love with the man, not the title. With his heart, not the crown.

But as I step foot in the Nation of Belmont for the first time as the Crown Prince's fiancée, I'm reminded of exactly who he is outside of the bubble we built around ourselves.

I'm reminded of exactly who I'll need to become if I'm to survive this tangled web of antiquated rules, constant media attention, and negative publicity from a country that hates the idea of an American marrying their future king.

This may be a life of privilege and excess, but I soon learn that with notoriety comes jealousy.
With fame comes enemies.
With a crown comes a gilded cage.

I've always dreamed of being a princess. I didn't realize our happily ever after would come at a price.

Pre-order *Tangled Games* today:
www.tkleighauthor.com/tangled-games

<h1 style="text-align:center">Playlist</h1>

Blow Me (One Last Kiss) - P!nk
Fall - James Arthur
Peer Pressure - James Bay, featuring Julia Michaels
Good Stuff - Griff
Reason to Stay - Sody
Can You Hear Me - Anson Seabra
Route 66 - Chuck Berry
Fade Into You - Mazzy Star
Either You Love Me or You Don't - Plested
Have a Little Faith in Me - John Hiatt
Photograph - Cody Fry
Break My Heart Right - James Bay
River of Tears - Alessia Cara
Rush - Lewis Capaldi featuring Jessie Reyez
Fall on Me - A Great Big World featuring Christina Aguilera
Already Gone - Sleeping At Last
Tell Me It's Over - Avril Lavigne
Hurt - Lady Antebellum
Someone Saved My Life Tonight - Elton John
Favorite T-Shirt - Jake Scott
BRKN - Madison Ryann Ward
Superman - Ronan Keating
I Love You - Marcus Johns
Satellite - Ben Abraham
Always & Forever - Lily Kershaw
Consequences - Camila Cabello
Bitter Pill - Gavin James
Need You Tonight - Welshly Arms

Hate Me Too - Emily Burns
Covered In Chaos - Billy Lockett
Mixed Signals - Ruth B.
Heaven - Julia Michaels
Everything I Wanted - Billie Eilish
Colour Me In - Damien Rice
Addicted to Love - Florence + The Machine
Please Stay - Francois Klark
Reason to Stay - Sody
Homesick - Declan J Donovan
Revival - Gregory Porter
Finally // Beautiful Stranger - Halsey
Beautiful & Brutal - Plested
Let's Fall in Love for the Night - Finneas
Explain You - JP Saxe
Last Time I Saw Sorry - Kane Brown, John Legend
I Choose - Alessia Cara
New York - Jake Isaac
I Love You's - Hailee Steinfeld
Square One - Tom Petty

Acknowledgments

Up until a few days ago, I'd planned on starting these acknowledgments celebrating the end of another series... Because up until a few days ago, this *was* supposed to be the end of this series. That's when my betas talked me into doing something I already knew I'd have to do... Continue Nora and Anderson's story.

When I first outlined their story, the first half was the road trip with the second half being Nora's struggles to adjust to what life as a royal would be like, as well as Anderson's continuing struggles with MS. Well, as you all probably know by now, things don't always go as planned. I didn't want to rush Nora's journey on Route 66 with Anderson, because I truly believe it was important for her to take her time and finally make peace with her past. So I made the decision to have that be the focus of this book instead. But as my lovely betas pointed out, their story isn't over. In fact, this is just the beginning. So there will be one more book in this series — Tangled Games — where we'll be off to the royal world of Belmont, and I can't wait to get started.

You know that saying that it takes a village to raise a baby? Well, it takes a village to raise a book baby, too. And none of this would be possible without *my* village. First and foremost, a big thanks to my husband, Stan, who's always supported me in my writing. When we drove Route 66 eleven years ago, I never could have imagined I'd eventually use our travels as the basis for a royal romance novel. Hell, I never could have imagined I'd write a single book, let alone twenty-six (I think). His unwavering support to this crazy career of mine has made all of this possible.

To my nannies — Brooke and Lauren. Thank you for loving and taking care of Harper as if she's your own.

To my fantastic PA — Melissa Crump. You're a rockstar. Thanks so much for all you do for me so I can spend less time online and more time writing. I couldn't do this without you.

To my amazing editor — Kim Young. Thank you for all your amazing work on every single one of my book babies. You're the only person I'd trust with my manuscripts. Thank you for all the care and expertise you show in your work.

To my author BFF — A.D. Justice. I love you. Thanks for always being there for me and always giving your honest advice, even if it's not what I want to hear. (But I've known you long enough to pretty much always know what you're going to say.)

To Emily and the entire gang at Social Butterfly PR. Thanks so much for all your help with this release. You make publishing infinitely easier.

To GB — Thanks for letting me pick your brain about your MS diagnosis and everything you went through and are still going through, not just physically but psychologically. It really helped me shape Anderson's character and gave me a grasp of what his mental process was. I can't thank you enough for all the time you spent answering my questions and assuring me I'd captured those early days after a diagnosis correctly.

To my beta readers — Lin, Stacy, Sylvia, Vicky, and Joelle. Thank you for always dropping whatever you have going on to read my stuff. I sincerely appreciate it. And you win. You're getting more.

To my admins — Lin, Vicky, Lea, and Joelle. Thanks for keeping an eye on my social media and reader group so I can stay offline and write.

To my review team. Thank you for all your unwavering support over the years and for always fitting my books into your schedule.

To my reader group. Thanks for being such a fun group, allowing me to pop in for a laugh when I need one.

And last but not least, thanks to YOU! Whether this is your first T.K. book or your twenty-sixth, thanks so much for taking a risk on my work. I have so much more planned in the years to come. So stay tuned. This is just the beginning for the Royals of Belmont.

Love and peace,

~ T.K.

Books by T.K. Leigh

ROMANTIC SUSPENSE
The Beautiful Mess Series
A Beautiful Mess
A Tragic Wreck
Gorgeous Chaos
Chasing the Dragon (Deception Duet #1)
Slaying the Dragon (Deception Duet #2)
Vanished: A Beautiful Mess Series Novel

The Vault
Inferno

Heart of Light

CONTEMPORARY ROMANCE
The Redemption Series
Promise: A Redemption Series Prologue
Commitment
Redemption

The Dating Games Series
Dating Games
Wicked Games
Mind Games
Dangerous Games
Royal Games
Tangled Games

ROMANTIC COMEDY
The Book Boyfriend Chronicles
The Other Side of Someday
Writing Mr. Right

MATURE YOUNG ADULT
Heart of Marley

For more information on any of these titles and upcoming
releases, please visit T.K.'s website:
www.tkleighauthor.com

About the Author

T.K. Leigh, otherwise known as Tracy Leigh Kellam, is the *USA Today* Bestselling author of the Beautiful Mess series, in addition to several other works ranging from sexy and sinful to fun and flirty. Originally from New England, she now resides in sunny Southern California with her husband, beautiful daughter, rescue dog, and three cats. When she's not planted in front of her computer, writing away, she can be found training for her next marathon (of which she has run over twenty fulls and far too many halfs to recall) or chasing her daughter around the house.

T.K. Leigh is represented by Jane Dystel of Dystel, Goderich & Bourret Literary Management. All publishing inquiries, including audio, foreign, and film rights, should be directed to her.